James Henry is the pen na~~me~~ ̶̶̶̶̶̶ who
has long been a fan of the original R. D. Wingfield
Frost books and the subsequent TV series. He works
in publishing, and enjoys windsurfing and long lunches.

After a successful career writing for radio, R. D.
Wingfield turned his attention to fiction, creating the
character of Jack Frost. The series has been adapted for
television as the perennially popular *A Touch of Frost*,
starring David Jason. R. D. Wingfield died in 2007.

Also by James Henry

FIRST FROST
FATAL FROST

and published by Corgi Books

Morning Frost

A DS Jack Frost Investigation

JAMES HENRY

CORGI BOOKS

TRANSWORLD PUBLISHERS
61–63 Uxbridge Road, London W5 5SA
A Random House Group Company
www.transworldbooks.co.uk

MORNING FROST
A CORGI BOOK: 9780552168533

First published in Great Britain
in 2013 by Bantam Press
an imprint of Transworld Publishers
Corgi edition published 2014

Written for the Estate of R. D. Wingfield by James Gurbutt
Copyright © the Estate of R. D. Wingfield 2013

Addresses for Random House Group Ltd companies outside the UK
can be found at www.randomhouse.co.uk
The Random House Group Ltd Reg. No. 954009

The Random House Group Limited supports the Forest Stewardship
Council® (FSC®), the leading international forest-certification organisation.
Our books carrying the FSC label are printed on FSC®-certified paper.
FSC is the only forest-certification scheme supported by the leading
environmental organisations, including Greenpeace. Our paper procurement
policy can be found at www.randomhouse.co.uk/environment

Typeset in 11½/15pt Caslon 540 by
Kestrel Data, Exeter, Devon.
Printed and bound by
CPI Group (UK) Ltd, Croydon, CR0 4YY.

4 6 8 10 9 7 5 3

Morning Frost

Prologue

She shoved the pushbike behind the hedgerow, checking to make sure it wasn't visible from the road. She felt hot, despite the damp autumn air, and her heart thumped rapidly beneath her sweater, but this was solely due to the exertion of pedalling uphill, and nothing to do with the job she had to carry out.

A narrow, winding lane fifty yards down the hill led to the club, and was the only way to reach the place by car, but on foot there was a track that peeled off from a public footpath through woodland that backed on to the building. Despite it being early November, the trees still had an abundance of brightly coloured foliage. A morning mist hung in the air as she made her way through the autumn mulch.

The rucksack felt heavy, but within ten minutes she had reached the clearing at the back of the club; she made a dash to the rear of the building and hid behind a stack of empty beer crates. Briskly she swapped her damp canvas Dunlops for a pair of red heels from the rucksack – not too grand, just a couple of inches for effect – and whipped off her baggy sweater, revealing a tiny white top that left little to the imagination. After deftly pinning back her auburn hair she produced from the bag a platinum-blonde wig. She used a small compact mirror to check it was straight; satisfied, she snapped it shut and slipped it back inside a red, sequin-studded handbag, next to a Beretta automatic pistol and a lipstick.

Having wedged the rucksack tightly between the stacked crates she slid silently round to the front of the building. Nobody was about. Now it was showtime. She confidently rapped on the door. She made an effort to focus her mind on the job in hand, but really this was a trifle, for the money only, and if anything, her mind was on her next task, something more personal, something she simply had to do before her final bunk to Spain. That detective. When so many of her own had died or been maimed – all thanks to *him* – it was unacceptable for him to still live. She knew he was looking for her, determined to bring in the last of the gang, but it wasn't fear of capture that fuelled her desire to exterminate him, it was revenge, pure and simple. Yes, there was only one way for her to find peace of mind: she had to kill Jack Frost.

The door was opened by a goofy young lad of little more than eighteen. He squinted at the bright morning light, but once his eyes had adjusted they goggled at the sight of her provocative appearance.

''Ello, can I 'elp?'

'I'm sure you can, love,' she purred, seductively. 'I'm here to see Harry.'

Thursday (1)

There was a freshness to the early November morning, and drizzle hung in the air, but a tepid sun was starting to peek through the vast bank of grey and allow the wet headstones to glisten. Stanley Mullett, the superintendent of the Denton police division at Eagle Lane, shifted his weight uneasily in the wet grass. There was no denying it, he felt uncomfortable standing by the graveside of a woman he didn't know. It didn't help that she was the wife of a detective sergeant he could hardly bear to be in the same room with, and would willingly dismiss at the drop of a hat if he could. But duty was duty.

Mullett glanced surreptitiously at the Rolex his wife had given him last month for his fiftieth birthday. Eleven thirty. The church had been cold and draughty, and now the moisture from the sodden grass was starting to penetrate the leather of his highly polished

Loakes, but Mullett knew that his discomfort and inconvenience was far from over. There was the wake to follow. Yes, he thought, almost the whole day will be given up to Mary Frost. The vicar's voice floated over the remaining mist, a suitably ethereal backdrop to the ample crowd of mourners at the graveside. The deceased's immediate family stood solemnly beside the casket: elegant mother, respectable-looking father, well-dressed sister and new husband. And to the side, a pace removed, the widower, Detective Sergeant William 'Jack' Frost.

Frost was barely recognizable in his smart attire of black tie and heavy overcoat, and though it hadn't occurred to him to shave, his unruly, sandy-coloured hair for once had a side-parting chiselled into it. These superficial fineries of mourning served to heighten the changes in Frost that even Mullett had noticed develop towards the end of his wife's illness – the weight loss, the sunken eyes, the greyish complexion. Mullet sniffed contemptuously; though not wholly unsympathetic, he couldn't help but think that Frost had contributed to his own bad luck.

Alongside the DS were his Eagle Lane chums: the overweight DC Hanlon, Frost's pal of many years who knew the region inside out, though in reality added little to the department beyond acting as Frost's driver; and next to him, good old Desk Sergeant Bill Wells, always dependable but failing the CID entrance exams with stoic consistency. Mullett observed how Frost appeared closer to these oddballs than to his own in-laws; it seemed that along with the other CID rabble, Waters, Clarke and Simms, they formed Frost's real family. The superintendent reflected sadly that sacrificing family ties for the sake of the job hadn't done much to make Frost a better policeman. Or perhaps it wasn't such a sacrifice. Mullett shivered as Frost suddenly caught his eye with a look suggesting he could read his mind.

The vicar finished his prayer and the casket was lowered slowly into the ground, as gracefully as was possible. Mullett glanced again at Mary's relatives; the two women, now in tears, huddled together, whereas the father remained stiff and resolute. A white-haired man in his late sixties, he suddenly appeared familiar. Where had Mullett seen him before?

Behind the front row of mourners, he noticed a number of Denton dignitaries – a bank manager, the mayor, the local MP. What on earth were they doing here? Frost's wife hadn't worked, hadn't done much at all as far as he could make out. The father was a City banker, unlikely to be on close terms with the local worthies. Surely they couldn't be here on Frost's account? Or had Mullett misjudged Frost's popularity? He'd always assumed he rubbed the town's back up as much as he did his own. So what was the connection?

The alarm clock sounded, but Detective Constable Sue Clarke was only half asleep anyway. After a nocturnal stake-out she only ever managed to doze. She reached to shut off the buzzer then realized it wasn't the alarm but the electronic telephone. Christ, she felt groggy. It was hardly surprising; having returned to her poky flat just before 7 a.m., she had made the mistake of pouring herself a large glass of Blue Nun. The bottle was a birthday present from her mother and had sat there unopened for over a month, but having just spent eight hours lying in a field of stinging nettles she'd been desperate for something to numb the itch. Clarke thought the whole operation a waste of time; she had spent three nights on the look-out for stolen electrical goods being shunted through an old warehouse out at Rainham, in the back of beyond. The station was understaffed, and those who opted for extra shifts were paid overtime, so she'd been fairly amenable – until now. DS Waters, who was looking to move out of police digs, had done the same and had been on a similarly unrewarding stake-out. The wine had seemed to help, but halfway through a second glass she was struck by a powerful wave of nausea and rushed to the bathroom to throw up.

It was now getting on for midday. Clarke picked up the telephone.

'Hello?' she croaked, reaching for a glass of water and not finding one.

'Didn't wake you, did I, love?' It was the tired but kindly voice of Night Sergeant Johnny Johnson.

'It's all right, Johnny, I was just dozing. What's up?'

'It's just you're the only one . . .'

Everyone else from CID was at Mary Frost's funeral. In the meantime the station was being manned by a skeleton staff including Johnson, who'd accepted a double shift.

'It's fine, honestly.' She scratched beneath the covers at a nettle sting. 'What's up?'

'Nev Sanderson, the old farmer, found something unpleasant while out on his tractor.'

Fields again. Hell, no. The last thing she wanted to do right now was tramp across a farmer's field.

'I'm sorry?' She yawned, fearing she'd not taken in a word he'd said. 'What was it he found?'

'A *foot*. He found a human foot.'

Harry Baskin smelt bad, he knew it. He stank so bad that no amount of cigar smoke would mask it, although he was giving it his best try. He grunted behind the desk, and poured himself half a tumbler of Scotch. The little card game he'd run through the night was a brilliant wheeze, although he knew that having it on a Wednesday, with the busiest nights of the week still in front of him, would take its toll. But times were hard, he mused to himself, and recession meant you had to work all the harder, to squeeze out every penny from the punters, and get them in beyond the usual Friday and Saturday, even if it meant the hassle of staying up all night, and at his age too. He grunted to himself. Who was he kidding? He might tell the wife it was a hardship, and an economic necessity, but in truth it was just an excuse to stay out gambling and boozing with his pals. He looked down at the pile of banknotes and sniggered again.

Suddenly a sharp knock on the door disturbed him from his thoughts. 'Come!' he rasped. The jug-eared youth poked his head in. 'The girl's here, boss.'

'Which girl, Cecil?' Baskin scratched his expansive midriff. The pain in his lower gut had started to niggle again.

'The stripper, boss.' Stripper? He couldn't recall fixing to see a stripper. Reaching inside his tonic-suit jacket he yanked out another wad of notes, which flopped with a soft sigh on to the desk. Grinning smugly at the sight, he leaned down to open the safe beneath the desk; best not to leave all this cash lying around.

'Remind me, son, what's she like, this bird?'

'Cracker, boss, huge bristols.' The lad puffed out his cheeks.

'Cecil, sunshine, there's more to women than tits. It shouldn't be the first thing you think of,' he admonished with a wagging finger. The boy looked forlorn. 'Never mind, never mind. Where is she?'

'Right here, boss.'

'Well, show her in.'

His words coincided with a deafening blast. Cecil careered across the room. Baskin had barely taken in the sight of the boy sliding down the filing cabinet, blood seeping from his chest, when the pistol swung before him and fired. The big gangster keeled over, banknotes flying through the air like confetti. As he lay slumped on the floor, he thought that Cecil was right; the girl was racked; then everything went black.

*

Frost stood in the grand entrance hall of George and Beryl Simpson's luxurious Rimmington home and felt as much connection with his in-laws as would a stranger. Should there not be more of a bond, after the experience they'd shared? He paused for a moment; everyone was here for Mary, his Mary. Theirs had not been the perfect marriage by any stretch, but in his way he knew he had loved her; he couldn't give a monkey's what anyone else thought. At the end he was with her night and day, and he felt they were reconciled; she even teased him about not being able to dress himself without her there. He smiled sadly at the memory.

Now she was gone, and he was rattling around in that house on his own. What would he do? Hell, what did it matter. He felt . . . how did he feel? *Empty*. He went through the open doorway of a large reception room and walked straight to where the drinks were laid out, at the far end of a buffet table, nodding vaguely to one or two guests as he did so. Seizing a cut-glass tumbler he poured three fingers of Scotch and drank swiftly. A sigh escaped his lips.

The last few guests had now arrived and a quiet throng hovered around the finger buffet. Mourners drifted past Frost towards the lounge; he was keen not to engage, affecting a distracted demeanour and avoiding their eye by focusing on *The Horse*, an impressive painting on the far wall at the foot of the staircase.

His reverie was short-lived.

'You might've shaved, William.' Frost could feel the scornful gaze of his mother-in-law upon him. She put particular emphasis on the first name he avoided using.

He chose to ignore the rebuke. 'Popular girl, our Mary,' he replied instead, but the word 'our' jarred uncomfortably. He surveyed the bustle of guests, of whom only a fraction were familiar.

'Yes, there were plenty who loved her.' Beryl Simpson observed him with cold eyes and exhaled cigarette smoke. 'What will you do now?' she asked, the remark carrying as much concern as if she were enquiring which entrée he'd chosen.

'Oh, I'll be fine.' He said it to himself as much as in response to her question. His attention had already wandered. Who was that chatting to his brother-in-law, Mary's sister's husband, Julian? Some strange, swaggering, foreign type who stood out a mile among the ordinary Joes gathered here. Nobody from Denton wore a cravat. Apart from Julian Brazier himself, of course, but then he was a used-car salesman. Together they looked a right pair of Noddies . . .

Beryl Simpson sighed. 'Of course you will.' Abruptly she turned, and with a steadfast clip-clop of heels across the chequered marble floor she made off towards the drinks, leaving a cloud of smoke and a faint trace of perfume in her wake.

'Suit yourself,' Frost muttered, patting himself down for cigarettes. Then he remembered that the pockets didn't work on this cheap black Marks 'n' Sparks suit. He'd only worn it once before, at his mother's funeral less than a year ago. And now Mary was gone. He was truly alone in the world – quite a depressing state of affairs if he stopped to think about it. So he wouldn't. End of. He went in pursuit of his mother-in-law to cadge a cigarette.

Superintendent Mullett, sipping his sherry, watched the exchange between Frost and Beryl Simpson. He wondered what they could be talking about. The Frosts' marriage had been in tatters – that fact was common knowledge (although Mullett himself was one of the last to find out, being rather crudely so informed by his secretary on hearing of Mary Frost's passing). It was a bit late, but maybe the detective was penitent in some peculiar way? He did seem a shadow of his former self, and looked slight standing next to the haughty older woman. Mullett hadn't yet spoken to her, but something in her bearing exuded a certain class. Plus there was the quality of the domicile; situated in the most expensive street in Rimmington, its decor was worthy of a glossy interiors magazine. The paintings alone must be worth more than the Mullett residence in its entirety. How could the Simpson girl have married so far beneath her station? What had she been thinking? Frost wouldn't know a Stubbs from a—

'Superintendent Mullett?' The departed's father had unexpectedly sidled up.

'Yes, indeed,' Mullett said stiffly. 'Very sorry for your loss.'

The old fellow sighed through a neatly trimmed, whitening moustache. 'Yes, yes.'

Mullett was struck again by the sense of familiarity. Where the blazes had he seen him before? Wait, was it . . .

'Yes, I thought it was you,' said Simpson in a low voice. 'Although, we haven't seen you square . . .'

'*Square?*' Of course, the Lodge. George Simpson was a Freemason. That would explain the score of town dignitaries at the funeral. Having made the link, Mullett was anxious to ingratiate himself further, but before he had the chance the crimson face of Desk Sergeant Bill Wells appeared at his shoulder. Damn. To Mullett's extreme vexation the Master slipped away.

'Fine woman, Mary Frost,' Wells said as the super-intendent watched Simpson top up the drinks of various guests, all of whom seemed to give him a knowing glance.

'I can't say I knew her,' Mullett remarked. 'I thought they . . .' he began but then curbed his intended comment on the state of the Frosts' marriage, sensing it might seem inappropriate, and instead said, 'She was clearly well loved – there's quite a few here.'

'Yes,' Wells concurred. 'Good family, too. I bet the mother was a looker in her time.'

Mullett glanced again at Beryl Simpson and found himself nodding in agreement; she was trim, attractive even, and clearly took care of herself. Perhaps the coloured hair was in a style too young for her years, but it was a minor blot on what was overall a fine example of the mature English rose. Bitterly he downed his schooner of sherry. How on earth Frost had managed to worm his way into such a superior family was a mystery, and, of course, staggeringly unfair. But now death had broken the connection, and he regarded it almost as an act of poetic justice.

Thursday (2) _____

Nev Sanderson pointed authoritatively with a large wooden stick. 'That there is a foot.'

'Yes, Mr Sanderson,' said DC Clarke as she winced, 'I'm inclined to agree.'

She took a tentative step forward, her feet sticking in the mud.

'Do you think you could get your dog away? It won't help the lab if the' – what *was* the right word? It couldn't really be classed as a corpse – '*object* is drenched in dog saliva.'

The Border collie snuffled enthusiastically around the pasty limb as though contemplating taking a bite.

'Fenton, here, boy,' the farmer said half-heartedly. He was swigging from an unmarked bottle she took to contain some form of scrumpy. He certainly had the complexion to match. The dog continued to sniff the prominent big toe. Sanderson leaned on his stick and smirked.

'Constable, remove the dog,' ordered Clarke. She was tired and had no patience for the farmer's lack of respect. Ridley moved to grab it, but at Sanderson's slap of his thigh the dog came to heel.

'Ah,' Clarke said with some dismay, looking across the field at the SOCOs trudging in the distance and what was likely to be Maltby. Not used to being first on the scene, she desperately needed to make some useful observation before Forensics arrived and disturbed the crime scene irrevocably. Frost always lectured everyone on how important these early moments were, although he qualified this by his own admission that he himself was seldom first anywhere.

'When did you first see the foot?'

'I see it from tractor o'er there,' he said, pointing to the becalmed machine twenty yards away.

'How? You must have pretty incredible eyesight to have spotted it from that distance.' Clarke frowned.

'It were the birds. The gulls. They were fighting over it.'

'I see. So you didn't unearth it, then? You're saying it was sitting on the surface?'

'I guess so.' He shrugged, his attention now drawn to the approaching entourage.

Perhaps it was left here last night, she thought. But, why here? And where was the rest of the body – dead or alive?

'Wait a minute. You said "gulls". But we're at least seventy miles from the coast. Are you sure they weren't crows?'

Sanderson rolled his eyes. 'I know the difference, ma'am. Reckon maybe they came from the reservoir.' He nodded towards the horizon. Denton reservoir, yes, of course, although there was nothing to see from this aspect; it was somewhere beyond these acres of softly undulating arable farmland.

'Yes, perhaps.' Clarke sighed, struggling for inspiration. Frost also said to take in a crime scene fully before focusing on the body, so as not to be unduly influenced in any way by the sight of the corpse. But this was just a field, and this was just a foot. She stepped forward. Yep, it was a foot, all right. She regarded the naked, lily-white limb, flecked with abrasions. What the hell should she do now? The farmer coughed impatiently.

'Detective Clarke,' wheezed a familiar voice.

'Doctor Maltby.' She was glad it was someone she knew. Next to him stood a visibly unimpressed young SOCO with a whisper of a moustache.

'Is that it, then?' the lad said, looking from Clarke to the foot and back again. Clarke raised her eyebrows and shrugged; she instantly loathed this upstart, pathetic bum-fluff and all.

'This does not constitute a "body",' added Maltby irritably.

'Well, I didn't call you,' Clarke countered defensively, but she was distracted by Sanderson, who had turned his back on them and was making for the tractor.

'Mr Sanderson, wait . . . Mr Sanderson . . .' The de-parting figure paid her no heed.

The Forensics men regarded her expectantly.

'Well, don't just stand there,' she snapped, furious with everyone, including herself. She mustered some latent authority and, raising her voice above the roar of the tractor, shouted, 'Bag it, then!'

After begging a fag from Beryl Simpson, who quickly moved on to an ancient aunt, Frost found himself standing with the Braziers and the cravat-wearing stranger. Frost groaned inwardly; he didn't like his brother-in-law at all, never had done. A tall, sort of handsome but smarmy individual with greying, bog-brush hair, Julian Brazier had always irritated the hell out of him.

'So, Julian . . . how's business, then?'

'We're doing great, aren't we, Jules?' Elizabeth, Mary's less attractive younger sister, cut in. 'Opening another showroom, here in Denton, aren't we, darling?'

Frost reached for the nearby Scotch bottle and poured himself another drink. He offered the bottle around, well aware they were drinking wine or sherry.

'Yes, so I heard. That place on the Bath Road. I nicked the last motor dealer to have it.' He knew the reference would rile them, but Jesus, 'showroom' was an exaggeration even for them; a shabby Portakabin with a forecourt were the sum of it.

'William, allow me to introduce you to Charles,' said Brazier, ignoring the remark. 'Charlie is from France.'

'Hello, Charlie from France.' Frost took a limp hand. He knew that the Braziers had friends in France, and Mary had been to stay with them in the Dordogne before she became very ill. 'It's very kind of you to come all this way.'

'He's come for more than the funeral, Will,' Brazier said.

'Yes, my business partner and I have opened an antiques shop in Denton; we opened early last month.' The Frenchman smiled cordially.

'Really?' said Frost, unimpressed. 'Well, I'm not sure we've got the requisite clientele for such' – Frost searched for the words – 'overpriced knick-knacks.' Just then he felt a heavy hand on his shoulder and a blast of hot, boozy breath on his ear. 'Arthur, say hello to Charlie from France.'

Hanlon lurched forward and winked at the Frenchman. 'Spain: three–one,' he chided.

'Eh?' Frost said, baffled.

Charles smiled politely at Hanlon's remark, turned back to Frost and bowed gracefully. 'I'm sorry for your loss,' he said before rejoining Brazier, who was deep in conversation with some town official Frost vaguely recognized.

'What was all that about Spain?' Frost asked, spearing a cocktail sausage from the buffet table.

'The World Cup, Jack! You know, football? Just a couple of months back. England trounced the Frogs three–one. Where've you been?' Hanlon guffawed.

'Hospital, in the main.' Frost waved away Hanlon's

sudden embarrassment. 'Well, it wouldn't be the first time we trounced them in Spain. 1812. Salamanca.'

'Not with you, Jack.'

'Not many are, Arthur, not many are,' Frost said, feeling suddenly very alone.

Detective Constable Derek Simms, having dropped off DS Waters in Denton High Street, now found himself snarled up in traffic. He regarded the almost black Georgian buildings that lined the northern perimeter of Market Square; he'd never before stopped to consider how filthy the place was. Perhaps it really was turning into a dump, as his mother constantly bemoaned. Denton's former glory as a very pretty market town seemed a distant shadow, not that he'd remember – his parents always complained how it had been ruined by a splurge of building in the mid 1960s, transforming it into what government officials called a 'new town', the purpose of which was to generate new business and industry. Much of that 'transformation' started and finished with the Southern Housing Estate, a sprawling urban mess of council houses, purpose built for the London over-spill. Twenty years later, Denton's population had swelled and with it a tide of crime and unemployment, but very little in the way of increased prosperity, leaving the town very much the poorer relation to upmarket Rimmington, which remained untouched by the developers' hands. Not that Simms minded. The more crime, the more experience for him and the more fun the job; though he could curse the bleeding traffic.

Given the recession and high unemployment, why were there so many motors on the road?

And he needed a pee, badly. Prior to dropping Waters off the pair had stopped in at the Bird in Hand, to shake off the solemnity of the church service, and to warm up – St Mary's had been cold as a tomb. They'd reflected on how depressing it all was. Dead at thirty-six. Although, being only twenty-four, thirty seemed old to Derek Simms.

Frost had invited them both back to his in-laws' house for what by the sounds of it was going to be a full-blown wake, lasting the whole day, but they excused themselves on account of being technically on duty, even though Waters had arranged to see his girl-friend and view a flat. After only six months the pair were moving in together. Jesus, talk about a whirlwind romance. Wouldn't catch me doing that, Simms snorted, fumbling in his pocket for cigarettes. He figured the big man was on the rebound from his recent divorce, but wouldn't dream of saying so. They certainly had tongues wagging around Eagle Lane; interracial relationships were unheard of, especially within the police force. John Waters, the token black member of the Denton force, and diminutive blonde Kim Myles turned heads on a daily basis.

As Simms waited for the lights to change, Morrison's, the undertakers, caught his eye, causing him to reflect again on the morning. He had seen Mary Frost only once, years ago, when she had stormed into the station late one night demanding to know where the hell Jack

was. She'd been pretty but scary, with bright red lipstick and elaborate 1950s-style hair – fiery but somehow
still quite cute. She clearly thought Frost had been out
all night misbehaving; it transpired he'd been sleeping
in the cells. That was marriage for you.

He turned on the police radio, feeling slightly guilty
that he hadn't done it sooner, but then for all Johnson
knew he was still at the funeral. Within minutes it
crackled into life.

'Yep, Simms here.'

'Where the dickens have you been?' Johnson sounded out of sorts.

'At the funeral, Sarge, along with everybody else.
What's wrong, the daylight not agreeing with you?'

'Less of your lip, laddy. The service was over an hour
ago. You were supposed to be on call after that. You're
needed; Sue Clarke has gone off straight from her night-
shift to check out what might be a human foot in one
of Nev Sanderson's fields. And that's not the half of it.'

'Eh?' Simms scratched his head. 'OK, sorry, it was
hard to get away – you know how it is at these things.
Anyway, what else is up?'

'There's been a shooting,' Johnson stated coldly. 'At
the Coconut Grove nightclub. Two in intensive care.'

'You're having me on!' Simms's pulse quickened. A
serious incident, no one else on call, just him to pick it
up. It was a gift. 'The Coconut Grove, eh? Bet Big H
ain't happy about that.'

'Too right,' Johnson said sombrely. 'He's one of them
that got shot.'

'I know you turn your nose up at Julian and Elizabeth, William,' said Beryl Simpson. Her green eyes were misty, Frost wasn't sure whether from booze or genuine emotion; probably both. The afternoon was waning, and he wished it would all end. 'And despite what you think of us, and all this' – she waved the glass unsteadily around her – 'we're not precious about money. Certainly the girls were well educated, and that's because of George. George worked hard to provide them with opportunities he never had.' Mrs Simpson looked to the vicar for confirmation of this statement. Father Hill, of whom Frost was fond, nodded encouragingly, and then endeavoured to steer the conversation away from family feuds by clasping her shoulder and adding something about generous donations to the Church.

However, Frost's emotions were running high as well, and he wasn't finished with her yet.

'I've never said a thing, Beryl,' he replied, prompting Father Hill to give him a scathing look.

'You don't have to, it's in your manner,' she almost sneered, revealing the lines decorum and powder had hidden. She suddenly looked her age – just when he was almost beginning to fancy her again. 'And for all your high-mindedness you never took proper care of Mary. Whereas Julian' – her glass indicating the favoured son-in-law, lounging on the sofa with legs sprawled apart – 'he may only be a car dealer to you—'

'He *is* a car dealer, Beryl!' Frost exclaimed, looking expectantly at the vicar for a sign of solidarity. 'To everyone!' Father Hill studied the marble floor, unwilling to get involved.

'You know damn well what I mean – the point is, *he* loves Elizabeth . . . and . . .'

Frost stared intently. Don't you dare try and claim he's never cheated on her, he thought.

Beryl Simpson held herself, and touched her bottom lip, as if to check it was still there. He thought for an instant she was going to continue her tirade, but all she said was, 'Just get me another drink.'

'Do you mind if we discuss the particulars another time, Sidney? I don't feel it appropriate to go into such things here.'

'No, quite.' Mullett flushed. What was he thinking in pursuing it? He must've had more sherry than he thought. The elderly Mason had acknowledged him and that should suffice for now. So as not to add to the embarrassment, he didn't correct the old boy on his name.

'Besides, you could start looking closer to home,' Simpson added. 'The force is no stranger to our organization.'

A woman approached with a sherry bottle. She was slightly chubby but with a hard face, and Mullett surmised that she must be the other daughter, whose name he couldn't remember. 'Top-up?' she asked. He'd probably had enough but it was rather good sherry, so he grinned amiably and watched the bronze liquid flow. One more, then he really must be off to the station.

'You're Will's boss,' she said abruptly.

'Sergeant Frost?' He smiled as generously as he could. 'Yes, I have the honour of having *William* serve under me.'

She looked surprised. 'You call it an honour? We've been led to believe he's a royal pain in the backside, eh, Dad?'

Simpson senior merely raised his eyebrows.

'Well, he has his own inimitable style, and yes, we do have our ups and downs,' Mullett admitted. He took a proffered cigarette. 'But he is dedicated.'

'Oh.' Her look softened. 'So it wasn't all an act, then.'

'I'm sorry, I'm not with you,' Mullett said.

'Gave Mary a hard run, didn't he, Dad?' she said. The old man sighed. Mullett wasn't altogether sure he was listening. 'Good to know it was all for a reason; that he was just being good at his job . . .'

Mullett wasn't aware that he'd said that, but he was touched by how the young woman took comfort from his words. He suddenly felt a peculiar closeness to this grieving family, with whom his only connection was through a man who was the bane of his life. Perhaps it was a sign that to be around these kinds of people was his rightful place? Or perhaps it was just the sherry.

'I've got nothing more to say to you. You ruined my daughter's life, you selfish, selfish man.'

Beryl Simpson shook her bowed head, clutching the kitchen work surface. That wasn't true and she knew it – until the cancer had taken her, Mary was happy-go-lucky despite their ups and downs. Or so he'd convinced himself anyway. Frost felt his relationship with Mary was misunderstood. Perhaps it was time to address this with the in-laws, reassure them that Mary wasn't the unhappy, downtrodden victim they thought. He picked up the picture of his late wife resting on the dresser in a gilded frame; it had been taken some years ago – fiery red hair, the brightest red lipstick imaginable, lively eyes and a full bosom. She was a cracker all right.

'But for years . . . she, she carried on with that bleedin' plumber,' he said absently. He realized his mistake as soon as the words had left his lips.

'Get out! Out of my house. How could you say that?'

She broke down in sobs. Frost's head spun. He felt despair and frustration rising up inside. He had to leave – he needed air. On impulse he grabbed one of the many bottles of spirits on the worktop.

Frost barged through a throng of people still in the hall, drunken laughter ringing in his ears. If it wasn't for the prevalence of black clothing it could well have been a party, not a wake. Perhaps that was the way a send-off should be? Despite coming into contact with death on a regular basis, he'd attended very few funerals.

'Jack, you all right?' Frost had collided with a red-nosed Arthur Hanlon.

'Fine, fine, just need some air.' He could hear himself slurring his words.

'That much "air"?' said Hanlon, pointing to the bottle. Before Frost could respond an equally smashed

Bill Wells had clutched him to his chest, squeezing the wind out of him.

'We love you, you know,' Wells said to his scalp.

'Get off, you great soppy oaf. I'll be back.' Then, opening the front door, he muttered to himself, 'Hmm . . . or was he an electrician?'

Thursday (3)

Clarke pulled up at the Coconut Grove, next to DC Derek Simms's red Alfa Sud. Baskin and Cecil had long been whisked off in an ambulance to Denton General. Simms was outside the club talking to a girl in a red miniskirt.

The sky was overcast and there was rain on the way again, giving the place an even seedier air than usual. Clarke avoided the puddles as she made for her colleague.

'Who's this?' she asked. Simms turned away from the distraught-looking girl. Mascara streaked her puckered cheeks, and her hair was in disarray. A WPC patted her shoulder.

'The girl who found them,' Simms replied. 'Kate Greenlaw. She's a twenty-three-year-old "Exotic Dancer".'

Clarke rolled her eyes, although she was careful that

the girl didn't see it. She thought Simms looked pale. She asked him to show her the crime scene and he led her through to Harry Baskin's office.

Simms talked Clarke through the facts: 'The lad, Cecil Rhodes, was shot at point-blank range. From the doorway, here.'

A Forensics officer kneeled by the door, his tape measure stretching several feet from a filing cabinet spattered with blood. Clarke realized that Simms had been waiting for her; though his confidence over the last year had grown, he still valued a second opinion, especially in something as serious as a shooting. As things stood either one of the victims might die, and Eagle Lane would find themselves in the middle of a murder inquiry. It was a wonder that no one was dead already; there was blood everywhere.

'You can tell from the blood smears on the cabinet that he was hit from this angle,' the Forensics officer said.

'Were either Rhodes or Baskin armed?' Clarke asked, addressing Simms.

He shook his head. 'Nope.'

'Someone they both knew?'

'Or they were taken by surprise. Looks like a hit to me – see.' He gestured to the pile of notes scattered on the desk and floor. 'Unlikely to be a robbery.'

'Better get that accounted for,' she said.

Clarke had never been inside Baskin's office before. Oddly enough, it was not dissimilar to Mullett's – smaller of course, but wood-panelled with garish furniture and an over-the-top leather chair, trappings typical of the terminally self-important. However, the super's office had certainly never been sprayed with blood, and she'd never seen as much as a pound note in there either, while there must be at least five grand lying scattered around the desk and on the floor.

'Any witnesses?'

Simms was at the window, impatiently rattling the latch. 'The girl was the only other one here. She'd arrived with Rhodes at 9.30, him to admin the takings from last night and she to practise her moves. Baskin was already here when they arrived and she was under the impression he'd been here all night, slept in the office.'

'So, did she hear the shots?'

Simms finally opened the window, releasing the metallic stench that was starting to claw at Clarke's throat. 'Claims she didn't see or hear anything.'

'Silencer?'

'Possibly. Or maybe *she* shot them?' Simms proffered.

Clarke pulled a doubtful face. 'An old lag like Harry, it could've been any number of people. He'll have run up dozens of enemies over the years.'

A cigar, half smoked, lay resting on the blood-soaked carpet by the side of the oak desk. 'What sort of shape was he in when they found him?'

'Unconscious but alive. He's a tough old bird. He took a bullet to the shoulder. Just the one, though.'

'Just the one . . .' Clarke repeated, following Simms's

line of thought. 'If it was a hit, you'd think they'd shoot again, just to make sure.'

'Exactly,' Simms said, his brow furrowed. Then, for the first time since she'd arrived, he seemed to look at her properly. There was an awkward pause. 'How's your day been going?' he asked; though he must have known full well – Sanderson's foot was all over the airwaves.

'A foot in a field,' she replied with mock jauntiness. She wanted to ask about the funeral, knowing that's where he'd been, but she couldn't bring herself to do so.

'A foot,' mused Simms, as if it were nothing more unusual than finding a lost dog. He wasn't interested in her, she realized; he was consumed by the here and now, this bloody mess. She recognized that disconnected air, and knew he was determined – no, desperate – to elicit something from the scene, some clue. She took in the disarray in the office, the open safe, the scattered notes. The shooting, it would appear, interrupted something – Baskin counting his cash. The attack was unexpected, which would explain why Baskin and Rhodes had been unarmed; had it been a business transaction gone sour, they would've undoubtedly been tooled up as a precaution.

'Was the door open or closed when the girl found them?' Clarke said suddenly.

'Eh?'

'Was the door open or shut?'

'I don't know – why?'

'Maybe the attacker was in a hurry, that's why they didn't finish Baskin off, and if they panicked they wouldn't have shut the door.'

'Good point,' he conceded, 'I'll check with the girl. Then we'd best get over to the hospital, see if the fat bastard has survived.'

'That was a waste of bloody time,' said DC Derek Simms, resting his feet on the desk in the main CID office. The hospital could at least have mentioned when they radioed ahead that Baskin was still out of it. He lit a cigarette, watching Sue Clarke settle at the desk opposite. There was something funny in her demeanour that he couldn't put his finger on. She picked up the phone immediately without answering him, not that he required an answer. Though he did fancy a drink after today's peculiar chain of events. Never can tell what'll happen next in this job, he thought.

He retrieved a half-bottle of Scotch from the desk drawer, picked up a mug, peered inside and decided to take it straight from the bottle instead. After a couple of swigs he paused, watching Clarke nattering on the phone. They had recently called it quits on their on/off relationship. There had been some fun times – well, one or two at least – over the summer. He'd been keen to have her back at first, as there was no denying how well they got on, but he couldn't shake off the suspicion that she was with him only because Frost had ditched her, on account of his sick wife. The niggling fear that she was on the rebound wore away at him and made him bad-tempered, until eventually he called time on things.

But now, a month on, Simms suspected he'd made a mistake. He discovered he'd been wrong about Clarke's feelings yet again. DS Waters, who had become a great friend, was seeing Clarke's buddy Kim Myles; she'd told him it was Sue who had ditched Frost in May because she'd blatantly had enough, and at the time she'd known nothing of his wife's illness. Though he wasn't totally convinced she'd dropped Frost for good, as once Frost's wife's condition became common knowledge the pair did seem pretty close . . . Anyway, Clarke had decided to give it another go with Derek because, well, Derek was Derek. She'd told him as much, but he'd never really grasped the idea that she liked him for himself – it wasn't until he heard it from a third party and there was some distance between them that it finally registered, and he saw what a fool he'd been. Still, they were young, there was time. There was always time . . .

'DC Simms! End of the day already, is it?'

DI Allen's sharp tone snatched him from his musings. Jesus! He swung his legs off the desk.

'No, sir.'

'No, sir, indeed. Where the bloody hell is everyone?'

'Mary Frost's funeral, sir.'

Detective Inspector Jim Allen scratched his beard thoughtfully. Within the worn face his pale grey eyes flickered with mild irritation.

'Are they now. And Superintendent Mullett?'

'He was there this morning.'

'Well, that toerag from the *Echo*, Sandy Lane, is banging on the front door. He had a call from a farmer – something about a foot in a field. Brief the superintendent – we'll have to make a statement.' With an angry frown he disappeared from the doorway as silently as he arrived.

Clarke was equally perturbed by DI Allen's surprise visit. 'What the hell was he doing here?' she asked as soon as she hung up the phone. 'I thought he was on secondment to Rimmington on that abduction case?'

'Beats me. Don't like him one bit,' Simms reflected. 'I agree with Frost; never trust a man with a beard. Even if he is a DI.'

'Oh, don't be ridiculous. Besides, you've never agreed with Jack on anything. Ever.'

'Not true.'

Clarke chose not to pursue Simms on this point, although she knew he'd argue the sky was green if Jack said it was blue. 'Anyway, that was the lab.'

'Go on.'

'The foot found in the field was a male foot, and is, as Drysdale put it, "fresh".'

'What does that mean?'

'It means it was severed recently – in the last twenty-four hours or so. The wound is precise, so it's likely it was hacked off in one stroke, using maybe a machete, or large meat cleaver.'

'Christ!'

'That's not all. The condition of the tissue reveals the

body was most likely alive when the foot was severed. Which I guess is significant.'

'Yep.' Simms swigged from the bottle again. 'We're looking for someone with a bad limp.'

He held up his hands in apology for the dodgy joke. Clarke declined his offer of a swig, so he placed the bottle precariously on the desk and stretched. 'What a day. Well, Allen is right, the press will want a statement.'

'Bloody farmer, couldn't keep it to himself.'

'No surprise, really, a town this size – not every day a limb pops up in a potato field.'

He was right, of course, they'd be lucky if they could keep it under wraps for long. They sat in silence for a minute.

'How was . . .'

'This morning?' Simms finished her dangling sentence. 'Odd. Frost had left all the arrangements to Hanlon. Big Eagle Lane contingent – even Winslow from County – which seemed strange given that most of them hadn't even met his missus.'

'But you were all there to support Jack – surely that was the point?'

'I guess.' Simms's tone was dismissive. 'Still, I would've thought by now at least some of them would have made it back here. It's nearly three and the place is like a graveyard, if you'll excuse the pun.'

Charles Pierrejean was glad to be outside the Simpson residence, however briefly. What a bunch of ignorant fuckwits, he thought, as he opened the car door to retrieve a fresh pack of Gauloises. *Oh, you don't sound like one of those Frogs – positively one of us, hawhaw!* And all that crap about the World Cup . . . on a day like this. *C'est incroyable.* No respect. He was indeed as English as he was French, but when presented with such peasants he sank into detached embarrassment.

Pierrejean had been in Denton for six weeks. He had met the Braziers early last summer, in his father's family-run restaurant in the Dordogne. It was there one evening that Julian had posited the idea of opening a business in Denton. Charles had a passion for antiques, inherited from his middle-class English mother, far greater than the one for cooking Pierrejean senior wished to instil in him; but it was a passion that went beyond the fringes of legality. England had been hard hit by recession, but, Brazier argued, the flipside was that leases had become cheap, and the well-heeled, who were more affluent than ever, were eager for something to put their money into. Denton had its fair share of nouveaux riches, such as Brazier's own in-laws, the Simpsons, and was ripe for the taking, all it needed was someone with the right skills and contacts, such as he.

Pierrejean was well-educated, cultured but unscrupulous; he and his business colleague, Gaston Camus, knew they could exploit the boorish upper-middle class of provincial Britain and were looking for an 'in'. Somewhere out of the way, a place that wouldn't draw attention to itself, and in particular that wouldn't attract the scrutiny of the French authorities. Denton would be ideal.

The Simpsons were exactly the kind of people Pierre-jean and his shady contacts had in their sights. Thanks to over-inflated City salaries and bonuses enjoyed by Simpson and his ilk, they had money to burn and liked to advertise the fact with showy, expensive furniture and decor. However, the shop itself thus far was seeing little custom, hence he found himself here, cringing at a funeral wake of somebody he didn't know, which had no sign of ending, and with the most bizarre collection of people he'd ever encountered in one place.

He sniffed the English autumn air. Rain again. It was just coming up to three, and in the time it took to smoke his cigarette his hands were cold enough for him to wish he had gloves. What a miserable, wet country this is, he grumbled to himself, flicking soggy leaves off his Citroën windscreen. God, he thought, making his way back to the house, something better improve, either the weather or business – he could barely imagine anything more grim than a winter in Denton.

Thursday (4)

Mullett knew he should leave the Rimmington house – it was growing dark outside – but then he stiffened upon noticing his superior, the Assistant Chief Constable, across the room. He'd spotted Winslow at the church, but having not seen him afterwards he'd assumed he'd returned to County HQ. When the hell did he slip in here? As usual there was tension between them; the ACC was unimpressed with the lack of progress in a rape case involving a teacher from a Rimmington school. The incident had been reported on Monday and all Denton CID had managed so far was to trace the source of some crank phone calls to the victim to 'somewhere' on the Southern Housing Estate. Detective Sergeant Waters had then spent two days on surveillance amongst what Mullett regarded as 'the scum' of the estate, but with little to show for it. Winslow was furious to hear that an officer whose chief characteristic was standing out like a sore thumb had been chosen for surveillance. He berated Mullett for poor judgement and a row then ensued over the tiresome issue of resources.

The superintendent sighed. He scanned the room for any other hobnobbing opportunities. He'd put in a good hour sucking up to Sir Keith, the MP for Denton and Rimmington, and the mayor, a blustering old fool by the name of Francis. Old man Simpson's connection with the Lodge was the reason all these others were here, including Hudson, that great fat layabout of a bank manager. But in what capacity was Winslow here? True, he was a fan of Frost's, albeit from a distance (but close enough to be pressuring Mullett to promote him by the end of the year), but there'd never been any personal connection as far as Mullett was aware. Perhaps his presence was also down to the Masonic influence?

Mullett cursed as Hanlon and Wells moved towards the buffet table and obscured his view. He watched them with distaste, scoffing as if it were their last meal, although soaking up some of this alcohol was undoubtedly a good idea. He really should be getting back, but his curiosity about Winslow had given him another reason to stay. Of course, Mullett hadn't forgotten that the ACC had a skeleton in his cupboard: he'd been spotted leaving the unsavoury Pink Toothbrush sauna back in May. Perhaps this compromising information was something Mullett could use to his advantage? He moved unsteadily towards the two Eagle Lane officers.

'Ah, gentlemen, what a very sad day,' he said in a loud voice. 'I take great comfort in seeing so many of Denton's finest here, supporting our colleague in his hour of need.'

Hanlon reached his great bear's paw around the super's narrow shoulders, and pulling Mullett towards him said, 'You're all right, sir, you're all right.'

What an idiotic remark, Mullett thought. However, Wells was nodding in sombre agreement, emotion brimming barely below the surface. He conceded that they might both be steaming drunk but at least they were well-meaning.

Mullett gently extricated himself from Hanlon's grasp. 'Why thank you, *chaps*,' he said. 'What are we on here? One more for the road, eh? Wait, where is old Jack?'

Within a few minutes, as the Simpsons' grandfather clock chimed three, all thought of Winslow and Mullett's own Masonic ambitions had dispersed from his thoughts.

'A *hand*?' said DC Derek Simms, gripping the telephone receiver. 'Are you sure? Just a hand?'

'That's what the man said, son,' replied Johnny Johnson.

Simms had started to take down the details when he noticed a very pale-looking Sue Clarke making to go. 'Johnny, I'll call you straight back.' He hung up. 'Hey, where you off to?'

'Home.'

'But it's only just gone three. C'mon, you went to look at the foot earlier, this is your case. At this rate we'll have a whole body by the weekend.' He was eager to forgo a missing limb, just to keep the Baskin case all to himself.

'I spent all night lying in a field, remember? Besides, the whole of Denton CID can't all still be getting hammered – it's a wake, not a party. Anyway,' she conceded, 'I don't feel too good.'

'Oh.' He backed down immediately. 'If you're not well it's fine, I'll take it.' He had to admit, she didn't look too clever. He knew her health had suffered after the trauma of being stabbed in the leg earlier this year, and he didn't want a relapse on his conscience. 'You get off to bed.' He smiled encouragingly.

He watched his colleague shuffle off down the corridor, sighed and picked up the telephone receiver.

'Johnny,' he said, lighting another cigarette. 'Gimme the details, I'm all ears.'

'It's that same farmer Miss Clarke went to see earlier.'

Simms knew he should go after her. For continuity's sake she ought to take the call. Why the hell hadn't the whole sodding field been searched straight away? Clarke should have stopped the farmer in his tracks and sealed it off. This was a serious oversight. What was the matter with her?

'OK, mate, get an area car down there. Grab Sanderson's tractor keys until the field has been combed. I'll call the lab, put Drysdale on alert, then I'll be straight down there.'

*

Sue Clarke felt a dreadful wave of nausea; it must be my bloody hormones, she thought. She'd sat in the car for five minutes with her eyes closed before she'd started to drift off to sleep. Tired and emotional was an understatement – death-warmed-up was closer to it. She wondered if she had a temperature; she certainly felt feverish. She'd probably caught a chill from her night in the field. She should never have been sent on surveillance on a night like that, and in her condition too. Not that anyone knew, though.

She reversed the Escort out and was about to pull forward but paused instead, closing her eyes and resting her damp forehead on the steering wheel. Damn, she thought. She realized she'd made a mistake: she should have sealed off the field and had uniform tread through. As if Forensics would look beyond the immediate area; they weren't best pleased to be there at all in the first place. Genuine intrigue and commitment to duty were battling against her desperate need for sleep. She re-parked the car and got out. Have a strong coffee, that would help. She missed the nicotine which she'd often relied upon to keep her going, but she'd had to can the fags as they made her even more queasy. And she probably would have packed them in anyway as soon as she found out . . . And everybody else would find out soon enough – she wondered how long she had before it began to show. She'd had a scare six months ago, but this time there was no doubt. For what seemed the billionth time she cursed her stupidity and slammed the car door shut.

Frost was going to thump him. Wife's funeral or not, any minute now he would bust the bleeder's nose, just watch him.

He shouldn't have returned to the wake. After a stroll around the block to clear his head Frost had intended just to pick up his coat and car keys and leave, figuring he could make his peace with his mother-in-law some other time – if that were possible at all. But while fetching his coat he'd been collared by Winslow and agreed to have a drink in the study. Frost, surprisingly, got on fine with the bald, bespectacled ACC.

Unfortunately, a few drinks had had the effect of turning Winslow into a bore, and after the customary condolences Frost found himself on the receiving end of a lecture on the coming of the computer age. It was enough to send him to sleep, so when Winslow paused for a pee, Frost made a break for it. He exited the study, intending to leave by the front door, but on entering the hall bumped straight into his brother-in-law. By Frost's own generous standards Brazier had had a lot to drink. Rather like Winslow, this seemed to compel him to deliver lectures, but Brazier's chosen subject was Mary Frost's decline.

Frost endured it for a couple of minutes, but it was clearly an encounter that was never going to end well. He heard all about Mary's good breeding and the usual tosh about how he'd corrupted her. Usually he just shrugged off the views of people he considered idiots, but there was a faintly sleazy tone beneath Brazier's drunken reproach, as he talked about that lovely girl and how wasted she'd been on an oaf like him, that gave him the mounting urge to plant one right between Brazier's shifty eyes.

'. . . And then she started drinking – which, as anyone knows . . .'

That was it. Frost grabbed Brazier by the cravat and pulled down the leering face so he was level with it, and then head-butted him for all he was worth. Blood spurted from Brazier's smashed nose and he staggered back against the hall table, knocking over some poncey china clown figurine which smashed on the floor. Frost felt concussed from the blow and was sure he was going to topple over. But just then he felt a firm grip on his shoulder and a calm voice saying, 'Hey, Jack.'

Frost looked up into the concerned eyes of DS John Waters.

'John. Nice of you to pop by.'

'Time to go, Jack.'

'Probably should, eh?' He smiled.

'It's highly likely they're from the same body, and blood tests will corroborate this, though not prove it one hundred per cent.' Drysdale continued: 'They are, I think we can all agree, both from a male.'

Simms regarded the pale hairy foot in the tray before him, and beside it the upturned hand, which was large and thick-set. Both articles he was having difficulty registering as real body parts; they looked more like props from *The Addams Family*.

'We can also observe that the method of severing is consistent,' said Drysdale.

'The fingers look broken,' Clarke mused. Drysdale nodded enthusiastically. Simms was put out – why the hell couldn't he notice things like that?

'Yes, quite! Now look at this,' Drysdale added. 'See the toenails – manicured, clean. And the palm of the hand, soft, indicating no manual work. Someone with a comfortable life, perhaps?'

'I see,' responded Simms, racking his brain for something useful to say. 'Skin must tell you something, about age?' he offered doubtfully.

'Yes. Texture is a good indication.' The pathologist stroked the severed limb, almost affectionately. 'I would hazard that the victim is under thirty. There's a powdery residue underneath the fingernails – I will need to run some tests . . .'

'Any idea how long these have been lying there?'

'A matter of days at most. The cold weather would slow the decomposition, but as the detective rightly mentioned, they couldn't have been there very long as the birds would've had them. I shall be in touch with Forensics.' The pathologist looked quite excited; unusual for him, thought Simms.

*

'Thanks for coming, Sue,' Simms said quietly, holding open the door. The showers had ceased and the sun hung low above the pine trees that bordered the lab grounds. Simms had always found the tranquil, picture-postcard setting of the County lab to be at odds with the morbid secrets it held inside.

'No, not at all – I screwed up. I should have cordoned off the field when the foot appeared, I know that.' She smiled tiredly. 'Thanks for not making a meal of it – Mullett would have gone ballistic. Him and his procedure . . .'

'He need never know,' Simms reassured her, pulling out his cigarettes.

'Not for me, thanks.'

'Given up?' He flicked the Zippo top up, lighting one.

'Yep, sort of . . .'

'Lots are. At seventy pence a packet, no wonder . . .' He sensed something awkward in her manner. 'Right, I'll drop you off, you look beat.'

'What about you?'

'I'll head back to the station, see if the SOCOs have turned up anything interesting from the Coconut Grove, then wait for Harry to come round.'

'You want that case badly, don't you, Derek? I know they're all out and it seems like your chance – but don't get too excited; once Frost is back in the land of the living . . .'

Simms frowned at her unfortunate turn of phrase, but she misread it as boyish dejection and reached out to touch his cheek. He pulled back in surprise – she was never touchy-feely at the best of times, so he hardly expected that! He could never work her out. He looked at the dark smudges under her eyes and said, 'C'mon, you're shattered, we'd best get you home.'

Thursday (5)

'Thanks for that, John. Things might've got out of hand.' Frost slumped in the Vauxhall's passenger seat.

'What do you mean *might've*? You just headbutted your brother-in-law.'

'Nah, that was more of a smooch.'

His relief at being whisked away from the ugly scene at his in-laws' helped him make light of it, but inwardly Frost cringed at his loss of control. After Mary's death he'd assumed that his relationship with the Simpsons couldn't suffer any more damage, and might even be repaired, so he was furious with himself, particularly for having given that spiv Julian the satisfaction of causing his latest disgrace.

As they accelerated along the Rimmington Road towards Denton he pushed away these gloomy thoughts by turning his attention to Waters. 'Anyway, what are you doing here? Aren't you on duty?'

'Yep, but I thought you'd want to hear the latest news. Harry Baskin's been shot.'

'Bugger me!' Frost exclaimed, the surprise causing an unpleasant reflux of Scotch up his windpipe. 'Where?'

'At the Coconut Grove.'

'How bad?'

'We wait to see . . . he's only just come round. Simms and Clarke took the call earlier.'

'So are they at the hospital?'

'Nope, at the lab. A different case. A couple of severed limbs have been found in a field outside Denton. But anyway—'

'Severed limbs?' Frost puffed out his cheeks. 'Blimey, take the morning off to bury the old lady and chaos breaks out. Let's go and see the old blighter first – I could do with cheering up.'

Waters followed Frost past rows of beds towards the curtained corner at the far end of the ward. He watched the detective totter worryingly close to a medication trolley, and sneakily pat a nurse's bottom, causing her to jolt upright from tucking in sheets at the foot of a patient's bed. Perhaps it hadn't been wise to bring him here in his semi-inebriated state.

A uniformed officer looking bored sitting outside the drawn curtains indicated that this was their man. Baskin was to be moved to a private room later that day; the police presence was unsettling the other patients. Frost parted the curtains dramatically as if making a stage entrance.

'Harry!' he said loudly with mock concern.

Baskin shrugged. Aside from a slight pallor the corpulent gangster did not look remotely unwell, let alone like the victim of a gunshot. However, he did look profoundly pissed off.

'Bitch won't let me smoke,' he grunted. 'Says it's not allowed.'

'It's not good for you, Harry,' Frost needled, pulling up a visitor's chair, 'or so I'm told.'

'Neither's getting shot. What's he doing here?' He gestured with his chin at Waters who remained standing at the foot of the bed.

'You've met DS Waters, haven't you?'

Baskin narrowed his eyes. 'Monkeys aren't allowed in here either.'

'Rather a monkey than a fat white slug,' Waters replied. 'Where's the salt? Maybe we can put you out of your agony.'

'Now, Harry, no need for those kinds of comments, or I shall lose my sympathy very quickly. Where'd they get you?' Frost poked the gangster's bandaged shoulder sharply. 'Was it here?'

'Jesus Christ, Frost!' He writhed in pain. 'Bleedin' bullet's still in there.'

'Well, just you watch your tongue, and be a good boy.'

'All right, all right.' He nodded at Waters while gently rubbing his bandaged torso. 'Sorry, son. I'm not my usual rational self, for some reason.'

'Now.' Frost stretched back, placing his hands behind

his head. 'Why would anyone want to take a pot-shot at you?'

'Why indeed, that's what I want to know—'

'Could it have been . . .'

'It was some bird.'

Frost raised his eyebrows. '"Some bird". That narrows the field.'

Waters pulled out his notebook. 'Can you give us a description?'

'Didn't get much of a chance – it all happened so damned quickly.' Baskin winced irritably as he tried to adjust himself in the bed. 'Cecil says there's a stripper to see me, next second he's splattered across me financials. And I'm lying in a pool of me own claret. It was a bit of a shock, I can tell you.'

Frost got up as if bored and stared out of the window, tapping his foot impatiently. Was he listening? Difficult to say. He didn't make a comment, so Waters continued: 'But you must have noticed something – height, hair colour?'

'About five six or five eight. Blonde – peroxide blonde. A bob – with a fringe.' Baskin marked a line across his forehead. 'Striking cheekbones. Tasty bird; big hooters.'

'Only you would remember her breasts, Harry,' Frost said, turning back to him. His eyes looked devastatingly tired, the eyelids a livid red under the unforgiving hospital strip lights. Must be the booze, Waters thought.

'Me? Nah. Seen one tit, you've seen them all. Cecil alerted me to it – last words the poor bugger said.

There'll be hell to pay from my sister Phyllis for getting her boy shot. *And* from my wife.' He sighed.

'Age?' Waters asked.

'Couldn't tell you. She was well made up, a bit over the top, in fact. If I'd taken her on 'arf the warpaint would've had to go.'

'So she really was a stripper you think?' Waters asked.

'Could be . . . but why one would take a pop is beyond me; I've always been good to the girls, don't knock 'em around. There's been ups and downs over the years, but like any business, really. I've taken good care of 'em mainly.'

'Yes, like a kindly uncle,' Frost said with distaste, stepping back from the window. 'OK, let's ignore your chequered past for now; we start trawling through that we'll never get out of here. Let's start with who you could have annoyed recently, right? Where have you been in the last twenty-four hours?'

'At the Coconut Grove,' Baskin said sardonically.

'What, you've not even been home?'

'We had a card game going.'

'Cards.' Frost shook his head regretfully. 'So, you've been fleecing the punters.'

'No money was taken from the crime scene,' Waters interjected.

'Precisely, to allay any obvious suspicion that money was the motive . . . but it's unlikely anyone would rub you out over a little game of poker . . . unless you've moved into a bigger league, Harry?'

'Oi, I've not been rubbed out,' complained Baskin

from the bed. 'No, nobody I'd not played with before.'

'You're still with us, granted, but your nephew is not in such good shape, he's lost a lot of blood. Come on, I want those names. It's a start.'

Waters took the names down in his notebook, but he instinctively agreed with Frost; it seemed unlikely Baskin had been shot over a card game. These local types – Jeremy Tile who ran the bookie's in London Street; Raymond Shooter, the publican of the Bird in Hand; Harvey Evans, the alcoholic Welsh coach of Denton RFC, and Gavin Cribbs, a solicitor on Gentlemen's Walk – were hardly a threatening bunch. Plus they were all men.

'We'd better check out the girls too – disgruntled employees, any that have left under a cloud in the last month, and so forth. Where do you keep your personnel files?'

Harry snorted. 'Records are pretty sketchy . . . it's all cash in hand; part-time in the main. The women we get, very few of them are actually dancers.'

'Really?' Frost exclaimed. 'And there's me thinking they were trained by the Royal Ballet. So, what kind of women *do* you get?'

Baskin shrugged. 'All kinds, really; most do it for a bit of pin money, working the circuit – pubs, football club, Labour club and what have you. There's only two girls on the books full-time. Kate and Rachel.'

'Kate and Rachel?' cut in Waters, pen poised.

'Kate Greenlaw – she was there when it happened. Good girl, been with me two years, sees it as the route to something better. Lord knows what. Always practising her routine. And Rachel Rayner, a diamond, but getting on, doesn't get her kit off much these days – runs the bar.'

Frost smiled. 'Such a way with words you have, Harry. What do you mean by "getting on"? Early forties?'

'Nah, late twenties.'

Waters laughed. 'That's hardly getting on, is it? That's younger than me! When you get to Jack's age, that's when you're really over the hill.'

'Exactly.' Baskin sniffed. 'Nobody's going to fork out to see Jack in the buff, are they?'

After half an hour Baskin had grown tired, and Frost left him to doze. For all his light-heartedness, he was still in a state of shock and completely clueless as to who'd taken a pot-shot at him.

Waters had dropped Frost off on the corner of Eagle Lane and driven on to interview one of Harry's girls. Frost had to get back to the nick; a press frenzy was growing over the body parts found in a field. He'd spoken to Johnny Johnson on the squawk-box in the car and said he'd handle it.

Frost had decided to walk the remainder of the way to clear his head. He needed to take command of the situation. Mullett was AWOL, possibly still at his wife's wake, hard to imagine though that was. The weather too had cleared and the last of the sunset was a deep bruised pink. He passed the Eagle pub, the policemen's boozer, which he noted was getting a lick of paint. He

61

nodded approvingly to a man in overalls folding away a ladder. Eagle Lane was not exactly the prettiest of Denton's streets and could do with tarting up. The station itself, an eyesore of sixties design, loomed into view. Flamin' hell, was that a TV van parked up?

Frost slipped discreetly through the mob of cameras and microphones and up the front steps, where two uniform stood stoically to attention. This lot could easily be palmed off, he thought cunningly, and spun round to address the press.

'Afternoon, ladies and gentlemen. How can I help?' He beamed.

Everyone bellowed at once, like over-excited children eager for the teacher's attention. 'One at a time, please.' Frost pointed to a familiar face at the front of the crowd, 'Let's start with you – Sandy?'

'Is it true that body parts have turned up in a farmer's field outside Denton?'

'That's correct,' Frost said, lighting a cigarette.

'Can you say exactly what has been found?'

'Nope,' Frost said bluntly.

'Why not?' Sandy Lane asked, taken aback. 'Nev Sanderson said there was a foot and—'

'Why you asking me, then?' Frost snapped. 'Next – yes, young lady?' He singled out a young woman, admiring her lustrous hair – straight off the Harmony hairspray advert.

'Have you a body?'

'This is it. What you reckon?' He drummed his chest playfully.

'No, I meant . . .' She stuttered to a halt, embarrassed.

'Jack, c'mon,' Lane insisted. 'Got to be a murder inquiry, surely? Somebody hacked to death. Sanderson reckons—'

'Sandy! Not necessarily.' Frost held up his hand. 'We need to investigate this thoroughly; murder is a possibility, but first I want to rule out an accident.'

'Accident?' Harmony said.

'Yes, we will be conducting a thorough search of Mr Sanderson's farm and equipment. There's a chance that some poor sod got run over by his combine harvester – nothing more sinister than that.' And with that Frost turned on his heel and entered the building wearing a grin; serve the gobby farmer right, he thought.

Thursday (6) _____

'You're kidding,' Simms said sulkily. 'I'm gutted. Didn't you tell him I was handling Baskin? That I'd been to the Coconut Grove?'

'Don't shoot the messenger,' Johnson rebuked him from behind the reception desk. 'I said you were on it. But Waters and Frost have already been to the General. And that's as much as I know.'

Simms shook his head in despair. 'You'd think he'd take the bleeding day off. I mean, he has just buried his wife.'

'Not our Jack; he's back already – just been chatting with our friends the press.'

'I heard.' Simms sighed. 'Not sure Mullett will appreciate him announcing that some bugger has been mown down by a combine harvester . . .'

He strolled over to the noticeboard, and scanned the missing-persons list. Two children, a teenage girl and a seven-year-old boy. Very few adults, especially men, were ever reported as missing. 'Balls,' he muttered to himself. The owner of the severed limbs was hardly going to fall into his lap; he knew he'd have to cast the net wider, around the county for a start. It was only five; he could make a few calls before calling it a day . . .

Johnson was talking behind him. 'Sorry, Sarge,' said Simms. 'Didn't catch that.'

'I've got instructions to pin these up on the board, if you wouldn't mind moving aside.'

The blue of a five-pound note caught Simms's eye.

'What, giving money away now, are we?'

'Fakes,' said Johnson. 'Been a few found circulating in the county. I'm sure Mr Mullett will brief everyone in due course.' He handed one to Simms and fixed the other to the board, queen side up.

'They look all right to me.' Simms pulled the note taut and regarded the Duke of Wellington. 'Not that I see that many, at least not for long.'

'It's the texture. Feel.'

Simms found Johnson was right. Although the note looked sound, the paper quality was different; it didn't have the crisp, durable feel of a normal fiver.

'We've got to dish out a bunch. Must leave a note before I change shift.'

'What do you mean, "dish out"?'

'Give them out to shopkeepers, banks and so forth, so they know what they're looking for.' Johnson returned to reception and pulled out a Jiffy bag from underneath the desk. 'From Scotland Yard, no less. Here, you can sign for a dozen now.'

Simms took an envelope and slipped it inside his leather jacket.

'They were supposed to go out this morning,' Johnson continued. 'But what with the funeral and all . . . I must remind Bill,' he repeated.

'Well, I certainly won't forget sixty quid in my pocket. Cheers.'

DS John Waters wondered if he had the right woman; Rachel Rayner was certainly not 'getting on', to use Baskin's phrase. Sitting opposite him with her back to the breakfast bar of the smart, pristine kitchen was a remarkably attractive young woman.

'So,' drawled Rayner, 'someone finally got fed up and tried to plug the old bastard.' She took a languid drag of her cigarette, her eyes fixed firmly on Waters. Now she was facing him directly, he noticed a bruise over her right eye.

'Seems so,' he replied, sipping his coffee. 'Why would anyone feel that way, do you think?'

Her expression changed to one of suspicion. 'You're new around here, right?'

'Been in Denton six months.'

Rain began to patter on the window.

'Have you met Harry?'

'Once or twice. You're implying that it's no surprise Harry got shot. He's not exactly a Boy Scout, but we haven't discovered anything that would warrant—'

'*We?* What, Frost and the Keystone Cops?' She laughed, throwing her head back and running her fingers through short, raven-black hair. This boyish feature was offset by a pair of large pale blue eyes, the right one slightly bloodshot, and a plum-coloured pout. 'No, you're right. Big, cuddly Harry, he wouldn't hurt a fly.'

The tinge of bitterness in her voice intrigued Waters. 'How long have you worked for Baskin, Miss Rayner?'

'Ten years, on and off.'

'Harry told us you'd retired from the stage.'

'He did, did he?' She rolled her eyes. 'I manage the place – I don't *perform*.'

'He implied you were too old.' Waters said it with a clear look of disbelief.

She shrugged matter-of-factly. 'Harry likes them young.'

'You must see who comes, who goes?'

'I'm not his secretary. I told you, I manage the club, that's it.'

'What does that involve?'

'Hiring the acts. Running the bar; arranging brewery deliveries. It's not Camden Palace, but it needs looking after.'

'When you say hiring the acts . . .'

'The girls, Sergeant.' She lit another cigarette, gracefully uncrossing and recrossing her slim legs. She gave Waters a knowing look. 'He'd never get anyone to work there if I didn't handle it. Harry can't keep his hands off them; especially the younger ones.'

'Hold on . . . the girl who shot Baskin this morning, the boy told him she was a stripper.'

Waters pulled out his notebook and relayed what Baskin had said, along with the description.

'Doesn't sound like one of ours.'

'Would Baskin and Rhodes have recognized her if she was?'

'More than likely.'

Waters looked troubled. 'So Cecil just merrily lets in some stranger off the street. I know Harry's hardly Don Corleone, but if you think he had it coming, I'm surprised by the lax security arrangements.'

She considered this for a moment. 'Well, whoever it was knew that Harry can never resist a pretty girl, and Cecil wouldn't have wanted him to miss out. He's not the sharpest tool in the box, our Cecil, but he could hardly be expected to know she was packing.'

The woman looked at Waters. Faint wrinkles were just beginning to show at the corners of her pale blue eyes.

'And so, back to our original discussion. Who do you think might, in your own words, be "fed up" enough with Harry to want to wipe him out?'

'God, where would you start . . . Harry's mixed in dodgy company for years. Could be anyone.'

Waters glanced around the large, neat kitchen. 'Pay you well, does he?'

'Am I a suspect?' she snapped.

'No, we're just finding out as much as we can about Harry.'

'Of course, sorry – I'm just tired.'

'What are your hours, Miss Rayner?'

'Six p.m. to three a.m.'

Rayner gave an account of the previous night at the Coconut Grove. Her story checked out with Kate Greenlaw's statement. Nothing out of the ordinary had happened, and Harry was still at the card table when Rayner left at ten past three on Thursday morning.

'Whoever shot him knew he'd still be there at that time in the morning, and not at home. Did he often spend the night in his office?'

'I have no idea. I don't give him a kiss goodnight and I'm not there in the morning . . .'

'How would you describe your relationship with Harry?'

'I've put up with him for ten years.' She shrugged. 'That's about the best I can say.'

Waters wondered just how much Rayner's evasive manner might be concealing. He was about to start probing further when a telephone rang from somewhere within the house.

'Do you mind if I get that?' She slipped elegantly out of the room without waiting for an answer. Waters stood up and took in his surroundings in more detail, running his fingers across the granite work surface and admiring the shiny, German-made appliances. It seemed unlikely Miss Rayner could've kitted out this kitchen solely on her wages from Baskin's. Did she take on customers of her own, Waters wondered?

She returned and leaned alluringly against the door-frame, an amused look on her face. 'It's Harry on the phone, calling from his hospital bed. He wants to make sure I open up this evening as per usual . . .'

Waters raised an eyebrow; this Denton lot were a hardy bunch, he'd give them that. Someone had clearly wanted Baskin dead, but the wounded club owner's main concern was to keep his joint open. Waters was about to ask about her eye, then thought better of it; this woman was probably as tough as Baskin and would not welcome concern from a black copper she'd only just met.

'I'd best be out of your way, then,' Waters said, and slid his card across the table. 'But if you think of anything, give me a call.'

The street was deserted. Having claimed to know his way around Rimmington, Superintendent Mullett, head swimming with booze, was reluctant to tell his two companions that he hadn't a clue where they were headed. They'd been wandering down leafy avenues and picturesque lanes for what seemed like ages. One thing is clear, though, he thought with a pang, Rimmington is certainly a desirable place. Mr and Mrs Mullett had been all set to move to Denton's upmarket neighbour last spring, but unfortunately the sale of their house had fallen through. Mullett shuddered as he recalled the charges of robbery and murder against the estate agent who'd been handling it; it had tainted the whole business and they'd promptly taken their house off the market, cheering themselves up with a two-week vacation in the South of France.

The area he now found himself in wasn't even vaguely familiar. It was all very different on foot, he reasoned.

'Down here, guv?' said a wet DC Hanlon, indicating a cobbled lane to their left. 'I seem to remember a pub being somewhere around here.'

'I think you're right, Art,' Sergeant Wells agreed. 'The Barley Mow, I reckon.'

'Sounds plausible to me, gents,' Mullett offered lamely.

As they struck off down the lane, a relieved Mullett could indeed make out a pub sign creaking gently in the middle distance. It was at the superintendent's insistence that the three of them left the Simpson place to look for a hostelry to round off the day. A bit of bonding with the rank and file was just what was required after sucking up to that bunch of snobs, although the attraction had somewhat worn off after half an hour of bumbling around in the dark.

Once inside, however, Mullett felt better. The Barley Mow was a welcoming pub with a roaring fire, and somewhere there was a jukebox playing Elvis at a comfortable level. Hanlon went straight to the bar and got a round in with surprising alacrity, while Mullett and Wells took seats in the corner next to the fire, the heat of which compelled Mullett to loosen his tie and remove his jacket. They drank thirstily.

'So, men,' opened Mullett. 'Tell me, how exactly did the Frosts get together?' Emboldened by drink, he couldn't resist asking how Frost had infiltrated such a fine upstanding family, one that he himself yearned to know socially. By the end of his pint, he wished he hadn't bothered. To the ever-striving, unjustly rebuffed Mullett this unlikely couple's tale was as clichéd and unedifying as they come. Mary Simpson had, it seemed, fallen for the boy from the wrong side of the tracks mainly to annoy her father. Though William Frost was a policeman, ostensibly a respectable figure, Mary's father saw merely someone shambolic, uneducated and unlikely to go far. The young Frost had been a tearaway too – no surprise there, Mullett thought – and even before they married there was turmoil relating to drinking and infidelity. Sadly, marriage to Mary did little to curb Frost's wilder tendencies; instead Mary herself fell into increasingly bad ways – in fact, you might say Frost corrupted her.

'And then the other one, Mary's sister, she married a second-hand-car dealer!' exclaimed Hanlon. 'Now, there's a rogue if ever there was one.'

Mullett was distinctly nonplussed. Another round was in order. 'OK, men, my shout.'

'No, no, I'll get these, guv,' Hanlon piped up.

'No, I insist,' Mullett affirmed. 'You got the last round.'

Despite it being Mullett's turn, Hanlon followed him to the bar and gave a nod to the landlord. He was a veritable ox of a man with a full, yellow beard.

'Evening, squire. What'll it be?'

Mullett viewed the taps on offer. He seldom visited

public houses and plumped for the only name he recognized. 'Three pints of IPA, please, landlord.'

Having pulled the pints, the landlord, in response to a gesture from Hanlon, thrust his hand towards Mullett as though inviting a handshake. The superintendent thought it peculiar behaviour but reciprocated. The big man's grip was firm – Mullett felt a pronounced pressure from the man's thumb above his own.

'That'll be one pound twenty.'

Back at the table Mullett raised his pint. 'Cheers,' he said.

'Should've let me get that, guv,' Hanlon murmured quietly, taking his seat. 'Wouldn't have cost.' Hanlon and Wells exchanged furtive glances.

'I'm sorry – I'm not with you,' Mullett replied after a mouthful of beer. Then it suddenly clicked into place – the very issue that had been troubling him all day. 'Are you saying he's . . . that you . . . ?'

They both nodded ever so slightly. Good Christ, Mullett thought, whatever next!

Thursday (7) ────────────────

'I've checked the missing-persons lists as far afield as Reading. No males under thirty reported missing in the last two weeks.'

It was gone seven and Simms had been about to jack it in when Frost had wandered into the CID office, wanting the lowdown on the day's developments. 'Apart from Rimmington, that is, where they couldn't tell me. Their computer's swallowed the list.'

'Well, I don't think we need alarm ourselves just yet about a hand and foot; anyway, I fobbed off the press, to buy us a bit of time,' Frost said, slurping his coffee noisily.

'So I heard; old Sanderson was pretty nonplussed at having uniform wandering all over his farm.'

'He should keep his cakehole shut, then, instead of blabbing to the *Echo*. But nevertheless, leave no stone unturned. Might find something nasty in the wood-shed. Now' – he coughed – 'the Coconut Grove.'

As confidently as he could muster, Simms told him what they had, which wasn't much. The ballistics report would be in by the end of tomorrow.

'The question is, how did she get there?'

'I told you, nobody saw a thing.'

'If she'd come by car then surely someone would have heard her pull up. Baskin, for example – his office overlooks the car park.'

'Sounds a bit risky.'

'Exactly,' Frost confirmed. 'So, maybe she parked some distance away. But it's a narrow lane, no lay-by, and no parking on the main road either, so she'd either have had to leave her car somewhere really conspicuous . . .'

'Or come by foot,' Simms suggested. 'But if she did it's a bloody long way – out of the lane and then a good two miles down the Bath Road, back to Denton central . . .'

'So, she either walked or got dropped off.'

'So we might be looking for an accomplice,' Simms concurred.

But Frost had drifted off in thought. The room was oddly quiet.

'Err . . . how is Baskin?' Simms asked.

'He'll survive.' Frost shrugged. 'Not so sure about the boy.'

'Don't you think we should request that the super unlock the cabinet?'

'No, we are not tooling up.'

Simms knew Frost was anti-gun, but he nevertheless

persisted: 'But there's someone out there armed and dangerous – a wo—'

'A woman too, I know.' Frost rubbed his jaw anxiously. 'A further cause for concern, I agree, but until we have a fix on a suspect I see no reason to start dishing out shooters to you lot. That would only add to my worry.' Frost looked him in the eye. 'No, we'll follow procedure – unusual move, I know – and when we find who's responsible we'll call in those who know what they're doing: the firearms unit. Then and only then, if necessary, will we take the dubious step of arming ourselves.'

Simms knew it was pointless to argue and changed tack. 'I couldn't understand why she didn't finish off the job.'

'There're a number of possibilities.' Frost explained his main theory, that Baskin was hit for cheating at cards, so it was more punishment than murder attempt. This to Simms's mind seemed ridiculous, especially given that Rhodes was shot too. Frost proceeded to show him the names of four card players whom he wanted to question. Simms was on the point of objecting, but took one look at the tired, bedraggled Frost and decided he'd leave it until tomorrow, when after a night's sleep the overwrought DS might see the error in his logic. Simms would, however, draw the line at knocking up card players at eight o'clock in the evening, and was about to assert this when he was interrupted by the phone. Frost picked it up. 'This is not my phone,' was his inexplicable retort into the receiver before wearily hanging up.

Simms was once again about to protest when DS Waters ambled in.

'Wotcha, Sarge,' said Frost. 'What news of the retired stripper?'

Waters flopped down in the chair opposite. 'Well, for a start she says she's no stripper, never was, in fact. She didn't have much to say, except she's the one who books the girls, not Baskin.'

'Well, that's something. Does she recognize our hit-woman from Baskin's informative description?' Simms quickly interposed.

'Huh. Blonde and big knockers, yeah, right. Doubt it. But she said they weren't expecting anyone in.'

'Well, why did they let her in, then?' he pressed eagerly.

Waters yawned. 'Harry can't resist a looker . . .'

Both Simms and Frost concurred knowingly. The phone started to ring again.

'Forget it.' Waters waved the noise away. 'Baskin called while I was there to make sure she opened up tonight.'

'Ha! That's the spirit,' Frost clucked. 'What do you say to that?'

'I know! There's a pint of his blood still drying on the carpet!'

'Sergeant Frost.' A young PC appeared in the doorway with a vexed look on his face. The young constable was on the front desk, having just relieved Johnny Johnson. 'There's been a disturbance in a pub in Rimmington.'

'Rimmington? What's it got to do with me?'

'Superintendent Kelsey is on the blower.' All four looked at the angrily vibrating telephone. Simms had never met the Rimmington commander but knew that unlike Mullett he had a reputation for honesty and plain speaking.

Frost picked up the phone and cupped the mouthpiece. 'Right, you two are dismissed.'

Simms sat rooted, keen to listen in, but Frost was having none of it.

'Go on, bugger off!' He paused. 'Superintendent Kelsey?' Frost knew the station-commander only vaguely.

'To whom am I speaking?' came a broad Northern burr. Kelsey had been transferred to Rimmington the previous year after two decades in a bleak corner of West Yorkshire.

'Detective Sergeant Frost.'

'Ahh . . . Frost,' the man answered, seemingly satisfied by this. 'You're going to enjoy this.'

'Oh?'

'There's been an incident . . . involving Superintendent Mullett.'

Frost rather regretted dismissing Simms and Waters. 'An incident involving Superintendent Mullett? I'm all ears . . .'

'Ah. Come in.'

She was unable to make out where the voice had come from; the room was in virtual darkness save for a light directly above a snooker table. A tall, lean man with a bald head, aged around forty, paced lethargically, eyeing the baize.

'Over here, come and sit next to me.'

Once her eyes adjusted she spotted the glint of the light reflecting off his crystal glass.

'Come watch the game,' he murmured softly, patting the plush seat next to him.

A heavier man with a floppy curtain of hair now stepped up to the table, frowning anxiously.

'Kevin here is in a bit of a predicament.' She felt his stale breath on her cheek.

'Why?' she whispered, sensing tension in the room.

'Shh . . .'

The sharp clack of balls from the table made her jump. Her companion tutted, his heavy hand resting on her thigh. The floppy-haired man's shot had not gone as planned. She saw the lean one's face crease into a smile.

'Kevin has been a silly boy,' he whispered. 'Nobbled his opponent last week in the regional snooker finals. A pretty thing like you won't be interested in such . . . matters.' He paused to light a cigarette. 'It's only a game, but people take it very seriously. Especially where money is involved.'

'Of course,' she agreed, beginning to understand the situation; *his* money.

'The other poor bugger had to play with broken fingers.'

She noticed beads of sweat on Curtain's brow. The lean man was on the black.

'So, we're going to test just how good laddy here will be, under the same handicap.'

The final ball cannoned across the table and disappeared in an instant in the corner pocket, as though sucked down.

'Right.' Her companion got up slowly, groaning as though with back pain, and moved towards the table. She watched fear take hold of the defeated Kevin.

'Pumpy . . . *please*,' he pleaded. 'Pumpy . . .'

'Now, Kev, let's not be a baby about this.' He had something in the palm of his hand. 'Stick or ball?'

'Pumpy . . . please.'

'OK, never mind, let's do it this way. Heads, stick; tails, ball.' Moving into the light of the table, Pumpy tossed the coin he was holding. Seeing him properly now, she was struck by the sheer bulk of the man. He was enormous. 'So, what've we got?'

'Tails,' Kevin whimpered.

She watched the lean man's face erupt into a broad grin. His eyes were hidden behind tinted glasses, which somehow made him even more intimidating. 'Robert's favourite. Isn't it, Robbo?' Pumpy said, while Robert just continued smiling and toyed with something that looked like a sock.

'Ever seen *Scum*?' said the big man, addressing her. 'It's a film about a bunch of horrible little toerags at odds with the British penal system.'

She nodded, not that he could see her, but then he didn't need to. Almost everyone of her generation had seen it. She knew what was coming, and gripped the seat tightly.

'No, Pumpy, no!' Kevin backed into two heavies who had been lurking in the shadows.

'Raymond, help Kev place his right hand on the table, please.' A tall, crop-haired man stepped forward, as Robert knotted the sock, now laden with snooker balls. 'And you, young lady, come with me.'

She heard a sickening crack before the gangster pulled the door shut behind him. Poor Kevin wouldn't be playing snooker again for a very long time.

'Now then, what can I do for you, my lovely Louise?'

No longer disguised by the darkness of the snooker hall, the full brunt of Pumpy's pockmarked ugliness caused an involuntary shudder in her.

Thursday (8) _____

It was too good to be true. Mullett being arrested for drunk and disorderly behaviour would've made Frost's year, but the Rimmington station commander had been pulling his leg. All that had really happened, he soon explained, was that an area car had found Denton's own commander wandering the streets alone, lost and looking for a taxi. The officer had kindly driven him home. No, the real reason Kelsey wanted to speak to Frost was Baskin.

'I didn't take the call, I was . . . off duty this morning.'

'Of course. Forgive me, Frost. My condolences. It must've been a very difficult time.'

'Not a problem,' Frost replied, wondering how well known his affairs were in the county, 'but I did visit Baskin in Denton General this afternoon.'

'And?'

'He's in the dark. Thinks it was some would-be stripper—'

'And what do you think?' Kelsey cut in.

'We're talking about Harry Baskin,' Frost said, stalling, not really wishing to tell a man he didn't know, albeit it a senior policeman, his budding theories. 'Club owner, late fifties, been lord of the manor for the past twenty years in a quiet sort of way, ruffled a good few feathers but never really got seriously dirty – grubby, yes – but outright dirty, no. Friends in high places. Opened a sauna. Owns a successful building firm . . .'

'Yes, the Assistant Chief Constable has certainly helped that along.'

'How do you mean?' Frost asked disingenuously.

'Come on, Sergeant, you remember how Eagle Lane got rebuilt by Baskin's firm, after all the bomb damage last year – one of the first major contracts he was awarded. I heard that work dragged on for ages and went over budget. And then ol' Harry's sauna place was greenlighted, no questions asked.'

'Yes, I do remember.' Frost thought back to PC Miller spotting Winslow coming out of the Pink Toothbrush in May. Could the ACC be in with Baskin, as Kelsey seemed to imply? 'Maybe the ACC is doing his bit to fight the recession.'

'Quite.' Kelsey sighed, then after a pause added, 'And being gay in the police is hard work, no matter what rank.'

Frost raised his eyebrows at the extraordinarily indiscreet revelation, then smiled as he sensed things falling into place. Winslow – gay, of course. As is so often the way, once the truth dawns how obvious it all seems.

'Frost? Hello? Are you still there?'

'Yes, sir, just lighting a cigarette.' In fact he already had one lit. 'So, are you suggesting that the ACC had something to do with the shooting?'

'I'm not suggesting anything . . . though it does give pause for thought when there are shady goings-on behind the scenes, eh, Sergeant? No, my concern is what Baskin might be involved with. Drugs are becoming a problem with these underworld types, and it's not the sort of thing we want spreading through the neighbourhood. But if you think it's over some stripper he's shagged, I'll leave it with you.'

'Right you are, sir,' Frost said, relieved.

'And congratulations, Frost. I hear you're up for inspector.'

For the second time in two minutes Frost had learned something new. 'Am I, sir?'

'Yes. We've been saddled with that arse from Eagle Lane, Allen, so Mullett has no option but to promote you. He's been holding out, but the ACC has always had a soft spot for you . . . Well, goodnight, Frost.'

'Goodnight, sir.' The line had already gone dead. Frost pulled a bottle of whisky from the filing cabinet, still reeling from their extraordinary conversation, the contents of which would require some deep consideration. Why, he thought as he flicked an old teabag out of an old chipped Silver Jubilee mug, missing the bin, would Kelsey be concerned about an old Denton lag like Baskin? The mention of promotion he gave little heed to – it had been hinted at before by the ACC himself, but proved as yet elusive. It was now a year since his old boss and mentor DI Williams had been murdered; if it was going to happen, then surely it would have done by now. He poured a slug of whisky into the grimy mug.

And why call now, at this time of the evening? Normally a super would want to speak to someone of his own rank, but Kelsey knew Mullett wouldn't be around; indeed, his own men had practically tucked him up in bed. So had he planned to get hold of Frost? Wearily he rubbed his sore eyes; it had been a long day and his head was full of bad thoughts. He felt an urge to return to the Simpsons'; his other option, a cold, empty house, seemed suddenly far less appealing than trying to make amends for his earlier disgrace. He wasn't quite ready to let go.

'Champagne?'

Louise Daley needed a drink, but not champagne. She needed something way stronger.

'Ta,' she said nevertheless, taking the flute and moving towards the plate-glass window. In the hall below them were around two dozen full-size snooker tables. Abruptly she took a step back.

'Don't worry – it's mirrored,' he said from behind her, then added, brightly, 'So, how was your day?'

'Mixed,' she replied, sipping from the glass, unable to

turn round and meet his eye. She realized there was no point in beating around the bush so she took a deep breath and confessed: 'I'm not sure Baskin is dead.'

'Oh?' He was standing close behind her – there was a whiff of a familiar aftershave, Denim, maybe – looking down at the games drawing to a close as the evening ended. One by one the lights above the tables were turned off. The only sound was the fizz from their drinks.

'I shot him, make no mistake, he went down, and the boy who got in the way,' she said assertively, 'but the gun jammed, so I couldn't make sure. Later I saw ambulances. He might be in the hospital.'

'Well, if he is in the hospital, it's unlikely he's dead, is it?'

'I guess so.'

'Did he get a look at you?' he asked calmly.

She turned to face him. God, that black shirt and grey waistcoat was so old-hat – he looked more like a retired snooker player than a gangster.

'I was in disguise. It all happened too quickly for him to recognize me.'

He seemed satisfied with this. 'Well, I, as you know, am a disinterested party – and that's the way I'd like it to remain.'

'Fair enough.' What he meant by that, she had no idea. 'But the other job. Does that still stand? Something tomorrow? C'mon, Marty – there was cash all over that office and I didn't lift so much as tuppence . . . as I was told . . .' she pleaded, as the big man moved from the window and picked up the magnum. Actually lifting cash had never been mentioned; and she would definitely have lifted a few quid if the bloody gun hadn't jammed.

'But the job's not done. Someone else has to finish what you started. It'll cost more after your bodge. Who's to say you won't balls this up too?' He sat down heavily.

'I'll finish him off. Easy.'

'But how – aren't you off to the Costa del Sol?' He looked at her with faux concern.

She gripped her flute in annoyance. 'Not until Tuesday,' she said flatly.

'But if he's in hospital, then how?'

'Don't worry how. Now, about tomorrow – you promised . . .'

'OK.' He smiled, leaning back in the swivel chair. 'I promised your dad I'd look out for you, so look out for you I will.' He rubbed his red jowls with carefully manicured fingers. 'Not quite sure this is what he had in mind, still . . . Gregory Leather – an import-export outfit out on the Denton Industrial Estate.'

'Never heard of them,' she snapped irritably.

'Patience, Louise.' He flipped open the cigarette box and pulled out a thin, exotic Russian number. 'You know, if it wasn't for the cute way your nose wrinkles when you get agitated, there's no doubt you'd be in a ditch somewhere by now.' The deadpan delivery pulled her into check, and reminded her of who she was dealing with. 'Gregory Leather Ltd opened in January. At which time you, Pussy Galore, were holed up in Cardiff.'

Newport. She didn't correct him.

He continued: 'The business is straightforward – they import handbags from the Far East, slap a posh label on them and whack them out around the country; everywhere from Selfridges to the Littlewoods catalogue. Such an operation requires casual labour, ergo weekly wages in cash. You get the picture? Every Friday between eleven and midday a clerk picks up three grand in cash from Bennington's.'

Louise was about to ask a question, but he pre-empted her. 'You don't need to know more – suffice it to say, a disgruntled employee no longer picks up his sixty quid a week in a manila envelope. That's all I'll tell you.'

'The clerk goes alone?'

'Good girl. No, he takes a bruiser from the warehouse with him. You can't miss the pair – right odd couple . . .'

'Piece of cake.'

'All I want is a clean grand. The rest is yours.' That was a 30 per cent cut for him for doing bugger all. He wanted her for the job because she was a woman, and an out-of-town woman at that; she'd try and squeeze him a bit.

'Five hundred.'

The big man rocked back in the chair and laughed. '*Cheeky!* No.'

The door went. Palmer glanced over.

'Seven fifty,' she said quickly.

'No,' he said firmly. 'Now hop it – before I change my mind.'

'Are you sure this is wise?'

Frost ignored Waters' question, blinking at the glare from oncoming headlights on the other side of the Rimmington Road. He pulled his hip flask, which he'd refilled before leaving Eagle Lane, from his inside suit pocket and wound down the window a fraction.

'I mean, you did headbutt your brother-in-law before you left, or have you forgotten?'

'No, I've not forgotten.' Frost screwed the cap back on the flask and lit a cigarette. 'But I need to get the Cortina. The keys are in the in-laws' house.'

'The motor can wait, Jack.'

'It can't – gotta get it washed before I hand it back. Then on Monday it goes.'

'Goes where?'

'Auction, I guess. I get a new one. New model, a Tiara or something . . .'

'*Sierra*. Looks like a jelly mould on wheels.' Waters shook his head. 'One seriously ugly motor.'

'That's something to look forward to, then.' Frost pulled out the hip flask again.

'Go easy on that, eh?'

'Who are you, my mother?' Frost said testily, then regretted his sharp tone, as he was grateful for Waters' concern. 'Don't get me wrong, I appreciate you running me out here like this late at night.'

'Don't worry – I'm not doing you a favour. I want to check out a pub on the stripper circuit in Rimmington. Should just catch it before closing time.'

'Right. Was that a lead from the bird who worked for Baskin?'

'Nah. All I got from her was a couple of names.'

'I think it's unlikely Baskin was hit by a stripper, don't you?' said Frost. 'Call me old-fashioned, but if Harry had been tampering with a girl she'd have got her old man to sort him out. This is a different ball game, although it doesn't explain why he's still alive . . .'

'Rachel Rayner did say one thing,' offered Waters, 'along the lines of, if it wasn't for her he'd never get any girls to work for him. What do you make of that?'

Frost looked out into the blackness. 'Not much. If you were a nineteen-year-old girl, would you want to be leered at by someone old enough to be your grandfather?'

Waters grimaced.

'Here we are,' said Frost as they pulled into the Simpsons' road.

'Are you sure you want to do this? Haven't you had enough for one day?'

'Told you, got to pick up the motor . . .'

'Come with me instead. This boozer does after hours.' Waters gave an imploring smile as Frost pushed open the door. 'I've missed our cosy evenings together.'

'Yes, it's been a while. How about tomorrow, when I'm a bit fresher?' Frost paused, half out of the door, a plan hatching in his mind. 'Come to mine! We'll blow the dust off the chess board, flip on a couple of the old seventy-eights, order in a ruby . . .'

'Can't, pal, sorry.' Waters' head dropped slightly and he sighed. 'Promised Kim the movies – *Blade Runner* . . . but soon, eh?'

'Sure thing.' Without saying goodnight Frost softly closed the car door and trudged towards the house of his estranged in-laws. A warm glow radiated from the curtained front windows. It was almost 11 p.m., but to Jack Frost it could've been any hour at all, so tired and lost to the world was he on the day he buried his wife.

Friday (1) _____

Frost stood at the edge of an opening in the earth. The sky was bright orange, as if the horizon beyond the churchyard was ablaze. He took a step back, but the grave before him grew, swallowing up the surrounding grass, leaving his feet on the lip of an expanding black abyss. He felt unstable, and knew if he tried to move more than an inch, he'd topple into the hole. All the while a pain was growing more intense at his temples, like a tiny blade stabbing behind his eyes . . .

'William?' Mary's voice called up softly from the darkness beneath him. 'William, I need you. Help me . . .' Slowly her pale features came into view, her lips no longer the crimson shade she always used to wear but a green-grey hue. He felt perspiration creep down his neck.

'Come on, Frost, do something right for once in your life!' shouted Mullett from the other side of the grave.

The superintendent, whose complexion was even more of an angry puce than usual, was flanked by Frost's old boss, DI Williams, now deceased, and DC Simms. Both stood expressionless, their faces ashen white.

'William?' Mary called gently, a touch of seduction in her voice. 'Come here, you know you want to . . .'

Frost frantically trod backwards, but the soles of his shoes could find no purchase on the wet, slippery turf. Before his eyes, Mary was ascending weightlessly from the grave, calling softly, like a siren from mythology. She reached the point where she was close enough to touch; he stretched out his hand, and as he did so her features abruptly changed; the gentle, pleading countenance gave way to a malevolent smile revealing blackened teeth. Panic swept through him, he could feel himself crying, *No! No!*

'Flamin' heck!'

Frost cursed as he propped himself up on the cold, concrete patio, a metal swing-seat bashing him on the shoulder. It took a moment to register where he was, as it was pitch black, but it suddenly dawned on him that he was in his in-laws' gazebo. He pulled himself back up on to the rocking garden seat and used the Ronson to illuminate his watch: 3.45 a.m. 'Cheese and Scotch. Fatal mix,' he muttered, shaking his head. He was shivering, although fortunately heavy cloud cover had smothered the worst of the chill. He pulled the hip flask from inside his overcoat and took a deep pull.

'Ah, that's better,' he said to himself and patted his pockets for cigarettes, but couldn't find any. He rose unsteadily from the swing chair, a crick in his neck making him wince, and made his way slowly to the ghost-white oblong he knew to be the Simpsons' back door. To his surprise, it was unlocked. He tutted but at the same time couldn't believe his luck, thinking how nice it would be to get a couple of hours' kip on the settee before attempting to drive home.

Simms glared at the obstinate PC, who folded his notebook nonchalantly and tucked it inside his uniform. Two ambulancemen stretchered the dead boy to the rear of their vehicle and disappeared into it, leaving his bicycle lying innocently at the roadside. Twenty yards away, the motorist who had discovered the lad hovered uncertainly beside his turquoise Marina, while the uniform's partner manned one end of the roadblock. It was close to 8 a.m. Simms had been awake for barely half an hour; he had not been happy to be roused at seven thirty by Control.

Maltby got up from the pavement, brushing his hands on his cords with an air of finality. He made his way across to Simms and the PC.

'It's difficult to say,' was his disappointing response to their questioning looks. He pulled out a handkerchief the size of a tea towel.

Simms sighed loudly. 'Really?' he huffed. 'Because I could've sworn it looked just like a road accident.'

'I'm playing it by the book,' the PC countered, 'and the book now says, "sudden deaths" require a CID officer present.'

'Balls, not when it's this bleedin' obvious,' Simms snapped.

'But you can't assume the obvious,' rejoined the constable. 'As a detective you must keep an open mind.' Was the cheeky bastard smirking?

The recent decree from on high was vague, but following the case in Essex where a raft of murders had been discovered to have been wrongly pronounced suicides by uniformed officers on arrival at the scene, the rules of attendance had changed. As usual, they'd changed in a way that left little room for common sense, or so Simms reckoned. What made it worse was that in this case PC Watkins, he was convinced, was taking the piss.

'I'll tell you what is obvious – that someone here needs a clout round the lughole . . .'

'Gentlemen, please,' Maltby said, wiping a severely red nose. 'It's not really for me to say, but looking around you, you should consider the possibilities.' He swapped the handkerchief for a hip flask. Simms declined a swig, having seen the state of the hanky. 'The gradient of the road is such that a bicycle could easily reach forty miles per hour or more coming downhill, a speed which, if the descent was interrupted, could easily kill the cyclist.' Simms and Watkins regarded One Tree Hill behind the ambulance. The prow of the hill was a good mile off. 'But it's certainly curious that there's no hint of damage to the bicycle that would indicate a collision.'

'And no evidence of a skid. No tyre mark. On the road,' PC Watkins added eagerly.

'Hard to tell,' Simms countered. 'This road's just been resurfaced. And maybe a car clipped the bike rather than hit it.'

Simms took a step forward towards the bicycle, brushing shoulders with the ginger-haired and bearded PC as he did so. Next to the bike was the lad's holdall, copies of the *Sun* and *Mirror* spilling casually into the gutter. If he had indeed come off at speed, would they not be scattered more widely across the road?

'Maybe he just hit a stone or something and went over the handlebars . . .' he muttered uncertainly, reaching for the cycle itself – a Raleigh ten-speed racer – and pulling it upright. As he straddled it he recalled having had something similar when around the same age as the boy – 26-inch frame too – but he'd not been on a bike since. He flipped the pedal round and swerved uncertainly in the road as the two uniform and the police surgeon looked on. He made a wide arc, bringing the bike to a squealing stop in front of them.

'Brakes work all right, then,' Watkins said.

'Yep,' Simms agreed. He looked up the hill. The early morning sun reflected off the recently tarmacked road. The incline was steep, but was it really steep enough that a tumble at speed could have killed the boy out-right? 'OK, I'll take it from here,' he said resignedly.

Superintendent Mullett rubbed his head miserably. Hangovers were not something his constitution was designed to cope with. Worryingly, as he got older he'd started to suffer memory loss; the last few times he'd had one over the eight, he'd experienced a total blank the next day.

'Would you like me to run through that again, sir?' the polite young man in the lab coat asked. Mullett regarded the ugly object in front of him, which now consumed most of the space on his immaculate desk. No, he couldn't face another run-through, not now, not feeling like this.

'Perhaps later?' He smiled wanly.

'Of course, I'll be here most of today and the weekend, installing the others.' He blinked through enormous spectacles.

'Jolly good. Maybe turn it off for now?' The thing was frightfully noisy, whirring away.

The lad looked faintly dismayed. 'If you're sure?'

Just then the telephone flashed red, followed by a trilling ringtone that Mullett could swear was louder than usual.

'Mullett here.'

'Stanley, how the devil are you today?'

Assistant Chief Constable Winslow from County HQ. That was all he needed.

'Fine, sir. Tip-top.' The technician was still loitering in front of his desk holding a box of floppy disks. Mullett, finally out of patience, flapped him away angrily. 'Never better.'

'Really? I say, you have a remarkable recovery rate.' Winslow chuckled. 'Very impressive considering the rate you were putting them away yesterday afternoon.'

Mullett winced, feeling a ping of alcoholic queasiness deep within his system.

'Any news on the body parts in the field?'

'Early days, sir. We're searching the surrounding area. If there was anything more to be found we'd have uncovered it by now. A perplexing mystery.'

'Hmm, indeed.' A pause down the line; it was difficult enough to work the ACC out when he was in the same room, let alone down the wire at County.

'Now then,' Winslow continued, 'about Jim Allen. I think we must agree that a transfer to Rimmington is all but in the bag. After successfully implementing IRIS he picked up some casework over there, and being a man down, Kelsey has requested he stay until the end of the year.'

Mullett sighed audibly; he knew where this was heading.

'Now' – Winslow was chuckling again – 'you've had that little sexpot Myles, and the black chappie, with whom I believe she's entangled—'

'Yes, yes, Detective Sergeant Waters. Solid, dependable chap – very good,' Mullett cut in, eager to avoid discussing that particular liaison. 'Waters has requested a permanent transfer from East London, and we have him at least until December. So,' he concluded, as forcefully as he could muster, 'there'll be no need for any review of personnel until January at the earliest.'

'Now, now, Stanley,' the ACC berated. 'You cannot continue an inspector down indefinitely. Bert Williams has been dead a year now, and you're forever bleating about being under-resourced. Now the wife has passed away there's no reason not to press ahead. I saw him yesterday on the box, fending off those jackals from the press – you must admit it was a deft performance. *Promote Jack Frost.*'

Mullett was over a barrel. And based on the DS's recent behaviour, he had no good reason to protest; since Mary's illness had worsened, Frost had subdued his maverick ways – although his clear-up rate had slipped too.

'All right, all right,' he snapped, unable to suppress his annoyance, 'but surely not *today*, the day after the funeral?'

'No, make it Monday,' Winslow said with finality. Then he added, as if as an afterthought, 'I hear Harry Baskin has been shot.'

Mullett rubbed his creased brow. 'Baskin, really?' How the blazes had this passed him by? He glanced at his watch: 9.15. Why the devil had he not been told?

'Yesterday, at his club. Wake up, old boy! I rather like old Harry – get this one nailed, eh?' And with a click the ACC was gone.

Mullett tentatively sipped his coffee, as if it might be poison. Baskin shot! For most of his career, Baskin had been little more than a small-time nightclub owner, but in recent years his profile had grown substantially, and his notoriety along with it. His club, the Coconut Grove, named after the famous jazz club in Los Angeles, was a tawdry affair, boasting strippers and gambling. The council refused it a licence to operate in Denton town centre for fear of lowering the tone, so it was tucked away on the fringes at a discreet distance. The club had ticked along for years without drawing much attention to itself; there was the occasional rumpus, the odd raid, and an air of underworld seediness, but nothing that infringed too much on polite society.

Then earlier this year Baskin had opened a 'sauna' in an old laundry building, a site within spitting distance of Market Square, the town's respectable historic centre. Residents from nearby flats had raised concerns; there was suspicion that the Pink Toothbrush was, in fact, a brothel. Unable to tolerate so much as a whiff of impropriety on his patch, Mullett immediately had the place put under surveillance. Within a week he had incriminating evidence, although not of the sort he'd hoped for: ACC Winslow had been filmed leaving the premises in the early hours. Though not exactly caught in flagrante, he had, presumably, been up to no good.

However, no sooner had this all come to light than activities at the Pink Toothbrush went quiet. There were no more complaints from residents, so no need for Mullett to act on this awkward information, to his great relief. He rubbed his chin ruefully, remembering the moment he'd squeezed the revelation out of Frost – and instantly regretted it. It had been the first week of June and Frost had sat opposite him, sweating copiously and wearing that smug, self-satisfied grin of his. 'Are you sure you really want to know what PC Miller saw that night?' he'd said. 'Might be best to brush it to one side.' It was like a red rag to a bull, as Frost knew only too well. Mullett had unwittingly fallen into his own trap . . .

As the superintendent placed the bone-china coffee cup back on its saucer, he noticed that his hands were trembling. He grasped the steel rule he used to assist with reading crime stats and flexed it pensively. Much as he loathed the vulgar club owner, instinct told him he'd be more of a nuisance dead than alive. He picked up the phone, turning to prise the blind slats apart with the rule; the car park was a whirlwind of leaves.

'Miss Smith, get me Frost, immediately.'

He'd be damned if he'd promote Frost on Monday; a wounded Baskin offered all sorts of opportunities to foul things up for the scrofulous sergeant. Turning from the window, he glared menacingly at the ugly grey box on his desk. And if not Baskin, he said to the machine, tapping the monitor playfully with the steel rule, *you* will be his downfall.

'I don't bloody care what it is, I don't want it!'

Clarke could hear Frost's bellow over the ringing telephone before she even reached his office.

'Superintendent Mullett's orders,' squeaked a boy in a white lab coat.

'Really? Well, you've been misinformed! Those orders don't carry this far into CID.'

'Jack, can I have a word?'

DC Sue Clarke stood on the office threshold, unable to enter any further as a mountain range of paper lay between her and the desk, covering most of the famously stained carpet. Dressed in a crumpled black suit, Frost was pacing like a trapped animal. On the desk sat an enormous monitor and an equally vast grey box, with leads sprouting out of them in every direction.

'Not now, darling, bit tied up. Mr Mullett wants me to learn how to play Pac-Man.'

'Sergeant Frost, this computer is not a toy.'

He snorted in derision. 'I may appear a Luddite to the likes of you' – he gestured wildly with a cigarette; it was a constant wonder to Clarke that he and the whole office hadn't gone up in flames – 'but I read the papers. I know all about Sir Clive Spectrum, the genius who's got every kid glued to a screen playing King Dong.'

'It's *Sinclair*, Clive Sinclair – Spectrum is the console. And I think you mean Donkey Kong – King Dong is . . .' Clarke watched the boy flush.

'Dong or Kong, I don't give a monkey's. Alan Turing will be turning in his grave . . . if, if . . . what are you frowning about?'

'Nothing.' Clarke shrugged. 'Just the World according to Jack Frost. Enlightening, as ever.'

'Cheeky mare.'

They both eyed the technician, who shuffled his feet uncomfortably, looking as much a spare part as the unwanted computer.

'I shall have to report this lack of cooperation to the superintendent,' he huffed, navigating his way around the paper mounds towards the door.

'Mind my filing system,' Frost called after him, then turned to Clarke. 'Honestly, though, would you believe it? Look at the size of the bloody thing! Had to shift all this junk off the desk; the floor's the only place left to put it.'

'I can see,' Clarke agreed, then added casually, 'How was yesterday?'

'Yesterday?' He looked confused.

'The funeral?'

'Ah, yes.' He vigorously scratched the back of his head, which she knew by now to be a sign of nerves. 'Went off all right, from what I can remember of it.'

She was about to ask why he was still in his mourning suit, but thought better of it. It wouldn't do to get drawn into Frost's chaotic world – it would only distract her from what she intended to say.

'Look, Jack, I really need to talk to you.'

'Fire away,' he said, fishing out another cigarette. 'Want one?'

She shook her head.

'Not here, I mean I can't talk to you about . . . Will you pick up that bloody phone!' she barked in frustration.

'If you want, but there's only one caller who's that persistent.' He picked up the receiver. 'Frost. Miss Smith . . . yes, yes, I've been here . . . Just been having trouble getting to the phone. Really?' He raised his eyebrows. 'Bear with a sore head, you say? How appealing. I'm on my way.'

He turned back to Clarke. 'Whatever it is will have to wait. Hornrim Harry requires an audience.'

As he traversed the stacks of paper he almost lost his

balance; he clutched at her shoulders to steady himself, kissing her lightly on the cheek as he passed her. She was left with the tingle of beard and a sense of growing frustration.

Friday (2)

Detective Sergeant John Waters took a sip from the plastic cup. The coffee dregs were bitter and tasted of Thermos flask; bearable when piping hot but undrinkable when cold. The first drops of rain hit the windscreen. He'd been staring at the vandalized telephone box on Brick Road since daybreak and the thing was now burned on his retina, to the extent that he wasn't even sure if he was really looking at it. And what a street: smack in the middle of the Southern Housing Estate, a row of scrubby, pebble-dashed council houses whose front gardens displayed everything from ancient television sets to a Ford Anglia up on bricks. Several were boarded up. Did anyone actually live here?

Cold and tired, he yawned and adjusted his scarf. His night at the Nag's Head in Rimmington had drawn a blank. The two girls he'd spoken to, who were barely nineteen, were initially shocked to hear Baskin had been shot. Both had performed at the Coconut Grove last Friday and were due to appear tonight, and their concern for Harry Baskin was quickly replaced with annoyance at the prospective loss of a tenner each, plus tips. Waters had been surprised at the youth of the girls, and he had to admit that in comparison, Rachel Rayner was indeed 'knocking on'. He'd quickly surmised there was no way either of these two could've pulled a trigger, but he hoped they might remember something useful – an argument late one night, a disgruntled punter maybe. He'd left them his card just in case.

Now stuck alone in a car on a miserable street, he pondered the usefulness or otherwise of rain to the current surveillance operation he was lumbered with; it certainly reduced the number of ordinary people using the phone box, leaving it free for weirdos and perverts with a purpose.

He tweaked the stereo up a bit. Jelly Roll Morton's 'Dead Man's Blues' had a satisfying, mournful resonance against the rainy backdrop. It put him in mind of the times he'd spent over at Frost's. Waters had come to Denton six months ago from the Met, and although there was a mutual respect between the two, he and Frost initially had little common ground for becoming friends. A short while later, Mary was hospitalized. As predicted by the doctors, her condition deteriorated rapidly, and the trauma of her sudden physical frailty had proved too much for the stoic detective sergeant, who took to the bottle with determination. He managed to hide it well; only those who were close were aware of the extent of his pain. Before long he stopped driving, although not through common sense – Clarke had repeatedly confiscated his car keys until at last he acquiesced. To preserve his privacy he took taxis rather than relying on colleagues, until one evening when the cab firm let him down and he allowed Waters to drive him, first to Denton General and then to his empty home, where Frost invited him in for a nightcap. It was the first of several visits.

Over the next few months, Waters spent many evenings listening to jazz with Jack Frost. The detective's mother had died in January, and working his way through her record collection, which he'd finally found a connection with, was his way of grieving for her. It also turned into an understated way for Waters and Frost to bond. A few drinks, the occasional game of chess and a shared appreciation of these early recorded greats had brought the two men closer than any in-depth conversation ever could have done.

They'd listened to the discs in chronological order, starting with the earliest recordings in Edna Frost's collection, by Ferdinand Joseph La Menthe, or Jelly Roll Morton as he became known, the self-proclaimed inventor of jazz. Both grew fascinated with this remark-able character. On the evenings they didn't play chess, they'd sit in silence listening to National Library of Congress interviews with Jelly Roll, captivated by this raw and heartfelt oral record of one of the period's most colourful characters. Frost was particularly smitten with this chancer from another age.

Waters had also discovered that Frost was a history buff. The shelves, and often the carpet, played host to numerous weighty tomes. Jack was reluctant to discuss his interest but Waters had deduced over the weeks that in order to relax and wind down, Frost needed to engage his mind – and his preferred topic was the intricacies of conflict, in the form of great military tacticians, from Alexander and Caesar, through to Wellington and Napoleon. The irony of this passion for strategists from a man as disorganized as Jack Frost wasn't lost on Waters. Maybe that was the point, he thought – the man who seemed so proudly maverick secretly craved order.

As Mary's demise grew nearer and the drinking took its toll, Frost admitted he struggled to concentrate on the hefty reference works. It was around this time the two began playing chess more often. Waters was not a skilled player but rose to the challenge, whereas Frost always opened strongly but lacked focus and made foolish errors, which made for interesting games.

During sessions of tedious surveillance with plenty of opportunity to think, Waters would reflect on why Frost had picked him out as a pal. He was in no doubt that he'd been 'selected', and his conclusion was that he, in the eyes of the great and good of Denton, was, like Frost, an outsider.

He lit a cigarette and felt a twinge of guilt over turning the guy down for this coming evening. He recalled him shambling off sadly in the darkness and cursed himself. What had gotten into him? He could take Kim to the movies any night – they were moving in together any day now too. The man had lost his wife, for Christ's sake, he could at least put himself out. He shook his head ruefully and realized that, despite their unique bond, when it had mattered Waters had simply reverted to the classic Eagle Lane view – that Frost was a tough old bird, a loner, a resenter of intrusion, and not in need of anyone or anything. He ought to have known better.

The rain was heavy now, but time was pushing on. The threatening phone calls reported had all been made between 9 p.m. and 9 a.m. It was now nearly nine thirty – damn, he'd managed to overshoot by half an hour. He'd been here since 5 a.m., relieving a uniform detachment. He stretched and turned the key in the ignition – his toes had been numb for hours now; time for a bit of heat.

'Ah Jack, there you are. Please come in and take a seat.'

Mullett smiled obsequiously and even found himself rising from behind the desk. This unprecedented civility arose purely from awkwardness; he felt unsure how to act in the presence of the newly bereaved man. Despite spending the entire previous day in close proximity to Frost and his in-laws, Mullett had barely uttered a word to him. Now, presented with him on a one-to-one basis, he could think of nothing suitable to say. He wondered with surprise if perhaps he felt genuine compassion for the man sitting opposite, still in his black suit and tie from the day before.

'If it's about the computer . . .'

'It's not about the computer—'

'Because if it is . . .'

'It's not about the computer,' Mullett repeated. 'It's about Harry Baskin. I want to discuss his . . . getting shot.'

'He does seem to have a lot of people around here worried. Very touching. He'll live. Not so sure about the boy; he's still in intensive care.'

'Wait a second, slow down.' Mullett was struggling to think straight. He popped a couple of Disprin into his water glass, and stirred it with his ivory letter opener.

'Headache, sir?'

Mullett ignored the remark. 'Worried about him? Who else around here is worried?'

'Superintendent Kelsey called late last night, having dispatched your good self in an area car. He enquired as to our progress.'

'Kelsey – what on earth has it got to do with him?' Mullett was momentarily vexed, although he quickly composed himself. Kelsey was not his sort of man – he'd spent far too much time in the field to understand modern policing – but he knew he shouldn't let that get to him, especially in front of Frost. 'Is he worried about reprisals?' Mullett suggested. 'Gangland activity?'

'Perhaps.' Frost shrugged. 'But as I say, Baskin'll live. What about the poor boy in intensive care? He could well die.'

Mullett had been unaware of any other casualties, not having checked the incident board, but chose not to let on. Very soon, thanks to the blessing of new technology, he'd have this sort of information at his fingertips, and the board would be a thing of the past.

'Yes, well, was it a . . . gang thing? Baskin has his fingers in so many pies . . .'

'Too many pies, I would hazard. He's no gangster, though. His entrepreneurial skills, such as they are, don't go much further than girls getting their kit off for next to nothing, and Irish navvies cobbling a few bricks together, and not very well at that.' Frost gestured vaguely at the refurbished office.

'OK . . . Well, keep me posted. And Jack . . .' Mullett hesitated.

'Sir?'

The words fought their way to the surface: 'I'm deeply sorry for your loss.'

'Sir.'

The door opened suddenly, causing them both to start, and instantly extinguished the tiny spark of fellowship.

'Miss Smith, I would appreciate a knock!' Mullett snapped.

'Sorry, sir, but Sergeant Frost is required urgently.'

'Why so?' Mullett enquired.

Liz Smith's powdered forehead was creased with worry. 'There's been another rape.'

'What, at this time of the morning?' Frost looked at his watch. 'Bit keen?'

'Where?' Mullett barked, ignoring Frost's tasteless remark.

'The school. Denton Comprehensive.'

'Flamin' heck,' Frost snorted, eyebrows shooting up.

'I beg your pardon?' Mullett rose, shocked. 'On school premises?'

He stared at Frost, now also on his feet and standing next to the diminutive Miss Smith. 'This is getting out of hand . . .'

'A child?' Frost asked.

'A teacher,' Miss Smith replied. 'A pupil found her in the lavatories in a state of distress.'

'I'd best be off then. Sir?'

'Of course.' Mullett nodded, reaching for the pack of Senior Service lying on the polished desk. Frost left hurriedly, almost knocking over Mullett's secretary. The superintendent lit his cigarette, dismissing the perturbed Miss Smith with a wave of the hand.

What in heaven's name was the world coming to? Half past ten on Friday morning, and a young woman raped *at a school*. He puffed on his cigarette indignantly. It was the second rape in a week. A woman had been attacked outside a pub in Foundling Street on Monday evening. She, too, was a teacher.

Uniform had wasted no time at all in tracing the dead paperboy's home address – in his back pocket there'd been an unopened wage envelope, with a number denoting his route, that he'd been given that very morning in Townsend's on London Street – and they'd already notified the parents of his death, but hadn't mentioned any possible suspicious circumstances. Simms wouldn't broach that topic until he had the lab report. Whilst foul play wasn't yet confirmed he felt it was worth a visit to the boy's employer. Philip Chilcott had picked up his bag at 6.30 a.m., as he did every day of the week with the exception of Sunday, when a lie-in was permitted. Gruelling work, Simms thought, remembering the round he himself had done as a teenager. According to Townsend, the newsagent, a West Country man in his late sixties, it was not a popular round.

'The route's spread out and covers a lot of ground. We call it the initiation round.'

'Meaning?' asked Simms.

'The starters get the toughest rounds. When a lad leaves, the other ones will all move to a less demanding round. Reward for long service.'

'I see.' Simms nodded. He approved of this man, who must've spent half his life getting up at five thirty and yet still wore a neat shirt and tie. Something about him – upright values, pride in one's appearance – reminded Simms of his own father. 'Is it a tough round just because it's spread out?'

'It's not just the distance. The posher places, the ones with the long drives, Wessex Crescent and the like, will want the broadsheets, and on a weekend those blighters get bigger and bigger, shoving more and more in . . .'

Simms again nodded in agreement, not that anything more demanding than the *People* accompanied his Frosties in the morning.

'The lads do like it over Christmas, though – lovely big tips.'

'But in the bag I saw a stack of *Sun*s and *Mirror*s,' Simms queried.

'A lot of them posh 'uns take both.'

'Why's that?'

'They'll all pretend to read *The Times* and what 'ave you, but y'see, they won't get their fix of smut and sleaze from there, will they?'

'No, I guess not,' Simms agreed, realizing he was getting unnecessarily embroiled in the intricacies of the newspaper readership.

'Where did you say 'e were found again?' said the newsagent, popping the top off a tin of Old Holborn.

'Bottom of One Tree Hill.'

'Aye, well, he'd have them flats on the Wells Road to do an' all. That lot settle for muck only – can't afford any pretensions and whatnot.'

'I see. That reminds me.'

Simms reached into the inside pocket of his leather jacket and pulled out the white envelope given to him by Night Sergeant Johnny Johnson containing the fake five-pound notes. 'There's an alert from Scotland Yard. Dodgy fivers. Here, whack this up and be on your guard.'

'Blimey, as if there in't enough to worry about,' the man grumbled. 'Got people trying to stiff you any which way.'

'That's life,' Simms replied. 'Thank you for your help, Mr Townsend. I'll be back if anything else comes to light. Here's my card in case you think of anything that might be helpful.'

'Right you are.' Townsend shrugged, licking a cigarette paper. 'Should've split the round perhaps. Often thought about it.'

As he left the shop and pulled out his own cigarettes, Simms resolved not to share this reflection with the poor boy's parents.

Friday (3)

'Mr Bickerton,' Frost asked. 'Have you ever, in a professional capacity, come across a Joanne Daniels?'

Clarke regarded Bickerton, the dusty, bald headmaster – the very same one who had once caught her smoking behind the bike sheds – as he rolled his eyes thoughtfully to one side, before slowly shaking his head. His office was festooned with team photographs, many black and white, and cluttered with trophies and what Clarke assumed to be cricket apparel – a miscellany acquired through decades of schooling.

'No, the name is not familiar.' His voice was soft but firm.

Frost offered no more information to jog the man's memory – it was his way, when searching for answers, to prompt as little as possible. He turned his attention back to the schoolboy who sat meekly to his left. They had been over the story once already, but Frost insisted on a re-run. Clarke studied the headmaster who in turn regarded the boy with scepticism, as if his story were the most unlikely chain of events imaginable. Neil Pearson concluded his account of escorting teacher Marie Roberts, in a state of extreme distress, out of the school lavatories, and how she clutched on to him desperately, refusing to let go in the safety of the headmaster's office – her trauma rendering her helpless.

'Go back a bit, to when you found Miss Roberts. Did you hear her cry out?' Frost enquired. 'Or did you find her upon entering the cubicle?'

Pearson was a twelve-year-old second year with a shock of blond hair. He wore black-rimmed glasses, which he had the habit of touching with thumb and forefinger, like a nervous tic, every adjustment accompanied by an involuntary sniff.

'Well,' he said very quietly into a small, clenched fist, 'she was just, sort of, lying there—'

'I'm sorry,' Clarke interrupted, 'do you mind speaking up. I know this isn't easy . . .'

'Excuse me, Detective,' the head suddenly boomed. Clarke paused. He resumed in a softer tone. 'Pardon me, if I may . . . but I would dearly like to know what exactly young Pearson here was doing in the staff lavatories.'

Frost looked surprised. Both he and Clarke had overlooked this particular detail. Because the boy had found the woman, they had both assumed, wrongly it now seemed, that the attack had taken place in the children's washroom.

'Not only that, why did he visit the toilets at nine fifteen, when lessons had already started?'

'I . . . I was in there all along.' The boy adjusted his glasses again.

'You what?' Clarke leaned forward, amazed. 'While Miss Roberts was being attacked?'

The boy looked sheepish.

'What the blazes . . . !' the head stammered.

'Sonny, what did you see?' Frost urged. 'Did you get a look at Miss Roberts's attacker?'

He shook his head.

'Nothing at all?' Clarke said softly.

'Come now, Pearson, stop buggering about and answer the lady! What were you doing in there?'

The boy, aware that this commanding tone was ignored at his peril, shifted his attention from his feet and looked directly at the headmaster. 'Making a spy-hole,' he mumbled.

'A *what*!' The head raised a white eyebrow, and, with gown sleeve trailing across the desk, reached over and thwacked Pearson's ear with the ruler. 'Stupid boy!'

Frost let out an inadvertent snort of laughter. The head settled back down, evidently calmer for having administered an act of violence. The boy's ear pulsed red.

'Listen, Neil,' Clarke said to the boy, ignoring the two men, 'did you hear someone enter the toilet?'

'Err . . . no.'

Frost was smirking. 'So, how long had you been doing DIY in there?' His levity rankled Clarke; a woman had been raped and there he was grinning at some schoolboy prank.

'About fifteen minutes.'

'Fifteen minutes!' cried Bickerton. 'What class were you supposed to be in, and why the hell did the teacher not wonder where you were?' The idea of a pupil freely absconding and flouting the rules of the school seemed more troubling to him than the claim that a teacher had been raped on site.

'PE. I got a sick note.'

Bickerton rose and went to the door to address his secretary. 'Miss Taylor, get me this halfwit's form teacher, we'll see about truancy at—'

'Mr Bickerton,' Frost interceded. 'If we may keep a focus on why we're here.'

'Yes, of course, sorry.' He returned to his seat.

'Now, Neil,' Frost said, slowly. Clarke could tell he was bored. 'You were in the teachers' toilets for fifteen minutes, from nine until nine fifteen, and in that time you were not aware of anyone coming and going?'

'No, sir, I was just hacking away at the cubicle wall, and then I heard a sort of muffled whining which then stopped, so I thought I'd better leave and so I came out and heard this big bang . . . which was one of them big frosted windows, like, so I went to have a look and there was Miss, all . . . all, undressed, and she burst into tears, like.'

'OK, sonny, that'll do. Just a word with you, sir, if we may?'

The boy looked to the head for permission to go,

which was granted with a curt nod. Clarke looked at Frost, trying to read his mind. He hadn't seemed concerned when they'd arrived about Marie Roberts being off the premises, having already gone home with a WPC in an area car.

'I do apologize for the lad,' Bickerton began. 'It makes you wonder how these children are brought up. Disgraceful. You have my full assurance he'll be caned to within an inch of his—'

Frost raised a hand and shook his head. 'Not on our account. Nothing wrong with a healthy interest in the older woman. No, what I'm more concerned about is the fact that it's now, what?' He looked at his wrist-watch. 'Nearly eleven. The incident took place at nine, was discovered at nine fifteen, but was reported only at half ten – why the delay in calling the police?'

Clarke realized that the time lag hadn't even oc-curred to her. Was she becoming so preoccupied with her 'condition' that she couldn't even analyse the facts of a simple case? She definitely didn't feel quite with it. She pinched herself surreptitiously.

'Good question,' Bickerton responded, banging a pipe aggressively on the edge of the desk. 'Miss Roberts did not, at first, wish to call the police.'

'Why on earth not?' Clarke asked.

'I couldn't say, Detective,' Bickerton replied casually. 'She was upset? Humiliated, perhaps?'

Clarke tried to imagine herself in Marie Roberts's position – what would she do? To be attacked in such a degrading, intimate way, and then to be discovered by an adolescent boy – the humiliation of having to relive it for the police would be powerfully off-putting. Nevertheless, she could never let a man who'd raped her get away with it.

'Perhaps,' she replied, 'but she'd want the attacker caught, surely.'

'And so she does, Detective. Please have the good grace to appreciate that she was in shock. I called the police after comforting Miss Roberts for an hour or so, until she had calmed down.'

'I understand,' Clarke said, quietly.

'How's that leg of yours?' the head asked suddenly, smiling and catching her unawares. Clarke blushed at the reference.

'Forgive me for appearing unsympathetic' – Frost torched the tip of a Rothmans – 'but if you had comforted Miss Roberts a bit sharper, we might have stood a better chance of catching whoever did this. Another woman, also a schoolteacher, was raped on Monday in the Denton area, and it would have been of some comfort to them, I imagine, if you were quicker off the mark. Now, if you'd be good enough to show us the cubicle where the attack took place.'

Frost turned the key in the ignition.

'He'll go far,' he said, puffing on another cigarette.

'Who will?' Clarke asked, winding down the window.

'That lad; remarkable initiative. Wish I'd thought to do that at school.'

'Jack, for heaven's sake, a woman's been raped!'

'I know. Took her time reporting it, though. Odd.'

'Well, if there was the slightest chance you could understand women, you might see it from her point of view; the humiliation . . .'

The head was an odd fish too, he thought, ignoring Clarke. His mind turned to Waters, who had been watching a call box on the Southern Housing Estate for the best part of a week; Joanne Daniels had been receiving dozens of crank calls from that phone box, and had then been raped outside the Bricklayer's Arms. As yet they didn't even know if the calls were connected to the rape. A pub at closing time and a school first thing in the morning – the scenarios couldn't be more different; but could it be the same attacker? The only link so far was that both victims were teachers. All the same, he felt justified in giving the headmaster a hard time. He reached over for the handset.

Clarke interrupted his train of thought. 'Jack, I need to talk to you.'

'Just a minute, love. Control? Frost here. Is DS Waters back?' He started to pull out of the school car park but found, as he had on many occasions, that it was pretty difficult to drive, smoke and speak on the radio all at the same time. No, Waters wasn't back, came the answer, but a number of other people were after Frost.

'Jack, *please.*'

'What's that?' he barked into the crackling handset. 'My mother-in-law? Tell her I'll call back as soon I can.' Beryl Simpson had been on the phone, apparently quite beside herself. There was also something about Mullett, which Frost couldn't quite make out through the static. 'You what? He's not . . . ? Well . . . what? Really. Flaming hell . . . OK.'

He let the handset drop to his lap, and turned in annoyance to Clarke. 'The super wants an end-of-week briefing.'

'I know, I heard.'

'It's not really on. I had my weekly quota of his horn-rimmed highness this morning. What's the matter, love?'

Frost saw something was up. He could no longer ignore the petulant pout, hoping it would go away. 'What's on your mind? You look troubled.'

'Pull over, Jack.'

He didn't argue. He pulled off the road into a bus stop. Whatever this was, it wasn't going to be good. Unless she was transferring to Rimmington; that might help them both . . .

'What's up?' He looked into her eyes, and could see she was on the verge of tears. God, he thought, it can't be anything I've done, surely? Burying the missus couldn't have upset her, could it?

'I'm pregnant,' she blurted out.

'*FuckinghellIdon'tbelieveit!*' he mumbled, choking on a cloud of exhaled smoke.

'I'm sorry?'

'Well, that's a surprise.'

He smiled faintly, but she didn't respond. He felt his breast pocket for cigarettes before remembering he had one alight in the other hand. Blimey, he thought, she must be telling me this because . . . knickers, she can't really mean . . . no, not a chance. He stared dead ahead through the windscreen, watching two schoolkids having a tiff by the bus stop – the girl gesturing indignantly, the boy coatless, shirt out, palms outstretched apologetically. Frost felt queasy and closed his eyes. When was the last time he'd slept with her? No, it couldn't be his – Mary had always said she had more chance of being impregnated by next door's cat, a neutered tom . . .

'Mmm, that's a surprise,' he repeated, opening his eyes and turning to face her.

She looked down at her nails, which were bitten short. 'Yes, it was a bit of a shock for me too, I can tell you.'

'Are you sure?' he couldn't resist asking, though he cringed as the words slipped out.

She raised her head and gave him a withering look as if to say, *Yes, you berk, of course I'm bloody sure* – but instead said, 'Who's ever sure of anything, eh, Jack?'

'What you got?' DS John Waters asked, seeing a disgruntled Derek Simms sitting smoking at his desk in the main CID office. It was just gone eleven. Waters was hoping to file his report then slink off home for a couple of hours' kip.

'A dead paperboy . . . and a couple of severed limbs.' Simms smiled sardonically. 'You?'

'A big fat zero. Frost has me staking out a phone box on Brick Road on the Southern Housing Estate. Which nobody ever seems to use.'

Simms frowned. 'Are you sure the box you're watching isn't out of order? There are two public call boxes on Brick Road, one at either end.'

'You what? He just said Brick Road. I thought it was deserted because of the rain!'

'When in fact it's probably not even working and your man's been using the other one all this time. Just a thought.' Simms was laughing good-naturedly.

Waters slumped, deflated, at the opposite desk and snatched up a Post-it note from Frost; he squinted at the barely legible scrawl. *Wheeler*, it read, *check Unsolved*. Wearily he dragged himself over to the bank of filing cabinets in the centre of the office.

'What about your body parts?' he said, trying to summon an interest in Simms's case, having just been told they may well have wasted the best part of two nights.

'We found a hand and foot in a field, but that's it.'

'And the paperboy?'

Simms frowned, betraying his uncertainty. 'Waiting on the lab report before I go wading in to add to the parents' grief, telling them their lad could've been murdered rather than hit by a random car.'

'Seriously, the boy could have been murdered? What've you got to suggest it's anything other than a hit and run?'

'Nothing concrete,' Simms replied, 'but I've got to check all the facts now that this clown in uniform has put the call in, you know how it is.'

'What do you think, though?' Waters felt his younger

colleague had matured in recent months; he seemed far more measured and less likely to blow a gasket at the drop of a hat.

'Maybe, who knows . . . but that git Watkins has given me the right hump.' He lit another cigarette, waving the match out aggressively. 'I mean, I don't need telling what the rules are . . .'

'Of course not,' Waters agreed, flicking through the files in search of *W*. He opted to change the subject. 'Cheer up, it's the weekend soon. Doing anything?'

'Seeing a band tonight with Sue.'

Waters fingered the file out. *Jane Wheeler, RAPE, May 1979.*

'Oh yeah, who?'

'A Wing of Plovers . . . some new-wave thing.'

'Man, your musical taste is getting more dubious by the day. Have you seen that dude's hair? Must cost a small fortune in hairspray.'

'Sue's choice, mate, nothing to do with me. Besides, who cares what they look like? Take Freddie, now he may look unusual, but there's no doubting the talent.'

'Yeah, yeah . . .' Waters knew better than to criticize Queen's frontman. 'His talent has never been in question; but this lot have one-hit wonder written all over them.'

'Never mind my superior musical taste, what you got there?'

'Note from Jack to check out an unsolved rape case. Jane Wheeler, three years ago. Wants me to check for links with the teacher attacks. Nuisance phone calls maybe.'

'I remember that case – I was in uniform. Been on the beat for all of six months. Not sure what happened, though; I was on . . . err . . . race relations training shortly after.' He smiled cheekily.

Waters waved the slender file towards his colleague with raised eyebrows. 'Looks thorough.'

'Hmm. Your sarcasm is hurtful, Sarge. Such a wafer-thin file could mean one of two things: we either caught the bastard pronto . . . or . . .'

'Or found absolutely sod all?'

'Wouldn't be the first time, and certainly won't be the last.'

Friday (4)

'Rain, *mon dieu*. Rain, rain, and more rain.'

Charles Pierrejean tutted, looking out on to Gentlemen's Walk from the dry interior of Avalon Antiques.

'Don't worry about it, Charlie, mate.' Brazier clapped his hands loudly, causing Charles to start. 'You'll get used to it. Besides, the rain encourages punters to come in out of the cold and wet, eh?'

Clueless buffoon, Charles thought. 'I shall take your word for it,' he replied gloomily.

A woman with a headscarf tied over her blonde hair stopped in front of the window to check her appearance; she wore a pair of enormous tinted spectacles and a beige raincoat. Then, stepping closer, she removed the glasses to clean the rain off, revealing a pair of young, glinting, greeny-brown eyes. She puckered her lips. Charles was bemused and then transfixed by what he considered rare beauty – sharp cheekbones and a tiny upturned nose with a dash of freckles across it, topped off by those mesmerizing eyes. *Vraiment magnifique.* He stared in wonder. Suddenly she caught sight of him beyond her reflection on the other side of the window and was gone. The vision of beauty was abruptly replaced by the bright attire and spiky garish hair of a pair of leering teenagers.

Charles continued the conversation where he'd left off. 'Though I'm not sure I'd want certain "punters" to take shelter here. What is it with the youth of this country? It seems everyone under thirty is some androgynous drone in make-up. One cannot tell girls from boys and boys from girls, so . . . unsophisticated. And please, Julian, don't call me Charlie. *D'accord?*'

'Roger that, Charles . . .'

'And don't sit on that chair, it's Queen Anne.'

'What can you do with a chair if you can't sit on it?' He laughed.

'People were smaller in the 1710s, more delicate – certainly not of your bulk. Some respect, if you please.'

'People won't buy them if—'

'Enough,' Charles said purposefully. Gaston would be here soon, and his friend's nervous disposition would be sorely tested by this English chump. 'People aren't buying anything as it is – we'll be lucky if we sell one porcelain thimble. Now, I'm busy. And though I appreciate your company, I have work to do . . . but I thank you for dropping by, and do thank Mr Palmer for the dinner invitation tomorrow; I have heard much about him and look forward to making his acquaintance enormously,' he said politely, though he had a feeling the man might have been in the shop when it first opened.

'And he has heard much about you and your delicate chairs,' Julian said, winking playfully.

Charles Pierrejean smiled in spite of himself and opened the door to allow the car dealer out. The truth was he didn't mind Brazier that much, as long as it was in small doses, and he certainly had his uses. He figured that business in general must be slack if the man had that much time to gas away. Upon shutting the door he flipped over the *Closed for Lunch* sign and hurried to the back office. Fortunately though, Charles was not entirely dependent on Denton punters to buy his antiques of somewhat dubious authenticity – he was cash rich.

Removing a key from the toby jug on the mantel-piece he used it to open his roll-top desk. Taking a letter opener, he inserted it under the far right edge of the green leather inlay, causing it to pop up. Beneath was a mahogany base. In the bottom right-hand corner was a faintly discernible plug, about the size of a halfpence piece, not something one would notice unless looking for it. Removing it with his fingernail, he revealed a tiny keyhole into which the ornate butt of the roll-top key slipped effortlessly. An identical lock was located at the top right. The chamber underneath was stuffed full of banknotes.

Pierrejean pulled out a wedge, replaced the top and took a bank paying-in book from one of the smaller drawers on the desk housing.

'Well,' he sighed. 'If nothing is selling, we shall have to pretend.'

A sullen WPC stepped back from the door, allowing Detective Constable Clarke to pass through into the tiny second-floor flat. Marie Roberts sat uncomfortably on the edge of a velour sofa, as though the act of sitting itself brought a degree of pain. Roberts's dress sense struck Clarke as awkward too; a blouse with a frilly collar that would look more appropriate on a woman twice her age, and a shapeless skirt neatly tucked underneath clamped legs.

Clarke had come solo. Frost had crime stats to attend to for Superintendent Mullett and had said that Clarke and a WPC would be more than enough – they didn't want to fluster the poor woman. If truth be known, that suited her; she'd rather not have him around her just now. He'd barely shown a flicker of emotion on hearing the news of her pregnancy. Then, when she'd dropped him off at Eagle Lane, he'd just tapped her gently on the shoulder and said that the best approach with rape victims was to start gently with a woman's touch. Patronizing git.

But in any case, here she now was with the pretty, strawberry-blonde teacher who, shockingly, had been raped a few hours ago at Denton Comp. Clarke took the only available seating in the cramped room, opposite the WPC and Marie Roberts, in what she quickly discovered was a rocking chair. Clarke met the victim's eyes for the first time. She seemed calm considering the ordeal she'd been through – Clarke imagined that having been violated in such a manner she herself would be suicidal. Though she looked pained, Clarke knew Roberts had refused an examination by a doctor. This in itself was not unusual. She had, however, taken a couple of Valium.

'Miss Roberts, I understand this must be painful for you, but please, if you can try and remember . . .'

'I don't think you have the first idea of how . . . how painful . . .' Marie Roberts took a cigarette from a packet resting on arm of the sofa. 'Miss . . . ?'

'Clarke.'

'Miss Clarke, do you realize it happened on school premises?' She gave a shudder. 'In the *lavatories*.' Clarke noticed a faint Scottish accent. The WPC placed a sympathetic hand on Marie's knee.

'Can you recall anything – anything that might help us catch your attacker?'

'It all happened so quickly.' She was shaking her head, on the verge of tears. 'There I was . . . a quick visit before class . . .'

'Before class? That would be, what? Before nine?'

'No, no. The bell had rung, the children were in class . . . I was running late.'

'I see.' Clarke noted the reported duration of the attack was from just after nine to nine fifteen; she was surprised that such a brazen assault would have lasted as long as ten minutes, maybe more . . .

'I know you have already stated that you can't give a detailed description of your attacker . . .'

'That's correct – he pinned me down before I knew what was happening . . . I . . . I was too shocked to take in what he looked like.'

'But perhaps you can recall something small, that may seem irrelevant – the colour of his shoes, a type of wristwatch, perhaps?'

Marie Roberts sat pensively for a moment. Clarke was desperate to get to the bottom of this mystifying attack. What she found most alarming was its sheer audacity, in broad daylight and in a busy place. Someone must've noticed an unfamiliar adult on school premises, surely?

Roberts shook her head.

'Miss Roberts, do you mind if I ask if you have a boy-friend?'

Roberts's pale grey eyes registered surprise at the question.

'No . . . I'm not seeing anyone.'

'It may seem an odd question,' Clarke admitted, 'but I wondered if perhaps you recognized any scent your attacker might have been wearing? Hence why I asked if you had a boyfriend, and might be familiar with after-shave.'

Again she shook her head.

'But was your attacker wearing aftershave, or was there any other smell you were aware of?'

'I'm sorry . . . I don't think so.'

She reached for a tissue from a box of Kleenex on the arm of the settee and dabbed at her eyes, which had started to brim with tears. She then got up. ''Scuse me a sec.'

'Of course.'

She paused in the doorway. 'Can I get you anything? Tea or coffee?'

'I'm fine, thank you.'

Clarke was impressed by the woman's ability to be so polite in such circumstances. A few tears aside, she seemed remarkably composed. On hearing the bathroom door close, Clarke got up to survey the room; the WPC remained seated in silence. There wasn't much to go on; two cheap veneered bookcases and a small portable television with a hooped aerial. She took a step closer to one of the bookcases which held a graduation photo of Roberts with, presumably, her parents. It must've been taken recently as she looked exactly the same.

'How old is Miss Roberts, Constable?'

'Twenty-three.'

Clarke looked at the spines of the handful of paperback books. The trashiness of the collection surprised her: Harold Robbins, Jackie Collins and a host of other 'bonkbusters'. She would have expected something more upmarket from a schoolteacher, not that she herself had read anything of note since *Lord of the Flies*. Wedged in between a large ornamental owl and a Jane Fonda workout book she noticed the familiar paper edging of some gig tickets – she herself had a similar pair.

'I collect owls.' Roberts had returned to the room.

'Very sweet,' Clarke said, although she thought the large owl rather ugly. On the shelf above she took in an array of others of various sizes.

Sitting back down, Clarke pulled out her notebook, and asked a series of standard questions concerning Marie Roberts's daily routine. There was nothing unusual to report; the young teacher appeared to lead a very ordinary life – it could even be described as boring. She'd moved down recently from Edinburgh and had no real friends in the area. Though pretty, she did her best to hide it. Why anyone would single her out was a mystery to Clarke.

'I don't want to press you any further now, miss, but if you think of anything, do let us know. You may be aware that another young teacher was raped outside a Denton pub earlier this week. We're trying to establish whether we're after two, or possibly just one, culprit.'

'Of course.' She sniffed.

Clarke made to go. 'One final thing. And please don't take it the wrong way. But why did you not scream or cry out?'

'I beg your pardon?'

'Why did you not shout for help? You were within earshot of hundreds of children. Did he threaten you? Or was it because of the way he forced himself on you? Was he excessively violent?'

Marie Roberts looked momentarily dumbfounded. The WPC looked at her uncertainly, unsure what to make of her confusion.

'Excessively violent?' she said eventually. 'Why . . . yes . . . he grabbed me here.' She showed the inside of her wrists.

'How hard?' asked Clarke. The pale, almost translucent skin didn't appear to be marked.

'Very,' she said, and pulled her hands back, hugging herself.

'Did your attacker wear gloves?'

'Gloves . . . ? I . . .' The young woman looked vexed.

Clarke wondered if she might be trying, subconsciously, to blank the event out. She tried a different tack: 'Have you recently experienced any unwanted attention from men, like obvious chat-ups? Or felt like you were being watched?'

'Nobody's even flirted with me,' she answered, 'and no one is stalking me, not that I've noticed, if that's what you mean.'

The complete denial did not strike Clarke as odd; the girl was clearly attractive but she dressed so frumpily, she looked like she'd be more at home in a library than out on a date. 'What about anything less immediately threatening; like the odd crank phone call, that sort of thing?'

She shook her head.

'OK, that'll be all. We'll leave you in peace.'

Whether it was psychological trauma wiping the event from her mind or just an unwillingness to talk, it left them with very little to go on. At the moment the boy's account was all they had.

Louise Daley dropped her cigarette on the pavement and put it out with a turn of her heel. She was standing beneath a dwindling sycamore canopy on the north side of Market Square, right by Gentlemen's Walk. She wore a large, shapeless beige raincoat and a tightly tied flowery headscarf over a wig, and she held an enormous man's umbrella. She checked her watch. As if on cue, a gangly youth in an anorak and a huge hulk of a man in overalls entered Bennington's Bank from the south side. Pumpy's info was good.

Again she mentally weighed up the risks of pulling a hold-up on foot – she would be vulnerable, but experience had shown that in a small town like this, a car was nothing but an obstacle and the phrase 'getaway car' a misnomer; in Denton last year, it had been the car, a flashy Jag, that had sunk them – it had been so bleeding obvious. No, this was better, she'd slip away unnoticed with the black umbrella affording cover.

About a mile and a half was her judgement of the distance to Gregory Leather on the industrial estate, having scoped out the factory yesterday on her pushbike. It was the first time in nearly a year that Louise had been out so openly in the centre of town. The northern side of the square seemed less grand than she remembered; the storefronts all looked a little tired. She was sure that the dreary haberdashery window display of Aster's, the department store, was the same as they'd had this time last year. The other side, with its ugly modern buildings boasting branches of Radio Rentals and Woolworths, was certainly the same, except the kids lolling around outside Woolies playing truant with stolen sweets seemed even younger; maybe because she was growing older. She shuffled her feet; the payroll clerk and his minder should be out soon. She locked in on the bank's entrance. Her decision to come back to Denton was dubious, but if she pulled this off, worth it. When she had called Pumpy to sound out whether she could risk coming back to see her poorly mother she couldn't believe her luck when he offered her two jobs (on the strict proviso that she flee the country afterwards for six months to a year). He knew she'd done a stint at the Grove so would know how to access the place. Both jobs were a gift – or should have been, if things hadn't got messed up. Then there was the other matter, which Pumpy knew nothing of; she was pretty sure if he'd known her sights were set on a revenge killing she wouldn't have got either job – especially if he knew who the intended victim was . . .

In less than five minutes the pair reappeared from the bank, and there in the big man's grip, as plain as day, was a banker's blue cloth sack about the size of two bags of sugar. Well, well. They made off the way they'd come: south, past London Street.

Louise folded her umbrella and placed it in the basket of the bike she'd chained last night to the railings. She pedalled off in pursuit of the Gregory Leather employees, overtaking them on Foundling Street. Foundling Street itself had definitely gone downhill; the pubs had always been rough and ready, but now thanks to the video boom there seemed to be a sex shop on every corner. One of the raincoat brigade stood on the steps of a blacked-out 'private shop' as she sped by. The rain had eased to a drizzle and the wheels made a soft hiss on the wet road. She turned into Piper Road, which after half a mile met the junction with Oildrum Lane, where the firm was based. Continuing past, she stopped at the footpath to the Rec, stowed the bike and walked back towards the corner to wait for the hapless men.

Friday (5) _____

'. . . Frost. *Frost!*'

'Sir?'

'Do I have your full attention?'

Frost looked up at Superintendent Mullett standing behind the lectern, firmly gripping his small officer's stick. His complexion seemed to have acquired a greenish hue. Was he ill?

'Yes, sir, of course.'

'Good. Try to stay with it, there's a good chap. Now, as I was about to say . . .'

True, Frost's focus wasn't on the ghoulish Mullett, but on the woman two rows in front to his right, the woman who this morning had told him she was pregnant. There she was, head bowed, diligently taking notes. Her hair had been hastily tied back and several strands were escaping on to the nape of her elegant neck. He heard the thwack of the stick on the lectern, causing him to jerk forward suddenly in the cheap orange chair.

'For heaven's sake, man, pay attention! Marie Roberts – do we think it's the same attacker as on the earlier occasion?'

We? Frost couldn't imagine the super thinking about anything much, other than the sharpness of the crease running down his uniform trousers, or whether his buttons needed a quick polish – certainly not anything relevant to actual casework. 'Sorry, sir, I've not met the victims, but I think it unlikely. Detective Clarke interviewed Miss Roberts.'

'Clarke!' Mullett snapped. 'What's the MO?'

'The victim on Monday, Joanne Daniels, was forced at knifepoint. Marie Roberts was held firmly by her attacker. Furthermore, Miss Roberts had not received any crank calls before the attack.'

'Waters,' Mullett bellowed, 'the crank calls – has that been reported in the press?'

'Nope,' replied the big sergeant in denims. He leaned nonchalantly against the window at the back of the briefing room, drinking a Pepsi through a straw. What a character, Frost thought, smiling to himself. He was pleased that Waters was still in Denton; he was the closest thing he'd had to a friend in a long time. Sadly, he couldn't say the same for Mullett, now frowning and scratching his moustache, always a sure sign of trouble.

'So,' the superintendent said with a sigh, his small stick hanging resignedly by his side, 'we could have two rapists at large, then.'

'We could indeed, Super.' All eyes turned to Frost,

waiting for some nugget of insight and wisdom that would help the case along and dispel the tension in the room. 'Perhaps there's something in the water.'

Mullett flushed puce. 'If you've nothing constructive to say . . .' He gripped his stick hard and with visible effort regained control of his temper. 'Never mind.'

As well as the bombshell from Clarke, another thing playing on Frost's mind was the meeting he'd just had with the family solicitor. Apparently there were 'issues' that would become clearer at the reading of Mary's will the following Tuesday. What on earth that was all about he hadn't a clue. Perhaps it was connected to the fact that Beryl had been trying to call him. He must find a moment to return her call; he'd slipped away from the Simpsons' unnoticed early this morning so he had yet to apologize for yesterday's breach of the peace.

Mullett redirected his attention to Waters. 'Sergeant, what news on the telephone box you've spent most of the week observing?'

'Zero,' Waters replied. 'Not a sausage. I'm beginning to think we've been given duff info.'

Mullett shook his head despondently. 'Moving on – Clarke, how about you? Anything to report on the stolen electrical goods at the Rainham warehouse?'

'Nothing.'

'How many nights have you been down there?'

'Three.'

'Whose hare-brained scheme was this?' Mullett scanned the room accusingly, his colour rising again. 'On whose information were you acting?'

Frost lit a cigarette and said nothing.

'Well, Clarke? Or do you just happen to enjoy spending your evenings lying in fields?'

'Sergeant Frost had a tip-off, sir.'

'Did he?' Frost could feel the super's beady eyes bearing down on him. 'Did he, indeed? Well, you ought to know how worthless they are . . . You're to cease that futile exercise immediately.'

'Wait a minute,' Frost complained. 'I squeezed that info out of a trusted source . . .'

'I don't care whether you squeezed it out of Princess Diana herself.' The room erupted in laughter at the super's unintentional humour, which he barely acknowledged. 'We don't have the resources to pursue some half-baked notion, no doubt the result of drinking all night in some seedy den. Just drop it and stop wasting everybody's time. What of the Baskin shooting, have we any leads?'

'Not yet,' Frost said curtly. He wanted to avoid being drawn into a pointless conversation with Mullett, at least until he had something.

'Nothing at all?' Mullett pressed.

'Flamin' heck – it was only yesterday mor—'

'We've ruled out most of Harry's immediate circle,' boomed Waters from the back. 'It's not likely to have been any of his card-playing mates, and we've interviewed most of the girls who work for him. There's just one or two who weren't there at the club last night to check on.'

Frost leaned back in his chair and mouthed the word

'creep' at Waters, although he realized it was true – between them they'd eliminated all but one suspect. Waters in return pursed his lips in the form of a kiss.

'Very good, Sergeant. Now, where is Detective Simms?' Frost saw the rookie DC lift his arm gingerly. Mullett shuffled his notes. 'Body parts surfacing on agricultural land – that appears to have made the national headlines, thanks to Sergeant Frost.'

'Hey, that's not my fault!' Frost piped up. 'That gobby farmer telephoned every hack from here to Timbuktu. Thought I deflected the attention rather well!'

'Yes, well done, Frost.' Mullett gave a resigned sigh. 'I have since deployed a thorough scour of the area from uniform; Simms, you're handling the CID end – what avenues of enquiry are you pursuing?'

No longer under the super's gaze, Frost's attention returned to Clarke. (It was strange how Mullett's briefings were often the only opportunity he had to think properly.) Could she be seeing Derek Simms again? Bill on the front desk suspected as much. Mullett had dismissed the body parts as low priority, and Simms was now waffling on about the death of a paperboy, but was interrupted by some contradictory information from uniform, sparking an argument and causing the super to bang his stick in fury. Some took this as a cue to leave.

'Wait, wait!' Mullett screeched above the hubbub. 'Remember the roster for computer training over the weekend. Staff are to be made computer compliant, with a debrief on Monday at nine.'

Even this couldn't dampen the air of relief that pervaded the room as most of them made their escape and headed towards their offices.

'Bleedin' computers,' said Frost to a young blonde WPC sitting next to him, folding away her notebook. She gave a polite smile before swiftly getting up and walking off.

He stood up and lit another cigarette. Clarke glanced back at him as she left the room.

'Wait,' he called after her quietly. 'OK, suit yourself.'

His stomach rumbled angrily. When was the last time he'd eaten? A prawn vol au vent about this time yesterday probably. He checked his watch and found it said 7.45. Blast! He held it to his ear – yes, it had stopped. The wall clock read two. He took the ancient Rotary off and wound it up.

'Ah Jack, there you are.' His tubby friend, Detective Constable Arthur Hanlon, entered the briefing room.

'Funny, Arthur, my stomach rumbles and magically you appear . . .'

'There's been an armed robbery. Gregory Leather on the industrial estate – their weekly wages nabbed at gunpoint.'

'When?'

'Half hour ago. There's a man down too. A factory worker took two bullets. And the attacker took a pot-shot at a passer-by.'

'Blimey, it's all kicking off – shootings left, right and centre!' Frost pushed the plastic chairs out of the way and exited the room at pace, Hanlon lumbering behind him.

'The gunman . . . was a woman . . .' Hanlon puffed, struggling to keep up.

'You're kidding?' Frost stopped in his tracks; his immediate thought was of the Baskin hit – surely it must be the same woman.

'How old?'

'Not sure – report has it she was in disguise.'

It was more than coincidence, Frost thought – but Baskin's office had been littered with cash and his attacker hadn't touched a note. Why would she then go out and commit armed robbery?

'Better rally the troops, then,' he said finally.

'That's not all.' Hanlon pursued him down the corridor.

'Really? Well, it can't be anything more dramatic than that.' Frost pushed open his office door to discover the computer man in the lab coat on his hands and knees beneath his desk. 'Go on, then, what else?' Frost asked Hanlon, grabbing his overcoat and hunting for his wallet; he simply had to eat at some point soon.

'Your mother-in-law called again. She got me this time. Their expensive painting has been nicked.'

'You what? When?'

'Well, they didn't notice it until about ten this morning when they started clearing up, but they reckon it was done last night. Right under their very noses.'

'Bloody hell. Now we really are in trouble.'

Frost took a deep breath as he entered the main CID office. The fact that he could joke about the theft of his in-laws' prize possession felt good. With the funeral behind him, a weight had been lifted, and the time was right for a team chat. Fortuitously, thanks to the afternoon briefing, most of CID and uniform casework staff were still at Eagle Lane.

'Right, everyone.' He clapped his hands and stood on the office threshold. 'Events are mounting up; on top of everything else, we now have an armed robber . . . but before we go any further, I'd like to say a few words.' He surveyed his audience. Paperwork was put aside and conversations died. 'I think it's fair to say I've been distracted for the best part of this week – longer, in fact – with personal difficulties.' Heads were shaken and mutterings made to the contrary, but he held up his hand to silence any further comment. 'Let me finish; you're a great bunch, and I thank you for your support – but I'm back in action and you have my full and un-divided attention, such as it is.'

This remark was greeted with a round of applause, sparked, he thought, by Waters.

'Enough . . .' Frost hated sentiment, and whilst glad to have acknowledged his predicament himself, he was keen to move on. 'Now, Arthur, you took the call from Control – what's the situation regarding this armed robbery?'

'Uniform are already on site, and area cars have all roads out of Denton covered, plus the surrounds with the assistance of Rimmington Division. The female gunman got away clean, on foot.'

'OK, we'd better get someone from CID down there.

There's some juggling to be done . . .' Frost mulled over the options. 'Mullett is on my back about the rape, so Waters and Clarke, stick with it. Simms, what you on?'

'The dead paperboy, and there's the missing persons routine to go through – and I was first on the scene at Bask—'

'Drysdale got back to you yet on the boy?'

'No.' Simms dragged on a cigarette. 'Tomorrow morning.'

'And the parents think it was an accident?' Simms nodded. 'OK, that frees you up for the rest of the day . . . You come with me.'

'On it, guv . . .'

Frost watched Simms grab his cigarettes and stuff them inside his leather jacket, muttering something in Clarke's ear as he did so. Whatever it was made her smile briefly and nod.

Clarke turned to Frost. 'So who's handling Baskin?' she said stonily. Surprised by her tone, Simms stood looking at both of them, intrigued.

'Me and Arthur. I was just about to go and see one of Harry's mates – Hanlon will have to go on his tod.' He gestured to the overweight detective, who was finishing off a pasty in the corner of the room, oblivious.

'But Derek and I were at the crime scene,' Clarke insisted. 'Wouldn't it make sense—'

'While I was at a funeral,' Frost reminded her gently. Although she was confronting him he couldn't help loving her spirit. 'And you and Derek are required elsewhere.

Besides, Arthur knows the manor and characters better than anyone.'

'Right, I'm off to see the super!' Hanlon announced as he walked past, wiping his lips with satisfaction.

'What the bleedin' hell are you on about?' Frost exclaimed, spinning round in surprise.

'Got to see the super at three,' Hanlon replied.

'Hornrim Harry? What business have you got with him?' Frost asked in exasperation, to which Hanlon accorded him a brief tap to the side of his nose. The DS rolled his eyes; he could hazard a guess – Arthur Hanlon would have only one use to someone like Mullett . . .

Friday (6)

An armed robbery on the industrial estate – what next? And a *woman* gunman at that! Mullett dismissed the duty sergeant with barely concealed irritation; how would Denton ever regenerate and attract new business with a crime rate like this? Snatching a factory's weekly payroll of all things; it was like the Wild West out there. He shook his head and popped another two Disprin into his water glass. At least he was beginning to feel human again. He picked up the phone and dialled internally – where was Hanlon? It was gone three. The phone rang and rang, which was odd, as he knew that following the briefing most of CID were still in the building. He sometimes suspected them of knowing it was him calling and purposefully not answering. He sighed; perhaps they were all out on the street, hounding criminals, which is exactly where they should be, given the current crime wave. He prayed that at least *someone* was on verge of a breakthrough and they hadn't all just skulked off to the pub as was often the case once the Friday briefing was over. Then he recalled that he had just deployed a five-mile-radius search of Sanderson's farm – well, at least that partly explained it.

October's crime stats were still in front of him; the situation was going from bad to worse. There was a rap at the door.

'Come.'

'Detective Constable Hanlon for you, sir.'

'Thank you, Miss Smith.' His secretary stepped aside to give the portly detective room to enter. Strewth, he must be eighteen stone at least! Odd, Mullett thought, that he didn't recall noticing it last night. Then again, there was an awful lot about last night he was unsure of . . . hence this follow-up meeting. Hanlon's purported position in the Lodge seemed so outlandish in the cold light of day that he simply had to get clarification.

'Ah, Arthur, please take a seat.' Hanlon did so without uttering a word. 'A hive of activity in CID?' Mullett opened tentatively.

'Rushed off our feet.'

'Really?' Mullett felt his eye twitch involuntarily; he'd never seen Hanlon rush anywhere. 'And where is everybody rushing to?'

'Payroll job on the industrial estate.'

'Of course . . . well . . . no, no.' Mullett paused; no need to get sidelined – he was anticipating progress on the rape case, but Hanlon wasn't the man to assuage his worries on that score. 'Let's leave that for now. Right then, Detective, about last night.'

'If you don't mind me saying, sir, you were hammered,' Hanlon said, deadpan, without even a flicker of a smile.

Oh lord, what is he thinking? Mullett wondered, cursing inwardly. Engaging with this fellow would prove difficult.

'We'd all had a few.' Mullett smiled tightly. 'Very touching affair, and such a good turn-out . . . I was a little surprised to see so many attend . . .'

'Jack's a popular man,' Hanlon said, crossing his arms defensively.

'But, with all due respect to Frost, it was his wife's funeral . . . and apart from a number from the force, there were a surprising number of civilians there . . . in particular a wide range of dignitaries. Frost, for all his popularity, is not a social animal. They were perhaps there out of respect for the girl's father?'

Mullett's attempt to draw Hanlon on to the subject of the Masons by mention of Frost's father-in-law was met with silence. 'I'll cut to the chase,' he pressed on. 'There was a sizeable representation from the Denton and Rimmington Lodge there. Now, I understand that George Simpson, the deceased's father, is quite a bigwig, and that you yourself—'

Hanlon held up his hand. 'Sorry, sir, I'm afraid I can't discuss the business to which you allude.'

'Of course, of course,' Mullett said unctuously. 'However, Detective, we are in private . . . and if one wishes to be admitted one must start somewhere.' Mullett squirmed in his shoes; to think that he, the station commander, should humble himself – grovel almost – to this, this overweight . . .

'Your approach has been noted.' Hanlon sniffed. 'All in good time.'

'Yes, yes,' Mullett said impatiently, 'but this is the police force, damn it – it's my right. And, and . . . you, as senior warden, must let me in!'

Hanlon looked at him blankly, and then to Mullett's surprise yawned noisily. 'We'll have to see. There is one thing that might move things along favourably.'

'Yes?' Mullett asked cautiously.

'Bill Wells is a very good man.'

'Wells? He's *adequate* on the front desk.'

'Has a nose for things, you might say,' Hanlon said archly. 'Detection and the like.'

'Wait.' Mullett stood up. 'Are you suggesting that if Wells gets a position in CID, it will pave the way for myself gaining entrance to the Lodge?'

'I can't say for sure, but it might give your application the necessary edge, sir.' He tapped the side of his nose conspiratorially.

'What? By circumventing the examination procedure? The procedure the officer in question has failed no fewer than three times?'

Hanlon shrugged.

'I hardly think we'd be doing the force a service there, do you, Detective? Though' – he gave Hanlon a piercing stare – 'the system is not all it's cracked up to be, I must admit. Go on, out with you, I've work to do.'

This was not going as planned, Mullett fumed to himself as he watched the large detective leave the room. To think he would need to be subservient to that great oaf. He had his pride. Stuff the Masons.

While Frost chatted with a big, bearded sergeant from uniform, Simms ducked under the police tape and approached the crime scene. Crouching down on the stained pavement, Harding's assistant lifted something with his tweezers. Shell cases, presumably.

'There we go.' He held up a small brass casing.

'Any idea what was used?'

'Pistol. Nine millimetre. We've found three cases.' He retrieved a tiny transparent bag, shells glinting within.

'Well done,' Simms muttered to the young Forensics man, before walking over to the orange Maxi with the window shot out. The hysterical owner was fifty yards away, being comforted by a WPC. Another empty vehicle, bumper hanging limply, sat behind the Maxi. Simms looked over his shoulder – the Forensics guy was still scuttling about on the pavement – before opening the door of the Maxi and slipping inside. Glass was everywhere, but there in the door was a small nick. He pulled out a Biro and stretched over. In a matter of seconds he easily dislodged the lead bullet, which plopped into his open hand.

Outside the car he fished from his pocket an empty envelope covered in scrawled notes and placed the lead inside it. He knew it was unorthodox to remove evidence from a crime scene, but his curiosity had got the better of him. Feeling pleased, he slipped the envelope into his back pocket. Simms surveyed the quiet street. It comprised in the main a row of disused warehouses, set back from the road. Further off were a garage and a fruit wholesaler. It was clear to Simms that the area would not attract much in the way of through traffic, and certainly not on foot. Ideal for a grab-and-run like this. Unbelievably, this was the second shooting in as many days by a female gunman. Simms shivered; it was getting cold.

'She went that way.' Frost appeared at his side. 'Crossed the road about there and that was it, gone. Uniform are canvassing. But as usual, early afternoon, broad daylight, nobody saw a thing.'

'Apart from her,' Simms insisted, nodding towards a woman who had now returned to the orange Maxi, the passenger window shattered.

'Figure of speech,' demurred Frost. 'According to our witness, the person who shot out her car window was a woman dressed as a granny.'

'What, an old biddy? You're having a laugh!'

'I said, *dressed as*. Grey hair – probably a wig – head-scarf and granny mac. But she wielded a gun like Faye Dunaway in *Bonnie and Clyde*, and had roughly the same amount of make-up on, so we're not exactly looking for a master of disguise. Anyway' – Frost pulled out his notebook – 'you need to check in with the Gregory Leather general manager – chap by the name of Sutherland.'

'*Me?* Where are you going?'

'I'm going to call in on one of Baskin's mates.'

'But innocent people have been shot at here – Baskin brought it on himself – and look . . .' Simms gestured towards the damaged cars.

'Baskin'll live, but someone's kid, younger and spottier than you, is on a ventilator. Whoever did this will have gone to ground; screaming around all over the county with sirens blazing like a blue-arsed fly won't do any good now.' Frost turned to go. 'Until we at least have some idea of who we're looking for.'

'The super likes action, though.'

'Well, you get over there and find out what you can, and tell Hornrim Harry I'll be asking around in town. I'm heading there now.'

Simms found Frost baffling at times. He had a point, though; the kid shot at the Grove had been somewhat overlooked. Anyway, with Frost out of the way, there was more of a chance for him to get his teeth stuck into this case. He blew into his hands to relieve the chill and strode off in the direction of Gregory Leather.

Gavin Cribbs sat in silence. Frost was surprised that a man of this apparent stature was on Baskin's radar; but hats off to Harry if he could get someone this well-heeled into his club for a night of card-playing. Fleece him a few times a month and the bills would be covered. Cribbs's suit was of a class that even Mullett could only dream of wearing. Not that Frost knew much about clothes, but from the tailored fit and smooth cloth he could tell it wasn't off the peg at Marks and Sparks. Looking around, the solicitor's office had a similar air of affluence, with elegant furniture and a thick carpet. Here was a man used to money, one who could easily wave goodbye to fifty or sixty pounds over a poker game.

Beyond the plate-glass wall was a sudden flurry of activity as several of the staff tidied their desks, signalling the end of the working day and the beginning of the weekend. Laughter was heard as two secretaries, donning coats, teased an office junior. The disturbance caused the senior partner of Cribbs and Mayhew to stir.

'Well, that is a blow, I must say.' Cribbs linked his fingers and pushed his palms out towards Frost, joints cracking. He sighed. 'Swine was on a winning streak, too. Be a while until I see my five hundred quid back, then.'

Frost tried to hide his surprise at the stake involved. 'Tell me, Mr Cribbs, how frequent were these card games?'

'Not very – in fact we'd only just got into a routine; previously I would host the odd occasion at mine . . .'

'Where would that be?'

'Mount Pleasant, Rimmington. But Harry being Harry, he insisted on things moving to his grubby little club.'

The solicitor had a sallow complexion and dark, unfathomable eyes. He struck Frost as the sort of successful person who grew bored very quickly.

'Why would he do that?'

'Because he saw it as a way to make a quick, mid-week buck. By getting a game going for large stakes he could push some money through the club; attract a wealthier clientele and get them spending at the bar.'

'Really?'

'Either that or the poor soul was too idle to go out,' Cribbs said without the hint of a smile. 'Probably both.'

'And did it work? Did he attract a wealthier clientele?'

'As I said, it was early days. It takes a while for the word to get around that there's a big-money game in town. There were a couple of chaps from Rimmington the week before. I think H was hoping for further afield.'

'Did Harry play a straight game?'

'Ha! Sergeant, you surprise me – Harry might be strapped for cash but I doubt he would be daft enough to try and rip off his own punters. You don't really imagine that Harry was shot over a card game?'

'I don't know, but it was someone who knew he'd still be there early in the morning, so they must've known there was a card game on.'

'Yes, good point. Well, you're the detective.' He glanced at his watch, boredom beginning to show on his face. 'I'm afraid I have an appointment at five.'

'Just a couple more things.' Frost generally hated it when well-to-do types like Cribbs adopted that jaded 'you're inconveniencing me' manner, but having had a gutful this week he felt much the same. 'Did Baskin always sleep over at the Grove after a game?'

Cribbs rubbed his pointed chin and sighed. 'You

know, I really have no idea. This week I called a taxi at three, and the other two – Jeremy Tile and Evans – left by car at about the same time. Shooter had left much earlier, having lost nearly all evening. What Harry does after the games, I really couldn't care less.'

Frost, clearly unimpressed with the answer, shifted in the leather and chrome chair and said nothing.

'I'm sorry if I appear flippant . . .' Cribbs offered.

'You mentioned cash-flow difficulties?'

'It's no secret Harry was strapped – the sauna and manicure place in Market Square was burning a hole in his pocket.'

'The Pink Toothbrush?' Frost said, surprised. 'It's not been open much longer than six months – and he practically runs it on slave labour.'

'Indeed so, but, still, I'm not surprised.' Cribbs shrugged. 'It's not the labour, it's the rates. Why do you think the Chinese laundry went down? I'm not saying Harry's a slouch, but if those fellows couldn't make it work as a busy commercial laundry, how does he expect to make ends meet, painting the few toes that can afford it in Denton?' Cribbs raised a finger and mouthed something to a secretary gesturing in the doorway. 'Is there anything else? I'm terribly sorry, but I really do have an appointment waiting.'

Frost left Cribbs's office at the top of Gentlemen's Walk; all around him jovial people bustled as they headed into the weekend. A breeze had suddenly got up, so he sheltered in a doorway to light a cigarette and stood there, pondering. Was Baskin in financial trouble? He was always so confident, almost to the point of being smug. How much trouble must one be in to get shot? Frost pulled up his collar and jostled along with the crowd. Maybe that's why he was gambling?

'Detective Frost, now there's a stroke of luck!' He'd been tapped on the shoulder by a flushed, weasellylooking man in an ill-fitting suit and battered hat.

'Sandy,' Frost said, 'nice to see you again so soon.'

'My condolences, Jack. Been hard, I know. Didn't get the chance to say anything yesterday, all those other punters there.'

'Thank you, Sandy. What brings you out this way? You seem in a rush.' Behind him Frost noticed a skinny lad with dishevelled hair, looking vacantly down Gentlemen's Walk – the *Echo* reporter's photographer.

'Armed robbery in broad daylight – word's all over town.'

'Word soon gets out,' Frost agreed.

'What can you tell me?' Lane pleaded.

'What do you know?'

'Not a lot – had a bit of luck on the gee-gees, so we've been having a few in the boozer.'

Frost could well imagine; no wonder he had the look of panic about him – missing out on a story. 'Gregory Leather. Weekly payroll,' he said; he found Sandy useful sometimes if only for his reaction to such titbits.

'Only a matter of time,' Lane said dismissively, 'walking down the street with a bag full of cash.'

'You know about it?'

'Of course, everybody does! There's not been much new business round here to speak of, has there? They were queuing up for jobs when that place opened up on the industrial estate. Any idea who pulled it off? Desperate times – surprised it's not been nabbed before now.'

'A granny with an automatic pistol.' Frost lit another cigarette.

'Ha! Good one, Jack; like all that cobblers about a combine harvester yesterday. Tell me something useful for a change? We are pals.'

Frost shrugged. 'Like what?'

'A little bird at the hospital told me Harry B was in the General.'

'Really? Why don't you take him a bunch of flowers, then?'

'Can't get to him – in a private room. How about a quick snifter?' Lane gestured over his shoulder.

Though dying for a drink, Frost declined. Not that he had anything against Sandy – he quite liked him in small doses – just that the hack was already three sheets to the wind, which would make him hard work. Frost felt tired at the mere prospect. True, Sandy was some-times a good source of information, but for the moment Frost had enough on his plate. Besides, he'd promised Hanlon a catch-up later.

'Oh Jack, come on, just the one?'

'Maybe tomorrow afternoon.'

'Saturday?' he said, surprised. 'Well, all right. Where?'
'Come by the nick.'
'What time?'
But Frost had already moved off into the chilly evening.

Friday (7)

Simms drummed his fingers impatiently as he waited in the reception area of Gregory Leather Ltd on the Denton Industrial Estate.

'Would you like another cup of tea?' the pretty receptionist asked.

'No, thanks.' He forced a smile. He'd already leafed through the collection of handbag catalogues. Pricey items they were too. If I'm made to wait around much longer I'll get that ponce of a general manager to slip me a bag, he thought – it would do as a Christmas present for Sue, or whoever he happened to be dating next month . . .

'I'm terribly sorry to keep you.' The general manager appeared again, playing with the end of the red tie that refused to lie comfortably over his striped paunch. 'The accounts clerk will be with you very soon.'

'How much longer will he be?' Simms said impatiently.

'This is a very serious matter. Never mind the cash, some poor sod – one of your employees – has been shot.'

'Yes, yes, I know.' The man smiled apologetically. 'But the warehouse staff need to be paid, and Ian has insisted on taking care of it.'

Simms had heard it all already. After the robbery, in which he'd narrowly avoided getting shot, the plucky young clerk's first instinct was to rush back to Bennington's, although this time, taking no chances, the general manager drove him there himself. The lad then withdrew the same amount of cash as before, in the same denominations, down to the last penny. Manual workers, who made up half the workforce, were paid weekly in cash, and their largely hand-to-mouth existence meant that the company risked a riot if they didn't get their money, not to mention their families going without food. The office staff, such as the pompous nitwit in front of him, were paid through the bank directly.

'Yeah, yeah . . . I know.' Honourable as it all was, time was getting on and Simms had plans.

A pimply lad in a shoestring tie appeared. 'Ah, Ian, all done?'

The clerk looked no older than nineteen. His nod betrayed nothing of the ordeal he'd endured at the hands of the armed robber.

'Jolly good, jolly good. Now then, Detective Simms from Denton CID would like a word . . . Come, use my office.' He marched off with arms bent like a sergeant major on parade.

He led them into an office littered with graphs and charts. A visitor's chair was heaped with handbags.

'Just chuck them anywhere.' He beamed, settling behind a desk overflowing with paper. Not unlike Frost's, Simms thought.

'Just the young man, please,' Simms said sharply. The manager's face fell. 'You weren't present at the robbery, were you? And let me have details of any employees with criminal records before I leave.'

He huffed but didn't object, and left quietly.

Once the door was shut, Simms pulled out his cigarettes. 'Want one?'

The boy hesitantly took one. 'Mr S doesn't like smoking . . .'

'So what?' Simms shrugged. He eyed the lad; he'd been about that age when he joined the police.

'Tell me about your day, from the start. Right from when you decided on that dodgy tie . . .'

Simms listened, occasionally nodding, as the accounts clerk talked and smoked. He'd hoped that by getting the lad to retrace the events of the day up until the robbery he might spot something unusual in the ordinary Friday routine. But they had arrived at the point of the shooting and nothing untoward had passed. Simms then mentioned the Victorian method of paying staff; however, the clerk was dismissive – it was still common practice, he reckoned, as a lot of manual workers didn't have a bank account, even in this day and age.

'So, the armed robber,' Simms said finally, thinking this would be like looking for a needle in a haystack, 'she must've been expecting you. Is it always the same routine every week?'

'More or less, yeah. We have to fax the bank with the denominations first so they can count it out, then it's my job to pick it up, and Al – that's Albert Benson – comes with me as minder. We have to get back in time to pay the wages before the end of play, so there isn't much time to mess around. Mr S will sometimes go through the accounts if the overtime seems high, but not very often.'

'And the firm has been here, what, since January?'

'About that, yeah.'

'The assailant came on foot from behind. You're sure there was no car trailing you?'

He shrugged. 'Don't remember seeing one, but then I wasn't really paying attention . . . wasn't expecting to get robbed,' he said apologetically.

'OK, moving on to the attacker herself. Think carefully.' Only now did the boy's composure crack slightly. A tremor of fear passed across his face as he recollected the event. 'I know getting a gun shoved in your face is a shock, but anything at all might help,' Simms added.

'Oh, she didn't point the gun at me. Barely looked at me, in fact.' He frowned. 'I wasn't carrying the money.'

'What age would you put the robber at?'

'Hard to say – she was dressed like someone old . . . in disguise, I guess.'

'What do you call old?'

'Well, like a granny – headscarf, old person's coat. But there was stuff about her that made it obvious she wasn't old. It was the way she moved, I think – smooth and graceful, like a dancer. And her face was plastered in make-up.'

'Get a good look at her then, yeah?'

'Only briefly, it happened so quick.' He stopped and pondered for a moment. 'She had this flowery headscarf on like my mum might wear over weird grey hair. She reminded me a bit of a pop star in a video, the way she was all made up and wearing odd clothes, like Annie Lennox, you know?'

Simms wasn't at all sure what he was on about. 'Pop videos? Remind me – Annie who?'

'She was in The Tourists in the late seventies when I was at school. Not so much pretty but striking, like. Oh!' A thought occurred to him. 'She was on *Top of the Pops* last night, as it happens, with her new group. Classy video – did you see it? Maybe that's why I thought of her . . .'

Simms shook his head, scribbling furiously. At twenty-four it seemed he was already losing touch with popular culture. The Tourists he remembered vaguely, but not this singer the boy was on about. Being a detective left so little time for leisure – was he in danger of becoming cut off from everything except the job? He dismissed these thoughts, returning to the matter in hand.

'What about height and build? Short, tall, fat, thin?'

'About my height; tall for a bird. She was wearing this big, beige raincoat, so she could've been a cracker underneath but I didn't get a look.'

'Accent? Local?'

'She hardly said a word, something about calling an ambulance was all.'

'So we're looking for a pop-star granny,' Simms said, scratching the back of his head thoughtfully; whoever it was had done a pretty poor job of disguising herself, by the sound of it, although enough to make it difficult to nail important details. The temptation to assume it was the same girl who'd shot Baskin was powerful – gun-toting young women were hardly commonplace in Denton – but that girl had left a couple of thousand lying on Baskin's floor. It didn't add up . . . 'So, if you had to make a stab at her age, what would you say?'

The lad pondered for a while. 'Hmm . . . thirty, forty maybe?'

'How'd she hold the gun? With two hands, like this?' Simms clasped his hands together and stretched out his arms.

'No, with one hand.'

'Can you remember which one? Think back – what hand did she grab the cash with?'

The boy thought for a second, then said, 'She held the gun with this hand.'

'You sure?'

'Positive. When she grabbed the cash and ran, she knocked me on this side.'

'OK, great.' *Attacker left-handed*, Simms wrote in his notebook. 'And after she'd taken the money, which way did she go?'

'I didn't see. She yelled at me to face the wall, or I'd end up on the ground alongside Al.'

'Did you notice anyone else in the area along your route who might've been an accomplice or look-out perhaps?'

'Nah.'

'See anyone else at all, just before the hit?'

'It's deserted round there . . . Might have seen someone coming towards us as I spun round against the wall, but I might have imagined it . . . All happened so quickly.'

'OK. I'm going to send a police artist round to see you tomorrow, get a face, something to go on. That all right? Will you be at home?'

'In the morning.' He looked slightly troubled. 'Town are playing at home tomorrow afternoon.'

'The morning it is – best to do it as soon as possible. Your description is crucial, however vague. Given the state she's in, I don't think we'll get much from the mare who had her window shot out – so you're our key witness, young man.'

'That's a dead end, then.'

Waters replaced the phone in the cradle. Stiffly he stood up, and was surprised to see it was pitch black outside; so focused had he been on pursuing leads in this rape case he hadn't noticed the day slip into darkness. There was no connection he could find between the rape of Jane Wheeler in 1979 and the latest attacks, and since the earlier victim had emigrated to Australia without leaving any forwarding address the trail was now cold.

'Jane Wheeler's gone AWOL, and anyway, she was never a teacher.' Receiving no reply he glanced over at Clarke. 'Sue?'

'Sorry, miles away.' She pondered for a moment. 'Well, how do we know the teacher thing is significant? The girl attacked on Monday – Joanne Daniels – we have no idea if the attacker even knew she was a teacher. She was raped in an alley outside a local pub, so perhaps it was a random attack.'

'Except that if the crank calls she'd been getting were connected to the rape it must've been premeditated.'

'True,' agreed Clarke, 'so if we find out more about those calls we might finally be on to something. Where's that list you got from British Telecom?'

'I dunno that you'll learn much from looking at this,' Waters said wearily, passing her a sheaf of papers.

Clarke spread the sheets out in front of her and smiled encouragingly. 'Maybe the times of the calls might tell us something?'

Waters got up and moved to peer over her shoulder. The print-out listed dates and times of calls received by the victim from several local telephone boxes.

'Most of the calls are before nine a.m. or after nine p.m.,' Clarke said.

'Don't I know it, stuck in the motor at the crack of dawn. But that's just outside regular office hours, doesn't mean a thing,' Waters replied, disappointed. 'And some calls are as late as ten . . .' He ran his finger down the print-out, Clarke edging aside to give him space. 'Here, here and here.'

'Yes . . . but look what starts happening here.'

Waters looked closely at the papers. Suddenly he saw there were several consecutive days when calls occurred during the day.

'Strange – I wonder why the pattern changes,' mused Waters.

'Over these few days he suddenly decided to phone her at a different time. Why would he do that unless he knew she would be in?' Clarke smiled knowingly.

'But would she be in?' shrugged Waters. 'Why?'

'Half-term.'

A smile spread over Waters' face. 'So he must've known she was a teacher!'

'Quite possibly. So, if it does turn out that the caller is Daniels' rapist then we may have a link to the other attack.'

'Hmm, still a lot of ifs and maybes,' said Waters, returning to his desk and opening his notebook. He sighed; it was well over two hours since schools had finished for the day, while he was yet to even stop for lunch.

DC Derek Simms entered the Eagle Lane canteen hungry and edgy. His day had been a long and complicated one. He had found himself juggling cases like Frost did – first the dead paperboy, then the Gregory Leather shooting – and not only that, he'd fallen into Frost's trap of subsisting on cigarettes and coffee. Waters' cheery cool was beginning to grate a little; it was all right for him, he had his stripes – he wouldn't be unsettled by something like a raped schoolteacher. Simms was desperate for a break, a lead, *anything*. He now felt stupid for retrieving the bullet from the car door. Why didn't he hand it in? What was he to do with it?

But first he was desperate for some proper food.

Congealed scrambled egg and a solitary piece of fried bread was all that was on offer at the staff canteen. Jesus.

'Don't you sneer, young man,' admonished Grace, Eagle Lane's faithful catering retainer. 'If you will come in at six o'clock, then what do you expect? Give it another half hour and you could be first in the dinner queue rather than last for lunch.'

'Lunch? This looks like it's been out since four thirty this morning!' Simms disconsolately scraped the corner of the metal serving dish for the last of the orange-hued egg – the canteen's all-day breakfast clearly meant just that – and shuffled over to the till. Three uniform, Watkins among them, sat amidst a cloud of smoke, sleeves rolled up and ties loosened. It was the end of their shift and probably their week. Well, so what, he was still glad to be where he was, out of uniform and forging a career in CID, despite having not had a break. He sat down at a table and glanced at a tatty copy of the *Sun* that had been left lying open on page three. He stared at the paper lost in thought, imagining a woman very like the toothy beauty in front of him shooting Harry Baskin.

'Sorry to disturb your deep CID level of thought.' Simms jolted as a manila package was chucked across the girl's bare breasts. 'That's for you.'

'What's this?' he snapped at the lippy WPC.

'Ballistics report for yesterday morning's shooting.'

He signed for the package hastily, eager to take a look. It may be Frost's case now – every case was – but he, Simms, had been first on the scene at the Grove. Besides, he had always been interested in guns. Before deciding to follow Clarke into CID he'd originally hoped to get into the Firearms Unit or the Anti-Terrorist Branch, and he was one of the few at Denton qualified to use a firearm – though a fat lot of good it did him; Frost was so anti-gun.

Two transparent pouches slipped out of the Jiffy bag. One contained the shell cases – two 9mm shells had been found in Baskin's office. The Forensics note advised that the shells were probably ejected from an automatic pistol. No fingerprints were found on the cases. Simms recalled that the shell cases found at the roadside of today's robbery were also 9mm; and indeed the lead was in his back pocket. Coincidence? Simms knew that 9mm handguns were now commonplace in the UK; an influx of smart, powerful pistols had flooded in from Europe since the late seventies. It was only the police who continued to use shoulder-breaking Smith and Wessons dating back to the First World War. So perhaps it wasn't significant, except for the additional fact that both had been fired by a woman, not that their descriptions sounded too similar.

He pondered again his dilemma. The longer he left it, the more trouble he was likely to find himself in – but on the other hand there was the lead in the minder, shot on the scene – so perhaps it might not be over-looked . . .

In the second pouch was the bullet from Rhodes's chest (the other one, presumably, was still in Baskin's shoulder). *Striation marks consistent with Continental barrel – Beretta 92 model* claimed the accompanying notes.

Laughter at the uniform table broke Simms's concentration. He stuffed the packets into his leather jacket inside pocket – they would have to wait until later. He was due to pick Sue Clarke up at seven, and she wouldn't be impressed if he'd not had a shower and shave. He wolfed down his very late lunch; he'd better get a move on.

Friday (8)

'You all right, then?'

'Will be when we get inside.'

Sue Clarke was freezing but cheerful; the town-hall doors were still a way off, such was the queue. Unsurprisingly the gig was sold out; big names seldom came to Denton and A Wing of Plovers were riding high in the charts. In front of them, larking around, were a bunch of teenagers, and Clarke was secretly pleased to be one of the oldest ones there.

Derek had turned up promptly, hair back-combed, giving off a whiff of Denim. They'd even had time for a quick drink. He'd made an effort, and she was now well disposed for a nice evening.

They were finally through the doors; Simms immediately lunged for the bar, fighting past the lads in front of them as if it was his last ever chance for a beer. He's still so young, she thought; what would he do if he knew she was pregnant? But for the moment she was putting that aside. The town hall filled up, a Depeche Mode track was pumping through the speakers, and the atmosphere was one of young people in the mood for excitement. Outside it might be a miserable autumn night, but in here the weekend had started.

Clarke hadn't seen a band in ages, but she could hardly believe it when A Wing of Plovers announced a date in Denton. She thought Mike was dishy and loved his hair. All around were pale imitations of his futuristic-looking, forward-combed style, much to her amusement.

Suddenly she caught sight of a woman she recognized. Who was it? Average height, mid-twenties and strawberry-blonde, she was cuddling up to a man who was slight and shorter than her with longish blond hair, and laughing at something he'd said. Could it really be Marie Roberts, the teacher raped that very morning?

Simms sidled up to Sue. 'Here you go – sorry about the plastic cup. Vodka and Coke. Doesn't look like a large one but it is. Sure this lager is watered down, tastes like piss . . .'

'Derek, shh, look!' She tugged his sleeve. Suddenly all the lights in the hall went out, and they were momentarily in darkness before the stage was lit up in a spectrum of red, blue and pink.

'What?' he said irritably, but was distracted by movement on the stage. 'Christ, look at that lot!' Amidst a maze of stacked keyboards and mike stands the support act drifted on. Clarke had lost Marie Roberts as the crowd surged forward in the dark and involuntarily she found herself moving with it.

'Derek, listen . . . the woman who was raped this morning is here – with a fella.' Clarke distinctly remembered her saying she was single. And would she really be in the mood for a gig, after what had happened? 'Derek—' she persisted.

'So what, Sue. She probably wants to take her mind off it. Now we've got the night off, so relax, will you? I'm at the morgue tomorrow morning . . .' Simms drank deeply from the plastic cup, and edged forward for a better view of the band. 'Bet that geezer's trousers are PVC . . .'

But synthesized chords bursting heavily into life drowned out Simms's mocking of the frontman's attire. Sue Clarke thought him cute, in any case.

Frost unlocked the door.

As he crossed the threshold, he was struck by the almost damp chill within the empty house. He'd not been home since Wednesday, and prior to that he'd been generally too drunk or hung-over to register the state of his own home. Now, tired but sober, the stale air and feel of abandon hit him forcefully. It was nearly ten o'clock. He flicked on the hall light and picked up the post.

A glance in the lounge revealed a chessboard mid-game on the coffee table, flanked by an array of empty beer cans and overflowing ashtrays. Must hoover, he thought with a grimace. Continuing through to the kitchen, he dumped his takeaway bag – oil seeping through the brown paper – on the worktop and hunted for a clean plate, but it seemed that most of the crockery was stacked in the overflowing kitchen sink, still bearing traces of previous takeaways. With a fingernail he chipped a dried cornflake out of a breakfast bowl left on the kitchen table, poured in his prawn vindaloo, topped it off with pilau rice and stirred it all together. Delicious.

He opened the fridge to grab a beer but stared in dismay at the barren shelves. Half a pint of silver-top and a leftover sausage were all it contained. He certainly couldn't be fagged to go to the off-licence now, and in any case, it might even have shut at ten, so he sat at the kitchen table with a dejected sigh.

He tried to focus on the case of Baskin and the badly wounded boy, Cecil Rhodes. It was a far easier subject to contemplate than the prospect of fathering Sue Clarke's child. Try as he might, niggling thoughts about this unwelcome state of affairs kept creeping in, so he reminded himself it was only a slim possibility – he'd slept with her only the once in the last six months, at the end of September. It happened when Mary became very ill. Afterwards Frost had thought Clarke had felt sorry for him and he vowed never to let it happen again. Anyway she wouldn't have hung around, a pretty girl like her. He sniffed resolutely and reached for the salt. Next to the condiments was the pile of unopened post to which he'd just added more. That morning's *Denton Echo* caught his eye.

He unfolded the paper and glanced at the lead story: *CLUB OWNER SHOT.* Underneath was a grainy photograph of Baskin, wearing a bow-tie and standing with a pair of equally portly middle-aged men. Frost read the caption: *From the 1981 Gala Dinner for Local Commerce Initiative; l–r Harold Baskin, Michael Hudson, Martin Palmer.* 'What a trio!' Frost snorted. Again he reflected on the likelihood of debt as the cause of the shooting, but somehow it just didn't tally. He studied the glassy-eyed portrait of Michael Hudson, the bank manager, gurning up at him from the rag's front page. Well, my fat-cheeked friend, thought Frost, it may be worth a call on you tomorrow . . .

Something suddenly occurred to him: bet you're all apron-wearers too, he thought, and he found himself laughing softly in the silent kitchen over Mullett's desperate bid to join the Masons. Hanlon had regaled him with the story earlier that evening in the Eagle. What a hoot – he could just imagine Hornrim Harry fuming at being lorded over by the hapless Hanlon.

The telephone rang, interrupting his mirth. He groaned. It could only be Eagle Lane. Frost picked up the receiver in the hall with a sigh, expecting to hear Night Sergeant Johnny Johnson, but instead heard another familiar voice.

'Beryl!' Frost exclaimed, surprised.

'I've been trying to get hold of you all day, William.'

'Shit, I'm sorry. I . . .' He'd clean forgotten to call back.

'Don't worry, I'm not ringing to berate you for your disgraceful behaviour yesterday.' Frost's mother-in-law sounded distant, not just the few miles away in neighbouring Rimmington. 'No, the less said about that the better, though assaulting your brother-in-law proved useful in dispersing the guests . . . No, it's regarding another matter – we appear to have been burgled.'

'I got the message . . . the painting. That is terrible. I'm very sorry. Anything else missing? Any details, any clues whatsoever?'

'Just the painting.'

'Painful though it must be, you'd best let me have the guest list tomorrow. We'll run through the mourners with a fine-tooth comb.'

'Why? It would hardly be a guest!' Beryl Simpson was clearly shocked at the idea. 'I think it might have happened in the early hours of the morning, long after the last guest had left.'

'What makes you think that?'

'I heard a noise about four o'clock this morning that sounded like the back door. Didn't think anything of it at the time – thought I was just hearing things.'

Frost winced with embarrassment as he realized it was him she'd heard entering the house that morning.

'Who could imagine one's own home would be burgled just after burying one's daughter? The likelihood seems so improbable.' She sighed. 'I went back to sleep and didn't wake until gone nine. We discovered the painting was gone, and the back door was unlocked, at nine thirty this morning. Your very sweet desk sergeant, having failed to locate you, dispatched a few of your people who were padding around the house all afternoon.'

'Good, good,' Frost blustered, relieved Wells had jumped on the case.

'It's worth a tidy sum. I wouldn't say it's priceless, not now we've lost Mary – that puts things in perspective. But try and get it back, will you, William?'

Saturday (1)

A baby.

A baby. Derek Simms lay staring at the Artex ceiling, the ugly stippled surface slowly gaining definition with the early morning light. Sue Clarke, lying beside him, stirred in her sleep. After the gig he'd walked her back home for a coffee and nightcap. He should have guessed something was up when she insisted they stop at the off-licence and pick up a bottle of vodka, although something being 'up' did not really do justice to the news she imparted. They'd indulged in some energetic lovemaking, and then Clarke had finally dropped her bombshell at about 1 a.m. They'd gone on to talk until past three.

The post-lovemaking buzz and the fact he'd been tanked up on adrenalin and booze had helped deaden the shock, and he'd even felt a vague thrill at the thought of a family with Sue. However, after less than four hours' sleep his feelings this morning were not quite so warm. In fact, the more the events of the early hours resurfaced in his mind the more he felt a growing sense of alarm, bordering on panic. Never had the phrase 'the cold light of day' sounded so crushingly appropriate.

He slipped out of the bed, gingerly scouring the carpet for his maroon Y-fronts but unable to see them anywhere. Balls, he'd go without them – he daren't risk waking Sue. She was knackered after all that surveillance; it wasn't good for someone in her condition to miss out on sleep – that's what he told himself anyway, but deep down he knew the real reason: he was terrified she would quiz him on the promise he had made last night. The red digits of the digital alarm clock blinked seven o'clock. He didn't have to meet Drysdale at the lab until ten, but he didn't want to hang around. And he was starving; he'd nip down to the café and ponder the situation over a bacon sarnie.

He crept silently through the modest flat, past the chrome-and-glass table and chairs; she had good taste in some things, he thought, although he wasn't sure about the lava lamp that had been left glowing on the sideboard, illuminating a sultry black and white poster of OMD's Andy McCluskey, complete with oiled ringlets. Dodgy. But what did he, twenty-four-year-old Derek Simms, have to offer? Along with Waters, he was still living in police accommodation on Fenwick Street, although Waters would soon be off to bunk up with Kim Myles, leaving Simms with PC Miller and his extensive soft-porn collection. God, what was he going to do if the baby really was his? Move in with Sue? What would his mother say?

Such were the thoughts that troubled the young detective as he headed off along the quiet street, pushing complex CID matters firmly into second place.

Mullett stared in disbelief at such unbelievable rudeness.

'What in heaven's name do you mean, it's "duff"?' he blustered at the newsagent, unable to prevent himself from mimicking his West Country accent.

'It's no good. Funny money. A fake.'

'Now you look here, my good man.' Mullett leaned forward across the counter. 'I withdrew this money just this morning from Bennington's Bank on Market Square.'

'I don't care whether you were presented it from the Bank of bloomin' England isself, it's no good and you owe me eighty pence for the week's papers, and twelve pence for that there birthday card.'

Mullett was aware of a queue forming behind him and could sense a bustle of impatience. 'But how do you know?' he hissed, trying not to raise his voice.

'Young lad dropped this one off t'other day, from Scotland Yard. Can't trust nobody these days,' he said in a low voice to a woman in curlers who was next in the queue. She smirked in agreement and Mullett felt his colour rise.

'Do you know who I am?' he said through gritted teeth.

The newsagent remained unmoved. 'Aye, I know who y'us are.'

'Me an' all. Seen you on the telly,' the woman behind chipped in.

'Ahem.' Mullett cleared his throat. 'The young chap who left this other note with you, was he in uniform? What did he look like?'

'Not in uniform, no. Tall lad, leather jacket, moonish face, hair all swept back like Bryan Ferry. Were in asking after dead lad at bottom of One Tree Hill.'

Mullett nodded politely. What the blazes was Derek Simms doing handing out fake five-pound notes to a newsagent on London Street, *his* newsagent, no less? Why on earth didn't he know about it? There was Scotland Yard involvement, too. Surely he should've been briefed by County – how could he have been so blatantly bypassed?

'Excuse me, if you've not the necessary funds, mind stepping aside?' huffed the pompous woman behind him.

Mullett smiled tightly. 'Not at all, madam.' He needed to use the phone, but decided against asking for the shopkeeper's cooperation and opted instead for the call box outside. Someone would pay for this humiliation, he promised himself as he stomped out, passing a queue of disapproving eyes.

'Hello, son, what's the name of that snooker place in Rimmington – the Filthy Something or Other . . . ?'

'The Dirty Penguin, guv – opposite the train station,' replied young PC Ridley on Control.

'That's the one, cheers.' Frost hung up. The Dirty Penguin: he remembered Baskin referring to it snarkily. When Martin Palmer had opened up his snooker club Baskin had been envious. The idea was inspired: buy up a warehouse, fill it with snooker tables, and with unemployment rising you had a ready crop of idle young blokes between seventeen and twenty-four content to waste their days locked into endless games of snooker. With expensive club-price booze and low running costs – the place was almost always in darkness save for the table lights which came on only when a game was in progress – the Dirty Penguin turned a good profit for very little effort.

He went through to the kitchen, the tiles chilling his bare feet, and put the kettle on the hob. He felt grotty. A night off the beer had led to fitful sleep, and he'd not gone properly under until almost dawn. Now with the best part of the morning gone, it was too late to call in at Bennington's to probe into Harry's financial affairs. The bank liked to make it as inconvenient as possible for its customers to get at their hard-earned cash by giving them only a three-hour window on Saturdays. He'd have to try and pin down Hudson at home this afternoon; at least inconveniencing the podgy banker would give him quiet satisfaction. But first, he decided, he would venture to Palmer's club. As a mate of Baskin's, or maybe rival was more exact, with business dealings that tended towards the shadier end of the spectrum, Palmer seemed a good place to continue his enquiries.

The kettle boiled, and as he padded across the

freezing floor towards the stove he remembered he had no clean socks. No clean anything, in fact. He had some shirts at the dry-cleaner's, but that was no good to him here and now. He'd have to do some washing. The laundry basket was overflowing with clothes, and the washing machine had not seen action in what? Months? Not since Mary . . . He'd put a load on, and then what? A bath maybe? Well, why not, it was the weekend after all. If he kept it short he could still be in Rimmington by 12.30; the club was open all day, being Saturday.

He was halfway up the stairs when the phone went. He chose to ignore it, assuming it would be well-wishers offering condolences, which he could do without. Or worse, the mother-in-law again about the Simpsons' missing heirloom – the horse painting by Stubbs. That was a puzzle. What kind of thief steals nothing but a painting? One who knows its value. Forensics had dusted the wall the picture was hanging on for prints, that much he knew – but that was not worth reporting to Beryl. Of course, it could be the station on the phone, although he'd only just spoken to Ridley . . .

Frost turned and went back down the stairs and into the lounge, stepping over empty beer cans to reach the stereo. He took off the Count Basie 78 that rested on the turntable, placing it delicately on the armchair, and then slid out King Oliver's 'Canal Street Blues'. He turned the volume up sufficiently to drown out any further callers who might attempt to trouble him.

A few minutes later Frost returned to the kitchen clutching the entire laundry basket, which he plonked in the middle of the floor. He crammed as much of the contents as possible into the washing machine and then took a step back. The machine's array of knobs and symbols appeared to him like a series of hieroglyphics.

'Knickers!' he said to the machine. With a resigned air he shuffled down the hall and opened the front door, to be greeted by a chilly wind blasting up through the folds of his dressing gown. Unperturbed, and without bothering with shoes, he tramped across the overgrown flower bed and over the foot-high ornamental wall that divided the Frost residence from the adjacent property. He rapped on the lurid stained-glass front door of his neighbour.

A woman in her mid-thirties opened the door. 'Mr Frost!' she said with surprise.

'Hello, love. Couldn't give me a hand working the washing machine, could you?'

'As you can see, the break would indicate the head snapping back *thus*.' Drysdale used his forearms to push back against Simms's Adam's apple, causing him to gag.

'I get the picture,' Simms said, loosening himself from the pathologist's grip and stepping up to the light box. Intriguing though this was, his mind was not on it. Thoughts about babies and nappies kept flashing up instead. He tried to focus on the X-ray of the fracture, which, he saw, indicated that the break was clean. Drysdale had suggested it was caused by something akin to extreme whiplash from a car accident. 'So, was this the result of the kid coming off his bike or not?'

'I'd say so, but . . .'

Drysdale paused and scratched the back of his head thoughtfully. Simms found the snooty pathologist annoying. He had a patronizing air that implied everyone was an imbecile aside from himself and Superintendent Mullett. Simms, who lacked Waters' confidence and was unlikely to adopt Frost's couldn't-care-less attitude, struggled to overcome this. He knew he had to sharpen up if he was ever to earn his stripes.

'There is some slight grazing to the face, which is consistent with a gravel surface such as a tarmac road.' Drysdale rolled the boy's pale head from side to side.

Simms did wish Drysdale wasn't so difficult to deal with. 'You said "but"?'

Drysdale pulled the sheet over the boy. 'But it's more a question of how he landed on the road, wouldn't you say?'

'Yeah, I figured that out,' Simms agreed crossly, rubbing his stubbled chin. Drysdale was being as obtuse as that dickhead in uniform at the scene. Why was everybody being so difficult when he had so much on his mind?

Saturday (2) ──────────────────────

Sue Clarke stretched and rolled over in her bed to find the other side empty. 'Derek?' she croaked, slowly coming to. Her head felt heavy from a mixture of too much sleep and too many vodka-and-Cokes. For a moment she couldn't comprehend Simms's absence, but then she dimly recalled his mention of Drysdale and the lab. Yawning, she pulled herself up in bed and ran her fingers through her hair, but before she could move any further she was hit by a wave of nausea. Jesus, morning sickness again. How long would she have to put up with this? She reached for a glass of water and drank thirstily, then sat perfectly still for a minute. She was going to be OK.

As she pulled on an oversized Duran Duran T-shirt and a pair of tracksuit bottoms she played back the night's events in her mind. At first, when the gig was over, they had argued; she'd wanted to hang back and confront Marie Roberts, the rape victim, along with her bloke. Derek Simms was having none of it. His evening had largely been spent fighting his way to and from the bar – the band with their 'airy-fairy synth nonsense', as he'd put it, had proved decidedly not to his taste – and no way was he hanging around in the cold to ruin some poor cow's evening. In the end they had compromised: Simms would call in on the victim today, dropping the surprising sighting into the conversation, and Clarke, in exchange, had agreed to a coffee and nightcap round at hers.

Telling Simms she was pregnant had not been part of the plan – after what had happened with Frost she didn't think she was ready to – but on the way back to her flat the mood felt right. Simms had livened up and seemed to relish her company, making her laugh with affectionate jibes about her music taste and jokes about Mullett, Hanlon and Waters. They even stopped for a bottle on the way, such was the party mood. She'd worried he might freak out, but Simms's reaction was surprisingly mature and level-headed. Clarke smiled to herself. He really was a good boy and well-intentioned.

She glimpsed the bedside alarm clock and saw she had to get a move on. Though CID were chronically busy, and the rape case troubled her, there was something she had to do that couldn't be put off any longer, so for one weekend Eagle Lane would just have to do without her. No, the priority this weekend was to tell her parents, before it became general knowledge. It was the thing she most dreaded. Her parents were Catholics – lapsed, but pretty moralistic all the same – so of course a child out of wedlock was akin to a pact with the devil. Ditto an abortion, something she'd not even contemplated. Should she? In secret? She wouldn't mess up her career then. No, she couldn't, wouldn't think of it . . .

And what would she say of the father? Neither of the two men in question had doubted their culpability – not out loud, in any case. One had said practically nothing, no surprise there, and the other seemed thrilled at the prospect of fatherhood. In her own mind there was much confusion over the situation, and every time she tried to marshal her thoughts she found herself fretting wildly, so she chose, for now at least, not to think about it. She did, however, have a lengthy journey to Colchester to work out what exactly she would say to her mother.

At last, a possible lead. Detective Sergeant Waters slammed down the receiver, delighted at the prospect of hitting the streets. His eagerness to head off was due to more than just hope of a breakthrough; Mullett had forbidden the use of the heating until after midday at weekends, and Waters, who'd arrived at Eagle Lane at 8 a.m., had been crouched at his desk in a donkey jacket and was stiff with cold.

It was the landlady from the Bricklayer's who'd called. This was the pub Joanne Daniels had been drinking in prior to being raped. The attack had happened in the alleyway that ran across the back of the premises, and whilst the bar staff all had alibis – the rape had been before closing time – and were not under any suspicion, they were invaluable mines of information about the male clientele who frequented the pub, and had been interviewed earlier that week. All lived in North Denton, off the far-flung reaches of the Green Lane area. As well as the regular staff there were a couple of casual workers – two students – they used at weekends who the landlady had no addresses for. At the time Waters thought little of it as they hadn't been working a shift when the girl was attacked. Nevertheless, the landlady, an amiable West Country matron in her late forties, who seemed to have taken a shine to him, made a point of obtaining their details when the two had turned up this morning. She'd called him to pass these on. One lived on the Southern Housing Estate, on the very road where the crank calls had originated. Waters immediately thought it worth checking out.

Before leaving he'd called his girlfriend, DC Kim Myles, and arranged to meet her for lunch at the Bricklayer's. All this week Myles had been at Rimmington Division fiddling with computer cables and was there again this morning.

Waters heard the fax machine surge into life. He sprang from his chair excitedly. One of the reasons he'd come in, aside from the fact that Kim was working, was to pick up a fax from a pal at Scotland Yard. A convicted rapist, Frank Bates, had been released from the Scrubs last week, and the man had family in Rimmington. Waters had been promised his prints and address. As he tore off the glossy paper the phone rang for a second time.

'CID, Waters speaking.'

'John, it's Superintendent Mullett,' Desk Sergeant Bill Wells said urgently. 'He's in a right lather – something about fake five-pound notes and complete humiliation in the newsagent's on London Street.'

'What's that got to do with me?' Waters drained the dregs of a mug of coffee.

'DC Simms is handing out fake fivers and stoking up shopkeepers, apparently.'

'Again, Bill, what's that got to do with me?'

'He wants to speak to someone urgently. I don't know what he's on about. It's nothing to do with me either!' Wells had clearly borne the brunt of Mullett's anger and was agitated – unusual for the generally unflappable desk sergeant.

'OK, whack him through . . .'

The pips went. Waters heard cursing and the subsequent banging of small change into a payphone.

'Hello?' he ventured.

'Who's there?' barked an exasperated and distant-sounding Mullett.

'Waters, sir.'

'Where's Simms?'

'I'm sorry, sir, I have no idea.'

'Well, you'll have to do then, I suppose. Now listen carefully . . .'

But Waters quickly zoned out from Mullett's rant as he scoured the Denton area map for the address on the fax, the home of Bates's parents. A twitch of irritation fluttered through him; the address was in the very block of flats he and Kim had looked at on Thursday. He'd be damned if he wanted to live next door to a pervert, or a pervert's parents at that. Mullett was still sounding off, but Waters had missed half of what he'd said. The super stopped; he was waiting for a response.

'I could lend you a couple of quid if you're strapped, sir?' Which was the wrong answer.

'We were like brothers. I'm gutted.'

Gutted indeed, thought Frost; well, you could do with shedding a few pounds. Martin 'Pumpy' Palmer had the build of a retired heavyweight boxer. Easy living had softened the big man, but he could pack a punch if necessary, of that Frost had no doubt. He was sat opposite Palmer in his office above the Dirty Penguin hall. The room was in almost total darkness.

'Really, that close, were you?' Frost said cynically, leaning over to grab Palmer's lighter. 'Well, you'll be delighted to hear he's on the road to recovery.'

'Figure of speech,' Palmer replied. 'Is he on the mend? Glad to hear it.'

'But the same can't be said of the nephew. Not looking good.'

'Didn't know him . . . Phyllis's boy, isn't he? Shame.' Palmer paused as if thinking, but Frost suspected it was for effect; eventually he continued. 'Not too sure that I can help you, Sergeant.'

'Well, do you know anyone who might hold a grudge against Baskin, for instance?'

Palmer leaned forward into the light, his pockmarked

face ghostly pale and doleful, as befitting someone whose days were spent mouldering away in semi-darkness. 'A grudge? Why would someone hold a grudge against dear old Harry? Upstanding pillar of the community that he is . . .'

'Rivalry, perhaps?'

'Why would I be envious of that grotty little club, the Coconut Grove?'

Frost had not aimed the question at Palmer personally, but that was how he'd taken it. He came across this sort of paranoia time and again from those on the fringes of legality. Despite professing friendship, Palmer clearly had one eye on Baskin's empire, and Frost was more than happy to pursue this line.

'You may recall that in May there was some up-set around Harry's new venture, a sauna place. Then somebody left a dead man in the car park there. Harry thought someone was out to besmirch him . . . and mentioned you. So what exactly is it with you and Harry, Mr Palmer? Are you friends or enemies?'

'Are you pulling my plonker, Mr Frost?' Palmer grinned, revealing yellowing teeth. 'If I have issues with someone I don't pussyfoot around making obscure gestures – this ain't *The Godfather*.'

There was a snigger from the far corner of the room. The gloom was such that Frost hadn't noticed the presence of anyone else and was taken aback. 'I didn't realize we had company.'

'Robbo, show yourself,' Palmer commanded without turning round. A tall, bespectacled figure with a shaven head stepped into the light and nodded. He looked the type that Waters would call 'a right hard geezer'.

'And you are?' prompted the DS.

'Robert Nicholson,' Palmer answered for him.

'And what do you do? Chalk the cues?' Frost asked.

'Makes the tea,' Palmer said stonily. 'Now, if there's nothing more . . . I'm a busy man . . .'

'Quite.' Frost shuffled to his feet, stubbing his cigarette out carelessly on the dainty, saucer-like ashtray. 'Hope you don't mind me asking . . . just for the record, of course – where were you on Thursday morning at approximately nine a.m.?'

'Denton Golf Club, with some business associates.'

'And your teaboy? Caddying, presumably?' Frost didn't let on, but whilst he'd never set eyes on Nicholson before he knew him by reputation, which was one of extreme violence. As a pair he and Palmer were a notoriously brutal double-act that went by the name of 'the Pumpy and Knuckles show', a comic-sounding tag that would instantly bring a shudder to anyone in the know. Pumpy himself, in Eagle Lane parlance, was Teflon: nothing would ever stick. If the stories were to be believed he was an out-and-out villain on a grand scale, in a quite different league to poor old Harry. From stolen electrical goods to contraband cigarettes, Palmer was alleged to be involved, but never put a foot wrong. Frost had had Clarke staking out that Rainham warehouse that was said to be owned by Palmer, but he'd never set foot within a five-mile radius of the place.

'Maybe' – Nicholson stepped forward and reached

for the gold cigarette case on the desk – 'it was the boy they were after.'

'How do you mean?' Frost asked.

'Good point, Robbo. The boy's in a critical condition, right?' The leather squelched complainingly as Palmer leaned forward also to take a cigarette. 'Maybe Harry was winged just to put him down, and really the boy was the object of the hit. You'd be surprised what the youngsters of today get up to.' He shook his head woefully.

'Well, it's a possibility,' Frost said. *As if*, he thought. Cecil Rhodes? An effete, gormless lad of eighteen, whom Harry had been nagged into giving a job by his sister and the wife, because the poor kid had been on the dole since he dropped out of art college.

'Don't dismiss it out of hand,' Palmer continued, as though reading Frost's mind. 'He may look a wet blanket . . . but even wet blankets can misbehave.'

'What are you suggesting?'

'Weed. Today's kids, they go for the soft option: can't get work, so they smoke grass, get into debt . . .' He paused. 'Don't get involved with drugs myself. Filth. Leave that to the coloureds. But it wouldn't be the first time a kid has got behind with payments or, worse, thieved for their habit – even one as useless as this.'

'All right, I'll look into it.'

'Now you must forgive me, Mr Frost, I got a club to run.' The leather gave a sigh as Palmer pushed himself out of the chair. 'If anything comes to mind, I'll be sure to let you know.'

'Very good of you.' Frost offered his card, which was waved away.

'I know where to find you,' Palmer said, dismissively.

Saturday (3)

Simms spun the Alfa Sud around the car park of Eagle Lane Station and pulled in tightly next to the green Vauxhall, from which Waters was grinning mischievously. What's tickled him? Simms wondered, popping open the door.

'Wotcha, what's happening?'

'The super has been seriously humiliated' – Waters wagged a finger mockingly – 'and you're in the frame.'

'Eh? What you on about?' Simms was bemused.

'Know anything about dodgy fivers?'

Simms thought for a second. His mind was a blank – but after a moment he remembered. 'Yeah, I do. Got a wad here,' he said, patting his leather jacket.

'Seems you're the only one around here who does; you and the newsagent on London Street, that is.' Waters tapped a Bic lighter playfully on his car door. 'The one who refused our very own Mr Mullett when he attempted to settle his paper bill this morning . . .'

The fact hit Simms suddenly – there had been no mention of the Scotland Yard brief at the meeting on Friday. 'Jesus, that Noddy Johnny Johnson must have forgotten to pass the instruction from the Yard on to Bill.' He shook his head. 'Am I really the only one who knows?'

Waters smiled in confirmation. 'Sure are. If you would sort it out, the super would be ever so pleased.' He started to wind up the window.

'Wait – what's it got to do with me?' Simms frowned, annoyed. 'I'm not responsible for some communication cock-up on the front desk!'

A car horn tooted. Frost's filthy Cortina groaned to a halt alongside Simms's pristine Alfa. Why did he have to park so close?

'Have a nice weekend,' Waters said.

'Wait, where are you off to?'

'Off out of here before Mullett comes in . . . A sound thrashing puts me off my tea.'

'Aye aye, bit parky for a mothers' meeting out here, isn't it? Or have we lost our keys, boys, is that it?' mocked an annoyingly chirpy Frost.

'Err . . .' Simms was momentarily thrown and didn't know what to do first. He couldn't run off just because the super was on the warpath. It wasn't his fault and he really ought to clear himself. 'Guv, can I have a word? Oh shit . . .' A navy-blue Rover turned into the car park.

'Full house,' Waters quipped, starting up the Vauxhall.

*

'But it's on the noticeboard . . .' Simms whined to his unimpressed superior.

Mullett had not glanced at the noticeboard in months. Alerts about Colorado Beetles and Rabies were all it ever displayed as far as he was concerned.

'The noticeboard is for notices,' he replied gravely, flinging open his office door. 'The arrival of counterfeit money in the county, is, is it not, an incident – and *after* being reported at a briefing in accordance with procedure, it should find itself on the *incident* board.' The three accused men trooped into the oak-panelled office, first Simms and Frost, followed by Desk Sergeant Bill Wells, who had been caught napping on reception and started babbling excuses. Mullett ignored him and continued. 'Though this is all immaterial; as of Monday the incident board will be consigned to the museum. This is the computer age, gentlemen. As of Monday the IRIS system will be fully operational.'

The officers regarded the super warily as they seated themselves opposite the expansive desk. Mullett flung his Barbour down on one of the guest chairs. It promptly slid to the floor and he didn't bother to pick it up. He slunk down into the plush leather comfort of his own chair.

'Incident Resource and Information System,' he pronounced reassuringly, patting the lifeless grey box that took up a surprising amount of space on his desk. 'But that can wait until Monday.' He shot a look at Wells. 'Now, Sergeant, please explain to me the reasons for this total breakdown in communication.'

As Wells burbled on Mullett felt his interest evaporating and his anger waning. He regarded the other two: Simms – who seemed remarkably complacent considering his involvement, with rather bleary eyes and a misbuttoned checked shirt; and Frost – with at least a week's beard and wearing, for reasons best known to himself, a high-necked pullover with a prancing reindeer on it. What a dismal state of affairs, the superintendent concluded, looking again at the blank monitor; no amount of technology could improve this rabble.

'. . . wife said he won't wake up,' Wells bleated, clutching several sheets of letter-headed paper.

'Quiet, man, you're giving me a headache. Hand me that,' Mullett snapped and grabbed from him the Scotland Yard instruction. He started to scan-read the formal paperwork, muttering to himself, but on hearing the faint sound of Simms whispering to Frost he paused and looked at the young DC icily. 'You, Detective Constable, have enough to contend with, without adding bad manners to the list.'

'DC Simms has just informed me of another possible murder,' Frost interjected. 'A young lad found dead at the bottom of—'

Mullett raised his hand abruptly in protest. 'One thing at a time! Have the good grace to allow me to digest this important missive from Scotland Yard, hmm?' He continued reading the communication. A number of fraudulent banknotes had been picked up in the Home Counties, some as far west as Reading and Slough; fake banknotes were not rare but there were

203

two unusual features here. Firstly, the notes were of uncommonly high quality – only discernible as fakes by the feel of the paper and serial numbers. The Yard suspected a printing press on the Continent might be responsible. Secondly, the notes had been seen only in semi-rural areas, never in a major city, which was a uniquely cunning way of releasing them by stealth into the economy. Mullett absorbed all this but was again distracted by whispering.

'Right.' He looked up at the three of them, as if for the first time. 'What are you all doing here today anyway?'

'Most of us work weekends – Saturdays, at least,' Frost answered, looking, Mullett thought, fresher than he'd seem him look in months, notwithstanding the need for a shave and a less seasonal-specific jumper. 'We have two possible murders, two rapes, two gunshot victims in the General, and two unclaimed limbs. Remarkable how everything seems to come in pairs . . . Only a matter of time before your dodgy fiver finds a partner . . .'

The phone began to ring and flash simultaneously and all eyes turned to it. 'Mullett here,' he said tentatively. It was Ridley on Control.

'It's Mr Hudson for you, sir.' Mullett groaned and glanced at Frost. 'Put him through. Michael, how are you?'

The bank manager wheezed down the line: 'Stanley . . . thank God. I've got a customer up in arms – claims we've given him a fake five-pound note!'

'Yes, it appears there's the odd one or two in circulation. Put it aside and CID will deal with it on Monday.' Mullett had little patience for the fellow at the best of times, and now with his hopes for the Lodge going nowhere he felt positively churlish.

'*Monday?* That will not do!' Hudson huffed. 'The bank's reputation is at stake.'

Mullett checked his watch impatiently. 'For heaven's sake, you've already shut – it's gone midday. Nothing more can happen today. Don't be alarmist, a pair of fake five-pound notes in Denton is hardly going to spark a bank run—'

'A *pair*? There's another? Not from here, I hope?'

Mullett wasn't about to elaborate by explaining his own predicament at the newsagent's. He was left with no choice but to humour the panicked banker. He pulled off the top of his Parker fountain pen.

'OK, Michael, listen – give me the details of the withdrawal.'

It proved to be a complicated story, but essentially the recipient had not in fact received the cash from Bennington's but from a third party who had withdrawn it from the bank earlier that week. It dawned on Mullett that all fingers would eventually point to one of Market Square's three banks, as the hubs for all cash-flow in Denton, and it was probably just chance that both of these cases led back to Bennington's – it could just as likely have been the Midland or National Westminster in the frame.

By the time Mullett ended the call he felt much

calmer. Somehow the personal anger that had brought him into Eagle Lane had dissipated; he'd regained his perspective. Looking upon the three shambolic officers he felt himself rising to the challenge of taking them in hand. There were pressing issues to deal with – murder, rape and robbery, to name but three. And of course Frost's promotion, which was never far from the forefront of his mind. Seeing him sitting there dropping ash on the carpet almost caused his hackles to rise again, so pushing the issue aside – though he knew he had to deal with it on Monday – he addressed Simms.

'What's this about a paperboy?'

'What the bleedin' hell was all that about?' Simms cried, grabbing Frost's lighter. '"The system will be fully operational", blah blah blah – who does he think is he? Darth Mullett on the eve of launching the Denton Death Star?'

Frost, noticing a smudge of lipstick on Simms's collar, said, 'You look tired, son. Give it a break this afternoon.'

'I'm fine.'

Frost shrugged and didn't argue. 'What did Drysdale have to say?'

'Inconclusive.' Simms looked vexed; a far cry from his usual cocky self, Frost thought. 'He thought the manner of death not necessarily consistent with being thrown off a bike. Though, of course, that in itself doesn't rule out an accident. Or a straightforward hit-and-run.'

'Well done,' Frost said, trying to make the boy feel

better but not really engaging with what he was saying.

'Cheers.' Simms took a long drag on the cigarette. 'What do you make of it?'

'I don't know, but don't expect the answer to leap out straight away. Canvass the area; get a fix on who'd had their morning paper and who hadn't, and you should be able to pinpoint the exact time of death. I know I always say this' – Frost paused and smiled – 'and am often unable to prove it, but *someone must have seen something*. Early birds: posties, milkmen, shiftworkers, dog walkers, etc. – you name it, it may have been early Friday morning, but it's the middle of Denton. We'll get uniform to do that.'

'All right, guv, thanks.'

'What about the robbery yesterday?'

'A tart with a shooter.'

'A tart? What, a prostitute? Are you sure?'

'No.' Simms shook his head wearily. 'I didn't mean that. She was made up – like a pop star.'

'Pop star?' In Frost's mind the word conjured up the pantomime glitz of Marc Bolan or Gary Glitter. 'What, like a glam rocker?'

'A what? No, no . . . Who did the kid say . . . Like Annie Lennox. But disguised as a granny.'

'Err, you've lost me.'

'Doesn't matter . . . but the point is, whoever she is, she's still in Denton – unless she made it across the fields or woods. Uniform were quick to respond, and had the main roads sealed off—'

'Excuse me.' A young PC with a manila envelope appeared next to them in the corridor. 'For Detective Simms.'

'That'll be him.' Frost pointed.

'Artist's impression of the glamorous granny,' Simms said.

'I think we need to share this in the privacy of my office.'

'Well, that's about as much use as a chocolate teapot!' Simms exclaimed, studying the sketch.

'How do you mean?' Frost leaned over Simms's shoulder to get a better look at the drawing of the armed robber who'd snatched Gregory Leather's wages. 'Well, if it's what he saw . . .'

'Could be anyone!'

Frost reached for the cigarette pack – empty – though he'd only just that second put one out, and studied the heavily made-up face with huge painted-on lips, crowned with a mass of hair and headscarf. 'Are you sure we're not after a man in drag?' Frost spun round in his chair. 'Ciggy, please, I'm out . . .'

Simms looked forlorn. 'If it's what he saw, it's what he saw – there's bugger all I can do about it. All that make-up – it's as good as wearing a mask.'

Frost took one of Simms's cigarettes. 'Now, that's not the can-do attitude Hornrim Harry likes to hear, is it?' Simms leaned over with the Zippo. 'Ta . . . Urgh! What are these you're smoking?'

'Silk Cut.'

'Blimey, girl's fags . . . What's come over you?' he teased.

'They're not mine . . . I was given . . . Never mind. OK, what are we going to do?'

'Get this circulated asap. See what turns up.'

'What, in South Denton? The kid reckons she made off through to the Rec, probably cut across the canal and—'

'No, no.' Frost stretched and got up, moving to the map of Denton on the far wall. What on earth is the matter with the boy? he thought. He usually has a bit of common sense. 'She's hardly going to be dressed as an old dear after pulling off the job, is she? No, stick copies up around Market Square.' He studied the map. 'My guess is she'd have come in from the north end of town – to reduce the chances of being seen . . .'

'How do you mean?'

'I mean to avoid retracing her steps – and triggering people's memories – she wouldn't have followed them up to the bank through Foundling Street and back again . . . No, I reckon she'd come at Market Square from the north either by way of the High Street and across, or, if it was me, Gentlemen's Walk – it's pedestrianized, so more foot traffic to blend in with, and brings you out at a good vantage point – and there's the path that cuts straight through the square. Yep, that's my best bet.' Frost jabbed the map with his forefinger. 'Fly-poster the whole square, but we'll direct uniform towards the north. Get them on it pronto. And what about the ballistics report?' Frost frowned. 'I guess we won't have that until Monday . . . Reminds me, I've not had sight of the Baskin gun. What's up with you? Looks like you're about to pee yourself!'

Simms was staring at Frost whilst feeling around frenetically in his pockets.

'What are you doing with your hands? I know I'm an attractive bugger, but try and control yourself . . . Go on, off you go . . . Get on down to Market Square.'

Simms hurried out of Frost's office patting his jeans desperately. *Fuck*, he muttered, leaning against the wall, hastily emptying his pockets. As soon as Frost mentioned the ballistics report, he'd started to scrabble around furiously for the two pouches he'd signed for yesterday – the bullet cases and the lead removed from Cecil Rhodes's chest. He sighed, retrieving from his jacket the package that he was handed yesterday by the WPC, but the bullet he'd pulled from the Oildrum Lane car was gone. It had completely slipped his mind – everything pre-Sue telling him her news was a blur.

Waters sipped slowly on a pint of lager while he waited at the bar of the Bricklayer's Arms on Foundling Street, one of Denton's less salubrious addresses, for Kim Myles. His lead from Scotland Yard on the released rapist, Frank Bates, had been a non-event. Frank clearly had more sense than to turn up at his parents' house, where in all likelihood he'd be lynched for every local sex crime it was possible to pin on him. His parents didn't even know he was out of prison, and didn't seem particularly keen to see him either.

He watched the three bar staff shuffling from pumps to dishwasher. The landlady sat on a high stool at one end of the bar, chain-smoking and chatting with the regulars, pausing every now and then between fags and banter for a swig from a bottle of Guinness. Someone had just put an old Nick Lowe tune on the jukebox. It was a typical pub scene on a Saturday afternoon.

'Wotcha, hon.' Kim Myles pecked him on the cheek, catching him unawares. 'What a nice way to spend the weekend!' she jeered. 'In the roughest boozer in Denton!'

'Hey, you had the movies last night, didn't you?' Though he had to admit that her lush blonde mane and sparkling sapphire eyes were at odds with the drab smoky interior of the pub.

'Yeah.' She smiled. 'But I didn't expect to spend my Saturday afternoon on the lookout for replicants hiding themselves in the midst of Denton lowlife . . .'

He waved for the barman. The nineteen-year-old student regarded him cautiously, as had everyone he'd caught the eye of in the pub that afternoon – perhaps his reputation preceded him and they realized he was a policeman, or maybe it was just the fact he was black that spooked people. Whatever the reason, this wasn't his boozer; he knew it, and they knew it. As the boy fetched Kim's vodka and topped up Waters' pint, the landlady nodded from the far side of the bar, indicating he was the lad to speak to.

'Talking of replicants, Mullett could do with some help on that front.' He held out a five-pound note, meeting the barman's gaze as he did so. 'Help him spot a fake from a straight.'

'What are you on about?'

'Tell you later.' Waters watched the boy clatter with the till. He was tall but spindly.

'There's a firework display on at the Rec tonight, can you get time off?' She rubbed his thigh affectionately.

'I'll try, but I doubt it, it's crazy at Eagle Lane.' The crowd of customers was thinning out as the clientele made for the bookies and the afternoon football, whilst in the far corner by the fruit machines an argument kicked off. 'How's Rimmington?' he asked, one eye on the three men involved.

'Oh, all right . . . quite interesting, really. The IRIS system went live this morning, so fingers crossed. It's funny how technology will change the way we work . . . but that Jim Allen . . .'

There were two bikers in leather jerkins, one fat and heavily bearded, the other small and wiry with a moustache; Waters watched the latter prodding a third man in the chest. He was stockily built and wore a sweatshirt. Waters thought he looked familiar.

'. . . pinched my bum! Hey, are you listening?'

Waters turned to his girlfriend. 'Every word, baby.'

Suddenly there was the sound of breaking glass.

'Christ!' Myles exclaimed. 'What the . . .'

'Guess this song gets people like that sometimes,' Waters joked under his breath. The pub had fallen quiet, apart from the jukebox.

The smaller biker copied his bigger buddy, cracking a Pils bottle against the side of the fruit machine and waving the jagged shards menacingly at the third man. What happened next was over in seconds: the intended victim made as if to tie his shoelace, but instead grabbed the leg of a stool and whipped it up forcefully to smack it against the back of the big man's head, at the same time thrusting his elbow into the smaller guy's gut, and then punching him across the bridge of the nose. Blood spurted as if from a fountain.

'Nice move,' Waters muttered, recognizing the ex-roofer Steve 'Mugger' Moore, who seemed remarkably spry, considering his professed back disability.

'Shouldn't we step in?' Myles tugged at the sleeve of his denim jacket.

'Nope, no need,' he replied as the hefty landlady waded in, fiercely reprimanding the brawlers.

He turned back to the bar, only to see that the boy had disappeared. 'Wait a sec.' He jumped off the stool and dashed out of the front entrance. He was greeted by a stiff wind and nothing else.

'Shit.'

'What's up?' Myles was at his side.

'Kid behind the bar . . . just pegged it.'

'Wait – over there. Look, John.' Across the road, in the entrance to Tile's the bookies, stood the student barman watching them. Was he waiting for them? Waters moved into the traffic at a jog. The boy walked off briskly, turning down a side road, but Waters easily caught up with him outside Baron's Court flats.

'Why'd you bolt like that?' Waters asked.

'I was scared you were going to ask me questions at the bar.' The boy was well-spoken, which, given his attire – shredded Punk T-shirt and granddad cardigan littered with badges – took Waters by surprise. Never can tell with students, he thought.

'Had me made for police, right?'

'You're famous . . .' The boy grimaced, then added, 'In a good way . . .'

'How, in a good way?'

'A cool . . . err . . . guy.' He hesitated. 'A very cool black dude.'

'How kind. But how?'

'You spoke to the sixth form at Denton Comp in June, just before I left, on racism . . . Brixton and that.' Waters remembered more about Mullett's cringing request to turn up than about the event itself.

'OK. And yet you couldn't talk to me in front of that crowd, right?' He gestured with his chin to the pub behind them. The boy nodded, ashamed. 'Wise move,' Waters appeased. 'They're a pretty short-fused bunch.' He offered the lad a cigarette. He thought the boy seemed overly nervous.

'Yeah.' He drew on the cigarette in the affected manner of the young. 'You're here because of the teacher who was raped. Doreen said you were after the bar staff's addresses.' He paused.

'And you live on the Southern Housing Estate. But they wouldn't lynch you for that. We're making enquiries, is all.'

'Yeah,' he sniffed. 'I share a flat there with two others.'

Waters pulled out his notebook from his jeans back pocket. 'Where were you on Monday night just gone?'

'Band practice.'

'Oh yeah, what's your band?' The boy gave Waters the full low-down on Mindsucker, a Crass-like punk band, and the names of all the members involved. 'OK, cheers, son, we'll soon rule you out.' Waters made to go, but sensed the boy had more to say – the reason he'd wanted to talk away from the pub.

'Wait.' He touched Waters' sleeve lightly. 'The landlord, our landlord – for the flat . . .'

'Yes?'

The boy looked nervously about him. 'You might want to have a word with him.'

'Oh yeah? Why's that?'

'He's . . . a bit odd. Always making excuses to come into the flat. Says it's to collect his post. Laura, that's one of the girls I live with, says he's really creepy . . .'

'In what way?'

'Look, I don't want to get into trouble or anything . . . I mean, we live there.'

'I understand – mum's the word.'

'OK; it's just, once she bunked off college with her boyfriend and she caught him going through her . . . you know.'

Waters took this to mean her underwear. 'Uh-huh. And what does this landlord of yours do?'

'Well . . . that's why it might be, you know.' He hesitated, clearly uncomfortable, drawing on the butt of the cigarette like it was an elixir; probably makes a change from roll-ups, Waters thought.

'Go on, the suspense is killing me.'

'He's a teacher at Denton Comp.'

Saturday (4)

Charles Pierrejean pulled the sheet away.

'*Et voilà!*'

'*Sacrebleu!*' Gaston Camus exclaimed. '*C'est un cheval vraiment magnifique!* But how?'

The pair were in the cramped attic above Avalon Antiques on Gentlemen's Walk. Pierrejean watched his friend inspecting the painting, the late-afternoon sun through the skylight framing his look of surprise. Having taken a close look Gaston stood pensive, thumbs tucked in a natty maroon waistcoat. Charles had known the half-Algerian Gaston since they were at the lycée in Paris together.

Gaston's father, a French diplomat, had fled Algiers in the sixties with his Algerian mistress. Finding himself despised by the patrician French, Gaston survived on wit and cunning, and his flair for mathematics and later finance enabled him to excel against the odds. Charles, himself of mixed blood, felt an immediate affection for the diminutive fellow and the pair soon became firm friends. Now, many years later, Gaston managed Charles's business affairs, but above and beyond that, Charles valued his erudite and lively companionship in this bleak country. Though of late Charles thought even Gaston was looking pale; the poor climate seemed to drain his vibrant Moorish blood.

'It was easy. These English cannot take their drink. Uncontrolled louts, the lot of them.' The irony of taking the moral high ground, having just committed grand theft, wasn't lost on him. 'Gaston, this' – he could sense his friend's bewilderment – 'will help the Simpsons overcome their loss – it will bring them back to the real world.'

'If you say so, Charles.' Gaston looked unsure. 'The police will be looking at all those who attended the wake, *non*?' Gaston's accent was strong and in an effort to shake it off, he insisted on speaking in English even when only in the company of Charles.

'Maybe.' Pierrejean clapped his arm around his friend's shoulder. 'But believe me, these snobs would not credit a Frenchman with knowing anything about *English* art. The beast is beautiful and will fetch a fortune in France, eh? If I decide to sell it, that is—'

'But you are an antiques dealer! They are bound to look here!' Gaston said, alarmed.

Charles shook his head confidently. 'As far as the bereaved were concerned, I left comparatively early. Around eight I made my farewells. However, unknown to anyone I went to the walk-in cupboard under the stairs and dozed until all was quiet. They even forgot to set the alarm, which was also under the stairs; a piece of luck, as both front and back doors were wired. So simple! I lifted the painting, like so, and slipped out of the back door, leaving it unlocked.'

The little man moved away, picking up from a bureau cluttered with English knick-knacks and a peculiarly ugly ceramic toby jug, regarding it with curious distaste. They had acquired this gloomy place through a friend of Charles's mother. 'This painting, if genuine, is worth a fortune, even on the black market; it's probably ten times more valuable than this collection of junk we have assembled.' He replaced the toby jug, and tapped his toe petulantly on the creaky floorboard. 'We could go home for the winter. Shelve our activities here. My contacts could place the painting with an oil sheikh, I'm sure. Consider it seriously, Charles; I fear we are too unfamiliar with this country and its ways.'

Charles knew of these concerns; a cultural barrier hampered their varied business activities. 'Gaston, you worry too much. Fear not; we have some coffee now, *oui*?' Just at that moment a flushed young girl appeared at the top of the stairs.

'Jennifer! I told you, we are not to be disturbed!' Pierrejean snapped, angrily.

'I'm sorry, Monsieur Pierrejean, but there are two policemen downstairs . . .'

Gaston shot him a worried glance. Charles felt his pulse quicken.

'Come, Gaston' – he touched his friend lightly on the elbow – 'maybe we have coffee with the policemen, eh?'

Pierrejean ducked under a beam as he entered the main foyer of the shop. The building, which was mock-Tudor, had low ceilings, and rather than remove their somewhat comical dome-shaped hats, the two English bobbies stood crook-necked. They looked ridiculous.

'Good morning, sir,' a lad of about twenty said. 'Sorry to disturb you.'

'Not at all.' Charles was aware of Gaston nervously hovering behind him, and was momentarily worried he would lose his nerve and make a run for it. 'How can we help?' he effused.

'We'd like your permission to leave this in your window.' The PC unrolled a pencil sketch of a woman's face, attractive but heavily made up. Pierrejean's immediate thought was of the woman who had looked in his window yesterday. Could it be the same one? If so, it didn't do her justice. 'Perhaps you've seen this lady? Visited your shop?'

'Let me take a closer look.' He couldn't tell, he'd been so preoccupied with her beauty he hadn't really taken in the details. The high cheekbones were there but the luscious mouth and hair were all wrong. 'May one enquire in what connection this lady is sought?'

'Robbery, sir.'

Pierrejean raised an eyebrow. 'I am afraid this means nothing to me . . .'

'The window?' The PC gestured.

'But of course . . . Jennifer, please help the officer.'

And within the space of two minutes, all fear of the law had vanished. The doorbell tinkled as Gaston pushed the shop door firmly shut, with a look of bewilderment.

The phone rang and rang. Frost sighed and reached for a cigarette, then remembered he had smoked his last one. Blast. It was three o'clock in the afternoon. And for now he was alone in Eagle Lane; Simms had a lead from a milkman on the One Tree Hill paperboy – the dairy had put them in touch and the milkman had confirmed seeing him at the start of his round. Frost drummed the desk, anxiously. Where was she? He had finally come to terms with Sue Clarke's situation – it had taken a day or so to sink in; he had no idea what he was going to do, but they could at least talk through the possibilities. If he was indeed the father – which he doubted. This doubt had given him the courage to make the call.

Strange couple of days, he mused, hanging up the phone; as one life ebbs away a new one comes into being – when you thought about it like that, there was a beautiful symmetry to it; maybe fatherhood could be good for him. So why did he feel like scarpering in the manner of a teenage lad? Perhaps he was on the brink of a midlife crisis? He looked at the mounds of paperwork strewn everywhere – nah, he didn't have time for a midlife crisis with all this stuff going on . . .

'Ah, Jack, still here, I see?' The superintendent appeared from around the corner.

'Flamin' heck, sir, you gave me a fright.'

'Glad to see you're all wired up.' Mullett regarded with approval the ominous grey console, then smiled and said, 'Apologies for this morning's little outburst.'

'Forgotten it already.' Frost was immediately on the alert – apologies from the super were to be regarded with extreme caution.

Mullett continued: 'Getting caught out with a fake five-pound note might not seem serious—'

'Get away with you, sir.' Frost waved the apology aside. 'Simms should've been on the ball more. And Bill too.'

'Yes, well, it's been a trying week for us all – especially you – but we do appear to be in the middle of a crime wave . . . yet again.' Mullett paused hesitantly. 'The Assistant Chief Constable has just been on the phone again.'

'County HQ? To you, here?' Winslow would have been impressed with that; Mullett in on a weekend. The super should be pleased, but he looked more shifty than ever. Frost felt a smile cross his face; what would Mullett make of Winslow's rumoured homosexuality? His sense of order would certainly struggle with that one.

'Yes, he's up in arms about the rape at the school. A blight on the community, and so forth. Nobody is safe.' His brow creased.

'Understandably so.' Frost rocked backwards on the chair. He was bursting for a cigarette. Perhaps Mullett sensed this; he took out his Senior Services and offered them up. He certainly did want Frost onside.

'I need you to give the rape case top priority. I know there's a lot going on – the Gregory Leather wages, for one . . . but nobody was seriously hurt.'

'A man was shot! He's on a ward on the same floor as Baskin as we speak.'

'Yes, but he'll live. And as for Baskin . . .' Frost was about to interrupt but Mullett motioned him against it. 'I know, I know – but just put this on hold until we have the rapist, OK?'

'Yes, sir.'

'Good, good.' Mullett remained in the doorway, a strained look on his face, as if on the verge of either collapse or elation. Something was bottled up in there.

'Anything else, sir?' Frost prompted.

'No, that's it.' He made to go, then paused. 'No more limbs in fields, thankfully. The area has been combed.' Frost knew Mullett had orchestrated the search himself with uniform.

'Well, that's something, eh?' Frost said, cheerily.

'I suppose,' he said, but didn't seem convinced. 'But the rape case, Frost. Remember: the rape case is number-one priority.'

Mullett felt his colour rising as he walked at a clip down the corridor, such was his almost physical aversion to what he'd been asked to do. Though he was now in breach of orders, he'd found he couldn't, he simply couldn't do it. Having got wind of the school rape, Winslow had called fifteen minutes earlier; surprised to catch Mullett there, he'd insisted on the need for some positive news for the press conference on Monday morning: he'd repeated his instruction about Frost's promotion; however, the superintendent was to do it then and there, that very afternoon. Mullett had scoured his mind for some recent example of Frost's unworthiness, but he couldn't think of a thing, *not a single thing*, to pin on the wayward scruff. He was cornered.

He thought back to Frost, sitting there in his reindeer jersey in that disgraceful office. Was he being unkind? The man had, after all, just buried his wife. No, his total lack of discipline and disregard for authority outweighed any sentiment. If Mullett could just hold back until they had the computers up and running he'd have him for sure – there was no way on God's earth that buffoon would cope with the rigour of the IRIS system. It was the very definition of precision and order – or so he hoped. Maybe that was it: surely computer non-compliance should be made a disciplinary offence? If Frost failed to post his case movements on the system in accordance with the new ruling, he could be severely reprimanded and be made an example of to all the staff. But the system didn't go live until Monday, and Mullett was already overdue in granting Frost's promotion. He had to think of something . . .

Frost shook his head and picked up the phone. Something was niggling the super, and it was more than too much starch in his shirt. Nor was it this current crime wave – he knew how Mullett behaved under pressure, and this was definitely different. Maybe

Mrs Mullett is making unreasonable demands in the bedroom, he snickered to himself. Anyway, he didn't have time to dwell on it. Now Mullett had decreed the rape case should take precedence, he had to do some hasty regrouping. He wished he'd not sent Simms off fly-posting with uniform. If only he could get hold of Clarke – she was working the Marie Roberts case, along with Waters. And where the devil was he? Blast it! Frost moved aside the moulded-plastic computer keyboard. Forget the rape case for the moment, he was certain that the right thing to do this afternoon was to bother Hudson, the Bennington's bank manager, about Baskin, and he knew he was right in not telling Mullett his plans.

He flicked the Rolodex round to *H*. Since the incident with Hudson's nephew and a domestic-violence case last year he'd had the manager's home number.

A mousy voice answered.

'Ah, good afternoon, Mrs Hudson. I wonder if I might trouble your husband?'

'May I ask who's calling?'

'Detective Sergeant Frost of Denton CID.' Frost heard her muffle the phone.

'Frost?' Hudson barked abruptly, forcing him to hold the phone away from his ear. 'Frost?'

'Steady, sir, we're not all deaf. At least, not yet.'

'What news on the five-pound notes? More have been found; I knew it – well, there's more than one bank in Denton, you know, I—'

'Hold your horses – it's not about the forgeries.'

'What the devil is it, then?' he wheezed, having worked himself up into a state.

'It's about Harry Baskin.'

'Wha— Harry Baskin? Why the bloody hell are you disturbing my Saturday afternoon to talk about bloody Harry Baskin?'

'I'm worried about his financial affairs.' Frost assumed an air of concern.

'What would I know of his financial affairs?'

'You are his banker, are you not?'

'I . . .'

'And would therefore know plenty about his financial affairs.'

'That sort of information is confidential between the bank and the client—'

'And the police when the client is in hospital with a gunshot wound.'

'I heard about that.' His tone was now more measured. 'But what does that have to do with his dealings with Bennington's Bank?'

'That's for me to find out, isn't it? Was Harry brassic?'

'I'm not sure this is orthodox. It's certainly not information I wish to divulge over the telephone line. I'll have to run this by Stanley. Call me back on Monday.'

'Yes, I could do that,' Frost agreed. 'In the meantime, I could have a pint with my friend Sandy at the *Denton Echo*; just the one, mind; wouldn't want to get too juiced and spill the beans on Bennington's dishing out funny money—'

'You wouldn't dare.'

'Non-cooperation is enough to drive a policeman to drink, you know – a policeman with no leads is . . .' he pondered, '. . . easily bored.'

A deep sigh came down the line. 'Baskin has an extended overdraft facility.'

'Meaning what?'

'Meaning, Sergeant, he owes the bank money. It's no secret that the construction arm of his operations went under just after he opened his sauna.'

'"Construction arm of his operations"? You mean that bunch of Irish layabouts who pretended to rebuild Eagle Lane last spring?' Frost snorted in derision.

'The very same – the withholding of payment by the police authorities was, I believe, a contributory factor . . . and that's as much as I'm going to say.'

'Thank you, sir. One final thing – was he making the repayments OK?'

'Business has improved – where and how, you'll have to ask him. Now, if you'll excuse me, I will continue to enjoy my weekend.' And the line went dead.

Imagine that, thought Frost, replacing the receiver; Mullett holding out on paying the builders caused Harry to get plugged. He shook his head woefully and chuckled to himself.

'Gordon Bennett, what a tip!'

Frost looked up in surprise – it seemed his mention of the shady journalist to Hudson had conjured up the man himself. 'Talk of the devil. Chuck us a smoke, would you, Sandy?'

'And that jumper – get away! Are you some sort of grotto elf on the weekends?'

'I'll damage your 'elf in a minute, cheeky bleeder.'

As he took a cigarette from the pack held out by Lane, Frost winced – a thumping headache had crept up on him. He figured he needed to eat something. The Eagle did pasties – maybe they'd still have some left over from lunch. 'Flaming hell!' he cursed, almost tripping over the Smith Corona, which for some un-known reason had been chucked on the floor amidst a stack of papers. Did the arrival of the computer age mean the typewriter was consigned to the museum? Jesus, things were worse than he thought.

'How did you get in here, anyway? We're not a public convenience for every Tom, Dick and Harry to wander into when they feel like it.'

'I'm not just anyone, Jack. Told Bill Wells we had an appointment, didn't I.'

Frost reached behind the door and pulled his mac off the peg. 'All right, all right, let's get out of here and nip into the Eagle, and you can tell me all you know about Harry Baskin.'

'Me tell you?' Lane exclaimed. 'You're the copper.'

'Granted,' he said with a yawn, 'but despite an in-depth investigation, I've come up with bugger all, so a change of tack is required – indeed, I need to start raking through the squalor of gossip and hearsay . . . and what better place to start?'

'I resent that.' Lane sniffed.

'Oh come off it, Sandy.' He held the door open. 'You'd be mortified if I'd said anything less.'

DC Derek Simms stood on the patio as Toby Clunes forked the earth energetically in the last of the afternoon sun, watched by his five-year-old son. The boy wore a look of wonder, as though his father were performing a task of biblical proportions, such as unearthing a tomb, and not just digging manure into the veg plot. Could this be him in five years, with Sue Clarke and their child, in a terraced house in North Denton? The milkman was in his late twenties perhaps, so would have been around the age Simms was now when his son was born, and he looked contented enough. Simms examined his feelings . . . Was there a tug of longing there? He shivered involuntarily.

'That'll do.' Clunes wiped his nose with his sleeve. 'Run along inside to Mummy, Thomas, there's a good lad, while Daddy has a chat with the man.' The boy regarded Simms with caution, then, sidestepping him, scooted off behind him into the house.

'Sorry to keep you, but it's been stinking the place out all day,' apologized Clunes, spearing the ground with his fork and striding over to greet him. 'Dreadful shame.' He sniffed. 'Not an accident, you think?'

'We're exploring a number of possibilities,' Simms said non-committally. Frost had warned him to be careful how he phrased the paperboy's death so as not to bring about a panic and, as Frost had crudely expressed it, 'the total cessation of paper deliveries in Denton be-cause mums are keeping their cherubs at home'.

'I see,' said the milkman. 'All I can really tell you is I saw the lad most days, but only to exchange a nod or a "wotcha".'

'Around what time?'

'Like clockwork – about ten past seven.'

'So it would've still been dark?' Clunes nodded. The boy must have been killed not long after the milkman saw him. 'And where was this?'

'The top of One Tree Hill, Wessex Crescent – all round there.' Mullett's road, Simms knew that much.

'Why would the lad hoick a full bag all the way up that hill?' Simms mused aloud. 'Why not do the flats at the bottom of Wells Road first?'

'He'd do a circuit; up around the town hall and past the hospital. I saw him sometimes up over that way.'

'Gotcha.' Simms cursed himself for not properly checking the route. The newsagent had merely told him it was very spread out.

'They certainly make those kids work hard for their two quid,' Clunes commented, smiling at his boy who was waving through the kitchen window.

'Yeah, they do,' Simms agreed. 'Is there anything you can recall that was out of the ordinary that morning? A speeding car or bike, the sound of screeching brakes, something like that?'

'Not really.' Clunes shrugged. 'I'm on auto-pilot, really, in my own little world. It's starting to get really cold now – that morning frost has a bite to it – so I'm all for getting round as quick as possible. And at seven I'm at the end of the run and starting to feel it.'

'I understand, Mr Clunes, but, you do realize you were the last person to see Philip Chilcott alive – ten minutes after you saw him, he was found dead.' Simms waited for this to sink in.

'I'm racking my brains, honest. It's horrific . . . It was dark, you know?' he protested lamely. Simms felt for him: how could a milkman who'd got up way before dawn be expected to be alert for anything out of the ordinary.

'Well, if you do think of anything, give me a ring.' He handed over a card.

The man acknowledged it and said, 'The thing is, if anyone was going to do the boy in deliberately, they'd have seen my float beforehand, wouldn't they? So they'd wait until I was gone?'

'Maybe.' Simms sighed. Be that as it may, someone must have seen or heard something. He'd get uniform to canvass the whole area again.

Saturday (5) _____

As the daylight slipped away beyond the rotten window frame and a clear, crisp chill took hold of the rooftops of the Southern Housing Estate, Louise Daley flicked her hair back behind her ears and reached under the bed to retrieve a large suitcase. She heaved it on to the orange counterpane, swiftly twiddled with the combination and pinged open the locks. With the lid open the giant case took up most of the ancient queen-size bed. Inside were an impressive array of wigs, make-up and costumes, all neatly folded and arranged for the optimum use of space – this case contained her whole life, such as it was.

Moving aside a purple sequinned dress, she uncovered what she was after. She lifted out the uniform and laid it out on the bed. It had been a good few years since she'd last worn it; back in the days when she had just started out as a strippergram, before Baskin spotted her performing in a pub, and signed her up for the Coconut Grove. The nurse's uniform was the genuine thing – she'd bought it off a friend in nursing college – not some cheap sex outfit from the back pages of *Men Only*. Louise was always as authentic as possible, that's what made her so good.

Louise had never anticipated graduating from stripper to assassin, but a year in hiding – a fugitive from the law – had left her slim options for earning cash. It was surprising how in demand she, as a woman, was, and few were as young and as proficient as Louise Daley. Her reputation in the criminal world was growing; a cold, ruthless yet beautiful killer with a perfect hit rate. Until now.

And Daley had jumped at the chance of shooting Baskin; she loathed his sort. Initially she'd been surprised that Palmer would go after Harry – they were, as far as she knew, friends – but she didn't question the motive when the sum involved was mentioned. Palmer even gave her the opportune time; a card-playing crony of his had said that Baskin was often alone in the morning after staying up all night playing cards. But the gun had let her down. And then there was yesterday's fiasco, to compound matters.

But she had to focus on Baskin. She needed the money now. It seemed unlikely that he would be out of hospital before she left for Spain on Tuesday, so she had little option but to finish the job in this way. Sunday mornings in hospitals were the busiest for visitors, and yet this was the time she'd chosen – it was risky, but her strategy was the greater the panic created, the better her chance of getting away. Plus if she was really lucky, she might get Frost at the same time.

She put the nurse's uniform to one side, and held up the purple-sequin number. This would have to do for tonight. She was still uncomfortable about venturing outside the flat, but Marty had reassured her that everything would be fine – the dinner was at his place after all, and as if he'd put her in any danger. 'Think of it as a farewell dinner,' he'd said – though she suspected it was nothing of the sort. Rather, she was sure he intended to parade her in front of a couple of local businessmen. Palmer was just like Baskin, that much she knew: him being a friend of her father's made very little difference.

'Have a nice evening, madam.' Frost was still wearing an inane grin as the woman slammed the door in his face. He shouldn't have had that extra pint with Sandy Lane. On an empty stomach it had gone to his head. He turned and felt the first splashes of oncoming rain – the November weather kicking in with zeal. The Cortina was sprayed with sycamore wings loosened by the strengthening wind.

Cecil Rhodes's mother had not been appreciative of his call. Having been notified of her son's condition by uniform on Thursday, this subsequent call from CID in the form of Frost, and the unsubtle probing to elicit whether Cecil was in any way mixed up in activities on the fringes of the law (other than working for her dodgy brother Harry, that is) did not go down well.

And it only rubbed salt into the wound by drawing out how Cecil had ended up working for Uncle Harry in the first place. Mrs Rhodes had explained mournfully how Cecil's schoolfriends, who were blessed with more get up and go, had found places at Denton Tech, whilst her boy, having failed everything he sat at school then dropped out of art college, developed an addiction to computer games. He soon lost touch with most of his friends, all except for his one and only girlfriend, and even that had fizzled out.

Frost lit a Rothmans and flicked on the wipers. No, he thought, this boy may smoke a bit of weed, but he doesn't have the initiative or the energy to deal in it. Palmer was wrong on that count, of that he was sure. But a word with the ex-girlfriend might be worth it, to see if the boy ever talked about his lot with Harry.

That would keep until tomorrow, though – it was getting late, although not too late for a visit to Harry himself. Earlier that evening he'd called and left a message with Desk Sergeant Bill Wells saying he had remembered something important. An evening visit shouldn't be a problem as Baskin was now ensconced in a private room.

Frost didn't buy the theory that Baskin was a porn peddler. It wasn't his style. Compared to the hardcore nasties evoked by Sandy Lane in the pub earlier, the Coconut Grove was merely a cabaret. But he could see the demand for video cassettes and VCRs exploding. The Great British Public was straining at the leash to get beyond the three channels on the telly (although he had a vague feeling that, quite incredibly, some new channel had been added recently – what was it called now?); why settle for Susan Stranks in a tight T-shirt when the full exposure is on a Betamax from Scandinavia? Could that warehouse Clarke was watching be involved, though? Might it contain knock-off VCRs? However, so far her surveillance had produced a big fat zero. Frost felt a twinge in his stomach – the pasty and Guinness of earlier appeared to be at odds with his internals. And where the bloody hell *was* Clarke? Anyone would think it was the weekend.

DC Derek Simms waited at the door. He was knackered; he'd been on his toes all day, and now, standing in the cold outside the schoolteacher's flat, he felt dog-tired. It was dark and time for an early night. A firework crackled in the sky behind him, causing him to jump. He rang the doorbell again. She probably wasn't in – no lights were visible beyond the frosted glass. By now Clarke would be in Essex, delivering the news to her parents about her pregnancy, and Simms was fulfilling his promise to check out rape victim Marie Roberts's story; the teacher had claimed to be single and distraught, but Clarke reckoned she'd clocked her bopping around at the concert the previous evening with some bloke. It appeared that tonight she'd gone out on the tiles again; just as well, as he had no idea what he was going to say. He turned to go.

'Hello?'

'Err . . . evening. Detective Constable Derek Simms,

Denton CID.' Simms addressed a voice that came out of the darkness from behind the security chain.

'Yes?'

'Marie Roberts?' The woman didn't budge, which Simms thought odd – surely it wasn't that strange to find the police following up. He felt at a loss for words. 'This is just routine. My colleague asked me to check on you – following the interview yesterday.'

'On a Saturday night?'

Simms put on a soothing voice. 'I can assure you, Miss Roberts, that the night of the week is irrelevant in a serious case like yours. It's standard practice to follow up the day after, when the victim's mind is perhaps a little clearer and free from the initial shock.' He was impressed by his efforts.

'Oh, I see. You'd better come in then. But can you wait a minute? I'm not decent.'

She shut the door. Simms looked back over the balcony. The street was poorly lit.

The small flat was warm and airless; the heat was more uncomfortable than cosy. He wanted to remove his leather jacket, but felt it might seem inappropriate.

'Can I get you anything?'

Simms asked for a glass of water, and took a seat on the low sofa. The small TV flickered softly in the corner. Bruce Forsyth. Jesus, was that man ever off the telly?

'I'm afraid I don't recall anything more,' said Marie Roberts as she handed him a glass. Her dressing gown had opened slightly, revealing a hint of pale thigh at his eye level. Simms could not help but feel a stirring – he found her attractive.

'That's OK.' He cleared his throat hoarsely. This wasn't what he was expecting – Clarke had described her as dowdy. 'How are you – in yourself?' He was aware as soon as he'd said it that the question sounded trite.

'Bearing up, you know.' She flicked her long fair hair away from her face and sat down in the chair opposite. 'I feel sort of . . .' She let the words hang there.

'Sort of what?' he asked after a lengthy pause.

She brought her feet up on to the chair and hugged her knees. 'Lost . . . and sort of lonely.'

'That's to be expected,' he said uneasily, 'after what you've been through.'

'You think?' She looked over at him intently.

Simms was taken aback, that she should question the suggestion, which was matter-of-fact. He felt a twitch of discomfort. 'I guess.'

A sudden thud was heard from somewhere within the flat. Marie Roberts sat up straight. 'Bilbo.' She tutted.

'I'm sorry?'

'My cat.' She got up. As she passed him, Simms thought he felt the tip of her finger brush his shoulder but he couldn't be sure. A moment later, she returned with the hairiest cat he'd ever seen. Reseating herself, she stroked the furry beast languidly.

Simms felt he had lost his poise. 'Yes, it must be difficult – if you're alone. Have you no family or friends?'

'I'm not from round here – my family are from Scotland.' The cat jumped off her lap, dislodging her dressing gown. Simms found it hard not to look at her pearl-white thigh, which she left on view a fraction too long. Was she coming on to him? Surely not. 'I find it difficult to make friends.'

She was, he reckoned, about the same age as him, though, as he often felt with women, had the upper hand in maturity. But he wasn't stupid. 'So, you've not had anyone round – or been out?'

Marie Roberts tensed – or did he imagine she had? Stiffened perhaps; then in an instant her features softened and she sighed. 'I went out . . . needed to. No point staying cooped up in here, dwelling on it . . . Look, can I get you something proper to drink? It is Saturday night, after all.'

She got up again, not waiting for an answer. Simms was sorely tempted. What would Frost do in this situation? He reckoned he would take a drink; although it was a breach of conduct, he'd do it just to see where the girl was leading, and more importantly, why. Simms was not Frost, but he wasn't a stiff like Mullett either. Waters was where he wanted to be – but the guy was just too cool to work out.

'Err . . . just a small one, then,' he called out.

Mullett, attempting to relax, was distracted by the sight of his wife's pink fluffy slippers twitching along to the music. James Galway; how on earth could anyone be moved to even tap their feet to this penny-whistle merchant? Aggressively he snapped his *Telegraph* into shape. They were due to put a video cassette on at eight, as per their routine. *Jaws* again. It was all very well having one of these machines, but the choice at Denton Video was at best narrow. Still, it beat Bruce Forsyth hands down. If he joined the Masons perhaps they would get out more; he'd heard several mentions of 'Ladies' Nights' . . .

'I say, darling, would you mind . . .'

His wife looked up quizzically from her crochet.

He knew it wasn't really her feet, or indeed the Irish flautist, that was irritating him. It was an unpalatable mix of Frost and the Masons, plus blasted Denton itself. Mullett reached out of the armchair to turn down the hi-fi only to hear in its place the doorbell chiming. Who on earth? 'Dear? Dear . . . ?' he pleaded. His ever-patient wife placed her work to one side.

As she went to the door Mullett sipped his German white wine. The Piesporter tasted dreadful, and his throat burned as though he'd swallowed surgical spirit. Mosel Region my foot, he thought; Panzer-tank brake fluid would be closer to the mark. Why he had let himself be talked into joining a wine club, heaven only knows.

'Poppet, it's the police.'

'My dear, I *am* the police.' Unmoved by this, his wife stood uncertainly at the lounge door. Her cheek twitched nervously, a sure sign of worry. Maybe it was bad news? 'Show them in,' he said.

In his dark uniform, the tall officer looked utterly incongruous against the flowery soft furnishings of the Mullett living room. It felt like a violation. This must

240

be how Joe Public feels, thought Mullett fleetingly. He almost picked up the young officer for not taking off his shoes.

'Yes, Baker, what is it?'

'Sorry, sir, didn't realize this was where you . . .' The young PC tipped his helmet deferentially.

'Never mind that, you're here now – what's this to do with?'

'A young lad was fatally knocked off his bike at the bottom of One Tree Hill on Friday morning.'

Mullett waited for more, but Baker offered nothing else. 'And?'

'We're doing a door-to-door – all the streets on the boy's round.'

Mullett glanced at his wife. 'I see,' he said finally. Until now it had not occurred to him that it might be his paperboy who had been killed.

'Just to see if anyone saw anything—'

'Yes, quite.' Mullett cleared his throat. 'And the time of the . . . death?'

'Ten past seven.'

'Well, Constable, I would still be here – I don't leave the house until seven thirty.' Mullett expected this to be adequate, but PC Baker stood firm. 'Sorry, will there be anything else?'

'Your good lady, sir?'

Mullett glanced at Audrey, who stood to the right of Baker, looking peculiar. 'Yes, my dear? What time do you leave for the hospital – a little after seven, isn't it?'

Saturday (6)

Detective Sergeant John Waters was less than pleased to be still at Eagle Lane Station at nearly nine o'clock on a Saturday night, but the tip from Scotland Yard about Frank Bates had opened a can of worms, and he now found himself knee-deep in enquiries from across the country on unsolved rape cases. Desk Sergeant Bill Wells, who could read his annoyance, made misguided attempts to placate him.

'You're not the only one working on a Saturday night – I'm here too.'

'But not for much longer, Bill – Johnson will be here to relieve you any minute.'

'OK, well, Frost's gone to see Baskin.'

'And Simms and Clarke?'

'Err . . . no idea.'

In any case it didn't really matter where they were,

just that being the last man standing he had to pick up all the late nonsense on his lonesome.

A drunken holler echoed down the corridor. 'How can people be so – so drunk this early in the evening?' But he already knew the answer before Wells pronounced it.

'Town were at home today. And they lost three–nil.'

'It doesn't matter whether they win or lose, the outcome is the same.' The doors went and two PCs struggled in with another drunk, presumably the one Waters was expecting. 'If they win they simply get even drunker . . .' He sighed. 'This my dude?'

There had been a fight at the train station. Denton supporters had hidden in the Ladies and ambushed the jubilant victors when they thought they were home and dry, waiting on the homebound platform. As if the fight itself were not enough, an inebriated fan had exposed himself twice, once to a member of the station staff and once to a woman who'd discovered him asleep in one of the Ladies' cubicles.

'This the one?'

'Won't give his name, will you?' PC Collier said, propping up a lad in his mid-twenties.

'Gone all shy, have we?' Waters stepped up to the lad, who was frowning intently and trying his best to focus. Having had his Saturday night messed up, Waters was lacking in sympathy. Another roar came from the corridor. 'Bill, go check that out, will you? Sounds like a riot . . .'

The drunk grinned. 'Up the Town!'

'You like that?' Waters toyed. 'Now then, why are you too shy to give me your name when you're so comfortable showing old ladies your willy?'

'I think he's drunk, Sarge,' Collier said.

'No! What makes you think that? Well, maybe this'll sober him up a bit . . .' Waters reached between the man's legs and squeezed hard, producing a squeal akin to a cat's when having its tail trodden on.

'What's happening?' Wells returned from the corridor, aghast at yet more noise.

'Not sure, Bill – just trying to find the source of our problem, but have drawn a blank.'

'He looks in pain,' Wells observed. Collier staggered as the drunk almost went over.

'He's just tired out; people think it's *playing* football that's hard work – all that running about – but it has nothing on actually watching the game. All that drinking, shouting, fighting – exhausting. Chuck him downstairs.'

'We can't – no room at the inn. There's several being detained in the interview rooms as it is.'

'You're kidding. They'll just have to share cells, then.'

'Mr Mullett's not keen on that,' Wells replied. 'Always ends in trouble.'

'This isn't the Yorkshire Ripper, men, just some kid who's had too much to drink. Jack's done this tons of times.' Although he knew that wasn't necessarily the best rational argument. 'Talking of which, I hope he's scooting back soon.'

'Queen of diamonds.' Baskin sighed, sliding the thermometer from one side of his mouth to the other. 'You're a sly one, Jack Frost. Your deal.'

Frost picked up the cards from the hospital bed, while Baskin removed a pencil stub from behind his ear and marked the IOU on the pad.

'Not as sly as you, Harry.' He shuffled the deck proficiently. 'Important information, my arse.'

'Don't be like that, Jack.' Baskin looked woeful. 'It's lonely in here – and the missus isn't talking to me. She's very fond of Cecil.'

'I'm not surprised she's peeved.'

'It's not my fault my sister's boy got plugged, it's their fault for foisting the useless worm on me in the first place. It could have been me six feet under, how'd she feel then?'

The door went.

'I wouldn't like to speculate on how she'd receive that piece of good fortune,' Frost replied idly. A red-headed nurse entered the low-lit room without a sound and removed the thermometer. Frost eyed her and pondered for the millionth time why a girl in uniform seemed instantly desirable. Judging by the smile on his face, Baskin was equally appreciative, but this switch into 'lecherous old uncle' mode surprised Frost. Harry had always pleaded immunity to female charm due to over-exposure. The young girl, oblivious to all of this, or simply disinterested, shook the instrument.

'You're doing well, Mr Baskin. There's some colour in

your cheeks too.' That'll be the vodka, Frost thought.

'Thank you, nurse. I must admit I'm feeling pretty perky.' Baskin grinned.

'Well, we'll see how you are tomorrow morning, but I think we might be able to let you go home after breakfast.'

'Really, nurse, that would be grand.' She picked up the water pitcher and made to top up the two glasses on the table. Harry swiftly covered his. 'We're fine, thanks,' he said, a little too hastily.

'Very well. But don't be playing cards with your friend all night.' She glanced at Frost with a faint trace of a smile.

'I promise not to keep the old boy up all night, nurse.' Frost smirked.

As soon as she closed the door behind her, Harry whipped the Smirnoff bottle out from underneath the covers.

'"Friend" is pushing it a bit,' Frost scoffed.

'Ahh, come on, we rub along.' Baskin smiled, topping up the glasses.

'Tell me, was there any chance the lad was in debt? Drugs?'

Baskin shook his head. 'Nah, might have done a bit of weed – would certainly explain his lack of spark – but nothing to warrant getting taken out.'

'What about his girlfriend?'

'What about her?'

'She know anything, you think?' Frost dealt the cards.

'Nah.' Baskin squinted at his cards. ''Ere, pass me my specs.'

Frost reached over and took the spectacles off a tatty copy of *The Ipcress File*.

'Tell me, Harry,' Frost mused. 'If it was *you* trying to shoot you, how would you go about it?' He had left it until now to quiz Harry properly. He figured that now he was calm and out of danger he might be thinking straight.

'How d'you mean?'

'Well, first of all, where would be the best place to do it?'

'At the club. It's in the middle of nowhere, so precious little chance of witnesses.' The Grove was in an isolated spot down an unsurfaced road that stretched away for half a mile or so; there were woods on one side, fields on the other.

'But there's only one way there, along that narrow road,' said Frost, 'so more of a risk of being seen, surely?'

Harry ruminated. 'Ah, but there's a path; runs out from the back of the club through the woods, along between the field and the hedge. Can't see it from the back of the club – need to know it's there. Bert Williams would certainly have remembered it from back in the day. The girls used to use it when we got raided, before we had a licence . . .'

'Girls?'

'Yeah – runs all the way along to the main road. They didn't always need to go that far – sometimes they'd hide by the hedgerow, wait till they'd see the flashing blue light bomb back up the road – then double back and pick up where they'd left off.' Baskin laughed in a soft, gravelly tone.

'Don't you see then, Harry, it *must've* been one of your girls who plugged you?'

He shook his head. 'She couldn't have come that way. This bird was dressed up to the nines . . . heels, the works. Not the sort of clobber for traversing ploughed fields and the like.'

'But did you hear a car pull up or anything like that?'

'Can't recall it.'

'Tell me, where exactly does this path join the main road? I might just go for a ramble tomorrow. Breath of fresh air might do me good. Hospitals: unhealthy places, wouldn't you say?'

Brazier filled his French friend's wine glass right to the brim, as only one unaccustomed to drinking wine with meals would do. Typical of this primate of an Englishman, thought Pierrejean. The red liquid, only a fraction lighter than the gaudy dining-room interior, was unpalatable.

'Good stuff this French vino. Brought this bottle along myself – Piat d'Or. The right stuff, or what?' D'Or was pronounced *du oar*. Pierrejean smiled faintly; to him this watery table wine would be an insult to children – still, this French invasion had opened doors to entrepreneurs like himself.

'So,' began the large, pockmarked man sitting next to

him. 'How do you find the antiques business in Denton, Monsieur Pierrejean?'

'Charles, please.' He shrugged. 'Flat, but it's early days. I'm sure there are many hidden gems out here — one just has to familiarize oneself with the county.'

'I wouldn't be so sure.' The girl who was seated next to Brazier smiled. 'Anything valuable within a twenty-mile radius of Rimmington Marty's already stolen.' The girl — and it was *the* girl; there was no mistaking her beauty — had remained quiet and aloof during introductory cocktails, but the third-rate plonk had brought a glow to her cheeks and she had relaxed her guard a fraction. Yes, it must be the woman who had checked herself in his shop window. Though her hair was blonde then; not the short auburn look now on display.

'Is that so,' he replied, gently pushing away the rock-hard melon starter. The glacé cherry alone was enough to make him nauseous. 'But Mr Palmer is a shrewd businessman with a snooker club to run, he has no time for what are really no more than baubles.'

Palmer snorted loudly.

'You'd be surprised at what he dabbles in,' the girl cut in before Palmer could speak, reaching over and clutching his podgy fist, 'though watch it . . . He's a wily one, and not always reliable, are you, eh, Pumpy?'

'Too much drink is bad for little Loulou — careful, my sweet; we want you to wake up tomorrow.'

Pierrejean, who now even dreamed in English, found

he was lost at Palmer's remark, which had wiped the smile off the girl's face in an instant. He attempted to lighten the mood. 'Tell me, Mr Palmer, how does one acquire such a *cute* nickname?'

'I can tell you that, it's—' Brazier burst out.

'Quiet, Jules!' exclaimed his wife in alarm.

'See that cabinet in the hall?' Brazier blurted out, topping up his own glass.

'Cabinet?' Pierrejean was confused.

'Yeah. Well, it's a gun cabinet. Shotguns.'

'I see.' The connection still eluded him.

'Your usual crim round here favours a sawn-off – but not Marty. When it comes down to business, he settles for nothing less than a Remington or Winchester pump-action.'

Pierrejean sensed Palmer stiffen next to him.

'Darling, enough,' Brazier's wife hissed. The table had gone quiet. Only the girl looked amused.

A waiter entered the room and started to collect up the plates.

'You mustn't listen to tittle-tattle, Charles,' Palmer said. He noticed the waiter clearing barely touched melon. 'Our fruit not up to French standards?'

'At least we've got some decent French wine,' Brazier insisted.

'The wine's piss, Julian.' Palmer snapped his fingers at the manservant. 'Cable.'

'Sir?'

'Fetch something expensive from the cellar, would you?' He wiped his hands on a napkin and tossed it over his shoulder. 'Not much I can do about the fruit, but I can at least make amends for the wine.'

Pierrejean felt obliged to say something complimentary. 'I did detect a most divine aroma from the kitchen – something familiar, although I couldn't quite place it.'

'Duck à l'orange,' the girl said with a flourish, her good mood seemingly restored.

'Really?' He rubbed his taut stomach in a sign of appreciation, then noticed his host's considerable distance from the table, enforced by his voluminous paunch, and stopped.

'And Marty had a hand in it himself.'

'Louise is not wrong,' Palmer confirmed with glee. 'Shot the buggers myself. Serves 'em right for straying from the lake out back.'

Pierrejean saw a comic opening. 'So in England, they stuff a chicken and "pump" a duck?' As laughter erupted around the table the waiting staff appeared with the aforementioned waterfowl.

The Frenchman took the opportunity to quiz his female tablemate. 'And what, if I may enquire, do you do, Louise?'

'I used to be a dancer.'

'Oh really? What kind? Ballet? Disco? Flamenco?'

'Glamour,' Palmer said sniffily. 'Burlesque.'

'Not much glamour at the Coconut Grove now!' Brazier chuckled. 'More of a blood bath.' He lit a cigarette even though the main course had just been placed in front of him.

'What's that?' Pierrejean raised an eyebrow towards the car dealer.

'It's a tatty nightclub just outside Denton. The owner and a lad were shot on Thursday morning. Nasty business. Of course, the police haven't a clue.'

It was the first Pierrejean had heard of that shooting. And it was not the only shooting in Denton – they also had to find an armed robber who had made off with a payroll, as he was currently hearing. Both crimes appeared to have been perpetrated by a woman.

'The women in Denton,' Charles said aside to Palmer, though his gaze was on Louise, while Brazier prattled gaily on, 'are handy with a gun, eh?'

'Some more so than others,' Palmer said, then added, 'But yes, I wouldn't trust them – dangerous bints, all right.'

Charles thought he hadn't followed Palmer's words but he wasn't concerned; happily Denton Police appeared rushed off their feet and his own crime seemed very 'small beer' in comparison. The wine relaxed him and he studied Louise chatting energetically. So, she was a common stripper? In spite of this tawdry fact he still regarded her as a beauty, and not just for the obvious reasons, although he could hardly ignore the frankly magnificent cleavage bursting out of a sparkling purple dress that seemed more appropriate for a discotheque. She and Brazier were heatedly discussing the club, Louise having rallied to its defence.

'Come off it, you two. Let's not dwell on this rather sordid event – Charles, tell us what you've been up to this week?' Palmer brought him back down to earth.

Pierrejean gave a deferential nod to Elizabeth Brazier. 'As I'm sure you're aware, Mr Palmer, it's been something of a solemn week.' Palmer shot Elizabeth a sympathetic look, having just put two and two together.

'Apologies, yes.'

'Sorry, have I missed something?' Louise enquired.

'My sister . . .' Elizabeth started.

'Elizabeth's sister, Mary, was buried on Thursday,' Brazier said soberly.

'I'm so sorry, I didn't know.' Louise flashed a look at Palmer as if to say, why didn't you tell me?

'It's all right – it wasn't sudden,' Elizabeth Brazier replied, regaining her composure. The waiter offered her the wine to try and she gratefully accepted.

'Your parents' hospitality was exceptional,' Pierrejean soothed.

Brazier patted his wife's cheek supportively. 'Yes, it was, as they say, a bit of a do. Although rather too many policemen there for my liking.'

'That was unavoidable, Julian,' his wife admonished.

'How so?' Louise said casually; Pierrejean watched her intently. Just how cool was this woman, he wondered?

'Mary was married to one of Denton's finest – Detective Sergeant Jack Frost. A colourful character,' Palmer explained. 'Wonder how he'll cope.' Pierrejean didn't really know his host, but gauged the remark was made with little concern for Frost's welfare.

'He'll be just fine,' Elizabeth replied. 'I doubt he'll even notice.'

'Why's that?' Charles asked, his interest piqued, having briefly met the man in question at the wake.

'Married to the job,' Palmer said. 'Tenacious bugger – never at home. Only the other week, one of my boys found him asleep in his car out on the Denton Road.'

'All the more reason he should give back the house,' Elizabeth said bitterly. She saw the others needed an explanation. 'My parents lent them the money to buy it. A substantial Victorian semi – very nice.'

'Oh really, where's that?' Louise asked innocently, her greeny-brown eyes flashing over her wine glass.

'Vincent Close, on the outskirts of Denton, off Green Lane.'

Charles Pierrejean was beginning to change his mind about Denton. He sensed it was an extraordinary little town and was intrigued to see how things would develop. He took a healthy swig of the Pinot Noir, which was, to his surprise, first-rate.

Frost didn't notice the water as he crossed the threshold, leaving the key in the door and clutching a Kung Po Extra-Ping from the Jade Rabbit. Nor did he even flinch as he splashed down the dark hallway. He was thoroughly shattered, and it was not until he flicked on the kitchen light that the sensation of wet feet connected with the flooded room.

'Balls,' he said softly. He surmised that the washing machine had broken down. It was ten-ish, so there was nothing to be done about it now. He scrabbled around for a corkscrew, then picked up the spoon out of yesterday's dinner bowl and shoved it in his back pocket.

He glanced into the lounge, where the standard lamp had been left on since the previous evening. The room was also sodden, but he breathed a sigh of relief – at least he'd picked up the records from the floor yesterday. He grabbed volume five of Oman's exhaustive history of the Peninsular War from the settee and wedged it under his arm – he could do with hearing of a win, and Wellington's decisive victory at Salamanca in 1812 would be just the ticket, should he manage to stay awake for more than a minute.

He felt the draught as he re-entered the dark hall. Flaming heck, he cursed, I can't even remember to shut my own front door. But no sooner had he thought this than he became aware of a presence in the doorway. Too tired to pussyfoot around, Frost brazenly marched up to meet the figure.

'You left the front door open.'

Frost's hand brushed by the intruder's shoulder as he switched the light on.

'There's a bell!' he pointed out to a pasty Derek Simms.

'Jesus – you're flooded!'

'You'll make a detective yet, son. Come upstairs to the temporary dining quarters.'

'Don't you want to know what it's about?'

'I imagine it's of some crucial urgency, otherwise it would surely wait until the morning.' Frost paused on the second stair. 'However, I have a crucial urgency for this Kung Po Extra-Ping, and a discounted bottle of French plonk.'

'It can wait, I guess . . . Sorry to disturb you,' Simms said hesitantly.

'Come in, you're here now – here, hold that, and come get a glass.' Frost passed the book over, and sploshed towards the kitchen to grab the bottle and takeaway. 'Picked up this little French number from the offie – buy two, get one free. Not bad . . . never used to be able to get decent wine in Denton.' Frost was glad of the unexpected company, but sensed something must be troubling the lad for him to make a trip out on a Saturday night, and wanted to put him at his ease. 'Now, what's the problem?'

'Well, it's not much – it's thanks to bad luck I'm here; the car broke down at the crossroads, I knew you were nearby, so chanced it you'd be in and I could call a cab.'

'That little red number of yours?' Frost ushered him into the upstairs study, thinking it unlikely that he would be the first port of call unless something really was on Simms's mind, given the pub on the corner.

'Yeah, the Alfa. Bloody exhaust just fell off.'

'Well, it is a bit of a hairdresser's car,' Frost joked, flicking on the desk light. The boy looked like he felt, exhausted, though it wasn't much after ten. 'Take a pew.'

Simms sunk into the old armchair, quite literally; the seat had gone, it need restuffing and recovering, or perhaps, now Mary had gone, throwing away. Frost passed him a glass of wine and tucked into the luke-warm Kung Po, having offered the first orange spoonful to the young DC, who shook his head.

'Marie Roberts,' Simms started uncertainly. 'I think she's lying.'

Frost nodded, but said nothing; he'd had suspicions from the instant he'd left the school that something didn't stack up. Simms went on to elaborate about how Clarke had asked him to check out the woman's story about her movements on Friday night.

'Of course, there's nothing wrong with her going out, even if it did seem surprising after what she'd been through that morning, but Sue reckoned she'd been so adamant that she'd had no interest from men, so it was worth checking out . . .'

'Fair enough,' Frost said, taking a gulp of wine. 'And where is DC Clarke? Do you know?'

Simms was looking towards the floor. When he lifted his head his expression had changed. 'In Colchester, in Essex.'

Where her parents live. That much Frost did know; and he now suddenly clocked the true motivation behind Simms's visit. He held Simms's eye and with his best avuncular smile said, 'And perhaps that's the real reason you're here?'

Simms left the Frost house shortly before twelve. It was a grim, foggy night, and being a Saturday the wait for a minicab would have been an hour plus, so Frost had kindly lent him the Cortina. He'd originally offered him the spare room, but Simms felt that was overstepping the mark.

He'd been wrong about Frost in many ways, and was pleased he'd chosen to confide in the older man about Sue's pregnancy. Frost had, after all, had a fling with her on and off, and between the three of them there'd been an underlying tension at times. But as is sometimes the case, he thought, it takes unexpected events to bring emotions into focus.

Simms stopped at the end of the garden path, realizing he'd not told Frost about the lost forensic evidence: the bullet. He turned to see the upstairs light go off. It could wait; the sergeant had aged years since his wife's illness and his eyelids were drooping by the end of the evening; he'd be sparko in a matter of minutes.

Unlocking the Cortina, with a warm feeling from the cheap wine and the relief of a burden shared coursing through him, Simms, although dog-tired, was happy. He was reconciled to the thought of a future with Sue, and the prospect thrilled him. He planned to propose when she arrived back in Denton tomorrow afternoon. This was the last thought Detective Constable Derek Simms would ever have. His body, in such a relaxed state, barely registered the blade entering, and not until it was twisted did he become aware of what had happened to him. Unable to cry out he slid down out of the car and slumped on to the wet cold pavement.

Sunday (1)

Detective Sergeant John Waters rubbed his bleary eyes, to snap himself awake. It was 3 a.m. and he was down in the cells at Eagle Lane police station, yet again.

'Any more out of either of you and I'll slap you both with a breach-of-the-peace charge.'

'How's that work, then? We're banged up already – whose peace are we breaching?' The football hooligan was less drunk but more red-eyed than six hours earlier.

'Mine!' Waters snapped. He held up the other man's head; the wound appeared superficial. The man sneered at him through bloody teeth.

'He started it,' the other said limply.

'I don't give a damn,' Waters said angrily. 'Jesus, how old are you two – seven?' He could curse Bill Wells for putting supporters of opposing teams in the same cell. That was simply asking for trouble. Waters turned to the duty officer standing in the cell doorway.

'Constable, if there's so much as a peep out of the children, cuff them, OK?'

'Cuff them?'

'Yeah – arms behind their back, in the most uncomfortable position possible.'

Waters, limbs aching, made his way wearily back up to the CID office. The big detective sergeant hadn't realized the lateness of the hour until he'd been summoned downstairs again, so lost had he been in cross-referencing rape cases. He returned to a pile of witness statements and sipped his lukewarm coffee. He had something here, though: two teachers had reported attacks in the West Country by a man with a description similar to the one Joanne Daniels had given – below-average height, slight build. But did it tally with the Roberts girl's description? He looked to Clarke's notes – which said nothing. Strange; the attack took place in broad daylight – Roberts must have made out something, colour of his hair, for example. All Clarke had pencilled in was: *Victim seems vague – shock?*

Waters switched back to the other file; one of the teachers in the West Country had noticed a yellow sports-watch strap; she'd not recognized the watch brand itself, but as her attacker had pinned her to the wall she'd caught a flash of bright colour. The method of attack was similar to the Joanne Daniels case, outside a pub in an alley, but Daniels had not identified any such article—

'Sergeant Waters?' Night Sergeant Johnny Johnson's appearance made him jump.

'Johnny, you spooked me!'

'Sorry, mate – didn't know there was anyone here, I just tried to patch a call through – saw the light on.'

'I was downstairs.' He sighed. 'Think that's my lot – I'm off home.'

'There's been a body found in Vincent Close. I just sent an area car.'

Waters put his coffee cup down. 'Vincent Close? That's Jack's street.'

'So it is. Knew it was familiar. Just called him, but got no answer, then I tried Simms, no answer, then Clarke . . .'

But Waters was no longer listening. He belted out of the office and down the darkened corridor.

The knock at the door was loud and purposeful. Frost jolted awake. He was not a deep sleeper, more prone to hovering in a dream hinterland that could be easily punctured, especially after drinking late. He had thought he heard the phone but it was a sound he heard all too often in his sleep, so he'd rolled over. But the noise at the front door was very real and unmistakable.

The brass knocker thudded again. Was that Simms returning? Could he have only just left? He may have forgotten something, though Frost recalled he'd arrived empty-handed. It must be the motor. Frost groaned; the cheap wine had done its job, leaving his head dutifully foggy. He rolled over in the bed and opened his eyes. Beyond the nets – the curtains themselves had not been drawn – a familiar sharp blue whorl was rotating in the darkened street below, indicating an area car on his doorstep. Frost was not unused to being disturbed late at night, or in the early hours like now, but he sensed that something wasn't right. Why, he couldn't say, but his heart had begun to pound. Instinctively he knew something bad had happened. He flung off the counterpane and scrambled out of the bed. In nothing but pants and vest he stormed out of the room, kicking over a half-empty wine bottle on the landing in his haste to get down the stairs.

He opened the door, his booze-fettered mind unable to remember why his feet were wet – to be greeted by a sombre PC.

'Sorry to disturb you, Sergeant Frost, but there has been an incident of the most serious nature,' the uniform said. Frost didn't recognize the officer; his features were in shadow, obscured by the lip of the Custodian.

Frost stepped out on to the path. Beyond the skeletal tree bathed in blue light was an area car parked behind his own Cortina. But he'd lent the car to Simms? He hurried towards the garden gate, ignoring a cry from the PC imploring him to clothe himself first. The road was still, the far reaches of it bathed in an orange glow afforded by the occasional street lamp. As he approached the area car, his feet prickling on the sharp, cold ground, he could see a figure crouching over the pavement next to his own vehicle, which was dusted with a morning frost – the car had clearly not been moved from where he'd left it, hours earlier.

Frost dimly perceived his next-door neighbour –

still in her nightie – holding huddled against her her fully clothed teenage son; she was talking softly to a WPC. As he came up to his car the PC stood up and stepped back from the body. Frost knew that before him lay DC Derek Simms. He knelt towards his fallen colleague and took hold of his lifeless, bloody wrist, just as a screech of brakes pierced the icy silence with such severity that Frost thought his own heart might give out and he would join the dead man on the pavement.

Superintendent Mullett was having difficulty processing everything that had occurred over the last twenty-four hours. He'd slept badly as it was – worrying about all manner of things – only to be woken just before dawn with the news that the CID officer in charge of the dead paperboy's case had been stabbed to death outside Frost's house. It was vexing in the extreme.

He hadn't managed to ask his wife directly whether, on her way in on Friday (why on earth did she still insist on shift work at the hospital?), she had accidentally clipped the lad on his bike. He just couldn't bring himself to do it, for a variety of complex reasons that weren't yet clear to him. He knew it was a *possibility*, and for now that would suffice – his ratiocination did not call for further probing. Mrs Mullett's driving record was far from unblemished; prior to his arrival as superintendent in Denton he had had to brush under the carpet several embarrassing incidents. Until yesterday evening, when a uniformed officer rapped on the white-gloss door of 7 Wessex Crescent, Mullett had been unaware that

DC Simms had instigated a further scour of the area. And now, bizarrely and alarmingly, Simms was dead, knifed whilst getting into Jack Frost's vehicle outside the latter's home on Vincent Close. What the devil was going on?

As if he hadn't enough to contend with. Mullett's mind had churned restlessly throughout the night. Should he promote Bill Wells to get into the Lodge after all? It might be very useful if he did subsequently find himself in a tight spot thanks to his wife. But that could wait at least until Monday. Mrs Mullett bustled into the kitchen. He realigned his thoughts to the events of the small hours of this morning – the murder of Detective Constable Derek Simms.

Waters had already been assigned the case – Frost, due to his proximity to the crime, could not investigate it, and as a matter of procedure he would have to be formally ruled out of having any involvement in Simms's demise.

The Sunday papers were placed silently on the kitchen table in front of him, and his tea was dutifully topped up; his wife was tiptoeing around him this morning, but he was too preoccupied to acknowledge her. Simms and Frost. Simms *murdered*. Was the maverick sergeant in some way implicated? Could it be that what had started off as a sociable evening between two off-duty policemen had turned into a horrible drunken row? Frost's neighbour's inebriated son had stumbled on the attack after a Saturday night in Denton boozing with his pals. He'd been in no state to identify the attacker, who had pushed the boy over and disappeared into the dark. The boy, who had hit his head on the kerb and passed out, had eventually staggered up out of the gutter and woken his mother, who in turn had gone to summon Frost, but it was not until an area car had arrived on the scene that he'd opened the door.

Mullett knew in his heart that Frost, even at his most volatile, had never so much as raised a hand against a fellow officer, not even Jim Allen, whom he loathed, and to suspect that Frost was in any way involved was just wishful thinking. But there would have to be an investigation, a very thorough investigation. During which time the ACC couldn't possibly insist on promotion for the detective. In the meantime, he would put pressure on Frost to close the paperboy case; to say he simply fell off his bicycle, or something.

'More toast, my love?'

Mullett eyed his lady wife furtively. 'Yes, my dear, I could manage another slice after all.'

The superintendent bit smugly into his toast, not for a moment troubling to think why Simms might really have been killed, so lost in his scheming was he.

Sunday (2) _____

'So, am I under suspicion?'

'Hey, man, you know the drill,' Waters said calmly, glancing at Mullett who stared out of his office window, not rattled in the slightest, a paragon of self-control. And controlled was the only way to do this; it was a matter of form, but it needed to be done delicately. Mullett was right, Frost had to be questioned and ruled out of any possible involvement in Simms's death before they could move on. It required the finest skills of both men to pull this off swiftly. Waters watched Mullett sip his tea. Being the new man, he'd been surprised that Mullett had wanted him to handle this, and not his old favourite DI Allen, who would take extreme pleasure in trying to pin something on Frost.

'The guy was killed beside your motor, and you were the last one to see him alive. Man, you gotta answer some questions.'

'Yes, quite,' Mullett huffed. 'The teenage boy has no idea what he saw,' he added pointedly.

'Eh? What's that supposed to mean?' Frost retorted.

'Nothing,' Waters soothed. 'We just need to ascertain Derek Simms's frame of mind when he left you, you know that.' Waters was concerned for Frost, but re-assured himself that there'd been no positive ID from the kid next door. Mullett had grilled Waters on the phone earlier a little too excessively; Waters had repeated to Mullett that there actually was a witness, but in the end had had to say point blank, *There is no way this is Jack*, to silence the divisional commander.

'I know,' Frost agreed. 'I'm gutted for the poor lad. It's odd – we never quite hit it off, but we had a nice evening, you know?'

Frost, who looked as though he'd been up all night – and more or less had – went into detail about how the evening had panned out in a matter-of-fact, measured fashion. Waters made the odd note.

After ten minutes, Frost had concluded his account. Mullett sniffed and nodded his approval, but Waters had the nagging feeling that Frost was holding out – not lying as such, but leaving something unsaid. Waters didn't know the ins and outs of their relationships with Sue Clarke, but given the past connection between the three, it seemed very unlikely that Simms would stay for nearly two hours just chewing the fat or assessing the Marie Roberts case, as Frost had suggested, and not mention Clarke. It struck him as a strange omission.

As if reading his mind, Mullett chimed in, 'And where is DC Clarke?' The super was always anxious about his top female officer, but in a somewhat detached way.

'It's the weekend,' Frost said. 'Her whereabouts are anyone's guess, young girl like that.'

'No doubt,' the super replied. 'DC Clarke is also on the Marie Roberts rape case. If there's any credence to this story that the victim might be lying, as per your conversation with Simms, it's one less case to worry about. What do you think, Frost?'

'If you're asking if I think it's possible she was caught having a quickie in the loo, then yes, I'd say things are pointing that way.'

'I wouldn't put it in such base terms as that,' Mullet said sharply. 'Wait until Clarke is back and then confront the girl. Clear this one up.' The superintendent sat down behind the desk and, craning around the edge of the huge computer screen, leaned across towards them both. 'But Simms's murder requires a position more quickly.' Waters could read between the lines at the intent directed towards Frost. 'A comment will be required; "mindless thuggery" or "premeditated murder" of a member of the force.'

'Maybe robbery was the motive; the attacker was interrupted before swiping Simms's wallet or Jack's motor.' Even as he said it Waters didn't believe it. He felt sure it was deliberate murder, but was Simms really the intended victim?

'Cobblers,' Frost interjected. 'Vincent Close is a quiet cul-de-sac full of respectable punters who don't make a habit of strolling about after midnight, weekend or not. The attack was targeted. The killer was lying in wait for Simms.'

'Not necessarily Simms,' Waters said.

'Explain?' Mullett prompted.

'It was a dark, murky night. Derek was getting into Jack's motor. Could be mistaken identity.'

'Mistaken for who? Me!' Frost exclaimed. 'Why me?'

'Come off it, Jack, it's far more likely to be you than the boy, he's barely out of short trousers. You'll have offended far more people over the years.'

'Hear, hear,' Mullett agreed, brightening. 'Indeed, it will be difficult to know where to start.'

'Charming.' Frost blew out his cheeks.

'It's got to be someone you've banged up. Someone with a grudge, who recognizes the motor but not you at close quarters – a hit man?' Waters suggested.

'I've only had that motor three years – I've not changed that much, put on a few pounds maybe, but certainly not grown six inches . . .'

Mullett pulled out his cigarettes and offered one to Waters. 'Yes, but think of all the people you've annoyed and irritated over the years.' Mullett exhaled wistfully, warming to his subject. 'Ex-cons, wrongful arrests, harassments; and that's just the lowlifes. Think of all the respectable members of society you've offended with your brash, uncouth manner. And that's without considering the vast number of members of the opposite sex you've abused over the years.' Mullett whistled. 'That's quite a list there.'

'Where were *you* late last night, sir?' Frost asked, eyebrows raised.

The superintendent smiled an indulgent smile.

'Well, if that's all, I've an urgent call to make,' Frost announced after a silence. 'A plumber.' Waters and Mullett both looked surprised. Waters wondered for a moment whether he meant a solicitor.

'OK. Dismissed,' said Mullett, his normal stern demeanour returning. 'There'll be the usual press conference tomorrow afternoon.' Waters rose, anxious to be out of Mullett's office.

'Who'll notify the boy's parents?' Frost asked.

'I shall. As Divisional Superintendent, the matter falls to me,' Mullett said, deadpan. 'And need I remind you both that a police officer's murder is the most heinous of crimes and will undoubtedly make the national news.'

'In general, I'm not a supporter of drinking in the morning,' Frost announced as he opened his office door, 'but today, I will certainly make an exception.'

'I'll second that,' Waters said, following him in.

'Out!' Frost barked at the computer technician who was sat at his desk.

'But it's Sunday!' he whinged. 'How am I supposed to do this when you're always here!'

Frost had a sudden twinge of empathy; after all, the man was only trying to do his job. 'Give us half an hour, son, and it's all yours, OK?'

Placated, the technician left them in peace. Frost

pulled the bottle out of the filing cabinet and poured two large measures into empty coffee mugs.

'Thanks, John,' he sighed as he flopped into his chair.

'For what?'

'It didn't occur to me until we were sat in there' – he thumbed in the direction of Mullett's office – 'that if it became general knowledge about us and DC Clarke, Simms's demise might be viewed altogether differently.' He didn't want to spell it out but Waters understood – the facts could easily suggest a drunken squabble over a woman.

'Jack, it *is* general knowledge to the world at large – but unless it reaches the pages of the *Telegraph* it's not going to trouble the super. And anyway, Jack, wasn't that all over ages ago?' Waters asked hopefully. 'I mean, you wouldn't have been spending your time playing chess with me if you had a better alternative . . .'

'Wouldn't I?' Frost said amiably. 'I'll have you know I value our intimate evenings very highly.'

'Well, don't get too cute on me,' joshed Waters, lighting a cigarette. 'Mullett is right on this one – we've got to find out who did it, and be snappy about it.'

'I know, I know.' Frost ran his fingers through his unwashed hair.

'Think, Jack. Is there a connection with Baskin? Were you two up to something?'

'What, someone wanted to bump us both off? Nah, we weren't – *aren't* – up to anything . . . And we're not even close to resolving who did the hit on him.'

'Anyone who might have a grudge?'

'Can't think of anybody – after all, my clear-up rate is rock bottom, even the super would testify to that,' he joked lamely. In truth, Frost knew of a number of people who might have it in for him, but he had never allowed it much head space; how could a policeman do his job if he constantly agonized over potential reprisals?

'OK. I've never seen the super that excited about anything, though.' Waters sighed. 'Maybe we're barking up the wrong tree. Maybe somebody did have it in for Simms. Knew it was him getting into your motor – was following him, knew he was with you?'

'Thanks, mate – nice to know that as a last thought, after, one, me killing him; two, somebody wanting to kill me; that three, it crosses your mind that Simms himself might have been the target.'

'C'mon, Simms is much less obvious. Awkward sod like you, guaranteed to rub everyone up the wrong way. But maybe Simms just upset the wrong person. Think – what's he been working on?'

'The paperboy, which is probably just an accident or hit-and-run, and the robbery at Gregory Leather.'

'Nothing conclusive there, is there? Have a serious think, will you, Jack?' Waters looked gloomy. 'I'm off to the lab now. Simms's post-mortem.'

'Yes, off you scoot. And you can tell Drysdale I'll be along later – official or not. I don't care what Hornrim Harry says, the boy was my responsibility.'

'If you're sure it's a good idea.'

'It's never a good idea,' Frost admitted, suddenly deflated. 'Listen, what are you doing this afternoon? Fancy a ramble through the countryside?'

Waters rolled his eyes. 'My cup runneth over,' he groaned.

'What's up, sunshine?' Frost teased, trying to lighten the mood. 'You seem a little fractious this morning.'

'Are you kidding?' Waters stood up and stared. Frost blinked back at him, unmoved. 'The job, man, it gets to me – especially when a copper takes a dive. I'm not as tough as some.'

Frost knew this was levied at him, but chose not to respond; it wasn't that he was heartless, but he firmly believed that emotions added nothing to the job. At the same time, he was aware that trying to hide his own feelings, such as while his wife was ill, had made him disagreeable to work with.

'Hey, you're right. Apologies.'

Waters waved it away. 'Forget it. I'm a lightweight when I don't get much kip – had drunks fighting in the cells in the middle of the night before I was called out to your gaff.'

'Leave them to it, I would.'

'Me too; never mind.' Waters smiled wanly. 'I would dearly love to go for a ramble with you this afternoon but I got a lead on the Joanne Daniels case.'

'Joanne Daniels?'

'The girl raped outside the pub, Monday night – remember, you had me on a stake-out by the call box on Brick Road?'

Frost topped up his Scotch. 'Yeah, yeah, I'd forgotten about that. What you got?'

'This kid – also lives on Brick Road – works in the pub where she was raped; reckons his landlord's a bit of a perv; he's been caught going through a girl's knicker drawer. Thought I'd check it out, given the origin of the phone calls.'

Frost grunted his approval. He liked the way Waters worked – relentlessly and clutching on to everything there was in the way of leads. He'd worked practically a forty-eight-hour weekend. Unlike some, he thought, his mind flipping to Clarke, who'd gone away for the weekend and who had yet to learn of Simms's murder. He winced at the prospect of informing her of the death of her colleague and lover. From what the boy had said before he died, he figured she'd take it pretty badly.

'You go easy on that, you hear?' Waters said, pointing to the bottle. 'Get something to eat.'

Frost ignored him; instead he picked up the phone and dialled Arthur Hanlon's number – a number he knew by heart; the pair went back a long way. Good old solid, dependable Hanlon.

'Arthur, it's Jack. Meet me at the Coconut Grove at midday.'

Louise Daley had slept like a log; long, deeply and peacefully. Waking at close to ten, lucid and surprisingly clear-headed, she realized what she'd done last night was risky; but she'd done what she'd set out to do.

Admittedly, she'd had a drink or two and that had

fuelled her enthusiasm, but hell, she'd have broken into that bastard's house and knifed him in his own bed, if necessary.

Daley played the events back her mind, with a smile on her face. On hearing Frost's address reeled off at Palmer's dinner table, she'd felt compelled to act. She'd been harbouring a burning desire to slay Jack Frost – in revenge for shooting her uncle Joe Kelly dead in Denton woods, and leaving her half-brother Blake Richards crippled for life – so when this crucial information was tossed in her lap it was too good to resist. She propped herself up in bed, her hands itchy. She looked at them with distaste, and in the half-light saw dark patches of dried blood.

Having left Palmer's at near midnight, Daley had driven back from Rimmington to Denton and parked round the corner from Frost's road, Vincent Close. She knew Denton like the back of her own blood-encrusted hand and had no problem finding the street. Daley couldn't recall Frost in person – she'd seen the odd press photo but had barely glimpsed him in the flesh – but that bloke at the dinner last night, the brash car dealer with the bust nose, had been ridiculing Frost's motor, so she knew which car to look for. The dealer was Frost's brother-in-law, and clearly hated him as well . . . Little did he know what his slip of the tongue had given rise to!

Daley went into the bathroom and filled the cracked basin with water. She picked at the dried blood covering her hands. As the brown flakes swirled in the scalding water she thought of the murder weapon – a bayonet lifted from Marty's cabinet. (She had not banked on such good luck, and so had left the Beretta at the flat.) Upon her arrival at Palmer's farm, ahead of the other guests, her host had insisted on showing off his extensive collection. And extensive was the word; it stretched well beyond his fabled assortment of shotguns and included all manner of weapons from both World Wars, such as the German bayonet she'd swiped on her way out.

In Frost's road she had spied the Cortina – but it was parked beside the kerb, not in a driveway. She didn't know exactly which house her intended victim lived in, so it seemed as if tonight's quest might be over. She had lit a cigarette, and stood in the shadows thinking. Just then the upstairs light in a house near the Cortina went off, and abruptly she heard a front door echo in the icy stillness of the road, followed by footsteps. There was no sound of laughter or farewell to suggest the end of a Saturday evening round at friends'. Who would leave a house at this late hour and slip silently into the night – a policeman on call, perhaps? Without a second thought she reached into the deep trench-coat pocket for the narrow steel blade as she saw a man walk towards the Cortina.

Wait. The Triumph. Her car. It was still parked a couple of streets from Vincent Close. That stupid drunken kid had bumbled into her, causing her to bolt on foot like a frightened animal, all the way back to the Southern Housing Estate. High on adrenalin, she'd got back to the flat and downed half a bottle of Cinzano.

Hell, she'd got away, though, and with Frost out of the picture chances were she could slip away without difficulty – apparently he was the only one at Denton nick with any intelligence, or so Pumpy maintained. She'd get her motor later. Pumpy had revealed that Frost had been hell-bent on catching her since she escaped after the shoot-out last autumn (if she was still at risk, why did the great oaf offer her the hit on Baskin? He thought that hilarious). She rubbed her hands furiously in the sink, and decided to run the bath too.

She had planned to finish off Baskin this morning. *She needed that cash.* When she'd tried last night to bring up the Friday job, Pumpy had put his finger to his lips and said business was not to be discussed in his home, only because that slimy butler was hovering . . . As the bath filled she started laying the nurse's uniform out on the bed, but was interrupted by the phone in the hall. She froze. Only one person knew the number. She waited and waited, but it rang on, commanding she answer it, knowing her to be there.

'Hello?'

'Louise, sweetheart, I was worried I'd missed you.'

'I was just running a bath, Marty, clearing my head.'

'Good girl, very wise. You certainly put it away last night . . . Now then. Change of plan,' he wheezed down the line. 'Visiting hours are cancelled for today.' He was referring to Baskin at Denton General. 'A rozzer's been murdered. Place will be crawling with coppers. Too risky.'

'Oh.'

'But swing your pretty arse down here later. You seemed well humpy last night.' He rang off before she could answer.

'Bollocks!' she cursed. She wasn't expecting that – Christ, she'd really screwed up. If she couldn't finish the Baskin job he wouldn't pay her. Palmer was keen on her but not that keen – for some reason her charm would go only so far with Marty, something she couldn't understand (given his reputation and the double-entendre behind his nickname). She sighed. Funny he didn't ask about the payroll job. Did he just assume she'd pulled it off? Nevertheless, she'd try and squeeze him later for some cash.

But in the meantime, why not work on somebody who *would* be susceptible to her charms. Tossing the nurse's uniform back in the case she dug through the pockets of her coat until she found what she was looking for, a bent business card. On the back of the Avalon Antiques calling card was a residential number in flowery script. Yes, getting money out of this man would as easy as a walk in the park . . .

Sunday (3)

'So tell me, mademoiselle, how come our paths have not crossed before?'

The 'mademoiselle' was purely for effect, but Charles cringed at himself for having said it – this girl exuded confidence and intelligence, and was unlikely to fall for any heavy-handed French charm. In truth he had never expected her to call the number he'd written on the back of his card last night.

'Oh, I flew the coop a long time ago. I only come back to Denton occasionally, to visit my mother.'

'And your uncle?'

'My— Yes, and "Uncle" Marty, of course.' She studied him with her sharp, green-brown eyes, tinged with tiredness perhaps, searching for a hint of sarcasm. The pair were in the poplar-lined pedestrian avenue that crossed Market Square; it was a space of such a generous size that on a Sunday, with reduced traffic at its edges, it doubled as a small park for the centre of town. Charles noticed that strolling towards them down the path was a policeman, the second he'd seen since arriving ten minutes earlier to meet Ms Daley. Without a word Louise linked her arm through his. The unexpected close contact gave Charles a small thrill. The policeman passed without noticing the attractive, well-dressed couple, he in his late thirties in a mohair coat, and his striking companion in her twenties with her short auburn hair.

'So, Charles, how do you come to know Marty? You seem to be from outside his usual circle of acquaintance.'

'Mr Palmer is a businessman, as am I. And he also has a passion for antiques.'

Louise laughed. 'I think you'll find that Pumpy's interest in antiques goes little further than weaponry. I saw the way you flattered him on that motley collection of tasteless old junk.'

'As I said, I am a businessman.'

'And what business do you have with me?' She stopped, and turned to face him.

'You are a very attractive woman, Louise. Intelligent . . .' He paused; the right words eluded him. Her demeanour, her behaviour last night, her connection to Palmer, everything about her told him she was dangerous, and in combination with her beauty that was a powerful attraction. He craved the thrill of courting such a woman. But, smitten though he might be, Charles was still sensible enough to realize she wouldn't have met up with him unless she wanted something too. And what was that likely to be? It could only be money. What else is there? he thought.

They crossed the top of Market Square, moving towards Gentlemen's Walk and a café that Gaston had his eye on. Charles's friend had talked about opening a bistro-cum-café on the pedestrianized street, though Charles himself was cynical; the idea of the British appetite evolving beyond eggs and bacon or fish and chips seemed to him unlikely, and even if it did, the climate would not support pavement-café culture for more than a week or so a year.

Charles's companion gave very little away about herself as they drifted up the empty street, and he found himself waxing lyrical about his property in France. In short, he was showing off.

They reached Billy's Café and Charles gallantly opened the door, but Louise stopped in her tracks, causing him to lose his hold on her arm.

'I'm afraid I must dash,' she said, removing her sunglasses.

'Oh,' he replied, disappointed. 'But we've only just met.'

'And very nice it was too; I'm just very shy – in public.' She fluttered her eyelashes coquettishly, to accompany the loaded remark.

He was quick to respond: 'Dinner tonight – my place?'

'I'm afraid I'm leaving Denton tonight.'

'Oh. An early supper perhaps?' He was suddenly

filled with a desperate desire – he simply had to get his fill of her before she left town.

She looked at him strangely. 'I'm a working girl, you know,' she said brightly, unabashed.

He might have known. Though he suspected she was after his money, he did not expect her to be a *fille de joie*.

'I see.'

'But yes, OK, early this evening would be dandy. I've quite an appetite.' And she ran her tongue suggestively along the bottom row of her perfect teeth – a gesture that was verging on the vulgar but that Charles found oddly alluring. 'But I value my time highly,' she added, lest there be any doubt.

'I would expect nothing less,' he replied, although his ego yearned differently.

She kissed him lightly on the cheek, having noted his address, and promptly left him. As he watched her hurry back along Gentlemen's Walk, he pondered why an intelligent girl such as Louise had stooped so low as to sell herself. The payroll robbery was one thing, for he was now sure it had been her – the *Denton Echo* reckoned the haul was in the region of three grand – but prostitution too? The British; he would never understand them. But it hardly mattered, since right now money was not an issue, especially when it came to one so beautiful. Having 'acquired' a painting worth several million francs, Gaston and he had decided they might as well quit while ahead, so they would soon be leaving Denton, but he would grant himself one last night of pleasure. Why not – they'd been few and far between since landing on these shores.

Frost stood alone in the cold, grey lab. Drysdale for once had the sense to give a few moments' grace to the weary sergeant, for which Frost was grateful. Waters had already been in, but the Chief Pathologist didn't quibble about the dead DC's superior officer paying his respects.

Here in the silent, lonely room Frost succumbed to the pressure of pent-up emotion. Only last year he'd lost his boss and mentor Bert Williams at the hands of bank robbers. To lose another fellow officer, especially one so young, was shocking, and dreadful for morale. There was no denying it, regardless of any police endeavours the world was growing into a more dangerous place. It was this rising tide in violent crime that Frost found difficult to swallow. Simms's plea for firearms only on Friday echoed in his head. 'Fat lot of good that would've done you, son,' Frost muttered to himself. It was clear that the young DC had not seen his assailant coming. A swift jab to the lower back, a slice up under the ribs through the liver, and then, as the man buckled, a slash to the throat.

Frost sighed. He took a little comfort from the knowledge that the boy had died believing himself the father of Sue Clarke's child. What, he wondered, did she tell him exactly? Frost naturally had kept to himself that he already knew about the pregnancy while talking things over with Simms, who had come to the decision that he would do the honourable thing and marry the girl. But what was Clarke playing at? It dawned on Frost that perhaps she was unsure who the father was. Why else tell them both? Again he grew vexed at the prospect of breaking the news to her of Simms's death. She would hold him responsible in some way, without a doubt.

'A shame,' said the tall pathologist who had joined him in the room.

'Risks of the job,' Frost said quietly.

'I suppose you know he always looked up to you?' Drysdale remarked.

'His mistake,' Frost replied in a sombre tone. 'Is there anything you can tell me that might be in any way useful?'

'I told DS—' But then Drysdale stopped himself mid-track, deciding to avoid a confrontation. Frost knew he was taking a gamble; the pathologist could pick up the phone to Mullett the instant he left the morgue and inform on him. 'Very well, I can approximate the time of death, to midnight last night.'

Frost grunted. The attacker had obviously been lying in wait. For the first time it struck him that it could have been him here, pale blue on the slab.

'The attacker was shorter, given the method of attack and the incision angle.'

'Hardly a difficult assessment to arrive at, given that the boy was six two. Anything else?'

'Blade was long and thin; length approximately eight inches.'

'Any idea what it could be? Kitchen knife?'

'Yes, as a matter of fact; and, no, it's not a kitchen knife.'

'Go on; don't keep me guessing.'

Frost could see he was undecided over whether to tell him, but knew he'd be unable to resist it; the pathologist loved to show off. 'I can't say for sure,' he began eventually, 'but the weapon was just that – a weapon – and not a domestic knife.'

'How so?' Frost asked, intrigued.

'Military blades, for instance, are designed for killing, and as such are bevelled to allow easier penetration into the body, which was bad news for our poor friend here.'

'I see, so we're looking for an army knife or dagger?'

'Perhaps . . . or maybe a bayonet, given the length and narrow width.' Drysdale rubbed his grey chin pensively.

'*Baïonnette*, French for a type of knife . . . know that?' Frost said, vainly trying to detach the pierced dead body in front of him from the chirpy young policeman he'd been drinking with last night.

'No, I didn't; nor did I imagine you knew any French,' Drysdale stuttered uncomfortably, perhaps having second thoughts about speaking his mind, but moving towards a brightly lit glass cabinet. 'Here is something I forgot to mention to Sergeant Waters . . . It has to do with the deceased's personal effects.'

'Yes?'

'These.' Drysdale held up two small pouches.

Stanley Mullett sheepishly reversed his wife's Midget out of the double garage and on to the drive. The suburban Sunday-morning ritual of washing one's motor vehicle, very popular in Wessex Crescent, was not an activity he would usually participate in, small-talk with the neighbours being something he preferred to avoid. Climbing out of the compact sports car he regarded it sternly.

Mullett pulled on a pair of pink Marigolds, nodded to the accountant across the road who was hosing down a Volvo, and plunged the sponge deep into the bucket of sudsy water. The MG Midget was a 1977 Jubilee special edition in British Racing Green; they'd bought it when he was made chief inspector five years ago. The car had many period features, such as a walnut dash, but it did retain the large, modern 'rubber bumper', as opposed to reverting to the chrome. One could plough into an elephant with one of these and pull away with not so much as a scuff, he reflected as he soaped the front headlights.

After a meticulous inspection of the front bumper – mercifully pristine – he made a quick show of splashing suds over the rest of the car. Relieved, he found himself breaking into a nostalgic whistle; an out-of-tune rendition of the Brotherhood of Man's '76 Eurovision winner, 'Save Your Kisses For Me'. He unwound the garden hose.

It wasn't until the soapy water had drained from the windscreen that he noticed a hairline crack running down the nearside of the glass. He looked nervously about the crescent. Volvo man and his pompous wife had just that minute shot off in their Sunday best, so for the moment all was deserted. He put his thumb to the end of the hose and directed the powerful jet across the large bonnet. The sharp autumn sun which until now had remained hidden chose this moment to reveal itself, and at the same time illuminate a slight but very definite impression on the bonnet of the Midget, as though a heavy weight had landed there.

Waters turned off at Brick Road and parked up outside the address he'd been given by the student barman from the Bricklayer's. The boy had been only too willing to help, and had arranged for his flatmate Laura to be home on her own. The girl would telephone the landlord and ask him as a matter of urgency to fix a leaky feed on the washing machine (Waters had got the idea from Frost's plumbing issues). The landlord was one Terry Windley, twenty-six years old and a supply teacher at Denton Comp. Windley had inherited the flat from his mother, who had died the previous year, and rather than sell it he'd opted to rent it out to students. Waters hadn't realized this part of the long street had private properties, unlike the partially derelict end by the vandalized phone box where he'd spent a couple of nights. Suddenly and with a groan he clocked a bright red call box outside a row of shops that were just beyond the flats; this one had all its glass and was yet to be adorned with graffiti.

To Waters' mind, any landlord prepared to come out on a Sunday morning at the drop of a hat was immediately suspect – most tenants would be waiting several days before a landlord even acknowledged the need to take action. He parked the Vauxhall, lit a cigarette and rolled the window down, letting in the damp autumn air. He felt slightly uneasy. A black guy sitting on his own in a low-rent residential area was bound to draw attention. During the early mornings when he'd been watching the phone box it wasn't so bad, but here he felt exposed. A curtain twitched in a ground-floor window, in the block where the students lived.

A skinhead came bowling along the pavement with a newspaper under his arm, walking a surly-looking terrier. As he came nearer he locked his eyes on the Vauxhall – or, to be more accurate, the black man inside. Waters could sense confrontation brewing. A blue Leyland Princess pulled up opposite, outside the flats. *Damn.* The landlord's vehicle. Waters didn't want a scene that would blow the element of surprise. He leaned over to the passenger seat and wound down the window, just as the skinhead – every inch the archetypal aggressive white male, with bulky torso and pale, skinny tattooed arms, bare even at this time of year – reached the car. He took the bait and leaned in to utter some curse or other, but instead quickly pulled away and, tugging aggressively on the dog's lead, continued up the street. Waters' police badge glinted from the passenger seat. He sighed with relief.

On the other side of the road a slight, wispy-looking man wearing a red body warmer over a tracksuit had got out of the Princess and was making his way towards the flats. He shot a look at the first-floor window, expectantly. The curtains were suddenly pulled open in a hurry – the signal.

Waters gave it a couple of minutes before slipping out of the car and crossing the road, so as not to appear to be on the man's tail. He rapped lightly on the door of the flat. A girl of eighteen or nineteen with long orange hair silently let him in. He nodded and she smiled coyly – pretty, if it wasn't for a nose piercing that looked infected.

In the kitchen the landlord was already crouched under the sink, body warmer riding up to reveal a pasty white back.

Waters looked to the girl and said loudly, 'Thank you for your time, Laura. I'd just like to ask you a few questions about last week – your whereabouts on Monday night, for instance?'

The landlord flinched, banging his head on the base of the sink as he tried to get up hurriedly. Waters reckoned he was little more than five foot four even at full height, and the slight frame and longish fair hair lent him a boyish appearance.

'Gave me a bit of a fright there!' He looked nervously from one to the other and then thumbed towards the sink. 'Nothing wrong there, Laura . . .'

'And who might you be?' Waters stared at him hard; he was perspiring, but that might be from the effort of being doubled up under the sink. He didn't appear to be wearing a watch.

'Terry Windley – I'm the landlord.'

'Is that so? And might I ask where *you* were on

Monday just gone, sir?' he asked politely; Windley's response was all he needed – one way or the other.

'Me? I thought you were asking *her*?' Windley was backed up against the draining board, now looking daggers at the girl.

Waters had taken an instant dislike to him. 'Yeah, and now I'm asking you. Well?'

'I'm a teacher,' he said defensively.

'I don't care whether you're an astronaut – a girl was—'

Waters caught the blow on his lower jaw – he could taste the metal on his teeth. He stumbled against a flimsy kitchen chair, which did nothing to break his fall. How did he not see that coming? His athletic build allowed him to spring up swiftly, only to take the solid weight of the wrench full in the face. The bridge of his nose exploded and blood sprayed forth, causing the hitherto silent Laura to emit a piercing scream. Although it was messy the pain was bearable, and Waters stood facing his assailant, who seemed unsure what to do next. Not wishing to give him another opportunity to swing the wrench, Waters dealt him a right hook, sending him crashing into the draining board, glasses and crockery tumbling off the drying rack and flying in all directions.

'There wasn't any need for that,' Waters said to the crumpled heap. 'You got a phone?' he asked the girl who nodded, dumbstruck, pointing to the doorway to the hall.

The supine Windley, blinking rapidly several times,

suddenly started screaming at the top of his voice, 'Help! Help! Police!'

Waters moved forward, about to kick the whining man in the crotch, but stopped himself, sensing vaguely that something had gone dreadfully wrong.

'What do you mean, Waters attacked him?' Frost's mind was on the road ahead, trying not to miss the lay-by, and he couldn't quite grasp what Desk Sergeant Bill Wells was telling him over the radio.

'It's what he's claiming – says there are witnesses.'

'Eh? He was following up a lead on Brick Road – he wasn't out picking fights.' He frowned, darting a glance to the left, thinking he'd missed it – he had. 'Bill, this'll have to wait. But on another matter, get on to Forensics for me: we're missing the bullets from the Oildrum Lane payroll robbery; Simms had the cases, but not the lead itself. The lead bullets – you got that?' But Frost didn't catch the response; chucking the handset aside, he laid both hands back on the steering wheel and screeched suddenly to a halt, prompting a barrage of horns.

'Sunday drivers,' Frost muttered under his breath, pulling a sloppy five-point turn which cut off the on-coming traffic. When he finally reached his destination he parked up facing a dormant articulated lorry. The lay-by, popular with truckers, was off the Lexton Road, the busy main artery out to the north of Denton. On flinging the Cortina door shut, it struck him that it looked completely different. He took a step back and worked out what it was: the vehicle had been cleaned.

Apart from the odd dint the trusty Ford looked as good as new, and he felt he was seeing it properly for the first time in the three years he'd had it; and, ironically, tomorrow was the day he was due to hand it in. Suddenly a cold shudder rippled over him as he realized the only reason the car had been washed was to remove the blood of his dead colleague.

He turned from the car and surveyed the bleak roadside landscape before him. This section of the Lexton Road was on the fringes of Denton; a carpet showroom and a large Rumbelows superstore occupied the east side, and a transport café stood five hundred yards up on the west side – the last stop before the motorway, hence its popularity with truckers. Plus the occasional area car; two had been stationed here following the armed robbery on Friday afternoon.

Dead Lane – the road to the Coconut Grove – was in front of him to the north; behind the café stretched acres of arable farmland, belonging to the Sandersons. Frost crossed the road, hopeful that Hanlon should be down there already, as it was already gone midday. The public-footpath sign was set a way back from the road, behind a worn kissing gate. With some effort Frost pushed it open and followed a path that ran alongside a ploughed field, bordered by a drainage ditch and hedge.

The earth was damp underfoot; Frost was optimistic that there might be footprints once the terrain grew less uneven. Baskin was right, it would have been impossible in heels.

Eventually, perspiring and short of breath, Frost

arrived at woodland, just as Baskin had described. The path, though smattered with fallen leaves, was not entirely obscured. There had been rain in the last couple of days but no heavy downpour for a while and Frost felt sure there was still enough of a canopy to protect any footprints – the clods in uniform had done a half-hearted search of the club's surrounds but he doubted they'd troubled themselves to go this far back. He trudged slowly, more due to weariness than diligent inspection, but it allowed for a meticulous combing of the path.

After five minutes his search was rewarded with more than he'd bargained for. Lying in some brambles was a woman's red stiletto. Frost sheathed his right hand in a plastic bag and gently retrieved the shoe.

'Dainty,' he muttered to himself before ambling further along the path. The rear of the club was edging into view between the thinning trees, which ended, along with the track, fifty feet from the back entrance. The rest of the way was smooth, damp earth. Frost scanned the ground until he found what he was looking for.

'Oi! Jack!' a voice beckoned.

'Ahh, Arthur, there you are,' Frost called, kneeling down and scanning the ground.

'Where've you been?' the tubby detective grumbled. 'It's half twelve. You said midday!'

Frost checked his wristwatch – it had taken him twenty-five minutes. Admittedly he wasn't the quickest mover in the world – far from it – but it would probably still have taken a younger, fitter person a good fifteen to twenty minutes. And allowing a minute for her to change her clothes . . . he took out his notebook.

'Where've you been?' Hanlon was looming over him.

'Careful where you tread!' Frost lightly brushed aside fallen leaves to reveal what he'd hoped for.

'Footprints?'

'Size three, to be exact.'

'Blimey, Jack, you can be that accurate?' Hanlon puffed.

'Trust me, Arthur. We're looking for a proper Cinderella.' Frost smiled, producing the red stiletto.

Sunday (4)

Frost jogged up the steps to Eagle Lane and pushed through the swing doors. He was aware the station would be on edge; the police airwaves were awash with the news of DC Simms's murder. He was back later than expected. Control had put through a call from Harding at Forensics – there was an evidence discrepancy at the Oildrum Lane crime scene. 'One thing at a time,' he muttered to himself.

Mullett had abandoned his usual fiscal prudence and pulled out all the stops; uniform were in on a double shift and double pay, canvassing the town. Initially Frost's own neighbourhood had come in for heavy scrutiny, but by this afternoon every pub and club in Denton had been shaken down. All the local grasses had been pulled in. But nobody knew a thing about the stabbing of Detective Constable Derek Simms.

Frost walked briskly through the foyer, not wishing

to be buttonholed. He caught sight of Desk Sergeant Bill Wells arguing with a civilian, a gobby solicitor Frost knew to be trouble. 'Afternoon, Bill,' Frost said, gliding by and making straight for the incident room.

'Wait . . . Jack . . .' Wells beckoned to him.

'Not now,' he called back. Frost had decided to address the men as soon as possible. Given that the incident had occurred on his street, he felt he should be seen to take the initiative, regardless of Mullett assigning the case to Waters. (Mullett would undoubtedly lay it on thick on Monday morning, and whilst the super had sucked in extra resources Frost didn't expect to see him again today. By now he'd be playing golf, or maybe polishing the Rover.)

He pushed open the incident-room door, killing the hubbub instantly. This might not be a breeze, he thought. Snatching a pretty WPC's coffee he made for the far end of the room towards the progress boards where the uniform duty sergeant had been coordinating the door-to-door.

'Ladies and gents, may I have your attention,' he demanded needlessly as the sergeant stepped aside. 'We could be forgiven for declaring ourselves in crisis. So I feel perhaps an impromptu assessment is warranted.'

He surveyed the team in front of him; a lot of them were unfamiliar. Hanlon and a couple of youngsters from uniform were all he recognized. He stubbed out his cigarette and paused a second, taking in the board behind him. Through a complex network of lines, cases and timelines akin to a plate of spaghetti, he couldn't help but notice his own address, a recent addition in bold marker pen.

Simms's murder was at the forefront of everybody's mind, but to keep things on an even keel and avoid emotion he decided to open in an upbeat way: 'Today we have made breakthroughs on several cases. Firstly, the Baskin case – important evidence has been found. And second, the Marie Roberts rape has turned a corn—' But he could see Hanlon was shaking his head slowly . . . where was Waters?

'So . . . the Coconut Grove, at least,' he continued. 'We have one fingerprint on a red stiletto found this morning in the woods between the Grove and the fields – which means we have the escape route for the glamorous would-be assassin and the approximate time she would have popped up on the main road.' Nods of affirmation from around the room. 'There will be an appeal for witnesses in tomorrow's *Denton Echo*. The print is downstairs, with Records looking for a match – knowing the approximate age and sex, we should have something shortly.

'Secondly, we have these.' He held up two pouches containing 9mm shells. 'Two found at Baskin's, and the others at Oildrum Lane, the site of the payroll robbery. Now, we can't be sure, but it's likely it's the same gun—'

'Why can't we be sure?' a uniform asked.

'Because we need all the bullets. We have the ones from the Grove, but not from Oildrum Lane. They appear to have gone missing.' The shells had been found with Simms's personal effects, but not the bullets. He paused to light a Rothmans. Harding's call came to mind. The hospital had, it seemed, mislaid the bullets pulled from Benson, the payroll minder. Apparently the police hadn't asked for them, and as the man wasn't in a critical condition it was possible they'd been thrown away. But more problematic was the shot fired in the car window on Oildrum Lane: a new recruit was on the scene from Forensics and he'd failed to inspect the car at the crime scene. When the car was later inspected at the pound, the bullet had gone from the door. There was much finger-pointing at this cock-up, but Frost in his heart suspected where the blame lay, although he dare not say. And where the shot was now was a mystery. He exhaled and continued, 'The Forensics bod reckons they were certainly fired from a similar gun, but to be sure he'd need the physical lead itself to match up the barrel-striation marks.'

'The country is awash with nine-millimetre automatics from the Continent and the States,' a Forensics officer cut in. 'Walthers, Berettas, Lugers.'

'Quite. But this is Denton, not New York. The proximity of the crimes makes it certainly possible, plus both were perpetrated by a female.' He pointed to the artist's impressions on the boards. 'Perhaps one and the same.'

'But they look totally different!' a WPC remarked.

'Our artist can't draw for toffee,' Frost snapped. 'Be thankful he's not colourblind too.'

'The descriptions are different, granted,' said the duty sergeant who was perched on the desk to Frost's right, 'but one consistency is that witnesses to both crimes reported the assailant to be heavily tarted up.'

Frost picked up the thread: 'So, under all the war-paint, it could be the same woman in disguise – not that you'd make that connection from these Rolf Harris doodles.' He gestured disparagingly at the artist's impressions. 'However, what do we make of the reported age difference? One's described as a girl in her mid-twenties – the one at Baskin's – the other at Gregory's payroll is said to be thirty or forty . . .'

'Jack, are you saying it's the same woman or not?' Hanlon asked, confused.

'Anything's a possibility! We should keep an open mind. No money was taken from the Baskin hit, so it seems odd that the very next day our would-be assassin would hold up a payroll. But remember, both these crimes happened very quickly, and in such circumstances that even a scant disguise could trick a victim. According to the payroll clerk's statement, though unsure of the attacker's age judging by her appearance, he did notice her youthful agility.' He paused to light a cigarette. 'Which brings me on to the fine young man who took that statement.

'As you will all know, Detective Constable Derek Simms was brutally murdered, practically on my own doorstep, shortly after midnight this morning.' As Frost recounted the sequence of events for the second time that day, it finally sunk in that the boy was dead, and he was truly sorry.

'OK, so, going forward, I will continue with the

Baskin case and take over the payroll robbery. DS Waters will continue on the two rapes with DC Clarke, when she returns. Officially DS Waters will take on DC Simms's murder, a point which no doubt Hornrim Harry will ram home tomorrow – but, unofficially, all of us are working on this one. Anything else?'

'Simms was working on the dead paperboy,' someone in uniform said.

'Noted.' Realistically there was no possible way Frost could take on anything more, and he certainly didn't want that case to get sidelined, but he had to prioritize – had to get a result. 'I'll look into it. Anything else?'

'Counterfeit money?' someone else offered.

'Balls to that,' Frost snapped dismissively.

'We're with you all the way, Sarge,' an unshaven PC, tie askew, said emotively. 'We'll nail whoever killed Derek Simms.' Miller, of course, Simms's mate from uniform, who shared a flat with him in police housing.

'Cheers, son, appreciate your support.' Frost noticed the mood had lifted. 'OK' – he clapped his hands – 'onwards!'

As the scraping of chairs signalled the end of the ad hoc briefing Frost leaned back against the wall, his arm nudging the board, and lit another cigarette. The sense that he had them on side made him feel pleased.

DS Waters had come late to the meeting, unseen by Frost, and was also standing with his back against the wall looking at the bustling room. He sidled up.

'Ah, John, where the hell have you been? Old Bill was babbling on about something about a punch-up?'

'Well . . . it's not how it seems.'

By now Frost had turned and clocked his colleague's bashed-in nose. 'Bloody hell, not again. Something about you, isn't there?'

Sunday (5)

After her weekend away, Detective Constable Sue Clarke felt good. She arched her back and stretched before getting out of the car. It had been dark for several hours and her eyes felt the strain of driving the long distance. She reached back inside the car and pulled out the duffel bag containing her overnight stuff. Shutting the car door with a contented sigh, she reflected on her time away as she climbed the stairs to her flat.

Her parents had received the news of her pregnancy better than expected. Clarke had been vague about why she was opting for motherhood so early in her career. She didn't say it was planned, and she didn't say it was an accident – but she conveyed such a sense of excitement that the rationale behind it was a matter of little interest. And yes, she really was excited. At first the heightened emotion had been produced for her mother's benefit, but she'd quickly found the reflected enthusiasm infectious, and before she knew it, she was gaily debating names over tea and scones.

On the question of the father, she answered truthfully that he was a policeman, and confessed that she was hoping to settle down with one Derek Simms. Travelling alone yesterday had given her time to filter her thoughts, and to get a perspective on life outside the police force, something she'd been immersed in since the age of sixteen. The warm welcome at her parents' reinforced this; there was a richness to family life that made her acknowledge for the first time her desire for it on top of her career.

Clarke had been born in Denton, but throughout her teens her mother and father had shuttled to and from Colchester to attend to her ailing grandmother, and eventually formed an attachment to the place. Following her father's retirement from his law firm, with Clarke at the police college in Hendon, they'd decided to up and move. It was irritating to have to go so far to visit them, and would probably be all the more so with a baby in tow, but she couldn't criticize them for doing what they wanted. She recognized that streak of determination in herself.

Wearily she forced the stiff Yale lock and shoved open the door. The light on the answering machine blinked manically at her from the small phone table in the hall. 'Yes, I will,' she whispered affectionately to the small bright red light, expecting it to be her lover; for she had decided she would marry Derek Simms. The euphoria had not diminished since Saturday morning, and though tired after a four-hour drive back from Essex, she dearly wanted to see Derek.

You have twenty-one new messages. Blimey, you are keen, she thought, pressing Play and moving across the flat to run a bath.

'Louise, darlin', slow down.'

She paced Palmer's office angrily, pausing to glare through the smoked glass at the youths around the snooker tables below as if they were in some way responsible for her predicament. She was furious he had cancelled her hit on Baskin that morning – killing Frost was one thing, but that was personal, and it didn't pay for a flight to Spain.

'Why didn't you say anything last night?' Palmer continued.

'I tried to talk to you and you said not to discuss business!' she snapped back.

'But you could have waited until Charles and Brazier left – they weren't here late. Why were you in such a hurry anyway?'

'Doesn't matter. I wanted to think things through.' Which was actually true to a degree. She couldn't understand it – why would Pumpy give the same tip about the robbery to someone else? Was he trying to stitch her up? She just couldn't work out his game. 'I did *not* rob the Gregory payroll; understand?' she spat out venomously.

'Well, who the bleeding hell did?'

She caught a glint in the shadows, behind Palmer:

Nicholson's spectacles. She hadn't even noticed that Palmer's number-two was in the room. Nicholson hated her, of that she was sure; although she'd never been quite sure why; perhaps he was jealous of Palmer's affection for her. Maybe they were lovers.

'I don't know – somebody beat me to it,' she explained. 'After they left the bank I followed them on a bike. I overtook them and hid the bike, but then came back to see another woman waving a shooter around: the minder was already on the ground, and the gun was in the kid's face.'

'Some bird?' Marty replied, surprised.

'Yes, "some bird".' Louise perched on the expansive desk, running a ruby-painted fingernail along the folds of his hefty jowls. Surely she could squeeze him for a couple of quid too? 'I just wondered whether you tipped off every girl who walks through here, that's all.'

He shifted in the chair. 'I don't know any birds with the balls you've got to pull off a job like that in broad daylight – that's a man's game.'

'Well,' she sighed, 'it wasn't a man – I saw it with my own eyes: a woman dressed like an old dear.'

'An old biddy?'

'That's what I thought, until I saw how fast she legged it across the road – a woman, all right, but not old. Uncanny disguise, though; she even had a headscarf on like me. I felt a right idiot.'

Palmer snorted. 'To think blokes are so unimaginative, just shoving on a lady's stocking when they're pulling a job. Girls have so much more panache – why not make an effort with a headscarf and a pair of shades.'

'I'm serious, Marty.'

'So am I – can't have jobs being pulled off round here that I don't know about.' A vertical eyelet of podgy white flesh winked at her through the straining black shirt as he rocked back in the chair. 'Still, if someone's dumb enough to walk through the centre of town carrying a big bag of money, then I guess it's to be expected. Forget about it, darlin'.'

'What about Baskin?' she said, anxious to get back on to the subject of her earnings.

'Forget about him too – for now. There's too much heat now that copper got done. Baskin is small beer, but keep your head down, Frost will be sniffing around – they'll be shaking every tree in the orchard for this one.'

'F-Frost?' Louise Daley couldn't help but stutter over his name. How could it be! He went down, she made sure of that. 'Frost?' she repeated in surprise – or was it another emotion, one she'd never experienced. *Fear.*

'Why, you look surprised?' The shadow, Nicholson, stepped forward.

'Nah, he's got it in for me – that's all,' she said.

'Where did you go, eh? After leaving Mr Palmer's last night?' he said quietly. 'I think she's been a very naughty girl, Mr Palmer. I reckon it's her that did that rozzer last night, thinking it was Frost.'

Why would he say that? How could he know? Louise moved away from the desk, feeling insecure. Palmer scrutinized her. She couldn't hide from his cunning, she knew.

'Marty, look, I just need some cash to get out of Denton, lie low . . . Don't listen to him, he hates me, you know that. Always has.'

'Pumps, you got to distance yourself – she'll bring the filth down on us and we can't afford that. She's already screwed up with Baskin.'

She pleaded with Palmer, but uncertainty clouded his face; fond of her as he was, he wouldn't allow her to put his business at risk, or himself in jeopardy. He said nothing. He didn't even enquire whether she really had killed the policeman; Louise read it as he'd rather not know. Palmer was doing as his henchman advised – he was distancing himself from her.

'You can have what I got on me,' he said finally, reaching inside his jacket for his wallet, 'then you'd best clear out for a while.'

A man of Palmer's stature had little need of cash – he had only sixty pounds in his pocket. Three twenties. Nicholson offered her nothing aside from a smile that resembled a sneer.

She pocketed the notes, and was about to embrace Palmer, but his stony expression stopped her in her tracks.

'Look after me mum, Marty?' she said hopefully as she took her leave. 'Please?' But the big man's attention was already elsewhere, beyond the mirrored glass of the office window.

Sunday (6) ──────────────────────────

Frost leaned on the cell door, squinting through the peephole.

'He doesn't look like much,' he remarked, turning to peruse Waters' injured face. 'What were you doing, dozing? Or chatting up the bird?'

'I didn't expect the little git to spring me with a monster wrench.' Waters massaged the plaster that spanned the bridge of his nose.

'Suits you.'

'They don't come in my colour – apparently we never bleed.'

Frost grunted, and turned again to view the wispy specimen sitting on the cell bunk clutching his knees. 'How did a little fella like that get such a clean swing at a big bloke like you?'

'Told you – I was caught by surprise.'

'Really? Not as surprised as his solicitor is claiming.'

'That's bullshit, man. He is one lying bastard.'

'I believe you, and the pretty girl says so too. Anyway,' Frost said, reaching into his trouser pocket, 'he'll be the surprised one in a minute when I slice off his goolies with this.'

Frost pulled out his Swiss army knife and waggled it behind his ear. He'd found it invaluable since his wife's death for everything from bean tins to bottle tops. To his mind the fact that Windley was a teacher at Denton Comp was more than coincidence; he was sure they had their man. Suddenly he felt the knife whipped from his grip.

'Yes, that would be just the sort of thing to do now, wouldn't it, Frost?' Superintendent Mullett stood behind him, tapping the Swiss army knife on his thumbnail. 'Threatening to castrate a schoolteacher?'

'Hello, sir, didn't hear you creep up.' Frost sighed. 'Rapists, though, best thing for them – one way to guarantee they'll never do it again.'

But Mullett ignored him. 'And you, Sergeant Waters,' he continued, 'I'm glad to hear you feel able to make light of matters.'

'Whoa there, sir,' Frost countered, 'that's just not fair—'

'Then what is fair, Jack?' Mullett was spoiling for a fight. Frost could see the colour beginning to rise around the superintendent's shirt collar. Usually Frost would goad him, but given the current circumstances he reined himself in. Mullett resumed: 'From an outside perspective your prisoner's actions seem perfectly reasonable – a landlord is dutifully fixing a leak when, startled by a large coloured man on his premises, he fears for his life and takes a swing.'

'What's his colour got to do with it?' Frost argued.

Mullett paused and looked at his shoes, then continued: 'Windley claims it was the shock of seeing a black man that terrified him into violence. He'd only ever seen people like Sergeant Waters rioting on the television.'

'And you believe that?' Frost said incredulously. 'Look at his face!'

'It doesn't matter what I believe, Frost.'

'The girl saw it all,' muttered Waters without much conviction.

'I don't give a tinker's cuss what the girl says' – Mullett's voice was reduced to an angry hiss, to avoid being overheard by the cell's occupant – 'the fact remains that DS Waters here did not have ID when he entered the flat – and here the girl agrees.' Mullett switched his attention to Waters. 'That's correct, is it not?'

'I left my badge in the car, but she knew I was coming,' Waters explained. 'She let me in.'

'That is not the point.'

'But—'

'But nothing. Sergeant Waters, I thought you understood by now that the suburbs of Denton are not the cosmopolitan melting pot you're accustomed to. That being the case, someone in your shoes, presuming they had a lick of common sense, would follow procedure to the letter, and hence avoid any possible misunderstanding.'

'Come off it!' Frost snapped. 'Any normal person doesn't go clouting people in the face with a wrench!'

'How could you possibly know what "any normal person" might do?' Mullett said in honest amazement.

'But the guy's bound to say stuff like that if he's guilty. C'mon, I got the result,' Waters insisted. 'If I'd played it by the book and knocked on his front door he'd have been composed and in control. What pushed him over the edge was twigging we'd already spoken to the girl: he realized we knew he was a knicker-sniffer—'

'You have *not* got a result,' Mullett countered. 'You may ask him where he was at the time of the rape attacks, but after that he's free to go. No reference can be made to his encounter with you. We're lucky he's not pressing charges for assault – and if he really is the man we're after, you'd better walk on eggshells – we don't want him going free on a technicality thanks to our bungling, hmm?'

Frost said nothing, shooting a glance at Waters who had his eyes on the floor, knowing the super to be right.

'I must say, I'm disappointed in you, Sergeant Waters. I fear you've been spending too much time in Frost's orbit.' And with that he turned on his heels and clipped off.

Before reaching the stairs, he looked back. 'In fact, I'm even surprised at you today, Frost.' His voice echoed down the gloomy basement corridor. 'It's regrettable that even after the death of one of your colleagues you can't manage some modicum of decorum.'

Frost rubbed his bristly jaw thoughtfully. 'OK, I'll deal with this, John,' he muttered. 'You go off and orbit elsewhere.'

Waters nodded and followed Mullett out, while Frost signalled to the PC at the end of the corridor to open the cell door. He had his angle pitched. If this man was the rapist who attacked Joanne Daniels they would need hard evidence; that Waters had spooked the pervert was not enough, especially in the muddle they found themselves in now. But if he could put the frighteners on him in connection with Marie Roberts, then he might just trip himself up.

'Ah, good evening, Mr Windley.' Frost shook the man's hand but ignored the solicitor sitting in the corner. 'I'm Detective Sergeant Frost. I'm terribly sorry about this morning's debacle—'

'So you should be – disgraceful behaviour, attacking a man in his own home! Police brutality on a most unprecedented scale!' Even Windley was taken aback by this outburst from his solicitor.

'Although Mr Windley is not actually living there, is he, Mr . . . ?' He didn't wait for a reply. 'And I think you'll find your claims are without foundation. Police brutality? Have you seen my colleague's face? Having said that, we have no cause to hold you, Mr Windley, as Sergeant Waters himself has waived charges. You are free to go.'

They clearly hadn't expected to get away that easily, in spite of the defiant claims of police wrongdoing. Frost allowed a moment or two for the facts to sink in, while watching each closely for a reaction. Windley, who had shown no sign of indignation, exuded relief.

The solicitor, on the other hand, felt the need to press the point, to justify his trip out on a Sunday: 'I should think so too. If Mr Waters is injured, then serve him right. The police are issued with ID for a purpose—'

Windley leapt off the bed and clasped his solicitor's forearm in an effort to silence him without making a show of it.

'I think, son, you ought to button it, before I change my mind,' Frost said, sternly.

'All behind us. We'll be on our way.' It was the first time the suspect had spoken. Windley was slight and unassuming, with undefined features and longish blond hair, striking Frost as vaguely effeminate.

'Very well,' Frost affirmed. 'Aren't you a teacher at Denton Comp?'

'I am.'

'Do you know Marie Roberts?'

'Yes, I do.'

'This is just routine, regarding another enquiry. It would save us both some bother if you answered a couple of questions.'

Windley looked at his solicitor.

'It'll save me having to call on you during the school day,' Frost persisted. The solicitor shrugged agreement. All Frost wanted to know was whether Windley had been on the premises at the time of the attack. He got his answer immediately. 'Yes.'

*

The Eagle Lane car park was verging on full. This added further to DC Sue Clarke's consternation; on arriving home less than an hour ago, Clarke had picked up an assortment of messages, all claiming to be urgent, but none of them giving any details of why the matter was so pressing. Bill Wells, Mullett's secretary, Frost at least a dozen times, and bizarrely, PC Miller, Derek's flatmate, but oddly none from Derek . . . though, of course, he knew she was away for the weekend. She tried returning the calls but couldn't get through to anyone, and so had decided to come to the station.

She didn't recognize the two uniform who glanced at her on the steps as she entered the building. In the lobby, Superintendent Mullett was in earnest discussion with Desk Sergeant Bill Wells. Wells stopped mid-sentence on spotting her. Mullett, too, turned her way.

'Evening all,' she said jovially.

'Detective Clarke,' Mullett said formally. 'There you are. We were beginning to get concerned.'

'Concerned? Why?' She looked quizzically at Wells, who managed a smile though looked uncomfortable. 'I've been away . . . Why, what's up?'

'Would you be so good as to notify your superior of your whereabouts, even at weekends, so that when something like this happens you can be accounted for,' Mullett lectured.

'Something like what?' She looked plaintively at Wells. What was Mullett on about, and why was he even here?

'It's Derek Simms, Sue,' Wells said softly, unable to meet her eye.

'Oh my God. What?' Clarke felt the ground go, and her stomach churn. 'No . . .' she uttered quietly. 'What . . . what's happened?'

She heard the words spoken by Bill Wells without understanding them. The only ones that stuck out were 'Jack' and 'Jack's house'.

'Yes, tragic,' Mullett muttered, stroking his moustache.

She turned and stared at him blankly as if only vaguely aware of his presence, and whatever he began to say next about a blight on the station she ignored and charged down the corridor towards Frost's office. Rounding the corner she collided with two men coming up from the cells. One was a short skinny man in a tracksuit, the other was a slippery-looking type in an ill-fitting suit – a solicitor, no doubt. She made her apologies. The man in the tracksuit with longish blond hair reminded her of someone, but her thoughts were interrupted by hearing a familiar cracked laugh in the incident room opposite.

Clarke pushed open the door. Inside were six or seven uniform, and at the back sat Frost, sharing a joke with Waters. Frost's face fell on seeing her enter the office.

'What's happened to Derek?' she asked flatly. 'Jack? Tell me, Jack?'

'Sue . . .' Frost half smiled.

Clarke zoned in on him; the room fell deathly quiet. Instead of explaining anything he just smiled at her, that cheeky little smile of his that normally softened her vehemence – but not this time. She walked straight up to him, past several bemused uniform, and slapped him squarely across the face. The sound – like a wet fish hitting a marble counter – resonated loudly in the silenced room. His cheek coloured instantly. For all she knew, he had absolutely nothing to do with Simms getting stabbed, but nevertheless she felt instantly better, while at the same time flooded with emotion that until now had been choked up. She hadn't even cried yet. She swiftly exited the room and ran out of the building.

Waters placed the coffee mug tentatively on Frost's desk.

'Bit harsh,' Frost said, rubbing his cheek.

'Sign of affection,' Waters said dismissively, picking up the uniform call log.

'You think so? Really?'

'No, not really.' He sighed. They'd been trying to laugh off Windley's self-defence line. But it wasn't really funny, and Clarke's appearance had brought them back to earth with a bump. The dismay on the girl's face had made something they'd tried to keep impersonal crushingly real. Waters turned his attention to perusing the results of the enquiries so far. The house-to-house calls on Vincent Close and the streets surrounding it had yielded nothing, despite their promptness. The investigation's main hope – often the lucky breakthrough in such cases – was finding the murder weapon which the killer might have tossed away in panic, so every garden in the close had been combed. Nothing.

Simms had been murdered in the small hours of Sunday morning. Did they really expect to trace the killer? Countless murders went unsolved in every part of the country, and Denton was no exception. In fact, their clean-up rate over the last six months was poor, and Waters knew that Frost felt this keenly. However, at that precise moment it was hard to believe it, as he sat there noisily slurping his coffee.

'Hey, what are you doing, man?' Waters said, annoyed. 'Get after that girl.'

'You think so?'

Frost made to go and clapped him on the shoulder.

Waters answered the trilling phone. It was Superintendent Mullett. Watching Frost march out stoically, cigarette clamped between his teeth and slamming the door behind him, Waters winced as Mullett lectured him again on Windley.

Sunday (7) ─────────────────────────

'But I don't get it, Jack. Why would Derek turn to you?'

Frost drained his pint. 'Another?' She nodded, and though coughing aggressively, helped herself to another of his cigarettes. Being a Sunday, the Eagle was practically deserted, but they'd elected to stay at the bar and not take a table. 'Oi,' he remonstrated. 'You've had half a packet in half an hour.'

'I'm upset, aren't I?' Clarke replied defensively. 'Answer my question – why would he spend the whole evening with you, even if his car had broken down round the corner?'

'A bit of fatherly advice – you know.' Frost nodded at her midriff.

'Oh, so he told you.' She bowed her head, and fiddled nervously with her cigarette in the ashtray. This fidgeting made Frost nervy himself. 'But you've not got children – why on earth would he ask you?' she protested, perplexed. 'He doesn't even ask you about police work; something you're supposed to know about.'

'I'm older, and he reported to me . . . He wanted to know how his career might be affected. To be honest, we only touched on that. In the main, we discussed the Roberts case. He'd been to see the woman, as you asked him to.' He was desperate to change the subject, knowing he was tired and bound to say the wrong thing. He reckoned that in the last four days he'd had little more than a few consecutive hours of sleep. That was pushing it, even by his standards, making his thought processes murky. Frost paid the barman for the drinks.

'Here you go.' He placed Clarke's glass neatly on the beer mat. 'Just what you need.'

'Ta. But Jack,' she persisted, 'why would he go to you? He didn't even like you . . .'

'Charming,' Frost snorted.

'You know what I mean. It's not like you and Bert Williams.'

Frost immediately reached for his cigarettes at the mention of DI Williams. 'It's almost a year to the day since Bert was murdered. Wait . . .' Frost pinched his eyes shut, his thumb and forefinger meeting at the bridge of his nose. Cigarette smoke snaked up his forehead, as he recalled his dream when asleep in the Simpsons' garden.

'What, Jack?'

'You'll think I'm mad.'

'I *know* you're half crazy anyway.' Her glossy eyes met his intently.

'I think I foresaw Simms dying. Dead, I mean . . .'

'What? Don't be ridiculous . . .'

'Well, I don't mean *foresaw* exactly, but I did have this strange dream – nightmare, really – where I was standing at the foot of Mary's grave—' He suddenly stopped himself. How ridiculous did he sound?

'Go on,' Clarke prompted.

'Nah, it was nothing – just the wife trying to torment me from beyond the grave.' He took a swig of his pint. 'Little firebrand – trust her to be coming up from the earth, not descending on a cloud with a pair of angels . . .'

Clarke looked at him as if he had taken leave of his senses. He reached across and patted her thigh affectionately. She recoiled.

'Anyway, Simms did mention the rape case you'd been working on, and that you thought the girl was fishy. Well, he paid her a visit and he reckoned your instincts were right.' Frost thought it indelicate to say why, the truth being her attempt to chat him up.

'Why, did she admit that she had a boyfriend?'

'Oh, not in so many words, but he suspected she rather liked men. His theory was that she was caught in flagrante on Friday morning by that pupil.'

'I knew it!' She downed her drink and then reflected for a moment. 'Poor, poor Derek. Did he say anything else?'

'Nope, that was it.'

'Nothing? Really?'

'Err, well, he did say he was really fond of you.' Simms hadn't actually said those words, but Frost thought it was safe to presume, and he knew it was what she wanted to hear.

'Why would anyone want to kill him?' she cried, suddenly overcome with emotion. Frost delicately patted her shoulder and smiled at the inquisitive barman polishing glasses at the far end of the counter.

'We'll get them, Sue,' he assured her. He realized that now was not the time to posit the theory that the intended victim was him himself. Clarke didn't yet know that Simms had been stabbed getting into his Cortina, and he wasn't about to tell her. He drained three quarters of his pint, deciding it was time to head off. 'Don't worry, we'll find them, mark my words,' he said, struggling to suppress a beery belch. 'Mark my words.'

Louise Daley lazily poured Cinzano into a Wombles mug and saluted a slim streak of notes on the yellow Formica kitchen table. A hundred quid was a hundred quid. And the Frenchman wasn't bad in bed either, if a little noisy.

There was no denying it, everything she'd done recently had been a disaster, but she was stoic, a trait her mother had taught her; if you accept your fate it will enable you to stay calm, avoid panic and make the best of the situation. Her plan had been to make a tidy sum from Palmer, exact her revenge and rub out Frost, and then do a bunk to Spain, letting it all blow over for a couple of months before returning to look after her sick mother. But it had all gone to pot. Both Frost and

Baskin were still alive, and someone else had made off with the payroll. Who the bloody hell had done it? As Palmer had said, there were few women ballsy enough to commit armed robbery in broad daylight.

It was her father who had put her in touch with Palmer. Andrew Daley had run with Palmer in the sixties, when both had been small-time crooks. They'd moved out of London in the seventies when drugs and racial tension began to change the dynamics; it wasn't a scene that two men in their late fifties wanted to be involved in, so they'd gone in search of a quieter life, winding up in Denton. When the Daleys' marriage had broken up, Andrew had relocated to Southall with a girlfriend, but he still kept in contact with Palmer.

Louise had no idea what Palmer's beef was with Baskin, and she wasn't interested – the less she knew the better. Despite his penchant for unnecessary violence Marty Palmer had been good to her and she couldn't blame him for making her skip town with only sixty quid of his. She had blown it, after all. She could've had five grand for the hit on Baskin which she'd failed to pull off; then he'd given her the payroll tip; if all had gone to plan, she would've netted over eight thousand pounds, enough to buy a place on the Costa del Sol and then split her time between Denton and Spain . . . but instead she had a measly £160.

She stretched and then reached to turn off the radio – on a Sunday night the listening choice was limited to obscure indie crap or classical music – and looked at the paltry collection of cassettes. She topped up her

Cinzano and slipped *Off the Wall* into the radio cassette player. She swayed playfully in the drab kitchen, day-dreaming. It wasn't all bad news: Spain might be off the cards for the time being, but as Charles dropped her off to get her car he'd mentioned he had a place in France. She'd be away at first light getting out of Denton, with thoughts of Paris . . .

'This is good!'

Frost hungrily poked a forkful of meat and potatoes into his mouth. 'Can't remember the last time I had a roast dinner.'

'Our pleasure.' Kim Myles smiled coyly.

'Now, tell me about this living together lark?' Frost grinned benevolently at them both.

Waters smiled across the tiny table at his girlfriend. It was an impromptu gesture, and Myles's idea at that – to invite Frost round for a late Sunday dinner. Waters should have thought of it himself, but luckily his mention of Frost's flooded kitchen had prompted Myles to come up with the suggestion. '. . . And John can't stay in that filthy bachelor den for ever with all the boys . . .' They had spoken about Simms's murder over drinks. Frost, Waters had noticed, did not wish to dwell on the young DC's death, and swiftly switched the topic to their flat-hunting. Guilt, he imagined, though Frost was reluctant to engage emotionally on any level. But talk of the police accommodation on Fenwick Street had unwittingly brought them back full circle to Simms.

Kim frowned slightly at Waters, sensing Frost was

uncomfortable. 'Anyway, how are you coping?' she asked warmly, topping up his wine glass.

'You know, muddling along. Glad it's all over, to be honest. We'd not had an easy run these last few years for one reason or another, but she was in a lot of pain, and in the end it was a relief.' Frost chewed thoughtfully.

'Great send-off, though,' Waters added, passing the dish of Brussels sprouts across the table. 'Who were all those people? For someone who never left the house apart from to go to bingo, Mary sure had a turnout.'

Frost shook his head. 'The old man,' he replied. 'The apron brigade.'

'The *what*?' Myles asked.

'Ah, the Masons,' Waters said. 'I should've twigged. That would explain Winslow, and Mullett too, I guess?'

'Winslow for sure,' Frost confirmed, spearing the remaining roast potato, 'but not being a chosen one myself, I couldn't say about Hornrim Harry. Certainly there are aspects that would suit him: the peculiar rituals would appeal to his sense of order – but he'd have to get past the Great Buffalo in charge of Denton Lodge.'

'The Buffalos are something else, Jack,' Waters corrected.

'Yeah, I know that – but this particular Mason could well be mistaken for a giant mammal of some description.'

'You know who runs the Lodge?' Myles asked in amazement. 'How?'

Frost paused in his chewing and took a swig of wine. 'I'm a detective, aren't I? I know these things.'

*

Very fond of you. The words had played round and round in Sue Clarke's head since she'd switched off the bedside light and tried to get to sleep. Now half an hour later her conscience pricked her: it was wrong to be more preoccupied with what Simms had felt for her than the fact he'd been murdered. *But* she couldn't shake the disappointment of hearing the phrase *very fond*. It meant nothing – people are fond of dogs, or aunties, or well-worn items of clothing, she thought. It was a million miles from marriage and planning a future together. Maybe Derek was too embarrassed to let on to Frost. No . . . he'd say nothing if that was the case. Maybe Frost was lying? But why would he do that?

The sharp trill of the phone pierced the black silence. Startled, she reached too quickly for the receiver, knocking over the glass of water that rested on the bedside table. She cursed as the glass rolled on to the carpet and under the bed.

'Hello?'

'Evening, Detective Clarke.' It was the soft tones of Night Sergeant Johnny Johnson. 'Denton General just called. Albert Benson has just had a heart attack.'

'Who?' Clarke didn't recognize the name. Was it the lad shot at the Coconut Grove?

'I believe him to be the gentleman who was shot on Friday – the payroll robbery. Delayed shock.'

Clarke rubbed her forehead frantically. 'I see – but why are you calling me? Doesn't matter . . . Where's Frost?'

'We can't locate Sergeant Frost.'

'I see. So am I needed at the station?'

'No, miss, just thought you should know.'

'Very good. Goodnight, Sergeant.'

'Goodnight, miss.'

Of course, as the man had died, it would up the ante from armed robbery possibly to murder, or at the very least manslaughter. Clarke gave an involuntary shudder in her cold room, the heating having long since turned itself off. The bodies were piling up. Granted, she was tired and emotional, but she couldn't help wondering whether she was cut out for police work, or perhaps better suited to something more sedate. Her mother was a librarian, and seemed happy on it, indeed looked younger than Frost, despite being ten years his senior. Did she really want to end up like Frost? Maybe pregnancy was affecting her state of mind; she'd not felt like this before. All the same, her mother wouldn't be troubled in the middle of the night by overdue library books, of that much she was certain.

Monday (1)

Louise Daley pulled into the National service station on the northbound carriageway of the Lexton Road.

She was anxious to be on her way. In the cold light of day, the seriousness of her predicament seemed very real. She would have gone on Sunday night after ditching the Frenchman, but being late on a Sunday, the petrol stations were all shut, and the Triumph drank fuel like it was going out of fashion. So she had to wait until first light. She told herself to be calm; once over the border into Wales she would be fine – it might as well be South America so removed did it feel from the rest of the British Isles. And then perhaps France in a month or two? She smiled fondly as she recalled Charles's parting words.

As she hung up the pump she clocked a bobby in the adjacent bay filling up an Allegro panda car, whilst his partner in the passenger seat ogled her. She smiled back coyly – he must be all of nineteen, twenty – and he grinned back and winked. They're barely out of nappies these days, she thought, walking briskly into the garage shop.

'Number two and twenty Consulate, please.'

She noticed behind the kiosk an 'information wanted' poster relating to an armed robbery. *Her* armed robbery. 'You've got my money,' she said to the sketch that should have been her.

'Five pounds twelve pence, love,' the attendant said, moving his gaze to the policeman now striding across the forecourt.

She handed over a fiver and counted out the change.

'Hey, what you doing?' she asked, as the cashier held the note up to the window.

'Got to check,' he said, pulling out a clipboard from beside the till. He raised his eyebrows. 'This here's a fake.'

'What you got there, pal?' the young policeman, now standing behind Louise, asked.

She felt a flicker of panic; she was trapped. *Stay calm*, she told herself.

'A fake note.'

'Oh, how terribly embarrassing!' Louise replied, cringing as best she could.

'Let's have a look.' The policeman reached over, taking the offending bill and perusing it. 'Do you recall where you got this note, miss?'

'You know, I really don't.' She looked the picture of innocence.

'I'll need you to come down to the station to make a statement.'

'Really? I'm in an awful hurry – can't it wait?' She gave him her most beguiling smile and twirled her hair between her fingers.

'Afraid not, miss. We won't keep you long.' She cursed inwardly. The other PC, the younger one in the car, she could have twisted him round her little finger. 'Maybe you'd like to make a call first?' he offered by way of compensation, looking to the cashier.

'There's a public phone round the back, next to the loos.'

'Yes, I wouldn't mind, if that's OK – I'll just call the office . . .'

Where the bloody hell did I pick up duff money? She couldn't believe it – had Charles really paid her in hokey notes? Of all the stupid things!

'Where shall I tell my boss you boys are taking me?' she asked gaily on the threshold of the garage shop, hoping against the odds it might be Rimmington and not Denton – they were between the two towns.

'Eagle Lane, Denton.'

'Fine.' She smiled, knowing that if she got within spitting distance of Frost there was no way she'd ever leave Eagle Lane a free woman. 'Is it OK if I just pop to the car for a telephone number?' The constable nodded assent, and she strolled across the forecourt to the TR4, in as casual a way as she could manage. Her handbag was on the passenger seat, the butt of the Beretta just nudging the zip. Louise opened the car door, reached inside to retrieve her bag and made a show of ferreting around for her pocket diary. Smiling, she brandished the Letts at the shop window and continued walking towards the phone box, which was close to the exit for the main road and not visible from either the shop or the panda car. She'd be making a call for sure – two, in fact – but not just yet. Waiting for a gap in the traffic she dashed to the central reservation – she reckoned she had five minutes max to make good her getaway.

'You're joking!' Frost almost choked. He, Waters and Bill Wells were just entering the car park at the rear of Eagle Lane.

'No, I'm not, Jack.' Wells really wasn't.

'John?' Frost said plaintively. Waters shrugged.

'But look at it!' Frost implored, gesturing at the new car.

'You'll get used to it,' Waters offered sympathetically.

'But it looks like a Noddy car – I'll be a laughing stock.'

'It's *aerodynamic*,' Waters said, patting the Sierra's bonnet.

'It's a new car is what it is, and you gotta sign for it,' insisted the desk sergeant, holding out a clipboard and pen.

Frost puffed on a cigarette, annoyed. 'I don't know, computers, new cars . . . where's it all leading? Not sure I can handle all this change on a Monday morning. Can't I just keep the old one?'

Waters saw that Frost seemed genuinely spooked by the march of progress at Eagle Lane, as if this exchange of old for new would destroy his equilibrium and impair his ability to function as a detective. Peculiar, given that Jack was only thirty-nine – what would he be like when he was forty-nine?

'No, you can't. You might want to buy a new pullover, though,' Wells suggested as Frost scribbled on the clipboard.

'What do you mean?'

'You've been wearing that reindeer one, since—'

'Blast, that reminds me, I've got to let the plumber in at nine-thirty.'

'Is it still not fixed?' Waters asked as Frost peered hesitantly inside the vehicle, as though fearful of finding aliens lurking within.

'No, I've been a bit distracted.' Frost climbed into the car. 'And Bill, if you think the jumper's been worn for too long you ain't seen nothing. There are some things that get a second lease of life when you wear them inside out – that's a whole extra week!' He adjusted his crotch manfully, grinning, before pulling the door shut and turning on the ignition.

'God forbid,' Wells said to Waters. 'Still, he seems pretty perky, all things considered.'

'Yeah, but what else can you do? Letting things get on top of you ain't going to solve anything.'

'Pity a plumber isn't going to shave him and wash his hair.'

Frost crunched the gears, put the car into reverse, and then stopped while he desperately tried to work out where the cigarette lighter was.

'The guy has just lost his wife—' Waters stopped mid-sentence, distracted by a uniformed officer running towards them, waving frantically.

Seeing the exchange between Waters and the breathless PC, Frost quit playing with the car and yanked the stiff new handbrake.

He caught the tail-end of a hurried conversation: a woman had been apprehended while trying to purchase fuel at a filling station with a fake five-pound note. On the pretext of calling her office she had legged it rather than answer a few questions at Eagle Lane.

'This girl who did a runner, how old did they reckon she was?' Frost asked.

The PC tugged his ear. 'Mid-twenties? Bit of a corker, too; short auburn hair and driving a Triumph convertible – the motor's still on the forecourt.'

'That so? And how much headstart did she have?' Frost asked, aware that whoever it was more than likely had more on their conscience than a dodgy fiver. His interest was piqued; good-looking women were top of his list today.

'What do you mean?'

'The time from when the girl left to make the phone call until your colleagues in blue woke up to the fact she wasn't coming back.'

The PC scratched his head. 'Five, ten minutes?'

She couldn't have got far – if they caned it, they might just catch her. Frost tugged Waters' sleeve urgently. 'Right, let's see what this toy car can do – John, hop in.'

*

It was ten to nine when Clarke sat down at Simms's desk in the CID office. The station was deserted. So much the better, she thought; usually Clarke was keen to know what was afoot, but today she just didn't care. She hoped that the peace and quiet would allow her to adjust, without people swarming around her commiserating over Derek (some tart in uniform had already broken down in front of her as if to suggest they were suffering in unison). Whatever spin was put on it, Derek's death had upset her deeply, and tossing and turning in bed until the small hours worrying in vain whether he had cared for her was only a small part of it.

She sighed and took a mouthful of coffee. Frost had said last night he wanted Waters to pick up Simms's work, but she'd been adamant that if she couldn't get involved with Simms's murder, which was clearly out of the question, then she could deal with what was left on his desk. In the end Frost relented; not that he had much choice, given how understaffed they were.

She flicked through Simms's notebook. A pang of emotion struck her at the sight of his neat, almost juvenile handwriting. Simms was a diligent note-taker – unlike his senior, Frost, who did not by any means lead by example. Most of the contents were familiar; a child knocked over, which looked to be hit-and-run – low priority – and the Gregory Leather case. That was a different matter, given that the minder had died last night.

Simms's phone rang. Clarke picked it up hesitantly. 'Hello?'

'Hello, Sue, there's a young lad on the phone, he's says he's got some important information about the lady who ran away from the garage this morning.'

Clarke didn't understand. 'I'm not with you, Bill.'

'A woman tried to pay with a dodgy fiver at the petrol station out on the Lexton Road – uniform had her red-handed, but let her get away. Jack went charging off after her in his new wheels.'

None of it made much sense to Clarke, though it did explain why the place was so quiet. 'OK, put him through. What's his name?'

'Won't give it – wishes to remain anonymous. And will only talk to a "detective". Only a young lad.'

'Jesus H . . .' Waters breathed, shifting uncomfortably in the passenger seat as Frost hoofed it on to the dual carriageway, narrowly missing the cab of an articulated lorry. 'Shouldn't you go easy a bit, you know, run the engine in?'

'You what? This is a police motor, not an Arab stallion . . . Besides, this should come broken in, don't you think?' Frost was hunched over the wheel like some crazed character from *Wacky Races*. 'Don't be such a baby – that truck was miles away.'

'If you say so – but see that stick thing in the middle, it's for changing what we call "gears". When clocking seventy miles an hour it is usual practice to move into a higher "gear" from that which you pulled out of the station in. The engine will thank you for it, believe me.' He knew it was pointless arguing. 'In any case, whack the siren on the roof if you're going to drive like that—'

'Siren?' Frost feigned bafflement. 'Here, light me a fag – not fathomed out where the lighter is in here yet.'

Waters wound down the window and lit a cigarette. 'Anyway, I'm not sure going like a bat out of hell will make any difference – she'll be long gone by now.'

'There were two area cars ahead of us – there's nowhere to run – bugger all round here: the garage, a brewery, and farmland either side. And they'd called ahead for assistance from Rimmington traffic police. Don't be so negative,' Frost admonished, pursing his lips around the Rothmans Waters passed over.

Waters shrugged. 'If you think this woman is in any way connected to the mayhem we've undergone this last week, it's very unlikely she'll be hanging around waiting for you to roll up – the woman or wom*en* we're after are way too smart.' He decided to change the subject; Frost was impossible to influence when he'd set his mind on something; besides, they were almost at the garage; arguing seemed pointless. 'How was Clarke last night?'

'Pretty perky, all things considered.' Frost flashed his headlights frantically at a three-wheeled van dawdling in the fast lane.

'"Pretty perky"?' Waters exclaimed. 'That surprises me – weren't they dating now? I would have thought, at the very least, she'd be pretty upset.'

'She'll get over it,' Frost replied resolutely, slowing down. 'Tough girl, that one. *Get out of the way!*'

Waters looked at Frost, surprised at his off-hand manner. 'No doubt she'll get over it, but she only found out yesterday evening . . .'

'Bloody hell,' Frost said, screeching abruptly to a halt, 'just look at those two gormless drips.'

Waters glanced at the two uniformed lads on the garage forecourt; their look said it all: they had lost the girl.

Monday (2)

Louise stared out of the window of the truck cab at the undulating countryside sweeping by, ploughed fields interspersed with the rich colour of woodlands in autumnal decline. She was not one to appreciate the beauty of the English countryside, but today she welcomed the dazzling array of colours and open space with a sense of relief as she left Denton behind. Yes, she thought to herself, I'll need a new look – orange and yellow with a hint of gold?

'Beautiful, those trees.' She sighed.

'What's that, love?' She turned to the bristly driver who'd picked her up twenty minutes ago on the southbound carriageway of the Lexton Road. 'Let me turn this off.' And with a tarantula-knuckled hand he leaned across and flicked off what she took to be a Citizens' Band radio which had crackled annoyingly with gibberish ever since she'd climbed in.

'Oh nothing, it's just nice to be out in the country.'
She smiled.

His glances at her cleavage were shameless, which she didn't mind – he wouldn't have picked her up if she looked and smelt like he did. Her gamble had paid off: she'd had to decide on the spot whether to try it cross country on foot or show a bit of leg and hope she'd get picked up in a matter of minutes, before the police had twigged she wasn't coming back.

'The only country I likes is sort of Country Music – you like Billie Jo?' He rattled a cassette box at her.

'Oh, I adore her – do put it on.' She couldn't abide C&W music, and couldn't grasp its popularity in this part of the world; Wiltshire was hardly Texas, but if suffering 'Blanket on the Ground' was the price of getting her to Bournemouth, it was a small one to pay for a getaway.

The trucker exhaled delightedly as he slipped the cassette in. At least the music would keep him quiet, and allow her time to think. It was reassuring that the only flashing lights she'd seen had been hurtling up the other carriageway, in the opposite direction. She thought she'd let a few miles pass, until they were outside the county, then request a stop for a pee so she could use the phone. She couldn't work out whether the ardent Frenchman would have knowingly slipped her duff notes. She'd call him, but not before trying Marty; OK, they'd not parted the best of friends, but she had met Charles through him, so he could at least tip her off if the bloke was crooked. She hoped not, though

– France was looking more appealing by the minute. What would the autumn season in Paris bring?

'Ah, there you both are.' Clarke greeted them with a triumphant smile, surprising Frost as he and Waters entered the general CID office looking deflated. Disappointed as Frost was at losing the girl at the filling station, he was glad to see Clarke smile. 'It would appear, gentlemen, that your luck is about to change.'

'I'm all ears.' Frost slumped down at the desk opposite, very much doubting it. 'John, stick the kettle on, I'm gasping. Losing a suspect always makes me thirsty.'

'A young local lad by the name of Simon Hope called just before nine.'

'Who the blazes is Simon Hope?'

Simon Hope, Frost now discovered, spent a lot of time tinkering with CB radio, and had been using an illegal AM radio to eavesdrop on police transmissions when he was meant to be getting ready for school. Clarke had taken his initially anonymous call: five minutes after hearing on police radio how a woman had abandoned her car at the garage, Hope, on switching frequencies, had overheard a trucker boasting over the airwaves that he'd spied a 'real cutie' to pick up on the roadside just outside Denton. Clever lad. It did finally seem their luck was about to change.

'I could kiss the little blighter!' Frost exclaimed.

'Well, you can't – I promised to preserve his anonymity.'

'What did he hear?'

'That Tricky Whiskers was Bournemouth bound.'

'*Tricky Whiskers?* What sort of name is that?' Frost spluttered.

'It's a handle – a name used on CB radio. A sort of nickname,' Waters said, handing him a coffee. 'Did you ever see *Convoy*? "Rubber Duck"?'

Frost, bemused, shook his head, and pressed on: 'Do we have any idea where this Mister Whiskers is now? I mean, she could jump off anywhere between here and Bournemouth.' Frost pulled the regional map for the South Coast from the shelf above his head, and thumbed through to the relevant pages, his forehead creasing as he squinted at the vexing mess of red and yellow squiggles.

'Nope, he went off air. Control have notified every traffic division between here and the coast.'

'Well, fat lot of good that will do – stop me if I'm wrong, but I doubt he's got "Tricky Whiskers" painted the length of his articulated, has he? I mean, how the flaming hell will we find him? This is urgent. He has no idea who he has on board.'

'Do we?' Waters asked.

'Yes. *We* do.' He reached inside his mac and produced a portrait photo, which he spun over to the opposite desk.

'A real cutie,' Waters said, repeating the truck driver's phrase with raised eyebrows. 'Who?'

'That is Miss Louise Daley.' Frost stood up. 'The traffic cops at the garage ID'd her.'

'Are you sure it was her, Jack?' Clarke said.

Frost detected disbelief in her voice. '*They* are sure,' he said pointedly. 'It's not me who saw her, remember?' He wanted it to be Daley, a point not lost on Clarke, but uniform's corroboration removed the suggestion of obsession on Frost's part. The escape of the last member of the gang that had caused the demise of Bert Williams had been haunting him for the best part of a year. He suspected now it was likely to have been her who had stabbed Simms, thinking it was him – but he said nothing of that to Clarke. 'And you can bet your arse it was her that held up the payroll on Friday. And we are not going to let her get away again.'

'OK, give me that,' Clarke said, snatching the photo. 'We'll get on to National and set up patrol cars between here and the South Coast – we'll get her this time, Jack.'

'I pray we do, but she's slippery as hell.' Clarke ran out of the office while Frost frowned at the map. 'Where are you? *Where are you?*'

'There's nothing we can do now, pal,' Waters said, 'but fortunately we have Mullett's briefing on the computer system at eleven to take our mind off things.'

'Yes, John.' Frost sighed, poking a cigarette between his teeth. 'Thank goodness you reminded me. Where would we be without the super's new toy?'

'Out solving crimes, maybe?'

'Perhaps,' Frost mused, 'but you know, I'm not sleeping much at the moment. The super's soporific tone might just do the trick – I could catch forty winks while he drones on about the Incident Reporting Whatchya-callit . . .'

'Have we gone "live"?' Clarke re-entered the room, breathless.

'Not you too?' Frost said, exasperated. 'That was quick.'

'All in hand,' she assured him. 'Uniform are on the case – we will get her.'

'We'll see,' he said, doubtfully. 'In the meantime, take a trip to Denton Comp and pick up that teacher – let's see if her memory's still on the blink.'

Charles sat in the attic room above Avalon Antiques on Gentlemen's Walk. Rain had started to patter on the skylight. Slumped in the old rocking chair, he was considering what he should do next, and whether they were in any real danger. Gaston's pacing in the dusty, cluttered room was not helping him focus his thoughts. Charles had just told him he'd given Louise Daley counterfeit notes. After she telephoned from what sounded like the middle of a main road, Charles realized he might have put them in a spot of trouble, so he'd come clean to Gaston (though withholding the nature of the transaction itself). Before arriving in the UK the pair had manufactured high-quality forgeries and had slowly been drip-feeding them into circulation. As their antiques business started to flounder, so they had upped the usage of fake money to maintain a respectable lifestyle while all around them were gripped by the recession.

'Gaston, please. That floor is several centuries old, but your incessant pacing is seriously reducing its chances of making it into the next one—'

'Ha! The next century! Eighteen years' time! By then this country may just be considering letting us out of gaol!'

'Don't exaggerate – we've taken liberties with the English currency, not kidnapped its queen. I'm sure the worst that can happen is we'll get deported . . .'

'Deported, then prison.' The little man paused in his pacing and frowned.

Charles was deeply fond of Gaston, and hated to see him fret so. '*Pah*, I doubt it,' he said. 'Your namesake in Brussels will recommend clemency – sterling work on behalf of the Common Market.'

'Charles, this is no laughing matter . . . and what about the painting? It will be seized for sure if the police start sniffing around here – we have nowhere to hide it.'

'Hmm, this is true. The situation, I admit, is not a good one,' Pierrejean conceded. He covetously eyed the Stubbs on an ancient easel before them.

'Tell me again – what is it this woman said to you?' Gaston persisted.

'She said she may call upon me for help. "You will not be incriminated," she said.' And a long line of expletives that he didn't feel required repeating. Louise had not accused him directly, but it was clearly implied in her tone.

Gaston sighed. Charles felt for him; he did not have the mettle for such risks. 'But that means nothing! Why, oh why, did you give her the money – when we'd agreed no more?'

'She was supposed to be leaving Denton last night.

I thought the risk minimal.' She had told him she was leaving that very night, driving to Wales initially, although yesterday evening vague promises had been made for a romantic rendezvous in Paris. She seemed genuinely to like him and took the money out of necessity – although her tune may well have changed since; the last thing he'd expected was her getting caught with the fake money at a service station not two kilometres from this very shop!

Any other girl would have simply gone along to the police station, made up some spurious story about receiving the money in some shop, feigned innocence and walked away. Charles in rather cavalier fashion had palmed off the forgeries on a woman who clearly had issues with the police. Why was he now surprised it had backfired? Instinctively he knew her to be trouble, so involving her covertly in their shady dealings had been a foolish risk; he cursed himself. His libido had got the better of him once again. He tried to placate Gaston. 'She did not suspect – she is a high-class call girl, that's all I know. I didn't think she'd run from the police for being in possession of a fake note.'

'*Mon dieu*, I cannot believe this. *Because she is wanted by the police!*' he shouted furiously. 'Most men in our present position would run a hundred kilometres from such a woman – but no, not you; she flashes her . . . her *bits* at you, and off you go!'

'It's not quite like that . . .'

Though he knew very well it was, and that he was very much in the wrong. They should have hopped it once they knew the police were on to the forged notes. He hated England, the weather, the culture, the men; why he found the women so alluring he had no idea. 'I only gave her a hundred pounds.'

'One hundred!' Gaston tutted; the poor fellow was on the verge of questioning how and why, but realizing it was pointless said, 'Charles, you have no reason to believe her word; we cannot risk hanging around here a moment longer. We should return to France immediately. Burn the money.'

'You're right.' Charles rose from the chair, and walked towards his friend and embraced him. 'We shall burn the rest of the money immediately. The painting, though – what shall we do with the painting? It is too valuable to risk leaving behind.'

'Painting? What painting?' A tall bald man in a dark suit emerged before them from the attic stairs.

Monday (3) ─────────────────

Charles was uncertain what to do. There could be no doubt that he was in more trouble now than an hour ago when he'd put down the telephone on Louise. When the unexpected visitor who now ushered them into the back of a black Mercedes had asked that they come immediately to see Palmer on a matter most urgent, Charles knew a refusal would not be tolerated.

The man smiled a closed, menacing smile; his very presence was threatening. There was something inherently sinister about tall, quiet men in dark overcoats and black gloves. It was the gloves that did it. Charles slid into the back of the car with Gaston, the door shutting after them with a confident German clunk.

It was too late to do anything now, but what would he have done anyway? Screamed for help as they were marched out of the antiques shop? And what would have happened then? The man was carrying a gun; of that he was sure – how else would that deathly cool be sustained? It couldn't just be his height, although he was several centimetres taller than Charles himself. Still, if they were really in serious trouble, wouldn't Palmer's men have grabbed the painting? As it was, the valuable Stubbs remained where they'd left it, on the easel.

Gaston shifted uncomfortably next to him.

All they knew was that Mr Palmer wanted to see them urgently. Which in itself should be nothing to worry about, except that 'urgently' did mean literally this minute, and there was no explanation as to why. Charles knew it could be only one thing. As they left Denton and powered up the Rimmington Road he felt slightly queasy at the prospect of seeing Palmer – since it was more than likely that he too had had a call from Louise Daley.

'Good morning, everybody.' Mullett stood at his groomed finest before a full briefing room. 'Today, as you are all aware, is IRIS day. Yes, the computer age has finally arrived in Denton. The Incident Resource and Information System is now fully operational. Uniform went live on Friday, and this week CID . . .'

Frost yawned loudly. However annoying Mullett was, he was nothing if not professional. Frost knew the super was just back from visiting Simms's parents, a task Frost himself would not relish, but there was Hornrim Harry up at the front, immaculate and unruffled. Mullett looked to the man in the lab coat standing next to him to corroborate his last pronouncement. The technician, who'd spent most of the last week scuttling around the building looking stressed, nodded apprehensively. Frost thought that this poor unlucky sod, to whom the majority of CID had been rude since his arrival a week ago – in particular himself – looked decidedly uncertain.

'. . . this means that from this day forth, the old incident board is obsolete, and going forward it is the responsibility of each individual to log his activity electronically. Failure to do so will result in disciplinary procedures.' Frost could see the super's beady eye sparkle as it focused in on him. Pathetic, Frost thought, he's doing this solely to annoy me. He lit a cigarette and ruminated on Louise Daley. How those clots in uniform could lose that girl at a filling station was beyond him. He stared at the creased photograph he'd carried on him for the past year. She was a stunner, all right. His conscience, in his tired bedraggled state, had no qualms in allowing him idle fantasies about her. The fact she'd more than likely murdered his colleague was temporarily shelved in his mind.

At the front of the room the superintendent's voice rose an octave. There was something sadistic in Mullett's obstinacy in refusing to move this blasted computer meeting; he knew Frost was bursting to get out after her. There was a good chance she was responsible for the mayhem in Denton this last week – did Mullet not see that? He ran his grubby thumb along the contour of Louise Daley's cheek.

Shaking himself abruptly, he ground out the cigarette

on the meeting-room floor, something Mullett hated, and pocketed the photo. What on earth was the super burbling on about now? Back-up routines and whatnot? This was getting *his* back up, all right. Procedure, procedure. But Frost was resolved not to be beaten – he would use the interlude to marshal his thoughts; compose himself rather than fly off the handle. He lit another cigarette and nodded sagely at the introduction of something called a Central Processing Unit.

Mullett pivoted himself round in his executive chair and glared out at the car park expectantly. Winslow, the Assistant Chief Constable, was due any minute from County HQ; according to Miss Smith he'd be here at twelve. The Denton super was unsettled by his visit to the Simms family home in Lexton. He lit a Senior Service and chose not to dwell on the encounter, but rather to focus on the here and now and the incoming ACC. He might have bothered to show up for the presentation on the IRIS system, thought Mullett. After all, the odious little man had turned up for the Rimmington 'go live'; indeed Mullett himself had been summoned to attend Superintendent Kelsey's tedious display at Winslow's insistence. Mullett was baffled by the ACC's preferential treatment of the bluff, uncouth Rimmington commander; maybe it was because Kelsey was as small and bald as he was. They were as eerily similar in looks as they were disparate in deportment.

He sighed loudly. Though he was pleased to see the modernization of Eagle Lane station, he wasn't convinced that a computer system would have prevented the chaos that in the last week had reigned over Denton. The collation and sharing of information was one thing, but would it replace men pounding the streets catching criminals? He doubted it, but he could already see the fiscal implications – the cost must be staggering; they wouldn't have a snowball's chance in hell of improving the station's manpower now.

'Ah, there you are,' he muttered, spying between the blinds Winslow's Jaguar cruising into the car park. He was quite prepared for the ACC now – let him try and browbeat Stanley Mullett – for the superintendent had been toying with letting slip what the surveillance operation outside the Pink Toothbrush sauna in May had surprisingly revealed.

He drummed his fingers on the highly polished desk. But the ACC should have no quarrel with Denton today. Louise Daley, a wanted felon, had been spotted just outside the town this morning. There was a good chance she was responsible for much of the recent crime wave.

Still, Winslow's sponsorship of Frost was a constant irritation. He buzzed Miss Smith for coffee. Loathe Winslow as he did, you *had* to respect someone who could make ACC when still the right side of fifty. He pondered again whether Winslow might be a Mason and whether it had been wise of him to dismiss Hanlon out of hand like that . . .

'Ahh, good morning, Nigel,' Mullett said, rising from his chair as Miss Smith showed in the ACC.

'Stanley,' he rejoined, removing his uniform cap and running his hand needlessly over his bald dome. 'All go off OK, with the computers and whatnot?'

'Tip top, sir. The whole of Eagle Lane is live and functioning. Uniform went live last Friday and CID today. It's a shame you missed it.'

'Couldn't be helped,' he said, making himself comfortable.

Mullett was instantly rankled by Winslow's lack of interest. Was an apology too much to ask for? But the ACC clearly didn't feel compelled to expand on the reason for his no-show.

'Yes, it's a shame – I was rather hoping you might have made it, to impress upon the men the importance of this system. I mean' – he paused as Miss Smith entered with the coffee – 'it will be a disciplinary offence not to log incidents in the prescribed fashion.'

Winslow sipped his coffee daintily, and smiled at Miss Smith. 'Of course, CID might be a problem – I can see that' – Mullett beamed at this response – 'however, there's all manner of viciousness going on out there, so don't come down on them like a ton of bricks straight away, eh, there's a good chap. Now, what have you to report? I know extra men were drafted in yesterday following the young detective getting murdered.'

'We have a lead, sir. A wanted felon was spotted this morning,' Mullett said proudly. 'The suspect has a history of violent crime and we are confident she's responsible for the havoc wreaked last week, including the murder of DC Derek Simms.'

'Jolly good, Stanley.' The ACC smiled a weak smile. 'You say "spotted"?'

'Yes, we've yet to catch her. But we will.'

'Well, that's good to hear. This division could do with a result.'

'The woman aside' – Mullett fiddled with his Windsor knot self-consciously – 'we're exploring all possibilities and the extra men will be usefully deployed fact-finding on the Baskin shooting. If there's the remotest chance of a gang war we need to stamp on it immediately, show them who's boss.'

'Well, quite. What did you have in mind?' Winslow arched a single eyebrow.

'We need to look at the comings and goings at both of Baskin's establishments. Just because he was shot at the Coconut Grove, doesn't mean we should rule out the Pink Toothbrush – that's the sauna in the centre of town,' Mullet said pointedly. 'Perhaps you've heard of it, sir? About six months ago we held the place under surveillance following complaints of seedy goings-on . . .' He left the remark hanging there.

The ACC didn't take the bait. The fact that he might be compromised, having been witnessed leaving the premises, appeared not to stir him at all. Instead he said, 'I wouldn't waste too much time on Baskin – if it transpires it's some feud between lowlifes you can bet there'll be no charges brought to bear. *Prioritize*, Stanley.'

'But this is all part of the investigation into Simms's murder,' Mullett said, crestfallen. 'Louise Daley consorts with the criminal underworld; who knows where this might lead—'

'No, your priority is the rapist, Superintendent, as I've told you before; I'm assuming you don't have this woman fingered for the rapes?'

God, I really do hate you, Mullett thought to himself as he stared into the small, mole-like eyes of his superior officer.

'The public, think of the public,' Winslow continued. 'The people need to feel safe. Nobody cares if some overweight club owner gets blasted, or for that matter if a policeman gets stabbed, but rape is bad. That and theft – the armed robbery in broad daylight – that in the eyes of the general public is borderline anarchy. And on the panic scale, a payroll is about as bad as it can get.'

'Quite,' Mullett concurred grudgingly. 'The minder did just die of a heart attack—'

'That's immaterial – stealing a payroll is the weekly wage packet gone: tantamount to taking food from children's mouths.' Mullett looked perplexed. 'If it's a bank job,' Winslow continued regardless, 'that's fine – it's the bank's money. It's not in reality, of course, but that's what the good citizens of Denton think. But I don't really need to tell you that, do I?'

'No, sir.' The ACC was fond of spouting off like some cod philosopher, and Mullett had little choice but to humour him. This sanctimonious twaddle was all very well now, but when it came to the end of the month and Winslow himself was getting it in the neck from the Chief Constable about clear-up stats, it would be a different matter, of that Mullett had no doubt. 'As I said, we have a suspect for the robbery.'

'You've got to catch her first, if I remember correctly?' Winslow said archly. 'Anyway, no doubt you'll have taken all this on board ready for your press briefing; I saw the vultures circling in the lobby.'

Mullett had not forgotten the weekly Monday-afternoon slot, and nodded resolutely.

'Anyway, that's not the reason I'm here.' Until that moment it hadn't occurred to the super to wonder why Winslow had even bothered turning up, having missed the IRIS briefing. 'No, the reason I came was to congratulate Frost on his promotion.'

'Ah, I'm glad you brought that up, Nigel.'

'Oh, problems?' The eyebrow went up again.

'The murder of DC Simms was practically on Frost's doorstep.'

'And?'

'Well, I thought it imprudent to promote Sergeant Frost while there's a shadow over him—'

'A shadow? How do you mean? He's not under suspicion, is he? You just told me you have a suspect, this Daley woman?'

Mullett speculated idly as to why some bald men's heads were as shiny as polished marble and others not, as the midday sun pierced through the Venetian blinds and struck his superior's endless forehead.

'Well, as you say, we've yet to catch her. I just thought it prudent to . . .' The superintendent was aware of his own contradictions as he tied himself in knots; he sensed defeat.

'Thought *what*? Piffle. Call him in now.'

Mullett hesitated, then picked up the phone. 'Engaged,' he said stubbornly.

'Come on, don't be so curmudgeonly; he deserves it and you know it. Do it, Stanley,' Winslow said sternly. 'Anyhow, I must be away.' He rose to leave. 'By the way, talking of Simms, it's a strange coincidence, but your one new recruit in uniform is a Simms. I signed the papers, just the other day. Perhaps they're related?'

'Perhaps. Very good, sir. See you soon.' Though hopefully not that soon, he thought, smiling tightly.

There was no 'perhaps' about it; when he visited the deceased's parents in Lexton a brave and proud father informed Mullett that his second son was on his way to Eagle Lane, and pressed him not to allow the same fate to befall him. 'Look after my boy,' the man demanded from the doorstep. Mullett frowned at the recollection. This was the last thing he needed, a relative to feel responsible for, and what if the lad now had a vendetta to let loose on Denton?

'Bingo!' Frost slammed down the phone. 'We've got a fix on our man. Dorset police will intercept the truck on the outskirts of Bournemouth, having lured an unsuspecting Tricky Whiskers to give himself away over the radio.'

'How do you mean?' Waters asked.

'Mister Whiskers is back on air and gloating across

the airwaves while the princess is sleeping. Dorset police have requested what's known as an "eyeball" – a butcher's to you and me – and consequently have got a fix on their location.'

The phone rang again. But Waters could tell Frost's mind was in Dorset.

'Shall I get that?' he offered.

'Hell, no. We're going on a road trip.'

'What, now? They haven't caught them yet.' It was close to twelve thirty; Waters baulked at the prospect of tooling down the motorway with Frost all fired up at the wheel of the new Sierra. He'd much rather wait until the Dorset plods held her – if indeed they caught her – before going anywhere.

'So?' Frost snapped. 'We should get our skates on so we can make sure she doesn't slip through their fingers, like she did through ours last year.'

Waters acquiesced, knowing Frost's fixation with the Daley girl. Reluctantly he pulled on his denim jacket and, feeling chilly at the prospect of what lay ahead, swathed his neck in the long multicoloured scarf Kim had knitted him for his birthday. It was going to be a long and probably cold afternoon.

'Nice scarf,' Frost joshed, his mood visibly improved since the ordeal with Mullett and the computer. 'Who're you aspiring to be, Doctor Who or Orinoco Womble? All you need's the floppy hat.'

'You' – he poked Frost in the back as they left the office – 'are in no position to say anything, dressed like some hairy reject elf . . . and an out-of-season one at that.

The Doctor, for your information, has traded his scarf for a stick of celery; and on that note we're stopping for food before we hit the motorway.'

'Good idea!' Frost grinned. 'I'll get Control to send an area car to the Codpiece and put our order in, as we're heading that way – we can have some fish and chips en route.'

Charles Pierrejean's stomach rumbled not with nerves but with genuine hunger. He and his business associate Gaston Camus had been sitting in the poorly lit room – there were no windows – with only a small lamp on the low glass table in front of them, and a dim green glow above one of the pair of snooker tables, for the best part of two hours, waiting for the arrival of Martin 'Pumpy' Palmer, the man who had 'urgently' requested their company.

When their black Mercedes pulled up Charles was initially relieved to see a familiar neon sign, the cigar-smoking penguin with cue nattily held between its flippers, and not some cowshed in a field where, in his vivid imagination, British villains did away with problems. However, upon entry to the club he was perturbed to find it shut until the evening and the place deserted – devoid of a living soul including their host, Palmer himself. Where was he?

The clack of snooker balls in the far corner of the room drew Charles's attention back to their two companions, the tall man and the driver, and not for the first time Charles considered just standing up and leaving. But fear prevented him from acting; what if the door were locked or the tall man moved to block them, then . . . then he would know it was serious. Thus far, a veneer of cordiality existed: Palmer had sent his apologies; drinks had been offered and consumed.

The door opened silently, allowing daylight to enter from the club foyer. Gaston fidgeted uneasily beside Charles on the leather couch. No sooner had the rectangle of light appeared than it was eclipsed by the rotund silhouette of the club owner himself. At last. Charles had decided that the best approach was to deny everything – he was French after all.

'Afternoon, gentlemen,' Palmer wheezed. 'Sorry to keep you waiting – had to visit the hospital.'

'Oh, nothing serious, I hope?' Charles asked in spite of himself.

'Nah.' The big man slipped down into a chair on the other side of the glass table. 'Just extending good wishes to a friend. Robert, turn the lights on, for heaven's sake.' Palmer took a drinks tumbler that was handed to him from behind. 'Cheers.' The cut glass twinkled in the grateful podgy fist. 'Now then, what's all this about funny money?'

'*Je ne comprends pas.* I am sorry, I do not understand.'

'C'mon, Chaz.' Palmer leaned forward. 'Don't play the innocent Frog with me.'

Charles could only just make him out – his stooge having still not turned up the lighting. He shook his head in ignorance.

'Yes, you do understand. Young Louise got nabbed

by a pair of rozzers at a petrol station, and she called you at that poncey little antiques shop you two front. Am I wrong?'

'Yes, she did call . . . but I didn't understand,' Charles bluffed. Only now did he wonder what had happened to her. He had presumed she was already in police custody – why else would he be here?

'I like you, Chaz, don't get me wrong. You might dress like a noofter, but I'm a progressive sort of bloke in the modern business arena. But one thing I can't abide is lies. I don't put up with them from people round here, like Harry Baskin, and I certainly won't have them from a pair of garlic-munchers like you.'

'C'est quoi un "noofter"?' Gaston whispered in Charles's ear, not being familiar with English hoodlum vernacular. Charles silenced him with a light touch to the forearm.

'Mr Palmer, why would I lie to you? We are both men of business, ourselves recently arriving in Denton to set up an honest antiques business – art and collectibles. Like you, we are men of culture. Why would we dabble in matters of fraud? Let alone the *mademoiselle*.'

Palmer sighed. 'Don't give me that old pony – you' – he pointed at him with a stubby finger – 'were poking her.'

Charles wrinkled his nose in an involuntary gesture of disgust.

'And you probably knew she was short of a bob or two.'

'We did meet, that much is true. I am, believe me,

very fond of Lou— Miss Daley, but I was not aware of her financial—'

Before Charles completed his sentence a soft thud, such as is made by a heavy cushion when dropped to the floor, accompanied the sight of Palmer slumping forward on to the glass table.

'Enough of this romantic bollocks,' the tall man said as the lights were finally turned up. Gaston emitted a tiny squeak. 'Right, you two, pick him up.'

'How?' Gaston exclaimed in shock.

'Don't argue – pick him up and put him on the table.' Charles and Gaston both looked at the prone man sagging across the tiny glass table. 'Not that table – that one.' He pointed towards the snooker table where the driver of the Mercedes appeared to be a laying a sheet of stainless steel. Another man appeared with two very large sports bags and pulled out two sizeable sheets of polythene.

'But 'e is so big,' Gaston said, drawing Charles's attention back to the unconscious club owner.

The tall man stopped and considered, as if for the first time taking in Palmer's true size. 'Trev, you'll have to give these guys a hand – we don't want to make a mess of the carpet.' He smiled and produced something that glinted from within his overcoat.

Charles felt himself go white with fear.

Monday (4)

'Sit down, Detective.' Mullett smiled broadly; he'd always liked Clarke – for a woman she was quite acceptable. 'Frost? Any ideas where he might be?'

'He's on his way to Bournemouth, sir.'

'Bournemouth?'

'After a suspect.'

'Ah yes.' Mullett stroked his moustache thoughtfully. He'd caught wind of this development and had heard the crunching of gears in the car park as he'd closed the door on Winslow. 'Jolly good, let's hope we get a result pronto. Now then, I believe the rape case has been assigned to . . .' He tapped a forefinger delicately on the computer keyboard and waited. He rocked back in his executive leather chair and looked expectantly at the blank monitor before him. Nothing. Then a groan was emitted by the grey box, as though the machine were straining with all its might, then a light started to wink frantically on the console, followed by a stream of green binary code shooting across the screen. 'Christ alive,' he mumbled to himself. Clarke leaned over the desk to try to get a peek. Mullett retaliated by twisting the monitor round further towards him. 'Security, Clarke. You don't have clearance for this level.' He tutted.

Clarke sat back, unperturbed. 'Sergeant Frost has assigned me to follow up the Marie Roberts case, if that's any use?'

'Good, good. I just had an earful from the ACC, who fortunately hadn't heard about Sergeant Waters' bungling of . . . Anyway, that's no concern of yours.' He stopped himself, then said, 'Well, I imagine the reassignment of Detective Simms's caseload has yet to be logged . . . That would be it.' He looked suspiciously at the machine that refused to give him an answer.

He noticed Clarke bow her head at the mention of Simms, which triggered a thought: was it her who had a thing with him, or was it that Myles, the blonde who wore her skirts too short? 'Shame about Simms. Promising lad,' he said pointedly, at which she smiled. 'Still, I gather we're to get his brother.'

'His brother?'

Mullett consulted his notepad, having followed up the ACC's mention that a relative of Simms was coming to Eagle Lane. 'Yes, Charlie – no, David – starts in uniform tomorrow.'

The girl looked thoughtful.

'So can we expect progress with the Roberts case very soon?'

'Yes, sir, we're on the cusp – we're investigating a likely explanation for the Marie Roberts incident. Though I'm not sure it immediately resolves the attack last Monday,' she said hesitantly.

But Mullett didn't care to split hairs – to clear up one would get the ACC off his back; solving two would be too much to hope for. 'Well, press on. Keep up the good work, Susan. And let me know the minute we make an arrest. Understood?' he said keenly. 'Send in Miss Smith on your way out, please.'

Disinterestedly he watched the girl's curvaceous rear leave the room. Sighing, he turned his attention to the now-dormant machine in front of him. If this blasted system wasn't going to work there was no hope of him nailing Frost on account of him not following procedure. He banged the side of the grey box in frustration.

'You wanted me, sir?' Miss Smith appeared anxiously in front of his desk.

'Yes. Blasted machine doesn't work.'

'Have you tried turning it off and on again?'

'I beg your pardon?'

'That's what Colin says.'

'Who the blazes is Colin?' he said, vexed.

'The young gentleman who installed the computers. Or there's a helpdesk number – would you like it?'

Mullett stared at the useless flickering screen; all he could see was a horizon strewn with problems and pointless, time-wasting nonsense, and all the while the clear-up stats list growing ever longer.

*

Louise played with her food; a transport café fry-up this late in the day was not particularly appetizing, and watching the way her companion mopped up his fried egg with a piece of bread did nothing to encourage her to eat, even if it had been hours since her last meal. But she wasn't about to grumble when Whiskers was picking up the tab, given her quandary about dipping into her own cash – what if she brought out another fake? Would the staff out here be aware of fraudulent notes in circulation? Possibly not, but there was no point risking it – especially not in a roadside café where there was always the chance of coppers pulling in, as before.

'Another cuppa?'

She nodded and smiled. 'Whiskers', as he was known, was all right, despite being rough around the edges; he had woken her ever so gently for fear of startling her when they had pulled over just outside Bournemouth, suggesting they stop for food.

She had been encouraged by her telephone call to Charles – he was mystified as to the fake notes but was willing to help. If she had to skip the country because of trouble, he had given her a name and address to call on in Calais. Funny he didn't question what sort of trouble she might be in . . . Pumpy, on the other hand, was guarded and difficult to read over the telephone; he said he'd check out Pierrejean. What that entailed she didn't quite know, but deep down she felt he'd lost patience with her and thought her too much of a liability. Fair enough, he could be forgiven for thinking that. She lit a cigarette. Whiskers had stopped to engage in conversation with two scruffy men in denims; other truckers, most likely. She snorted at their grubby appearance; personal hygiene was clearly low on their priority list. One had greasy and limp blond hair, and the other looked like he could do with a good scrub. Still, underneath the grunge there was something oddly attractive about them.

Whiskers headed for the loo, and the two men, who looked to be in their mid-twenties, made their way over to her table.

'Hi there, mind if we join you?' the fair-haired one asked.

'Sure,' she said, and slid over in the booth. They apparently had no food or drink with them – lecherous pair, only interested in one thing, she thought. 'Where you guys heading?'

'To the nick – with you, sweetheart.'

In an instant her face was slammed down into the plate of cold baked beans and her arm twisted behind her back so hard the pain produced the unfamiliar sensation of tears.

Clarke waited outside the school gate. Most of the children had gone; there were just a few left monkeying around by the bike sheds, tossing a lit cigarette around. It was the same in her day – the same bunch who were reluctant to go to school in the morning were the same ones who were in no hurry to leave at the end of the day. She herself had been a latchkey kid. The first of the teachers began to leave, in a red 2CV followed by a pale blue Morris Minor. Marie did not drive to the school – Clarke knew that from her interview on Friday. Clarke got out of the car in anticipation, slipping on her sheepskin – it was getting chilly as the afternoons disappeared more quickly now.

Clarke mused on the fact that Derek's brother would be joining them at Eagle Lane. She didn't even know he had a brother. Leaning against the car, it occurred to her she hadn't really known Simms at all – perhaps it would have been hasty to rush into marriage off the back of her predicament. She'd never know now.

Marie Roberts emerged from the main school entrance along with a young colleague. The pair paused on the steps laughing, she touching his forearm. Then the man, who was bearded and wore a tweed jacket with elbow patches, noticed Clarke leaning against the car and watching them. His smile vanished, prompting Marie to look in her direction. The pair said goodbye and the man scurried off to the staff car park.

Marie walked slowly but deliberately, clutching schoolwork to her chest. 'Hi,' she said with an affected air of surprise that instantly got Clarke's back up.

'Hi, Marie, how are you?'

'Bearing up, getting along, you know.'

'Yes, I do know,' Clarke said abruptly, causing Marie to frown in puzzlement. 'Mind if we take a stroll together?'

'No problem.'

'How was your weekend?'

'Quiet. Your colleague came by on Saturday to check

up on me. I must say, you're very kind to take so much care.'

Clarke stopped in her tracks. 'It's not so much that we *care*, Miss Roberts – it's more that we suspect you're not telling us the whole truth.' She deliberately did not use the word 'lie', although that's what she meant. Clarke had learned early on that an indirect statement could work wonders and avoided hysterical accusations.

'About what?' the teacher asked, the cold afternoon chilling her breath.

'In spite of what you said to me before, I think you do have a boyfriend, Miss Roberts.'

'I told your colleague—'

'My colleague is dead. Now, if you'd like to explain exactly who you were out with at the town hall on the evening after the rape.'

The sudden news of Simms's death clearly pulled Marie Roberts up short, and her cheery demeanour evaporated. 'Oh. I'm very sorry to hear that. Look . . . it's my call to press charges, isn't that right? Well, I think I'd like to let it go – put it behind me and move on.'

'Charges? We've not even caught your attacker.'

'Yes, of course, I'd just rather forget about the whole incident.'

'Really, why's that?' Clarke pressed the young teacher.

'You know, don't you?' Marie Roberts hung her head in shame. 'Terry Windley and I are lovers. Everything would have been fine if that little peeping Tom hadn't startled the hell out of me. I just want to forget the whole thing.' She burst into tears.

Clarke felt embarrassed. 'Be that as it may,' she said, 'there is a rapist at large, and as unconcerned as you appear to be about catching him, I'm sure the other, real, victim is of a different mind.'

'But what makes you think it's Terry? I mean, Jesus, Terry's not like that. I read in the paper the attacker had a knife!'

'I think we'd better go back to the station for a chat, don't you?'

Monday (5)

'Right, get to work. There's plenty of time. The club doesn't open until six today.'

Charles was panting with the exertion – they all were. It had taken all four of them to get the big man on to the snooker table. He must be 130 kilos at least. Then they had been made to squeeze into boiler suits, and what with the combination of shock, exertion and now the constrictive suit Charles felt he might pass out.

'What?' he managed to puff.

'Start chopping.'

A pair of meat cleavers lay glinting conspiratorially on the edge of the table.

'But . . . but he's still alive!' As if to confirm this fact, Palmer began to moan.

'Not for much longer.' Nicholson sniffed. They'd discovered that was the tall assassin's name; the driver had let it slip while straining to get Palmer on to the table.

Charles looked to Gaston; beads of perspiration covered his tanned creased brow. He wasn't sure his friend could handle this much longer: he wasn't sure *he* could handle it.

'I'll get you started.' Nicholson stubbed his cigarette out slowly on the prone man's hand, which fidgeted as if being galvanized by an electric shock. It dawned on Charles that he'd decided to wake the man up before he – or they – butchered him. Palmer's eyes started to twitch.

'Oi Pumpy, wakey, wakey,' Nicholson hissed in his ear, pulling on a pair of rubber gloves.

'My head . . .' Palmer slowly regained consciousness. 'Where am I?'

'On a snooker table.'

Charles noticed the big man blink rapidly in panic – suddenly savvy as to the significance.

'Yep, you know what happens now, don't you?' Nicholson shook Palmer's chubby jowls. 'You're history, sunshine . . . shh, no, you keep quiet.' Palmer had started to whimper, knowing he was done for. 'We've all had enough of your chatter – you listen to me. Can you do that, just once – listen? Good. See, Trev and I have had enough. You're too greedy, not willing to share . . . and you're behind the times. There's more to the world now than snooker and the occasional bank job . . . which reminds me, even when there's a tip-off for an easy job, you give it straight to some tart who walks in off the street. Well, not any more.'

'You'll never get away with it,' Palmer wheezed.

'Oh yes, we will.' Nicholson perched on the table, relishing his moment. 'We've had to wait. You're a cunning old goat – never leave yourself exposed like that fool Baskin, and never go too far – those fat little legs can't manage it. We just didn't know how to bump you off, until this pair of charlies turned up.' Nicholson pointed a meat cleaver at Charles and Gaston. 'You're a bit of a big lad, and to get shot of you, to get you to disappear totally, we need help. I've been biding my time. Pondering, you might say. But now you've given me no choice.'

'How do you mean?' Palmer stuttered.

'Not only did your girl bungle killing Baskin, she only then goes and gets herself caught by the rozzers with bent cash.'

'That wasn't her fault, mate, it's that French twa—'

'I don't give a monkey's about whose fault it was – but it means the police are on to her, and if they catch her, she's going to have to bargain with them.'

'She wouldn't breathe a word – I promise,' he pleaded.

'Course she would!' Nicholson shook his head in disbelief, and sighed. 'Trouble with your sort is, you can never see beyond the tits and make-up; she's lethal and smart.'

Charles was at a loss: he now understood Louise was caught up in something far more dangerous than he could ever have imagined – the rest of the conversation meant nothing, though he tried to follow what he could. If they ever got out alive, there'd be some explaining to do.

'Think the Denton rozzers wouldn't be banging on our drum?' Nicholson tutted as he ran the blade across the fleshy white neck. 'Stupid. But on the other hand *this* opportunity presented itself with these two berks.' He waved the meat cleaver casually in their direction again.

Charles saw Gaston's Adam's apple rise and felt his do the same. Nicholson spun round and sneered in Palmer's face. 'So ya see, Marty, I really have no choice.'

'But Kelsey—'

'Kelsey nothing, sunshine,' Nicholson said, priming his forearm.

'But Robbo! You know me,' Palmer rasped.

'Yes, I do, Marty, that's the trouble. It's too good a chance to miss. Besides, one thing you are is clever, you'd have us eventually . . . see, a compliment? It's my time now. Sorry. You're fishfood, mate. Bye bye, Marty.' Nicholson raised the cleaver, theatrically almost, pausing to let his victim take in his last second. And then it came swiftly down on the man's neck.

Charles thought he was going to throw up. Gaston, he could see, was. This Nicholson was clearly a psychopath who'd been biding his time, and although his plan had been to get Charles and Gaston to hack Palmer up, he couldn't resist the opportunity of slaying his boss himself.

After another swift slash, Nicholson stepped back from the snooker table to admire his handiwork, then tugged the corpse to the edge of the table, to allow the blood to drain into a container beneath.

'Right, you two.' He wiped a spray of blood from his brow. 'Off you go.' They both took a step closer to the table, the polythene crunching underfoot. 'Try not to make a mess.'

'May we have gloves?' Gaston asked with astonishing calm, wiping vomit from his lips.

'Gloves?' Nicholson smiled. 'Oh dear, only got this one pair.'

Clarke shut the door on Marie Roberts and shot round to the front desk to find Bill Wells. The foyer itself was practically in darkness, the sergeant sitting in a solitary pool of light.

'You wanted me, Bill?' Clarke asked.

'The reservoir – they've fished out something unsavoury.'

'Can't someone else go? I've got a nympho teacher in there, needs taking in hand.'

'Really? Sounds just like Jack's cup of tea.'

'What sounds like Frost's cup of tea?' Mullett appeared before them, in overcoat and uniform cap. 'Or do I really want to know?' he said, buttoning his coat.

'Nothing, sir,' Wells said hastily. 'Off anywhere nice?'

Mullett glared at Wells as if he were simple. Clarke could barely contain a snicker, though she wasn't sure why she should be so amused – the super was on most irascible form, and given it was only Monday, it didn't bode well for the rest of the week before them.

'To get something to eat, if you must know. I have deferred the press conference until tomorrow,' he said sternly. 'We may as well wait for Frost to return with Daley, and perhaps he'll have something positive to say for once. Do we believe Daley to be behind the money fraud too?'

He looked from one to the other and was met with blank stares. Clarke had no idea – she'd heard the gossip about Mullett getting caught out at his newsagent's, but that was the extent of her knowledge.

'Where's Hanlon?' Mullett asked.

'Sick, sir,' Wells said, evidently pleased that he could at least answer that question.

'I want to see him as soon as he's back, you hear?' And with that he marched out of the building.

'That answers my question too,' said Clarke.

'What, Hanlon being sick?'

'Yes, it explains why I'm running around like a lunatic. What's wrong with him anyway?'

'Dodgy guts.' Desk Sergeant Bill Wells leaned across. 'What's all this about a nympho teacher?' he whispered conspiratorially.

'Bill, I'm surprised at you.' Clarke grimaced. 'I always thought better of you – the rest of that scurrilous bunch you expect it from, but you, Sergeant Wells.'

Wells looked put out. 'I was only curious, Sue . . .'

'I'm joking with you.' She laughed briefly. 'Poor little Marie was not raped, far from it – she was having a bit of fun with a randy teacher, a certain Mr Windley, when she realized they were being watched through a spyhole and panicked. Randy Windley scarpered out of the window and things soon escalated. She's pretty miffed as she reckons the headmaster reported it to the police without her consent, knowing full well what was going on. Something not right, though; why didn't he dismiss her? Anyway, when she heard another teacher had been raped for real, she knew she was in trouble.'

'Bloody hell, silly mare, she must feel a right twit.'

'Not half as much as when she finds out her boy-friend is possibly in the frame for the rape of Joanne Daniels.'

'Eh?'

'Terry Windley, the pervert landlord who landed Waters one on the nose with a wrench. But that's by the by for now. What's all this about the reservoir?'

The uniformed officers stepped aside to allow two men in plain clothes to enter the room. CID probably, but not the two who had caught her at the transport café: a shortish, sandy-haired, bearded white man in a Christmas jumper, and a bigger, younger black man in a denim jacket with a plaster across his nose, like some sort of Apache warpaint. An unlikely-looking pair.

'Miss Daley, we meet again.'

'Do we?'

'My name is Detective Sergeant Frost and this here's my colleague, Detective Sergeant Waters.'

Of course, it had to be.

'Nice jumper.'

He looked down at his chest. 'Why, thank you.' He seemed genuinely pleased.

So this was the man she had set out to kill, the man

who had seen off the Kelly gang, killing her uncle Joe and crippling Blake.

'I'm afraid I don't recall the pleasure.'

Louise in fact remembered she had seen Frost once, fleetingly, when he had banged on her door in Carson Road. He'd been making enquiries after Steve Hudson across the road had knocked his wife about. It was hard to believe that what she saw before her was the source of so much trouble – she was expecting someone more impressive. The tenacious super-sleuth who had been hounding her this past year looked more like someone's dodgy uncle after a rough night.

'We exchanged shots in Denton Woods last October,' Frost prompted.

'Really? I must have missed you . . .' she said sardonically; she had certainly shot at a number of policemen that fatal night. Until she had a grip on what exactly the police did know she'd have to be careful what she said. There was always the chance she could slip out of this, a chance, however slim. 'Would you mind telling me how you caught me?' She smiled.

'Your trucker pal put a call out on the CB to say he was picking up a "cutie".'

'Ah, yes, the radio.'

Louise couldn't remember whether the radio was on when she climbed into the cab – there was a CB but all she could remember was the awful Country and Western music playing. But she did nod off on the journey. How stupid!

'Can't blame him – if I'd been lucky enough to pick

up such a piece of crumpet by the roadside I'd announce it to the world too.' Frost grinned.

'OK.' She'd had enough of bantering with the smug bastard; she cut to the chase: 'What are you charging me with? I presume it's more than possession of a dodgy fiver?'

'Armed robbery, for starters; the Fortress building-society job last year with Blake Richards sounds about right – wouldn't you agree?'

'No, I wouldn't – I was just the driver.'

'You can argue that in court. In the meantime, it's back to Denton for you.'

'Oh, that's a bore.' Anything not to be in a cell: out of doors there was always a chance of escape, and she wasn't cuffed. 'Can I make a call, then?'

They looked at one another.

'Just one? Surely I'm allowed a call; I've not made one yet. Ask them,' she said, pointing towards the two PCs, who shook their heads in confirmation.

'Of course. If you promise not to run away again?'

'Ha ha.' What a comedian, she thought. 'I'd like to call my brief, if that's all right, get him to meet me at Denton.' She had to try Pumpy – get him to spring her en route. He didn't have to get his hands dirty himself, but surely he could send some of his boys.

'OK, and then we're off home. I'll try and liven it up for you, though; John here hates my driving, which gives me a chance to have a cuddle with you in the back.' Frost beamed, dangling a pair of handcuffs in front of him.

377

*

Detective Constable Sue Clarke stood as close to the reservoir edge as she dared. Bubbles broke the surface intermittently, indicating the scuba unit beneath the black water. It was almost pitch black now, and the arc lamps were barely sufficient to keep track of the two frogmen – how they did what they did she would never know. To her left the elderly angler once again regaled the two constables with his fight to reel in the severed arm bedecked with weed that had lain at the bottom of the reservoir. Beyond him half a dozen other men in brown and green parkas were packing away their equipment and muttering amongst themselves. Clarke sniffed in the cold air; she could feel her nose starting to run. She could not think of a worse way to spend an afternoon than sitting here in the chilly damp in the hope of a nibble. It wasn't even a natural lake – rather an ugly man-made effort of concrete commissioned in the late sixties.

'I couldn't say for sure.' Maltby approached her, a dew drop hanging from his red nose. 'But it's likely it belongs to the same man – Drysdale will be able to tell you more.'

A frogman surfaced before them struggling to push a brown sack clear of the water's surface. A uniformed officer in waders moved to relieve him of what to Clarke looked like a coal sack, although presumably it wasn't full of coal. Maltby hovered uncertainly beside her, looking as keen as she was to be away from this watery grave.

'Thank you, Doctor, but don't disappear – looks like there's more to come.' The coal sack was far from empty given the effort the PC was making to get it ashore; he nearly toppled in and had to be steadied by his companion.

Monday (6) ————————————

'I want bail.'

'Bail? You've got to be joking!' Frost paced the cell angrily. They'd made good time and arrived back in Denton in under two hours, but he was tired and irritable now. Too much time in a car didn't agree with him, and now the chase was over, the excitement was fizzling out; it had been a long day. 'We've been after you for a year – I'm hardly going to let you go wandering off, having just this minute charged you for shooting club-owner Harry Baskin!'

'I want a lawyer.'

'But I thought you called one before we left Bournemouth? Where is he?'

Daley had not said a word on the way back; there seemed very little of her brazen demeanour left. She stared obstinately at the red stiletto on the table.

'I don't know,' she said finally, lifting her gaze from the shoe to meet his piercing green eyes. 'Maybe he's been shot?'

'Make life easy for yourself; confess to shooting Baskin now. Cooperate.'

She placed a painted fingertip on her chin and said, 'Thank you for finding my shoe – do you happen to have the other one?'

'You're only making this tougher on yourself.' He shook his head. Frost had placed the stiletto before her prior to getting the ballistics report back for the Beretta found in the Triumph, just to gauge her reaction. Stubborn and uncooperative.

'There's been all sorts of merry hell in Denton since you've been back. I would have a good hard think, if I were you, before we next have a chat.'

Louise did not answer. She was as smart as she was pretty and would see his obtuse questioning had a purpose – but she didn't know what they knew already, and he wasn't going to tell her. But she'd been careful and had alibis. She was going down, that much was certain, but for how long would depend on her cunning.

Frost pushed back his chair, which scraped on the cell floor, causing Louise to flinch. 'Constable,' he said, addressing the WPC minding the door, 'assign Ms Daley some legal representation. Her lawyer appears to have gone missing, along with her other shoe.'

'I didn't do it, you know,' Daley said in a controlled voice behind him as he made to go. He stopped at the door and looked back. 'The armed robbery of the pay-roll, where the minder died. I know you think I did, but I didn't. I heard all about it while waiting for you and your friend to collect me this afternoon.'

Frost turned and pulled back the chair. 'And the hit at the Coconut Grove – Baskin and the boy?'

'They'll both live, right?' Her cool green eyes met his.

'It was touch and go with the lad for a while, but yes, they'll both pull through.'

'Maybe we can make a deal?'

'What say you tell me exactly where you've been the last week – everything, down to where you've been for a wee – then I might listen to you.'

Frost closed the door of Daley's cell lost in thought. She was hoping that by confessing to shooting Baskin he'd cut her a deal. But he wasn't ready to play ball; he expected he would soon have enough evidence from the ballistics analysis to charge her, and the shoe might help. When questioned on her motive for the shooting she was taciturn; she vaguely alluded to a long-standing beef with Harry, but Frost didn't buy this; he reckoned she'd never grass and was prepared to take the fall.

He had questioned her long and hard about her movements on Saturday night; she claimed to have had a night of passion with a local businessman, a French-man whom she'd met at Palmer's that evening. If it all stacked up she'd have an alibi for Simms's murder, and they'd need solid evidence to get her.

He paused in the corridor. But the payroll robbery? She said not . . . and maybe that was true. The artist's impression looked nothing like her. And where was the cash? If she was making to skip town, surely she'd have the payroll cash on her? Doubts were beginning to cloud his mind as to whether Daley had pulled the Gregory heist, but he couldn't countenance the alternative: another bird running around Denton with a shooter? Flamin' heck, this was giving him a thumping headache.

'Oh! You made me jump, sir. That's the second time you've caught me unawares down here.'

Mullett frowned disparagingly. 'So, is this young lady responsible for the mayhem that's been wreaked over the last four or five days?'

'The *young lady*, one Louise Daley, twenty-five years old, formerly of Carson Road, Denton, wanted in connection with a spate of bank robberies that struck the region about this time last year.'

'Yes, yes. I know all that. But last week's disturbances – you have her for Baskin already, anything else we can pin on her?' he asked keenly.

Frost raised his eyebrows and said in a condescending tone, 'Well, she is an armed robber, and an automatic pistol was found in her car, so there's every chance she may have had something to do with the Gregory Leather snatch on Friday. Though she says not.' Frost was being truthful to some degree here, and thought it best to let the super think Daley guilty of the robbery until he had an alternative explanation. The DS lit a cigarette, and offered one to Mullett, who refused. Frost shrugged and was silent for a second before muttering, 'I'm sure I saw her mincing about in Denton in May, when we had that heatwave.'

Mullett tapped his toe in a familiar way indicating an increasing loss of patience. 'What about Simms?'

'I would think so, yes. Though there's no proof,' Frost said matter-of-factly. And this he did honestly believe. 'We still haven't found the weapon.'

'OK, well, take your time, Frost. Assess the facts and present your evidence – let's not balls it up at the last hurdle, eh?' And with that he moved off to address the duty sergeant who was nattering to the PC on cell watch.

'*Take your time?*' Frost muttered to himself. 'Never heard that one.' He moved to the spyhole, and viewed the prisoner. Louise Daley was supine on the bed, arms folded and eyes shut, like an Egyptian princess lying in state, perfectly calm. 'You are a beauty . . .'

'Thank you,' Frost said into the phone, giving the thumbs up to Waters on the other side of the desk. Forensics had confirmed that the bullets found in Baskin's nephew matched Daley's Beretta left in the Triumph at the filling station. 'And the payroll robbery on Friday – don't suppose the bullets have materialized?'

'No. Only the shell cases. Which are indeed from a nine-millimetre pistol. Without the lead it's impossible to say—' the Forensics officer started to explain.

'I know, I know.' Only the shell cases had been found

on Simms's body – and that was what Frost had returned to the lab for a match.

'I only have what you returned. The hospital haven't as yet found the bullets extracted from the Gregory Leather employee, and the bullet from the vehicle door is, as you know, unaccounted for. All evidence from both cases was signed for by Detective Simms.'

'But Detective Simms is dead,' Frost said, exasperated.

'I know that, Sergeant. He's here at the lab.'

Frost's grip tightened on the phone, and on the artist's impression of Friday's armed robber which he held in the other hand. It didn't look like Daley, no matter how hard he stared at it – a fact he was even more aware of after seeing her in the flesh. 'Can't you tell from your records?'

'No, we need the lead itself to match the striation marks with the barrel. You see—'

'I know what striation marks are, thank you.' Frost hung up and sighed.

'No good?' asked Waters.

'Flaming knickers. We can't match Daley's gun to the armed robbery. The bullets are missing. He waved the artist's impression at Waters, annoyed. 'Not that she looks anything like this anyway.'

'Where are they, then?'

'How the hell do I know? If I did, I wouldn't be wasting my time with that rubber johnny, would I?'

Frost stretched his arms across the desk, his wrists resting on the computer keyboard, prompting a whirr and ping from the enormous grey box.

'Useless piece of junk,' he tutted. 'Where are those bleedin' bullets!' He banged the desk angrily, scattering cigarette ash and paper everywhere. He wanted them badly to prove his gut instinct right . . . but if he was right, where else to look? Palmer? 'In the meantime, let's get a line-up together. Get the payroll clerk to give Daley a once-over, but I'm not hopeful. Judging from this.' He tossed the sketch to one side.

Waters looked across at Frost and noticed how bloodshot his eyes were. The man was stressed and not making a great deal of sense. Waters stretched over and levelled a tottering pile of paperwork. Frost, he was fast beginning to think, couldn't see the wood for the trees. Waters wasn't into psychiatry, but had begun to wonder whether Frost had suppressed his grief for his wife by obsessing over this very dangerous woman.

'Jack, keep things in perspective – we have Daley for Baskin, and more than likely for Simms's murder. Focus on that.'

'You're right,' he conceded, scrabbling for his cigarettes on the chaotic desk.

'Now, tell me what you know of Daley's movements – what has she told you?'

Frost slumped back in the chair and repeated the interview, pausing every now and then to check himself, and in doing so calmed down. Daley's Saturday evening as Frost told it seemed so implausible that it might well be true.

'Hell, man, that's some alibi,' Waters said after Frost

had finished. 'Is there a chance that if she's mates with Palmer, he put her up to murdering Baskin?'

'Maybe.' Frost shrugged. 'But if so, why offer him as an alibi, if not to hide some greater crime?'

Waters could see the logic – throw in Baskin to save her skin on something bigger. 'And the French geezer? In Denton?'

'He exists, all right.' Frost exhaled, wearily. 'He was at Mary's send-off on Thursday with my . . . err . . . brother-in-law, as was. Who, as I said, was also at the dinner on Saturday night.' Frost reached beneath the desk and pulled up a bottle. He seemed calmer now, having talked events through.

'Christ, man, close to home.'

'And therefore easy to check.' Frost gestured at himself. 'I shall pay a visit to my dear brother-in-law very soon, get him to corroborate the dinner party.'

'Don't forget to ask how his nose is.'

'You can talk. And take that plaster off – you look like Adam Ant in reverse.'

'That so? Well, that sorry excuse for a beard doesn't make you Serpico.'

Frost clawed at his jaw. 'Really? I was hoping the girls might go for it. Well, I might have to settle for Pumpy Palmer.' Frost got up, wincing as he did so. 'Right, let's see what Pumpy has to say for himself; Daley claims to be staying at a property owned by him, so that's harbouring a known criminal for a start.'

'She really is hanging him out to dry.'

'You don't say!' Frost coughed.

Waters realized it had occurred to the DS all along; it was impossible to make out the man's thought processes at times.

'We could squeeze him a bit. He's a tricky one, though – don't be fooled by his size, he's as slippery as an eel. Not easy on the eye, but very clever.'

'Why's he called Pumpy?'

'Two reasons: the most popular – with him, that is – is due to his fondness for weaponry, in particular pump-action shotguns.'

'Nice . . . And the other?'

'Please, not on an empty stomach!' He smirked. 'We'll go via the Bath Road, check in with Brazier at his car lot, then shoot off to the Southern Housing Estate and sniff around, see if Ms Daley has left anything for us apart from a Frenchman's pubes . . .'

'What an appealing prospect.'

'Not enough glamour for you?' Frost raised a cynical eyebrow.

'You're all the glamour I need in my life, buddy.'

Waters picked up his denim jacket and Frost grabbed his mac, spinning round into DC Hanlon, who had sheepishly ambled in looking green around the gills, his shirt open at the neck. Waters couldn't ever remember seeing Hanlon without a tie.

'Arthur, you old trooper, I thought you were poorly?' Frost ferreted in his mac for his cigarettes, offering one to Waters, who declined. Frost was chain-smoking, which he found too much.

'Mr Mullett called.'

'You've been spending a lot of time with him lately; is there something you'd like to share with us?' Frost grinned knowingly.

Hanlon raised his eyebrows wearily. 'Bugger's disappeared – press conference has been cancelled, or something.'

'That was hours ago. But seeing as you're here, you might as well do something useful.'

'Aw, Jack, I'm really not well.' Hanlon rubbed his prodigious belly. 'Been throwing up all morning.'

'Don't be such a baby. We're short-staffed as well you know – even worse than usual since the weekend . . . Here.' Frost tore off a page from his notebook. 'Go and brave this French gentleman – you'll recognize him from when we buried the missus on Thursday.'

'Don't remember any Frenchman . . .' Hanlon scratched at his unshaven jowls, glancing questioningly at Waters, who had also been at Mary Frost's funeral, albeit briefly.

'Yes, you do – you were winding him up about some football match, remember?'

'Oh yeah, foppy-looking fellow in a cravat.' Hanlon waved a limp wrist in distaste.

'That's him. Well, this is the address we have for him and his shop – Avalon Antiques.' Antiques? It registered for the first time. The shop was an antiques shop. The in-laws' painting sprang to mind; might it be as simple as two plus two equals . . . ? Fingerprints had been found on the hall wall. Frost tapped the side of his head, as if the act itself would encourage storage of the information. One thing at a time, though. 'Ask him politely to confirm whether or not he's acquainted with the bodily delights of one Miss Louise Daley. Probe gently – she reckons they spent Saturday night at it, so be vague and see what he comes up with . . . and get someone from uniform to drive if you can't manage the motor. And' – Frost pointed his lit cigarette at his sickly colleague, causing the other to step back – 'try not to throw up on him. They're funny about their clothes, these Continentals.' Frost shook his head in disbelief and strode out of the room.

Clarke was not happy. Simms's death weighed heavily on her mind, and coming here, to where she knew his body lay, upset her deeply.

She had followed the Forensics people back from the reservoir to the lab. She disliked Drysdale at the best of times, so to be here on her own this late in the day was particularly irksome. The lab was always a good few degrees colder than outside, even at this time of year.

'Blue chalk dust.' The pathologist sniffed. A lab technician with a trolley trundled past noisily.

'Are you sure?' she quizzed, not wishing to step any closer.

'That's what the analysis results say, my dear. Pool-cue chalk, to be precise.'

'Can you be so precise? Teachers use chalk on blackboards in all colours – white, blue, you name it.' Clarke's thoughts were of the putative rape case involving school staff.

Drysdale peered over his pince-nez with the haughty arrogance she'd come to resent; why he thought it reasonable to behave in such a manner she could never understand – it was his job to know such things and share the knowledge readily, after all.

'It's in the composition. Chalk in general is silicone-based, but the type that is applied to pool or snooker cues has a mix of adhesive, so that it sticks to the cue tip.'

'I see.'

'Modern science for you.'

Clarke looked at the array of limbs before her, displayed in an assortment of trays. 'But . . . are they all the same man?'

'Yes, we can assume so – although the body parts are at various stages of putrefaction, due to some being above and some below water. And this is the fellow you are looking for,' Drysdale said, lifting a cloth from the nearest tray. The stench made Clarke gag. 'The fish have had a nibble here and there, but—'

'A "nibble"? They've had more than a *nibble*.' Clarke looked at the hollow eye sockets, where all that remained could only be described as matter – be it brains or reservoir mud – oozing within.

'Well, you can tell he had blond hair.' Drysdale prodded with a scalpel beneath what was left of the nose. 'And wore a decent-sized moustache.'

Frost stood with Waters at the Dirty Penguin snooker-club reception desk. It had just gone 6 p.m. and it had only just opened. He felt they were being deliberately ignored. The pair behind the desk, a kid and an attractive blonde, could probably smell police and were accordingly disdainful. They would be familiar with the Rimmington plod, he guessed. Brazier had confirmed that Daley was at Palmer's farmhouse on Saturday, as was he, but could offer little more in the way of information; as he put it, he was with the wife so he paid the skirt no attention. He couldn't say whether Pierrejean knew Daley already; in fact he could barely recall the conversation, and crucially he didn't know what time she left. Pissed, no doubt, Frost thought. Though he did manage to recall they had arrived separately; the girl was there before any of the other guests arrived.

'Mr Palmer about?' Frost enquired when the acne-ridden desk boy finally drifted over.

'He's out.'

'Can I have a word with who's in charge?' Frost addressed his question to the strapping blonde in a tuxedo dishing out snooker cues to a pair of likely Herberts in their Sunday best.

'That's me,' the youth replied; he couldn't have been more than eighteen.

'And who might you be then, Spotty?' Frost snapped.

'I'm Mr Palmer's deputy manager,' the boy said unconvincingly.

'Is that so? How come I've not come across you before?'

The kid shrugged and said, 'You wouldn't pass our dress code here.'

Frost turned to Waters. 'Cheeky sod. I'm sure I've seen this one nicking sweets from Woolies.' Although he was jovial, Frost thought it a little strange that Palmer would leave his snooker palace in the hands of a boy. 'Where's Pumpy's sidekick, the tall, bald bloke?'

'Mr Nicholson is also out.'

'Where did you say they'd gone again?' Waters asked.

'I didn't.' He sniffed.

Frost wandered back to the entrance and looked out across the Dirty Penguin's car park. It was starting to rain, the sort of drizzle that hung in the air for days at a time. Palmer drove a Mercedes. There was a black Mercedes nearby.

'Isn't that Palmer's motor out there?'

The boy, remaining at his station, bit his bottom lip in a sneer. 'That's Mr Nicholson's.'

'Well, where are they, then? I've not got all day.'

'They didn't say.'

'When are they back?'

'They didn't say.'

'If you're Pumpy's staff, you'll know this lady.' Frost flashed the snap of Daley, and winked at the blonde as she bustled past. 'It's her we're here about . . . she might be in danger. We know Mr Palmer will be concerned.'

The lad shook his head. If Louise Daley had walked through the foyer naked he'd still swear blind he'd not seen her. Frost was impressed by the loyalty: Pumpy had his crew well trained, he had to admit.

'Maybe we'll have a poke around,' Waters suggested.

The blonde in the tuxedo presented herself. 'We can't stop you, but try not to frighten the punters. I'll manage the desk, Des, if you like.'

'Fancy a game?' Frost asked Waters.

'Only if you're quicker than when you play chess, otherwise we'll be here all night.'

The foyer was shiny and smart; for something that was done on the cheap it managed to avoid being too tacky. Frost caught a glimpse of the two of them in the mirrored wall and was surprised to see that he really did have a beard – how did that happen?

Away from the desk the lad assumed a new demeanour; he was courteous, as if showing around prospective members, highlighting the facilities and number of tables. They entered Palmer's office. There seemed to be little trace of recent activity – the place was neat and clean, as if the occupant had gone away on holiday.

Just before leaving Frost noticed a door labelled *Private Room* in elegant script.

'What's this?'

'A private-hire room. It has two tables in it.'

Frost rattled the doorknob. 'It's locked.'

'It's just a room.'

'Open it,' Waters insisted.

The boy fumbled with his keys, eventually finding the right one. He pushed open the door to the darkened room. 'Can never find the lights . . .'

Frost stepped into the blackness and sniffed the air. He'd picked up a faint scent; those few seconds in the dark had focused his olfactory senses just enough to allow the hint of a familiar, metallic smell to hit him.

'There.' The room was suddenly illuminated. It was large, holding two snooker tables and an alcove with a leather seating area. The snooker tables were clear of balls. The glass table in the seating area had three glasses half full. Waters picked one up.

'Scotch.'

Frost moved around the nearest table, running his palm around the rim. The smell had gone and all that remained was an empty room with some unfinished drinks. 'Ouch,' he said suddenly, catching his finger on a tiny splinter. Sucking his finger, he examined the nick in the polished wood. He knelt to eye level with the table and spotted a further two similar nicks in the edge. Strange, he thought. The baize itself also appeared to be stained, which was odd, given that this was a private room, and presumably infrequently used.

'If you gentlemen have seen enough, I have the club to run . . . As I said, Mr Palmer is not here.'

Frost stood up. 'You are correct, son. He is certainly not here. Thank you for your time. Be sure to give him my card and have him call me.' Frost reached inside his mac pocket, fingering all manner of unidentifiable objects but not the one he needed. 'Just have him call me – Frost at Eagle Lane. Tell him it's very important. Come on, John.'

*

Outside the Dirty Penguin Frost pulled a cigarette from the pack with his teeth and lit it. 'That last room,' he said finally. 'Did you smell anything?'

'Only the Scotch.'

'Other than the booze, I mean.' He took a long drag, the rain hissing at the cigarette. 'Did you pick up a vague hint of anything?'

'Nope.' Waters bent down to reach the flicker of Frost's lighter in the gloom. 'Amazed that hooter of yours can pick up anything, the amount you puff away.'

'Yeah, you might be right,' Frost conceded, 'but just for a second, while dopey was trying to find the light switch, I could have sworn I got a whiff of blood.'

Clarke had left Roberts in an Eagle Lane interview room while she attended to Drysdale at the lab. She'd decided she would let the secondary-school teacher go on condition she cooperated. Waters had briefed Clarke on the parallels with two other rape cases in the next county. Clarke believed that Roberts's indiscretion in the school toilet had unwittingly revealed a serial rapist. And now Roberts, having been shut in an interview room for three hours, had had enough time to realize the gravity of her situation. It was only half past six but the woman looked tired and pale.

'Tell me, Miss Roberts, do you know much about Terry Windley other than his prowess at making love in a confined space?'

Roberts didn't smile. Her mind, Clarke knew, was preoccupied with losing her teaching position, not to mention a possible conviction for wasting police time. Clarke stifled a yawn, feigning boredom and giving the impression that time was no object.

Roberts looked up. 'Not really,' she said, 'he's just fun. And fit – you know, athletic, teaches PE.'

'Do you know why he drifts from one post to another, not settling for anything permanent?'

'He's desperate for a full-time job,' Roberts replied, suddenly animated, 'but can't get one – he says all the jobs go to women. Says it's sexism in reverse. Terry gets really cross about it – makes me laugh when he loses his temper. Although he's well toned he's not a big man, and I can't take him seriously when he's angry.' A faint smile played on her lips.

'Really? Would he get angry enough to take revenge on women?'

The smiled disappeared. 'Oh, I don't know about that. Really, I don't.'

'Listen here, Miss Roberts.' Clarke leaned across the interview table, close enough to discern the other woman's foundation line. 'You want to keep your job and your good reputation, don't you? Do you realize how much trouble you could be in for what you've done?'

The woman nodded miserably.

'You help me and we will see what can be done. You hear?' Clarke had no authority to offer a deal like this and knew it, but this wasn't a formal interview – there were no witnesses. In all probability, if the press got hold of the story of Roberts's attempted deception a scandal would break out and she'd be finished. They both knew it, and Clarke was prepared to take advantage of this.

'Is there anything you could point to that's characteristic of Windley?'

'How do you mean?' She frowned.

'What he wears, for instance – shoes, or coat. A nice watch, maybe?'

'Not really. He's usually in a tracksuit at school. I haven't seen him that often out of school – and it's usually dark.'

'How about a wristwatch – he must have one, to keep track of lesson times – can you recall?'

'Wait a sec. He caught something climbing out of the window the other day – after we, you know . . .' she said, frowning.

'Try and think. As a PE teacher, was it a sports watch?'

The woman's eyes grew big. 'Yes, you're right, it was . . . I've seen it. Has a yellow strap.'

Bingo, Clarke thought. 'Right, Miss Roberts, we might be able to let you go home,' she said coolly. Relief washed over the other woman's face. 'Just one thing you can do for me before you leave.'

Back at home, the crashing reality of Simms's death struck Frost again. A colleague under his command had been killed on his very doorstep – he would get whoever did this if it was the last thing he ever did. As he went to answer the door, he reflected on how easy it would be for uniform, who'd been conducting the on-the-ground search for evidence, to miss something vital. The whole division was too overstretched to carry out investigations thoroughly.

Frost stood back to allow the plumber in, following him down the hallway. It was close to 7 p.m. He had missed the man that morning, having gone off to the filling station on the Lexton Road. He had tried to leave the key with his neighbour, but she'd been too spooked by Simms's murder and refused as politely as possible – even offering to take his washing in instead (a gesture he was too embarrassed to accept). So Frost had left a message on the plumber's answerphone saying he'd pay double if he called in again, this time later, at seven in the evening.

'Sorry about earlier,' Frost said. 'Got called away.' The man said nothing and marched through to the kitchen at the back of the house, his large toolbox bumping against the wall as he went. Frost padded down after him. 'Fancy a cup of tea?'

'I'll still have to charge you for the call-out twice,' the man said, ignoring his offer and staring at the kitchen floor, layered with sodden towels.

'That's all right,' Frost said, fumbling with the kettle. He felt uncomfortable letting a stranger into the untidy kitchen with its mountains of washing-up and beer cans mixed with cereal packets on the work surface.

'Two sugars.' The man had a big quiff, rockabilly style. In fact his general appearance – checked shirt, turned-up jeans, enormous metal belt – suggested more obsessive music fan than tradesman.

'You sure you're a plumber?' Frost asked uncertainly even as the sizeable toolbox was opened, and all manner of equipment was displayed.

'You sure you're a copper?' The plumber paused to roll a cigarette.

'I mean your attire.' Frost gestured.

'You're hardly out of *The Gentle Touch* standing there in a reindeer jumper and green trousers. More like something out of a grotto.'

'So I've been told. Had nothing clean. These trousers are for gardening, though I've never worn them for the purpose; unwanted Christmas present.'

'And the jumper was wanted?' The plumber grinned.

'A Christmas present from my wife.' Frost laughed in embarrassment; for the first time in his life his whole domestic situation struck him as laughable. He changed the subject. 'Yes, I'm sorry again not to have been here earlier; I expect you wondered where I'd got to.'

'Eh?' The man had slid the washing machine out and was looking disdainfully at the hoses. 'Wasn't there a copper killed around here over the weekend? I had an emergency callout not far from your road yesterday afternoon, and it was a nightmare trying to get through; it was all blocked off. And on top of it all, this bloody stupid woman in a sports car nearly ran me over while I was unloading. Though I wouldn't have minded a bit of a tussle with her, she was a right babe!'

'I'm sorry – babe in a sports car?' Frost's heart was in his throat.

'Yeah. Cute.' He heaved the machine back into place. 'In a Triumph.'

'Are you sure it was a Triumph?'

'Sure I am. I got an old TR3 in pieces in the garage, I'm doing it up.' He stood up and dusted off his hands, and then gestured at his outfit. 'Go on rallies, don't I.'

Clearly Frost was supposed to understand the connection between his attire and his hobby – needless to say, he didn't.

'What colour was her car?' he asked.

'Blue. It was a TR5 or maybe 4 – they're identical, except for under the bonnet.'

Frost had immediately suspected that it was Daley. 'Where?' he persisted.

'On the main road up from your place.'

She must have driven there on Saturday night. And waited. When she was surprised by the neighbour's boy she must have panicked and fled – preferring not to chance the time and noise involved in climbing into and starting the sports car. Thus she had returned to pick the car up the following day. Uniform would have checked for anomalies in Vincent Close, but were unlikely to check far beyond the street itself. He sighed.

'Cor, bleedin' hell, your drains pong – what you been eating?' the rockabilly plumber moaned.

'You may well ask,' he said, abstractedly. CID were already working on the principle she had panicked, and leaving the car behind would corroborate that – hence the search for a dropped weapon. All day yesterday men in uniform had been clambering through the dormant, carefully pruned rose bushes up and down the close. 'Hold on a sec. What did you just say?'

'Your drains. Pong something awful!'

They'd barely checked the street itself properly, let alone beneath it.

Monday (7)

'Have I missed all the action?' DC Hanlon asked, stepping into the glare of the arc light.

'Yes, Arthur, surprise, surprise.' Frost sniffed. It was a cold night to be standing in the street popping open manhole covers but it had been a swift and successful operation and Frost was in a jubilant mood. They had the murder weapon: a Second World War bayonet had been found resting on the ledge beneath the drain grate at the end of Frost's road. 'Where the bloody hell have you been? You only had to toddle over to Gentlemen's Walk.'

'Leave it out, Jack,' Hanlon sighed. 'The fog's not good for my condition.'

'Condition? What condition? I thought it was dodgy guts?' He patted his colleague's shoulder, which was damp. He watched two uniform slide a manhole cover back into the pavement, the grinding sound echoing through the quiet street. 'I know, I know, you don't feel well, poor thing – right, what did our Frenchman have to say for himself?'

'Couldn't find him.'

'What do you mean, you couldn't find him?' Frost asked.

'Shop was shut by the time I got there, so I tried the flat he's rented, across the square at Baron's Court. No answer. So I went back to the shop and spoke to a neighbour. She said she'd seen him and his friend leave at about half ten or eleven, and they've not come back.'

'Friend? What friend?'

'Some other Frog. Swarthy-looking, so the girl said.' Hanlon pulled out his notebook and glasses. 'Wait, here it is: *Gaston* . . . Can't read my own writing, something foreign – he's an accountant stroke business partner.'

'"Swarthy-looking"? What the bleedin' hell does that mean? Where did they go?'

'A little brown fella. Wears natty waistcoats. She didn't know where they went – some bloke turned up in an overcoat and they left with him.'

'OK, so the Frenchmen have just disappeared. *C'est la vie,*' Frost joked. As far as he was concerned they and Palmer were low priority now they had the weapon.

'Then I went over to Palmer's gaff, his farm,' Hanlon continued, 'only to be confronted with some oily butler who gave me the creeps, who didn't seem remotely concerned about where his master was.'

'Never mind, we can worry about missing snooker-club managers tomorrow. In the meantime, let's get a pint in.' Frost pulled out a five-pound note. 'On me – it's been a good day.'

Hanlon beamed. 'Wouldn't say no.'

'I thought you were ill?' Hanlon's face dropped. 'I'm pulling your leg, Arthur. Let's try my local.' He surveyed the close. There were lights on in every house, people curious to see what their oddball detective neighbour was up to. 'I doubt anyone will bother us.' Suddenly the large lamp overhead clicked dramatically off and they stood, blinking, adjusting to the half-glow of the street lights.

'After all the commotion you've caused round here they may not even serve you,' Hanlon said as they made off into the dark, misty night, nodding to the Forensics team dismantling the arc lights.

'Maybe they won't. And you know what, Arthur, it just might be time to move on.'

Clarke was satisfied with her handling of Marie Roberts, but she felt out of sync with her colleagues and very much on her own. She checked the incident room – empty – then wandered into the general office where the phone was ringing persistently. She flicked on the lights and picked up Simms's phone.

'Yes.' A caller wished to speak to Denton CID. 'This is Detective Clarke speaking.' A gruff male voice introduced himself as the desk sergeant at Rimmington. 'The missing persons case, go on.' Clarke nodded. She picked up a pen.

When Simms had put out a call for details on any

missing persons last Thursday Rimmington Division had not been able to help because of teething problems with their new computer system; basically, their records were up in the air – until now, it seemed.

'A woman reported her husband missing last Monday,' the Rimmington desk sergeant continued.

'Yes, go on.' Clarke was momentarily distracted by a young PC who entered and sat down at the opposite desk, facing Simms's old desk.

'Six two. Fair hair. Moustache. Name of Paul Game.'

'Really? Profession?'

'Accountant.'

'Oh.' Cigarette smoke drifted over from the uniformed visitor. Clarke gave a slight cough; her lapse on Sunday had added to her morning sickness in spades, now the merest sight of a cigarette made her insides churn. Less than a week ago she was on twenty a day. 'Accountant, eh?'

'Yes, but he was supposed to be at the qualifiers in Sheffield on Saturday, which was what caused the alarm.'

'Qualifiers, what's that? Accountancy exams?'

A laugh came from the other end. 'No, love, *snooker*. UK Snooker Championship at the Crucible, bloke fancied himself a bit. Was a regular at the Dirty Penguin, that's a club here in Rimmington.'

'Thank you, Sergeant.' Talk about fortuitous. She flicked open her pad to her notes taken at the lab earlier in the day on the remains dragged from the reservoir. 'I think there's a chance we may have found your accountant. Have you any further details?'

Clarke scribbled a few more scant notes and hung up.

'Hello, can I help you?' she said to the visitor in uniform opposite, who with his broad, moonish brow looked vaguely familiar.

'Hi, I'm David. David Simms.'

Tuesday (1)

'Well done,' commended Mullett. The station super-intendent had heard about last night's successful rummage in the Denton sewers and dashed in at the crack of dawn to meet Frost early – it was 7.30 a.m. He also knew that with this result he'd have to promote Frost without further delay. They had sufficient evidence to charge Louise Daley with shooting Baskin and his nephew, and the murder of DC Derek Simms. 'And the armed robbery of the payroll; you've not mentioned that – I assume you'll be charging Daley for that too?'

'Nah,' Frost grunted, 'not yet.'

'Excuse me? The same gun, yes?'

'Possibly.'

'Come on, man, that minder has since died of a coro-nary, can't you muster anything more than a shrug?'

'We can't be sure at this stage.'

'Why on earth not?'

'We haven't matched the bullets from the Gregory Leather shooting. Only the cartridge cases, which are from a nine millimetre—'

'Why not?' Mullett craned forward across the desk.

Frost shrugged. 'They went missing.'

'Missing? This is highly irregular.' Mullett was frowning heavily. 'Primary evidence can't just disappear.'

'I'm sure they'll turn up.'

'*Turn up?* Car keys or cigarette lighters turn up, not lead bullets from the scene of a crime.' Mullett reached for the phone. 'I'll call Harding – someone must be held to account . . .'

'No need, sir, I'm on it – the bullets should be on their way from Denton General, and Forensics officer Harding is out. In fact, he's on his way over to see me. We're pulling together a line-up for the payroll clerk to take a butcher's at.'

'But she was disguised as a pensioner.' Mullett grunted with disapproval at the lack of a conclusion; he had his press statement to prepare for later that afternoon, and it was vital that he had enough positive news. Daley might be in custody but there was still the rape – Winslow had been very specific about the rape.

'Enough of this' – he waved his hand vaguely, searching for the appropriate word – 'speculation. What of the rape at the school? And the girl outside the pub last Monday? We have a result there, I believe.' He pulled forward his notepad and plucked the cap from his Parker fountain pen.

'Sort of – the randy sod who shagged Marie Roberts

in the school loo is the knicker-sniffer who boshed Waters on the conk.'

'Are you saying the, err, intercourse at the school was consensual?' Mullett was sure that no other divisional commander had to suffer the same unseemly use of language from subordinates relaying case assessments.

'I am, sir. But we believe this same gentleman is connected with other cases, including the attack last Monday.'

'That's good. And do we have proof this man raped Joanne Daniels?'

'We have a lead. Miss Daniels has confirmed she knew him; he was a supply teacher in Rimmington six months ago, at the school where she works. And we think we might also have him for a rape in the West Country. And we also have an ID from a shopkeeper in Brick Road that confirms our man's been using the Brick Road call box.'

'Good,' Mullett said, capping the pen. 'It seems an arrest is imminent?'

'That's if he's not scarpered.' Frost lit another cigarette.

'How do you mean?'

'His tenure at Denton Comp finished on Friday. And you let him go, remember?' Frost leaned back in the chair, hands to the back of his head, as if stretching back in a deckchair on Brighton beach. He continued: 'Yes, according to Miss Roberts, his imminent departure was why they risked a bunk-up in the lavvy . . .'

Mullett was not going to rise to Frost's remark

concerning Waters' breach of procedure. 'Well, arrest him, then.'

'We don't know where he is. The address he gave the school is the flat he rented out to the students – you recall, sir, where he assaulted Sergeant Waters?'

'You'll find him.'

By the end of today this man was to hold the rank of Detective Inspector. Mullett knew he had no way out; the ACC would not tolerate any further delay. It may as well be now; his plan to bring Frost to heel by way of the new IRIS computer system was not going to happen any time soon – the new technology was proving as unreliable as the wayward detective.

'Are you going to keep that?' Mullett enquired, finally.

'What?' Frost said innocently.

'That beard.'

Frost scratched at his jaw. 'Hadn't thought about it, sir. Never trust a bloke with a beard is my rule . . . Why? Do you like it?'

'Do I . . . ? Heavens, no,' Mullett retorted. He looked down at the promotion letter that Miss Smith had typed up over the weekend and braced himself; and after an involuntary adjustment to his tie he began: 'Frost, as you know, Denton division has been a DI down for over a year. The Assistant Chief Constable very much feels, as do I, it's time to bring the division into line. Given the current staffing shortage and lack of experience across the force it is impractical to recruit from outside, leaving me no alternative but to promote from within.'

Here, Mullett paused; his very being was in revolt.

He looked across at Frost, whose attention appeared to be elsewhere. 'Frost, are you listening?'

'I was thinking about a shave, sir,' he replied, feeling under his chin.

Mullett couldn't bear it any longer. 'You are promoted to the rank of Detective Inspector, with immediate effect.'

Frost paused mid-scratch. 'Nice one. What's that work out at a month?'

'Miss Smith will fill you in on the particulars,' Mullett said sternly, 'and let me tell you, Frost, I have my reservations. Needs must, but I will be watching you like a hawk.'

'I'd be disappointed if it was any other way.' Frost smiled a bristly smile.

'Stand,' Mullett ordered, and standing himself, saluted and offered his hand. Frost stood straight for a change, receiving the handshake and adopting a serious air. 'Congratulations. That will be all. Keep me posted on further developments. Dismissed.'

Frost turned to leave.

'And that beard makes you look like a fisherman.' Mullett was reminded of the smug, unkempt know-it-all from *Jaws*; older perhaps, without the glasses but with the jumper. The superintendent felt a wave of relief; he had performed his duty. Now the burden had shifted.

'Why, thank you, sir,' Frost smiled. 'Talking of fish, a couple of anglers reeled in a snooker player in the Denton reservoir yesterday early afternoon.'

'Meaning? Do you mean a professional?'

'Well, he'll need to pull himself together if he's to stand a chance at the Crucible.'

Gibberish, as usual; Mullett tutted to himself as Frost yanked the door to behind him. To be expected; Frost would never change. So be it. And after all, Mullett had a division to run, and though he himself did not support Frost's move up he was sensible of the fact that Frost's promotion would give morale a boost following Simms's murder. Winslow was right about that if nothing else. For now, though, Mullett needed to turn his mind to the press conference.

Frost held the pathologist's report close to his face. He must get his eyes checked. Clarke had called him late the previous evening wanting to run through the 'jigsaw man' case. A poor pun on the body found in the reservoir and the surrounding fields.

'But isn't it a Rimmington division case – I mean, he was reported missing to them?' Clarke was fiddling with something in her hands, he noticed.

Frost sipped his scorching coffee. 'No, you're stuck with him, I'm afraid; we found the body. They'll work with us on it, I'm sure. Tell me again, why the delay in reporting the missing person to us?'

'A problem with transferring information on to the computer system, that's what the sergeant said.'

'Seems odd to me – wouldn't the wife be camping out on the doorstep, worried sick?'

'I guess – but she'd not reported him missing straight

away anyhow – it wasn't until the weekend when they were supposed to leave for a snooker championship in Sheffield that she grew concerned.'

'So he'd have been gone over a week; more like ten days, according to the path lab. Modern marriage for you.' Of course, in his day he himself had been known to 'slip away' for several days. Not a week, though. 'Odd that it took her that long.'

'Yes, if she loved him, but she might've been sick of the sight of him.' Clarke gave him a cold look.

'Only one way to find out – get over there and talk to her.'

She sighed. 'But I'm trying to sting Windley this morning – got to be at Brick Road at nine thirty.'

'It's only eight – you can get over to Rimmington and back before then. Early morning's always best; Game's wife might have a job – you'll catch her before she leaves.'

'I don't know where she lives. The desk sergeant didn't tell me.'

'*The desk sergeant didn't tell me.*' Frost mimicked cruelly. 'Oh, come off it, Sue – use the flaming phone book for a start; there can't be that many Games in there.'

'Right, so I turn up and tell her her husband was hacked to pieces and has been feeding the fish for the past ten days. Great start to her day.'

'Someone's got to do it – take a WPC. I'd come with you but I've got to write a crib sheet on Daley for Hornrim Harry, for his TV appearance later.'

'I want to see her,' Clarke said. Frost could detect the faintly concealed aggression in her voice.

'*No.*'

'But Jack . . .'

'No. And that's an order.' He looked her squarely in the eye. 'You have no reason to.' He knew no good would come of it. 'What's that you're fiddling with?'

Clarke held up a scrappy envelope. She tossed it at him and he narrowly caught it, clutching the packet to his chest. He squinted at the squiggles. 'Look inside,' she said.

'Where did you find it, under the bed?' Clarke coloured. 'Only joking. Get it over to the lab pronto – if you're going to Rimmington to see Mrs Game you can drop it off.'

Clarke frowned.

'Well, get a runner to take them over for you, then. Ahh, and here's one now.' A fresh-faced lad of about nineteen entered the room; he didn't look familiar. Perfect. 'Hello, son, you new?'

Clarke stood up. 'Jack, this is David. David Simms.'

'Oh, Simms? Any relation?'

'Brother. David came by yesterday. We had quite a chat. He's all up to speed on computers. And, interestingly, he was logging some house-to-house calls, pertaining to something Derek was—'

'Terrific.' Frost squirmed. He felt deeply uncomfortable. 'How about you do young Sue here a favour? We can talk about Space Invaders later, eh?'

Waters paid for the two coffees and nodded towards a free table in the Eagle Lane canteen. PC Simms took his lead, and the pair sat down. Waters noticed a table of young uniform heads turn at the new recruit sitting with a CID sergeant. Waters shook his head; surely those kids must understand a bit of decorum.

'Don't worry about that lot, they're just curious. Your brother was popular with those guys. It was only . . .' He was going to say it was only a year ago that Derek Simms was sitting among them still in uniform, but stopped himself, thinking it highlighted how young the kid had died. 'So was it by luck or design that you ended up here?'

'Bit of both, I guess.' The boy had an angry shaving rash, accentuating his youth. 'This part of the country is advanced in its use of computers – that's what I'm interested in, more than just as a hobby – so I'll be spending a bit of time collating and pulling together data from all sources.'

'Sounds fun.' Waters smiled. He was as cynical as Frost on technology matters but wanted to be encouraging.

'Yes, so much information is lost; take, for example, your day-to-day routine – or even theirs.' He indicated the crowd of PCs over his shoulder. 'Brief notes in pocket books, be it detailing first impressions from scenes of crime to routine enquiries – all can be used as courtroom evidence, but where else is the information held, outside of one of these?' By way of demonstration he slapped his own recently issued pristine notebook on the table.

'Superintendent Mullett is going to *love* you,' Waters said wryly.

'I've yet to meet the divisional commander, but he has quite a reputation.' Simms beamed.

'He has at that,' Waters confirmed.

'Tell me, Sergeant,' Simms said, suddenly earnest. 'You lived with my brother. Was he a good policeman?'

'One of the best,' Waters said, and then found himself starting to say again what only moments ago he had held back. 'See that crowd over there – your brother was better than all of them put together. He proved himself and moved on.' That satisfied the young policeman, allowing both men to talk at ease. Simms junior struck Waters as a bright, opinionated lad, without the chippiness his brother had often displayed; ambitious, but more suited to the science of police work than life on the streets. The young Simms explained that the way he saw police work evolving was through science, and that this was just the tip of the iceberg.

'I hear you,' Waters agreed, 'but someone has still got to catch these guys.' Suddenly the canteen hushed. Simms noticed it too; he darted a look over his shoulder. The immaculately pressed white shirt and the perfect Windsor knot, topped off with the manicured moustache: the superintendent had entered the room.

'What's up?' Simms said quietly.

'Nice chatting with you, David, but I gotta split.' He gulped the burning coffee. Waters' rendezvous with Clarke was pressing, and he didn't want to catch the super's eye.

*

DC Sue Clarke was out of sorts. For one, she wasn't sure about the logic of nicking Windley with Waters. Who knew what he might do when he saw his old adversary – lash out, or maybe freak and do a runner? Then there was the peculiar happening half an hour ago in Rimmington with the non-existent Mrs Game. Maybe she'd misheard what the sergeant had said last night. Her mind was a jumble. She could kick herself for flushing in front of Frost this morning, and then for standing by when he was rude to Derek's brother. Infuriating. And that bloody bullet. When tidying up this morning she had retrieved from under the bed a water glass which she'd knocked from her bedside table when answering the telephone on Sunday night. Behind the glass she'd found a used envelope containing a lead slug. The missing evidence from the Gregory Leather robbery must have slipped out of Simms's pocket on Friday night. Why he had it, heavens only knew. She had tried to see Frost first thing this morning, but he was in with Mullett – they had Daley for Simms's murder. Though Clarke had remained calm, Frost had refused her access to Derek's murderer – given half a chance she'd claw the woman's eyes out – but one thing at a time. She was currently sat with Waters outside a student flat on Brick Road waiting for Windley.

'I'm a bit worried about this,' Clarke said, shifting in the driver's seat of the unmarked Escort. Windley had yet to appear as scheduled.

'Don't worry, we'll get him,' Waters said. 'The girl will be safe. We're here.'

'What if he doesn't show?'

'He'll show.'

Suspected rapist Windley had yesterday evening given notice to his tenants – Clarke discovered this by chance when she called the letting agency to see if they knew where Windley lived (to which the answer was no, all written correspondence went through a PO box).

Windley had also requested access to the property today, which he was within his rights to do. Marie Roberts had said he'd been unsettlingly taciturn on the subject of the incident involving Waters on Sunday; Roberts now saw Windley in a different light and she feared he might exact revenge on the tenant, Laura, if he suspected she'd set him up.

'She's frightened. She should be at college. But she's too nervous to leave the flat,' explained Clarke.

They both looked up at the first-floor flat, where the young student stood at the window. She had been nervous throughout their earlier questioning. When Clarke and Waters had quizzed the student over contact with her landlord, she'd been edgy and not the confident young woman Waters had described on the way over – Clarke was expecting someone brash and cocky, but recent events had frightened her into submission. Clarke could imagine how the situation had changed in the girl's eyes: it's one thing to think your landlord is a bit of a perv, rooting around in your knicker drawer, something to laugh about with the girls maybe, but it's another thing for the man to then be questioned by the police about serious sex attacks. Clarke waved at the figure clutching the net curtain and wondered what went through these young girls' heads: as if it's normal for a grown man, a teacher no less, to be interested in teenage girls in that way in the first place?

'Here he is,' Waters said as a sky-blue Leyland Princess came into view.

But instead of slowing to a halt the car accelerated past them.

'Shit, he made us!' Waters exclaimed.

'Made *you*, you mean.' She started the car and turned the wheel aggressively. 'He's not getting away.' Waters picked up the radio and registered an alert.

The Princess swung a left out of Brick Road and hared off down Cromwell Road, leaving a cloud of black exhaust fumes hanging at the T-junction.

'Suspect heading east in a '79 light blue Princess. Registration—' Clarke spun the Escort round the corner after the Princess, cutting up a bus. 'Outta my way . . .'

'Whoa . . . we want to get him . . . where's your siren?'

'Haven't got one . . .' Windley had shot the lights ahead, causing a Granada to twist into the middle of the road. Clarke deftly dodged the car and sped after the Princess. Up ahead she could make out a removal van trying to pull a three-point turn in the road, leaving too narrow a gap for anyone to pass.

'He'll never get round that,' she said as the Princess mounted the pavement.

'You're right,' Waters agreed, 'there he goes.'

Clarke pulled up sharply behind the abandoned car.

Windley had vaulted a garden wall to get past his own vehicle.

'Quick little bugger,' Waters remarked.

'I'll catch him,' Clarke said, determined. 'You take the front of the van.' And with that she was off. Waters jumped out and rounded the Pickfords van. Clarke felt the blood pump at her temples; *I will have you*, she said to herself and channelled every ounce of her strength into the chase. Terry Windley now embodied every crime and ill she had recently experienced. The PE teacher was quick but lost ground by checking over his shoulder too frequently. Suddenly she was upon him and they both jolted painfully to the ground.

'Wow!' Waters said as he caught them seconds later. 'You are quick for—'

'For what? A *girl*?' Clarke snapped, looking up from the flower bed, flicking back hair from her forehead. But she was smiling.

Tuesday (2) _____

Charles rocked back and forth in the replica Gainsborough chair, tapping his fingers nervously on the briefcase. He tore his eyes away from the phone sitting on the bureau to glance at his wristwatch; still a minute to the hour.

Charles studied the card left by the policeman – *Detective Constable Arthur Hanlon* – resting against the phone. Hanlon? Wasn't he one of those drunken bores at the wake he'd been to with Brazier?

'Call them,' Gaston urged him, noticing his attention on the card. '*Now*. Before he rings.'

'What, give it all up?'

'The painting fell into your lap. Forget it – burn it with the money.'

'It's not the painting.' Charles stood up and paced the draughty attic. 'Don't you see, we'll be finished. Our reputation in tatters.' He sat back down despairingly and sighed. 'Never to work again.'

'But we'd be alive!'

At that moment the phone rang.

Gaston started to speak but Charles grabbed the receiver, which silenced him.

'Hello?' Charles asked tentatively.

'What's it to be, then?' Nicholson asked, his voice calm and controlled.

Charles clutched his forehead with indecision. The static of the telephone line hissed into his tense brain.

'C'mon, Charlie, you've had all night to sleep on it. The choice is simple: get me half a million for the horse painting or I drop those meat cleavers where they can be found – with your dabs all over them.' Charles heard him suck on a cigarette.

Charles stared at Gaston's dilated pupils. He didn't believe Nicholson for one minute; all right, the meat cleavers may have their fingerprints all over them, but Nicholson wouldn't settle for that – why would he? No, those 'dabs' would still be all over those handles with him and Gaston dead and out of the way, and not mincing about and disputing their participation in slicing up the big man.

'Agreed. We will pay you once the painting is sold on the black market.'

'I want two fifty thou – regardless of what you get for it. And don't think you two can stiff me and scarper across the Channel; I have friends in high places – Interpol will have your ugly mugs postered all over the Metro before you can say, Claude's your uncle. I'll be round your gaff in an hour to go over the small print.'

'Well?' Gaston looked at him expectantly as he replaced the receiver.

'He'll be here in an hour.'

'He's a psycho.' Gaston tapped the side of his head. 'He'll kill us; you know that. Call the policeman back – fob that madman off, appear cooperative, then let's get the hell out of here before he turns up.'

Madman was right. Nicholson, having flipped out at seeing the reservoir cordoned off the previous evening, had had the four of them lug Palmer's dismembered corpse just a short way into Denton Woods before he decided to simply toss the remains into the darkness. Yes, it was only a matter of hours before they were discovered. What Nicholson had done with the meat cleavers was of much more concern.

'Yes, I shall call the police now.' Charles agreed it was best to appear cooperative from the outset. 'Be ready to leave . . . We have everything?'

'*Oui*, the Citroën is carefully loaded,' he said quickly, meaning the Stubbs was secure. They must get away without further delay, given what they had witnessed the night before. Though was 'witness' the correct word? 'Accomplice' would be more accurate in the eyes of the law, and should they ever breathe a word to anyone, Nicholson would corroborate their involvement though conveniently omitting the fact there was a gun to their heads at the time.

Charles picked up the telephone receiver and dialled.

'Hello, may I speak with Detective Hanlon? My name is Charles Pierrejean.'

He smiled across at Gaston, with as much confidence as he could muster. He shivered at the chill in the empty attic.

'Good morning, Mr Pierrejean. Thank you for calling.'

'How may I be of service? I understand you called in.'

'We are making routine enquires – nothing to worry about. Would you mind popping into Eagle Lane police station?'

'I am afraid I have a very important business meeting scheduled, is it not something I can do over the phone?'

'I'm sure that will be fine.' A long pause ensued. Then: 'May I enquire what your connection is with Mr Palmer?'

'Most certainly – I am an antiques dealer. Mr Palmer is a collector.'

'What does he collect, anything in particular?'

'Yes, Mr Palmer has a fascinating collection of weapons.'

Frost tossed his promotion letter on to a heap of paper in the corner of his office. Promotion? He'd never given it much thought, and was reluctant to give it any serious consideration now – whichever way one looked at it, the move up was bound to be a double-edged sword. Politics came with promotion, that much he knew, and that was a game he could never play. The extra few bob meant nothing either; what with Mary no longer around to suck it out of him, what need did he have for money? The occasional history book and a takeaway from the

Jade Rabbit or Denton Tandoori was all he needed money for . . . He flopped down at his desk and pulled off a Post-it note from the blank computer screen. Frost had decided that the main purpose served by the new computer equipment was as a noticeboard; his screen was littered with half a dozen messages. Some in his own hand. One said *Solicitors Tues 10.15.* Flaming heck, he muttered – Mary's will. He looked at his wristwatch – he could still make it.

'Congrats, Jack. Well overdue.'

'Eh?' Frost looked up. 'Hello, Arthur, old son. How you feeling?'

'Still a bit off, but OK . . . So it's Detective Inspector at last, eh?' Hanlon smiled warmly, making himself comfy in the visitor's chair of the cramped office. 'Would love to have seen Mullett deliver that one – did you know it was coming?'

Frost lit a cigarette, and rubbed his cheek – Mullett's mention of his beard had caused him to become pre-occupied with it, and it was irritating the hell out of him. 'Promotion? No idea whatsoever. Hard to believe, but I'm not his favourite in CID, Arthur.'

'That you're not; but it's long overdue – well done him, I say, for finally recognizing what was rightfully yours.'

'I don't know about that – call me cynical, but I just can't imagine Hornrim Harry sitting in his lair thinking that. Anyway, what you got?'

'Got hold of the French chap. He called up.'

'Good. And what did he say?' Frost had all but

forgotten about the Frenchman entangled with Daley, so much had taken place in the last twenty-four hours.

'You were right.' Hanlon pulled from his pocket a squashed pasty and started delicately tearing the packaging.

'Right about what?'

'We did meet him at your missus's funeral.' He took a bite. 'We had a right natter now I remember, about the footie . . .'

'I don't give a monkey's fanny about the flaming football, where the hell was he on Saturday night?' Maybe it wasn't such a surprise he'd been promoted after all, Frost thought, given the dimwits surrounding him.

'Where you said – at Palmer's for dinner. With the girl.'

'Right. Has he made a statement?'

'No, he had business to attend to. He'll be in tomorrow.'

'Good, make sure he is – I want a chat about something else too. But that can wait. There's enough going on for now but we'll need a statement at some point. Now give me a bite of that. Daley was seen collecting her motor near mine, and we have the weapon, though where she picked up that antique bayonet God alone knows – she won't say a word.' Frost passed the pasty back.

'Palmer's, I'd guess.'

'What?'

'The French gent said Pumpy collects antique weapons.'

'Are you sure?' Frost said, surprised. 'I thought his interest was strictly shotguns and the like?'

'That's what he said,' Hanlon said confidently.

Frost sat back in astonishment. 'Why the bloody hell didn't you say so? Obviously Daley snatched it from there, meaning she was where she says she was; and Palmer does know her.'

'Week's shaping up pretty well,' said Waters, rubbing his hands together as he entered the CID general office. Clarke trailed behind him, head down. 'What next, *Inspector*?' Waters added, giving him a mock salute.

'Don't you start.' Frost cuffed him round the back of the head. 'Windley banged up?' he said, addressing nobody in particular.

'Tried to do a runner – but Ms Clarke here wrestled him to the ground.' Waters beamed.

'Really?' Frost raised an eyebrow at Clarke, looking trim in a tight trouser suit, but she didn't wear the demeanour of a victor. 'You're right, John, with a clean-up rate like this, we'll be able to take the rest of the week off.' The phone interrupted Frost with what seemed like intent. 'Frost here.' A young Forensics officer informed him that the lead bullet deposited at the lab earlier that morning did not match Louise Daley's gun. 'You're sure?'

'The striation marks aren't consistent with the barrel,' the young man replied.

Frost hung up the phone. 'The lead found at the pay-roll robbery doesn't match the gun found in Daley's car.'

'You didn't think it was her, did you, Jack?' Waters said.

'I did at first,' Frost confessed, 'but then I started to have doubts. This confirms it.'

'Something else is odd,' Clarke announced abruptly, closing her notebook.

Frost looked over at her. 'Yes?'

'You know you told me to check in on Paul Game's wife? The man we fished out in pieces from the reservoir yesterday.'

'Yes, love, it was only this morning.'

'He's not married.'

'I beg your pardon?' Frost said quickly.

'I said, he's not married – there is no wife,' Clarke repeated.

'But Rimmington police said it was *his wife* who reported him missing,' Frost said, incredulous.

'Yes, it is what they said – I just checked my notes.'

'You must have the wrong Game.'

'There were only two in the phone book.'

'Jesus!' Frost cursed. 'I didn't say take the telephone directory as gospel – he might be ex-directory.'

'I have the right man, Jack.' The colour started to rise in Clarke's cheeks. 'Stop snapping at me and hear me out, will you?' she stormed.

Frost backed down. 'All right, all right. Tell me.'

'There were two Games in the phone book. One of them *P*. Address: 15a Beasley Street, a nice row of modern terraced houses in Rimmington. No answer when I knocked, so I knocked all the harder – having hiked all the way over there. A housewife eventually poked her head out from next door to see what the commotion was. She confirmed that our Game lived there – or had – a blond bachelor in his twenties. And that she'd not seen him in nearly a fortnight, but didn't think it strange, assumed he was on holiday and had forgotten to cancel the milk. Confirmed he was an accountant, and that he played competitive snooker.'

'Right,' said Frost. 'Let's recap the call you picked up last night; what exactly did this helpful desk sergeant say?'

'He said that Game's wife had reported him missing a week ago – last Monday – but the records were all over the place due to their computerization. He'd been missing a few days, but she didn't get concerned until the weekend because of some snooker tournament.' This was exactly as she'd told him not two hours ago. Somebody was feeding them information: Frost knew of such instances where one police division would slip the neighbouring force a suspect. Usually, the suspect would have had dubious connections with the local plod, but for some reason the relationship had soured and the police wanted to sever the connection and have their man dealt with at arm's length. Clarke's call smacked of this; the only problem was the name they'd slipped them was a dead man's.

'And what was the desk sergeant's name?' Frost asked.

'He didn't give his name.'

'You didn't take his name?' Frost quizzed, annoyed.

Clarke ignored him.

'What do you think?' Frost shot a look at Waters.

'Something ain't right. That's for sure.'

'Somebody wanted us to know jigsaw man's identity – but probably not the Rimmington desk sergeant—'

'Just a second,' Clarke snapped defensively. 'He knew that Simms had called last week, and was aware of the computerization – he had to be a copper.'

'I don't doubt he was a copper, but probably not who he claimed to be,' Frost said. 'Or perhaps the desk sergeant was just the messenger boy. But there's more to it than that – they've identified the body, but fed us duff information too—'

'*Dis*information, like the KGB,' Waters interrupted, 'telling you something that's true – that a man is missing – and something that's not true, that the man is married and his wife reported him missing. Easy enough to verify: the man who told you the lie about the wife knew you would find out immediately.'

'Why?' Clarke frowned. 'I don't get it. I know Brezhnev just died, but stop me if I'm wrong, I didn't think the new guy in the Kremlin had extended the Cold War to Denton?' She went to pick up the phone.

Frost placed his hand over hers, preventing her from picking up the receiver. 'There's no point phoning Rimmington – what else did they tell you?'

'Jack's right,' Waters said. 'What else did he say? There'll be a meaning to everything.'

'That Game played snooker at the Dirty Penguin.'

'Right you two, get over to the Penguin. Check with

the club records – find out when Game last played there. And give Palmer a slap – he still hasn't returned our calls.'

'Are you going to call Kelsey?' Waters asked.

If anyone knew what lay behind the mystery of Game's disappearance, it would be him. Frost recalled the Rimmington superintendent telephoning the evening after Baskin got shot. Was there more to that call than met the eye? Nevertheless, calling Kelsey would be easy and something Frost wasn't prepared to do just yet. Not until he knew more, rather than be at the mercy of the senior man at Rimmington.

'No.' Frost pulled his mac from the back of the chair.

'Where are *you* going, then?' Clarke asked.

'Solicitors. Should have been there ten minutes ago.'

Tuesday (3)

Mullett's office door opened and in slouched the heavy figure of Detective Constable Arthur Hanlon. The station superintendent sighed; he didn't have time for this nonsense, he really didn't. He had the press conference at noon. He gestured to Hanlon to take a seat.

Mullett had pondered the importance of a Masonic connection long and hard; and if honest with himself, he'd lost more sleep over this issue than anything else. Neither Frost's promotion, nor even the remote (and he had convinced himself it *was* remote) possibility that his wife had knocked down a paperboy had troubled him as much. Joining the Masons seemed vital to entering the higher Denton echelons, but as soon as Hanlon came into view, Mullett's sense of propriety was confounded: that such a sad, even laughable specimen of a detective could hold a position of power in any organization seemed immoral and blatantly unfair. No, Mullett decided, he was not going to put Bill Wells forward for promotion, as Hanlon proposed, to unlock the door to a secret society – he couldn't live with compromise of this magnitude. If, of course, Mrs M found herself in difficulty with a driving offence and help was required then he might reconsider, but for now the disservice to the force was too great a burden.

'Funny you calling me in – I was hoping we might get a moment.'

'Were you indeed?' Mullett smiled through gritted teeth at the puffed-up detective. The use of *we* grated like fingernails down a chalkboard. 'Now look – I've given this an incredible amount of thought, but—'

Hanlon held up his hand and looked to the door, to ensure that they wouldn't be taken by surprise. 'Say no more, Super,' he said, leaning forward.

'I'm sorry?' Mullett frowned.

'You're in,' Hanlon said in a whisper.

'"In"?'

Hanlon tapped the side of his nose, then sat back in the visitor's chair. 'Yes – promoting Jack.' He beamed. 'It's all about helping your mates – it was beyond our wildest dreams you'd give Jack a leg up, so we thought we'd work you for Bill Wells, instead. Welcome aboard.'

Hanlon offered his hand, which Mullett took, speechless.

Frost turned his back on the grubby solicitors' office just off Market Square, and on the Simpson family, who wandered down the cobbled street in the opposite direction. When would he next see them, he wondered, if ever? Not that he cared, given the news he'd just received. Bastards – the whole lot of them. Still, he wasn't going to dwell on that problem just yet.

He lit a cigarette and instead thought about the jigsaw man case and the connection to Rimmington station. A dead accountant found in a reservoir, and the only thing they knew about him was he played snooker at the Dirty Penguin. That snippet of real information had been fed to them along with the misinformation that the man was married – therefore Frost reasoned that the Penguin itself must be significant. What vital clue was he missing? Palmer and the Penguin . . . Palmer also knew the woman who had shot Harry Baskin. What was Harry Baskin mixed up in? Baskin had dismissed any likelihood that Palmer would shoot him – not that sort of man, and so on – but everything was starting to point that way because of the Daley–Palmer connection. Which meant what? They'd underestimated Palmer? Frost had already told Waters to put pressure on Palmer – for harbouring Daley, a wanted criminal – now they'd really have to squeeze him for all he was worth. And he'd have to see Harry again as soon as possible.

Clarke looked abstractedly around at the opulent surroundings while Waters waited patiently for Nicholson to get off the telephone. They were, he assumed, in Palmer's office. These guys were a cut above Baskin and his mob. And the Penguin was somewhat posher than the snooker halls Waters was used to in London's East End.

Palmer was still apparently absent and Nicholson, his real number two, was in his boss's chair. Nicholson, a lean, hard-faced man, was a familiar type to Waters, a cool customer who seldom spoke, and tough. Frost hadn't liked him from the start, and Waters could understand why – he was in a different league to the usual Denton no-goods. Frost was reserved when faced with the unfamiliar.

'I'm sorry about that.' Nicholson replaced the receiver. 'Business. You after Marty?'

Waters nodded.

'Me too,' he said, spreading paperwork across the desk, whether to signal the end of the conversation or to affect nonchalance, Waters wasn't sure. Nicholson sipped from a glass of water, then after a silence added, 'May I ask what you want with him? Maybe I can help?'

'This Palmer's office?' Waters asked, ignoring the question.

'Yes.' He joined his hands in a priest-like manner, as if waiting patiently.

'He mind you going through his drawers?'

Nicholson removed his glasses. 'The business has to run. With Mr Palmer unaccounted for, I have no alternative.' He said it slowly, with a flicker of what might have been a smile.

'You seem unconcerned. Does Mr Palmer often disappear without leaving any word?'

436

'I'm not his keeper, am I?' Nicholson sighed. 'Last I heard, he was off shooting.'

'Shooting?'

'Yeah, shooting birds. Pheasants.' Waters knew Pumpy had a passion for blasting anything that moved on his farm, in line with his aspirations to be a country gent. 'That time of year, ain't it?'

'I wouldn't know. Do you partake?'

'No, I don't. We don't mix socially.'

'When was the last time you saw him?'

'Friday.'

'So you didn't dine with him Saturday night?'

'"Dine with him"?' Nicholson sneered. 'Forgive me, Officer, but are you listening to me? I last saw him Friday and I don't socialize with him. Get it?'

Waters was unfazed by the barely disguised aggression; he was trying to slowly draw the man out from behind the tinted lenses. Attempting to bully such a character wouldn't work; irritating and teasing him might prove more successful than heavy-duty tactics. Waters jotted down a line in his notebook. 'You're absolutely sure?'

'Are you trying to wind me up? Wait—' Nicholson, on the verge of losing his rag, suddenly calmed down. 'This in connection with Baskin getting shot?'

'What do you think it might be to do with?'

'Ha ha, you might be smart in Denton, Sergeant, but this is Rimmington. Superintendent Kelsey knows we're not trouble.'

What was that, Waters wondered – an allusion to

police protection? 'OK, say it is Baskin we're concerned with . . .' Waters felt there was no need to mention Daley; Nicholson might tip Palmer off and they'd never get to the club owner himself.

'Right. There was one of your lot here Friday, asking questions. You think something's happened to Marty? Like what happened to Harry?'

'The sooner we find him, the sooner we'll know he's OK,' Waters said diplomatically.

'I see.' Nicholson rocked back in his boss's chair, thoughtfully. 'Excuse my firing off there.' He smiled. 'Nobody likes to be harassed by the old bill, especially when they're busy. Look, you might want to tap up these French geezers Marty's taken a shine to.'

'Frenchmen, in Denton?' Waters said in mock surprise. 'Have you a description?'

'They run an antiques shop in Gentlemen's Walk, right pair of dandies.'

Waters was struck by a contradiction; if Nicholson didn't socialize with Palmer, how would he know he kept company with a pair of French antiques dealers, or know where the store was? 'OK, we'll check them out. Sue?' He turned to Clarke who'd remained quiet. 'You have a few questions for Mr Nicholson.'

'We're also enquiring about a member of your club – one Paul Game?'

Waters saw Nicholson's right eye twitch ever so slightly. 'Doesn't ring any bells.'

'Can you check whether Game was a member? And if so, when he was last here. It would be a big help.'

'Of course.' He picked up the phone and called the front desk. 'What did you say the name was again?' Nicholson muttered into the phone, then looked at Clarke. 'Been a naughty boy, has he?'

'You might say that,' cut in Waters. 'We want him to help us with our enquiries.'

Nicholson replaced the receiver. 'Yeah, we have a Game on the books.'

'But not a regular player, then?' Clarke asked.

'How d'you mean?' Nicholson smiled broadly, displaying badly stained teeth.

'If you don't recognize the name.'

'I can't see who's playing from sitting here, can I, dear?' he said sharply.

'It's not your desk, remember?' Clarke said, getting up. 'Besides, there's the mirrored glass.' She wandered over to the far wall. Nicholson's gaze pivoted round to follow her.

Waters kept his eye on Nicholson. 'You didn't ask when Game last played here.'

'Huh?' Nicholson grunted, watching Clarke at the plate glass.

'I said, you didn't ask the front desk when he last played.'

Nicholson stood up aggressively. 'Well, you're welcome to check the register on your way out.'

Waters flicked through the Dirty Penguin log book; all manner of barely legible scrawl affronted his vision. He began to wonder whether holding a cue precluded you from holding a pen. The 'PRINT YOUR NAME' column was nothing but a collection of smudges and stains.

Waters had to marshal his feelings: Nicholson was a wrong 'un; he smelt bad – Waters was streetwise enough to know this, and what's more, Nicholson knew he knew.

'John, over here,' Clarke called from the rear wall. The foyer was like a hall of mirrors, apart from the back wall, which featured free-standing trophy cabinets. Waters joined Clarke, who was peering at a team photo.

'Check this guy out.'

'Looks miserable there too,' Waters said, recognizing Nicholson standing at the edge, holding a cue.

'Not him; the blond guy next to him.'

'It's not – surely?' And then he read the caption beneath the photo.

Tuesday (4)

'Louise Daley?'

'Yeah – used to work for you a few years ago.'

Baskin frowned, and pushed the noxious lunch tray to one side, unfinished. 'Nah, doesn't ring a bell. So many sorts tramp through the Grove, be hard pushed to remember them all.'

Frost shifted in the visitor's chair to avoid the sharp sunlight piercing the blinds behind the hospital bed. 'She was mixed up in that spate of bank robberies about a year ago.'

'Oh, yeah!' he said excitedly, then broke into a violent coughing fit and beat his chest with a club of a fist. 'Bleedin' nurses – if they didn't confiscate me fags I wouldn't have this cough. Sorry, yeah, I remember Louise; smart. Too smart to be getting her kit off for the likes of me.'

'Quite,' Frost agreed. 'Did you treat her roughly?'

'Eh?'

'You know, knock her around a bit.'

'Most certainly not!' Baskin protested vehemently, as Frost sat back, fearing another coughing fit. 'What do you take me for!'

'Sorry, Harry, had to ask.' Frost grimaced. 'Well, there must be a reason for her to take a pop at you?'

Baskin shrugged. Frost continued: 'Daley is pals with Palmer; the most obvious suggestion is that Palmer paid her to bump you off. Are you sure he didn't have a reason to nobble you?'

'Nah, can't think of anything.'

'What about that warehouse you tipped me off on – that wasn't something to do with Palmer? You know, where you reckoned stolen electricals were being stored?'

'Nah; told you – I got no beef with Marty, and would never rat on him. Got a low opinion of me, eh?' The wounded man looked hurt. 'The Pumpster was in 'ere only yesterday as it 'appens. Nice of him to pop by.'

'What did he say?'

'Not a lot. Come to think of it, he was a bit subdued.'

'Maybe he's worried it might be him next.'

'Maybe. But I don't think it was him that done it, as I said.' Baskin sniffed.

'All right, Harry, just trying to piece things together,' Frost said. 'What was the deal on the warehouse out at Rainham, anyway? I got that tip from you. Palmer owns that warehouse.'

'Err . . . Does he? But it's nothing to do with Pumpy;

apart from the snooker. The tip came from an accountant.'

'An accountant? Snooker? What about snooker?' Frost leaned forward excitedly.

'An accountant who was working for one of the big electrical stores. Game, his name is. Paul Game. Told me there was gear leaving his store for this old place out by Rainham. Someone was "leaving the door open" as it were, making it easy to have it away with stuff.'

'Why'd he tell you?'

'He was drunk at the Coconut Grove one night and told me and Rachel that these guys he'd met at the Dirty Penguin were strong-arming him to half-inch stuff out of his own store. But it was getting a bit much for him.'

'Sorry, you've lost me – "a bit much"?'

'They were making too many demands on him – getting him to nick more and more gear.'

'But we staked the place out and saw bugger all.'

'Maybe they knew you were on to them. Like my flowers?' Baskin said, changing the subject and indicating the bouquet on the table, arranged in a vase. 'Missus brought me them.'

'Lilies,' Frost pointed out. 'Maybe the wife wasn't expecting you out.'

Silence descended on the small hospital room.

'Harry, why didn't you tell me all this before?' Frost resumed eventually.

'I didn't see it as relevant. The accountant wasn't going to take a pot-shot at me.'

Frost suddenly twigged. 'So you offered to help the

accountant out. By snitching a leak to me. And what's in it for you?'

Harry sighed. 'The retailer in question is out on the Lexton Road – Rumbelows.'

'Which happens to back on to the fields not a million miles from the Coconut Grove. Let me guess: you said to him, Slip me a few VCRs out the back and I'll help you out in return. Meaning, you pocket the goods and tip me off about Rainham, stitching the guy up?'

'I didn't see it quite like that, Jack. I didn't stitch the guy up; we agreed you'd come back to me if you found anything, before making an arrest. It was covert.' Harry started coughing in earnest.

It was weeks ago and Frost could barely remember, though it sounded plausible. 'Maybe.' He fetched his cigarettes out of his mac, took one himself and tossed one on to the bed. 'You said "they". Who are "they"?'

'Nobody I'd heard of or remembered. Some fellas he met playing snooker. Small beer.'

'You sure it wasn't Palmer himself?'

'I told you, his name never came up.'

'And where is this accountant now?' Frost asked, though already knowing the man's fate.

'Gone to ground – reckon someone put the frighteners on him.'

'So he's a bleedin' liar,' Frost said crossly. 'Why didn't you haul him in?'

'On what grounds?' Waters countered, unsure why Frost was so angry he'd not arrested Nicholson. 'Might

444

as well wait until we have something more substantial, after we've checked out these French dudes. Why are you so crotchety? Things are going well.'

'Solicitor put me in a bad mood.'

'Anything you want to talk about?'

'Nope.'

Waters could see something was up, but if Frost didn't want to talk he couldn't make him. 'Well, I'll head over to Gentlemen's Walk, then—'

'Wait.' Frost stood up. 'We have grounds.'

Waters stopped in his tracks.

'We have grounds to pull in Nicholson, I mean. Remember last week Clarke was staking out that warehouse at Rainham – nicked VCRs and the like?'

Clarke looked up from her paperwork.

'Yep – she saw fuck all, bit like me and my phone-box monitoring on Brick Road.'

'*She?* I am in the room.'

Frost smiled wanly. 'The gear came from a bean counter at the Rumbelows superstore on the Lexton Road. The bean counter is none other than one Paul Game.'

'You're kidding.'

'Game got himself in too deep dealing with some blokes he met at the Dirty Penguin; but it wasn't Palmer – Harry confirmed that much. There's every chance this Nicholson character is behind it.'

Clarke drove the new Sierra fiercely down the narrow country lane. The jubilation she'd experienced knocking

Windley to the ground had passed as briefly as the moment itself; now on their way to a warehouse in the middle of nowhere that she'd already spent several cold nights watching she felt nothing but an irrepressible anger.

'What's up with you?' she snapped at Frost, who was slumped in the passenger seat staring disinterestedly out of the window. Usually he'd be ticking her off about her erratic driving.

'I'm in a reflective mood.'

'That's a new one; privilege of rank, is it?' They'd hardly spoken since their session in the pub on Sunday night. He'd not mentioned his promotion and she'd not congratulated him. Her disappointment at his apparent indifference to her personal situation in the light of Simms's death had been held at bay whilst dealing with the onslaught at Eagle Lane, but now, out of the station and in close proximity to each other, she felt it rise to the surface. He offered her nothing more, which niggled her further. 'I can't imagine what such a mood might reveal.'

'Eh? Oh, nothing.' He snapped out of his reverie as though suddenly realizing where he was.

'Come off it, Jack. What are you going to do?' She swerved to miss a cyclist; the lanes were as hazardous during the day as they were at night. 'I mean, more importantly, what am *I* going to do?'

'Do?'

'Yes, *do*. With Derek gone and this baby . . .'

'I see. Now is hardly the time. Hey – slow down.'

Frost craned forward, clutching the dashboard. 'Down here. Park up. We don't want to lose the element of surprise.'

The warehouse itself was screened off by a wall of conifers, the roof just peeking above the trees. Clarke wrenched on the stiff new handbrake. 'How many times have I heard that,' she sighed. 'For starters, that poky little flat of mine isn't a fit place to raise a child; not enough room to swing a cat, no garden . . .'

'Don't look at me.' Frost opened the door gently, his attention on the warehouse. 'I'm homeless; the old harpy of a mother-in-law is selling the house.'

'What?' Clarke hissed, but Frost shushed her.

DS John Waters strolled up Gentlemen's Walk at a swift pace. A chilly autumn wind funnelled forcefully down the narrow pedestrianized street. Hanlon had spoken to Charles Something-or-Other this morning; Waters reckoned he'd been fobbed off – especially now, subsequent to their bracing chat with Nicholson. He knew where Avalon Antiques was situated: between tatty little Keith's Records, which he loved to browse in when he had a spare moment, and Tile's the Bookmakers, which he also visited from time to time, and usually left the poorer as a result of one of Sergeant Wells's 'hot' racing tips. He remembered the antiques place opening and although he welcomed the new lease of life – the premises having been boarded up for six months after the previous occupants went bust – he had been surprised. The shops in that row were cramped inside – not ideal for housing large items of furniture. Still, what did he know about antiques? He pushed open the door, which set off a tinkling bell.

A young girl hurried to greet him, leaving an elderly couple mulling over a bureau.

'Police?' she asked anxiously.

'That obvious, huh?'

'Well, you don't look like you'd be interested in Queen Anne furniture.'

'What, because I'm black?'

Her face fell, and panic spread across her features. 'I didn't mean . . . No, I, err . . . what I thought . . .'

'I'm joking.' He pulled out his ID to reassure her.

'Me too, sorry.' She breathed a sigh of relief. 'I meant the police have been in here quite a lot lately.'

'How do you mean?'

'There was the armed robbery, for one.' She pointed at the artist's impression Sellotaped to the window. 'And a chap called only this morning . . . and there was this other man . . .'

Waters could see the girl was flustered. 'Mr Pierre-jean around?'

'No, they've left.'

'Left? What, for the day?'

'Charles said they were going for a long weekend – the car looked full.'

'"Long weekend"? It's Tuesday lunchtime! Can you describe these gentlemen for me, miss?'

Waters listened as the woman explained all about her two employers – one white with slicked-back hair, the other a fussy dresser of North African descent – how she had come into contact with them, the interview, and her thrill of working for sophisticated foreigners, who knew 'simply everything' about antiques.

'They sound charming,' Waters replied. 'Tell me, how were they when they left?'

'How were they?'

'Yeah, you know, what sort of mood were they in?'

The girl pulled at her bottom lip nervously. 'Very anxious. Very, very anxious. About what, I couldn't say . . .'

'Business not going well?'

'As far as I'm aware, business is not great. We've hardly sold a thing.' She glanced over at the couple in their seventies whose attention had now turned from the Victorian bureau to the intimidating presence of Denton's only black man. 'When I asked were they off with the police again they said no, they were going to view a house sale in Lexton.'

'Whoa there, "off with the police"? When was this?'

'Yesterday. A tall, bald man in an overcoat came and escorted them off. I think it was him that telephoned, just before they rushed off today.'

'Are you sure he was a policeman?'

'He didn't say he was a policeman, no; it was his bearing and his manner . . .'

'Can you describe him in any more detail? Did he wear steel-framed specs, for instance?'

'Yes, he did, with tinted lenses – is he a colleague of yours?'

'Not really; can you remember any details of the conversation you overheard—'

The doorbell went behind them. A breathless uniformed officer entered, tipped his helmet and said, 'Ah, Sergeant Waters, Control said we might find you here.'

Waters looked to the girl and said, 'You're right – the police do have a liking for this place. Yes, Constable?'

'You are required urgently.'

'What for?'

'Not in front of the young lady.'

Waters excused himself and stepped outside with the bobby. 'What's up?'

'A body has been found – hacked to pieces – in Denton Woods.'

The wipers were at full tilt. It seemed to Charles that the strained pulsing of the Citroën's windscreen blades matched the pounding of his anxious heart. The situation was hopelessly out of control.

Nicholson had telephoned the Frenchmen immediately after he'd got a visit from Denton CID. He was seething with anger, even throwing the phone receiver to the floor mid-conversation. After enduring a full minute of ranting, cursing and phone abuse Charles had the gist of the argument: Nicholson could not understand why the police were on to Palmer's disappearance so soon, and the only explanation was that someone had ratted on him, *him* in particular. In short, he believed Charles and Gaston had put the police on his trail.

Charles had asked what the police had actually said, which triggered another string of expletives, from which he deduced that one detective had been black and the other female, although these weren't quite the terms Nicholson had used. His suspicions were aroused because the policeman didn't say *why* he wanted Palmer, just that he was wanted in connection with their enquiries. Nicholson kept mentioning some fellow called Baskin, who Charles recalled vaguely from the conversation over supper on Saturday night, and another called Game (the latter Charles had never heard of). Thinking of the dinner party, Charles then suggested tentatively it might be in connection with Daley's arrest. This was news to Nicholson, and the villain burst into frightening and seemingly uncontrollable laughter. Anyway, the deal was off; Nicholson was going to drop the murder weapons in the centre of town, and wished them both luck. It was at this moment Charles's decision was made to leave the country. They were driving out of Denton and heading west with the Stubbs painting, removed from its frame, hidden above the Citroën's roof lining.

Gaston asked for the umpteenth time, 'What was it he said again?'

Charles sighed. 'He said: "Miss Daley, yes. Well, she may be guilty of many things, stupidity being one of them. But she won't be the one Denton police will be after for Marty. See you soon, boys!" Then he hung up.'

'Can't you drive this crapheap any faster?' Gaston urged anxiously.

'Yes, yes . . . Fear not, they won't come this way look-ing for us – they'll expect us to head for the South Coast and France.'

'I curse the day we ever came to this piss-drenched excuse for a country,' Gaston muttered, frowning at the road atlas on his lap. 'What on earth is this place – *Fishguard*?'

France was out of the question for now. It would be the first place the police would go looking. It was a ferry from Wales and then a spell in Ireland for them, staying with Charles's sister. *Ireland*. Charles sighed. It might be a bleak godforsaken bogland peopled with half-drunk peasants gabbling away in a peculiar, impenetra-ble dialect, but at least they were to be lauded for their fierce hatred of the English.

Tuesday (5)

Frost poked his head gingerly round the trees.

'That's Nicholson's motor, all right,' he said, having spied a black Mercedes alongside a white van.

'It's a bit out of the way,' Clarke said, concerned. She should know, the amount of time she'd spent out here, just her and a bored technical surveillance officer. 'Don't you think we should call for back-up?'

'Probably.' She might be right. Frost was surprised to find Nicholson here – Waters had described him as cocky to the point of insulting, which Frost recognized as the manner of one who considered himself above suspicion. However, perhaps his bravado was a bluff, even the pointed reference to Kelsey. If Nicholson was guilty of Game's disappearance and he knew the police had discovered he was missing, of course he'd scarper down to clear the warehouse. Frost saw he'd been foolish to think he could just casually mosey on down here – the solicitor's this morning must've scrambled his thinking. Everything pointed to this being one dangerous individual; Frost felt very uneasy.

A woman appeared, bustling backwards out of a side door with a stack of white cardboard boxes. She was about thirty feet away from where they stood behind the trees. She made for the Mercedes.

'Who's that?' Clarke whispered.

'No idea.'

'Are you sure that's Nicholson's car?'

'A black Mercedes is a black Mercedes,' he replied quietly. Judging from the printed labels, the boxes contained VCRs. The woman loaded them into the car and opened the driver's door.

'Might as well make a move, before she drives off.'

'Wait!' Frost hissed as Clarke moved forward and into the woman's view. She had not got into the car, but instead had retrieved something from the door pocket. She pushed the car door to, and confronted Clarke as she pulled her badge from her sheepskin. Frost hesitated, wondering whether to reveal himself, then stepped back as the woman called out to someone behind her.

A tall man appeared from behind the white van, dusting off his hands. Nicholson. Frost could see Clarke flinch. *Don't look for me*, he mouthed. She didn't. The man approached Clarke slowly, all the while scrutinizing the surroundings, looking for her partner. Frost hunkered down in the undergrowth. Nicholson stopped only inches from Clarke – she held her badge high, but he ignored the ID and instead gripped her wrist and twisted her arm tightly behind her back. Clarke buckled and fell to the ground. Frost winced and turned away, his cheek touching cold grass. *Think, think*, he urged himself. If he rushed in he might never find out the pair's intentions – and possibly put Clarke and himself in more danger.

He looked up; the woman was now standing over Clarke holding a pistol. Nicholson had disappeared from view. This was serious – Frost was unarmed and Clarke's life was now at risk. Frost pulled himself to his feet, but remained behind the trees, cautious. Could he reason with them? He doubted it – they had the advantage, being at this remote location. The Sierra was sixty feet behind him; could he make a dash for it? But what could he really do? They were, as Sue said, miles from anywhere. Nicholson reappeared from behind the transit, carrying two jerrycans. Frost's pulse raced as the woman shoved Clarke with the butt of the gun towards the warehouse door. He could see in an instant what was about to happen; he scrambled in a panic for the Sierra.

As Frost, on hands and knees, recited the Mercedes registration and their location into the police radio, he prayed he had enough time.

Waters halted, half out of the Vauxhall, at the visitors' entrance to Denton Woods. He'd just caught the tail end of an alert from Eagle Lane and turned to tug the radio cord. 'Control, give me that again.'

'Inspector Frost called an all-cars to pull over a black Mercedes last seen leaving Fir Tree Lane out by the village of Rainham. And for the fire service to attend a warehouse off Fir Tree Lane.'

'And Jack himself?' Waters watched the Forensics men carry large plastic containers through the trees towards the crime scene and winced. 'Don't move anything!' he hollered after them. 'Control – are you sure he's all right?'

'He didn't say. He just gave an alert to stop a car. Registration: Tango November Tango three five four X-ray. Exercise extreme caution, suspect is armed.'

For Frost to put in a call like that, and not tackle the culprits himself – he hated using uniform – was strange. Had something happened? 'Unusual,' he said, unintentionally aloud.

'Yes. Superintendent Mullett was jumpy at the mention of firearms,' answered the voice at Eagle Lane. 'He wanted more details, but the inspector has gone off air.'

'Come on, Sergeant!' the Forensics officer in overalls called out, standing amongst the trees with an empty plastic container, poised for action. Waters was concerned, but there was nothing he could do out here. He figured Frost was big enough and ugly enough to take care of himself. He chucked the handset on the seat and jogged over to the two Forensics men.

Not far from the path were several coal sacks, wrapped in plastic. One of them had been torn.

'Fox, probably,' the young Forensics officer said,

reading his mind. Waters knelt down. Inside was what could only be described as a bloody mess. 'Could have been a badger,' the officer continued, 'although something bigger would have probably carried this off when startled.'

'This?' The Forensics man pointed at something in the long grass. Waters turned and grimaced at the podgy hand lying there, still with a heavy gold bracelet around the wrist. 'Nice.' He crouched down and, with a pen, nudged the hand over to reveal the identity plaque on the bracelet, with the word *Pumpy* engraved on it.

Waters propelled himself up and said, 'Whoever did this didn't seem too concerned with hiding this guy's identity – or taking much trouble to hide the remains.'

'Yes, they're practically on the path,' a man in a Barbour said.

'Who are you?' Waters asked. He hadn't previously noticed the two men in green standing back from the path.

'I'm Marcus Archibald,' answered the first one, a large, serious-looking man with a moustache.

'And I'm Patrick.' His shorter companion beamed. 'Drink?' he said, offering a hip flask.

'Thanks,' Waters said uncertainly. He realized these were the two who had stumbled across the remains. He took a gulp of whisky, stepping aside to let the Forensics men move in, as the liquid burned his throat. 'And what are you doing here?'

'Looking for the Lesser Spotted,' said Marcus.

'You what?'

'Woodpecker,' Patrick chimed in, taking a slug from the flask.

'These gents are birdwatchers,' the Forensics man explained.

'Of course,' replied Waters, eyeing them curiously. 'Well, be careful where you "watch".' Turning his attention to Maltby, the crime scenes doctor, who was himself drinking from the flask, Waters asked, 'How fresh, Doc?'

Frost spun the car backwards. He could smell petrol even from this distance. The Mercedes had sped off. He didn't have a great distance to gather a run-up. There was a sharp turn through the trees along the lane and then an area of 300 square yards for loading and unloading. The warehouse was of wooden construction, with old-fashioned barn-style doors, fifteen feet high.

He revved the engine, determined but doubtful. The flames were already licking the upper reaches of the main doors. The small office window and the door that Nicholson and the girl had exited from were already consumed with fire. If he left it any longer they'd both perish. He released the clutch, and the Sierra shot towards the flaming warehouse. At the moment of impact Frost on reflex shut his eyes. The doors gave with a splintering crack and he found himself inside a dark warehouse. He leapt from the car.

The space was quickly filling with smoke and it clawed at Frost's throat as he scrabbled around frantically; he'd hoped to see Clarke right away in the glare of the Sierra's headlights but all he could make out was an empty, cavernous shell. The office – she must be in the office. There was a prefabricated structure within the main shell of the building to the right of the doors. It looked to be totally engulfed by fire. He ran, choking, towards the small door – it was open. The office was thick with smoke; Frost ran in and was almost overcome – but the room was tiny and Clarke obviously wasn't there. Maybe he'd got it wrong? He'd jumped to the conclusion that Nicholson would leave her to perish in the torched building. Where was she? He ran back into the main building. Did they take her with them? he thought in alarm.

He ran towards the far wall, away from the car. The corners of the warehouse were shrouded in smoky darkness and it was only when he got closer that he discerned feet thrashing about underneath a stack of cardboard boxes. He charged over to find a bound Sue Clarke struggling to free herself. Panic in her eyes switched to relief. He freed her quickly by severing the ropes with his penknife. As she pulled him to her desperately, the fuel tank on the Sierra blew, and with it the entire front entrance: doors, wall, the lot.

Superintendent Mullett stood on the front steps of Eagle Lane police station before the press and television cameras. The divisional commander opened his speech with confidence and authority, and felt he had solid justification for doing so. There had never been such a fine result in Denton in such a timescale, certainly not in his tenure. Daley's capture was a credit to him and to Eagle Lane.

For once he found he need not dodge questions, and could answer frankly and openly. That was until a blasted siren cut him off mid-sentence. The fire brigade, and it seemed to be getting closer. Heavens, he cursed, looking over the assembly of press and camera crews, what was the meaning of this? There was no visible sign of an emergency in the vicinity. He was losing his audience's attention as the vehicle neared the police station.

A green car screeched to a halt, narrowly missing a BBC van. Waters? Seconds later the fire engine arrived. Out climbed Frost and Clarke. By now all attention was on them. But Frost didn't stop – the newly promoted inspector hopped into Waters' vehicle, and after a cursory wave in Mullett's direction, shot off again. The sheer audacity; what on earth was he playing at? The sirens were silenced, and the press were now engaged in attempting to interview the fire crew.

'Excuse me?' Mullett beckoned to his audience, tapping the microphone. But he couldn't regain their attention, in fact, quite the opposite – some were packing away hurriedly and jumping in their cars.

DC Clarke limped up the steps looking rather haggard.

'Clarke!' Mullett buttonholed her as she passed. 'A rather dramatic entrance? Where have you been – and more importantly, where's everyone off to?'

'Uniform have cornered Nicholson,' she said wearily.

He caught a waft of some familiar smell as she passed by.

'Nicholson? Who on earth is Nicholson?'

'A man who tried to burn me alive.'

Petrol. He realized he could smell petrol, but before he could ask more, Clarke had entered the building.

'It's a stand-off, Jack – says he'll shoot the woman.' Waters handed over the binoculars. 'You know, I recognize that girl from somewhere.'

'Her name is Rachel Rayner. I think you went to see her?'

Uniform had Nicholson and Rayner trapped at a railway crossing on a seldom-used lane out towards the hamlet of Two Bridges. Frost's alarm call had been acted on quickly, and the Mercedes was spotted entering Denton. Why they were headed towards Denton was a mystery, but their direction played straight into the police's hands, and after a short pursuit, they were caught on the town outskirts as an express train rocketed through Denton. The lane was bordered by dense hedgerow, and with the barrier down the pair had nowhere to run. Nicholson, in a fit of desperation, had turned a gun on his partner. The stalemate had started almost an hour ago, even before Sue Clarke had guided herself and Frost out of the blazing warehouse. (Had Nicholson known it was her on surveillance duty of the site he would probably have shot her there and then – she'd done a thorough job, and knew all the entrances and exits of the building.)

'Rachel Rayner? Yeah, I remember her,' Waters said. 'I interviewed her the afternoon after Harry got shot; Coconut Grove manager or something.'

'That's the girl,' Frost confirmed. 'Here, what are that lot doing here?'

Waters turned to see the armed response unit crawl stealthily through the drainage ditch and ease themselves through the hedgerow.

'He has a gun, Jack, protocol dictates.'

'Only as a last resort. Who put the call in?'

'Hey, I was with you, remember? They're from Rimmington – we're almost on their turf.'

'He won't do it.' Frost shrugged and started to move forward. 'I just saw them drive off after torching that warehouse. They're in it together.'

'I don't doubt they are, mate, but wait.' Waters touched his colleague's sleeve, frowning through the murky drizzle. 'I'm not so sure he wouldn't shoot. I think he knocks her around.'

'What makes you say that? Just because he killed Game and probably Palmer, doesn't mean he'd shoot his own missus.' Frost looked at him quizzically. 'Though I was often tempted myself in the past, admittedly.'

'He's a nasty piece of work.' Waters dragged on his cigarette, the tip fizzling slightly in the damp. 'When I saw Rayner she was heavily made up, you know, the way some women are more because they have to than want to.'

'I see.' Frost adjusted his mac. 'Well, even so, I got to give it a go.' And with that he walked slowly beyond the police line towards the man who was holding a gun to his own woman's head.

Waters watched through the binoculars. As Frost drew nearer to the pair he pulled his hands out of his mac and held them at head level to indicate he was unarmed. Nicholson clutched Rayner firmly by the neck, an automatic pistol pressed to her temple. She looked terrified. This is going to go badly, Waters thought to himself.

As Frost approached down the centre of the road, Nicholson shifted the gun away from Rayner and pointed it at him. Through the binoculars Waters could see the crazed expression on his face; Nicholson looked fierce and desperate. *He's going to do it.* Waters felt anxiety crawl all over his body. He wanted to shout out, to run out to Frost who had stopped only yards away from the gunman. The DI had his back to the police support, so Waters was unable to guess what he was saying, but whatever it was, it appeared not to be working. Nicholson became even more agitated, spitting out what Waters could only surmise were angry demands for freedom. The gun barrel was no more than a few feet from Frost's head. But then, Nicholson's expression changed; a smile crept across his face and he spun the gun round in his hand and tossed it into the road.

'Jesus H!' Waters exclaimed softly to himself as he lowered the binoculars.

Two marksmen stepped out from the bushes and moved towards Nicholson who'd slumped back against the Merc, hands held above his head.

Frost turned round, lighting a cigarette, and shrugged at Waters as the girl careened past him screaming hysterically. Waters jogged up to his pal standing on his own in the middle of the road.

'What did you say to that maniac to change his mind?'

Frost shrugged again. 'Not much. I told him everyone thought he was going to kill his girlfriend anyway; we knew he beat her up and didn't give a toss about her.'

'That it?'

'Then I said, she was going to do a runner, so he may as well shoot her. That just got him mad.'

Waters watched the girl, handcuffed and with mascara-smeared cheeks, bowing into the back of an Allegro panda car. 'So I saw,' he said.

'He then said he could kill me. I said, be my guest.'

Waters looked at Frost hard, and saw in his eyes that he meant it. 'I see,' he said. 'Well, thank fuck he didn't.' He clasped his friend by the shoulder, and walked him back to the Vauxhall.

Tuesday (6)

Mullett's brow creased in consternation. 'Extraordinary,' he said, tugging a shirt cuff free from underneath his tunic. 'Run the robbery by me one more time.'

Frost's face was smudged with soot, but he appeared perfectly calm after what had been a harrowing day. 'Nicholson was seething that Palmer had tipped Daley off to the payroll job, so much so that he vented his spleen to girlfriend Rayner about how ridiculous it was to share such an easy, lucrative job with Daley.'

'Why did Palmer do that, anyway?' Mullett asked, getting up from behind his desk; the portrait of Margaret Thatcher had gone askew on the opposite wall.

'It was an easy job – but risky,' Frost continued, 'and Daley reckons that if she'd got caught Palmer could easily have distanced himself from her as she was already wanted for armed robbery.'

'And the Rayner girl?' He adjusted the Prime Minister to his satisfaction.

'Was desperate to get away from Nicholson; this job would have given her a wedge of cash with which to do a bunk. Unfortunately for her, events escalated too fast for her to make a move.'

'You're sure it's her?'

'The heavy make-up fits and we're having the gun checked now.'

'And this Game character? How does an accountant from Rimmington wind up at the bottom of Denton reservoir? Surely not for cheating at snooker?'

'The crooked snooker matches were how it all started; Game was a good player, a keen amateur, but apparently suffered badly from nerves. Pumpy realized this so nobbled a couple of opponents to allow Game to climb the ladder, which he duly did. Nicholson knew about this too, of course, but was also wise to Game's day job – a senior accountant at Rumbelows on the outskirts of town; to be more precise, Game looked after stock control. Nicholson leaned on him to nick stuff.'

'I see.' Mullett sniffed. 'And Game lost his nerve?'

'Exactly; as Nicholson upped the orders, Game panicked – he was terrified he'd lose his job; his nervous disposition didn't suit swindling his employers.'

'But to kill him – seems a bit extreme, even for a violent thug like Nicholson?'

'Nicholson thought Game had ratted on him to us – and indirectly he had: that warehouse Sue Clarke was watching was where Nicholson stored his stolen gear.' Frost paused. 'Nicholson must have clocked Clarke's surveillance, explaining why she saw bugger all. Nicholson immediately thought Game had dobbed him in.'

Mullett felt satisfied. There was a rap on the door. 'Come!' he pronounced regally. Things really were looking up. A young uniformed officer entered the office. 'Yes?'

'A pair of meat cleavers have been found in North Denton, sir.'

Mullett looked at Frost expectantly. 'Who found them?'

'An old tramp, rooting around in a bin.'

'Tramp?' Frost broke in.

'Yes, Inspector: Reeves.'

'God, don't let him touch them.'

'You know this character?' Mullett asked.

'Nicky "the Weasel" Reeves.' Frost nodded with disdain. 'Always flashing his willy at the ladies, sir.'

Mullett fidgeted uncomfortably in the leather chair.

'You're right to look appalled, sir, I've said to him before just because it's big doesn't mean you have to show—'

'All right, Constable, that will be all,' Mullett snapped. Frost was clearly saying this deliberately – he knew Mullett couldn't abide smut. 'Well, you'd better get over there, Frost – the murder weapon is vital. Do we have any clue as to the motive behind Palmer's murder?'

'Blackmail,' Frost said confidently.

'Blackmail? Are you sure? Over what?'

'Palmer was a fairy.' Frost reached for the heavy ornamental desk lighter.

'A what?'

'You know: bats for the other side.' He winked.

Mullett winced with distaste. 'I see.' Though he didn't really; homosexuality was on the very fringes of his ken; something seen at a safe distance on the television set, or experienced at public school (so he was led to believe) – certainly as far away from Her Majesty's Constabulary as it was possible to imagine. 'Are there others involved?' He felt it appropriate to ask, despite having absolutely no desire to know.

'But is there anyone else involved?' Waters pressed Frost as he sat, sipping his tea contentedly. They were in the incident room, alone apart from the tall blonde WPC who was clearing the board and walls of the events of the last seven days. A telephone rang, obstinately ignored by all.

'Possibly.' He raised a wry eyebrow. The WPC finally moved towards the telephone. 'Leave it,' Frost said. 'It'll only be the press fishing for a comment – always is after Hornrim Harry does a TV stint. Someone should tell him *Opportunity Knocks* ain't on any more.'

Waters recognized the ring to be an internal call, but continued to ignore it. 'Don't be such a tart. You know more than you're letting on.'

Frost smiled a broad bearded grin. 'Superintendent Kelsey at Rimmington.'

'What? He knows?'

'For certain, I reckon.'

Frost was being obtuse, and his attention was on the WPC, who wasn't remotely interested in the looks she was getting from the frazzled inspector. 'You're having me on.' Waters shook his head. 'Explain?'

'Nicholson knew, and had a squeeze on him and Pumpy – you know you asked me about his nickname, well, it seems it wasn't only referring to the guns. He went to great lengths to project some sort of Lothario image, but it was all a front. He was horrified by the thought of it being made public. We have his oily manservant in – if that's the right word – and he's confirmed it.'

'But *Kelsey*?'

'Yep. You remember he called me last week? What I didn't tell you was that he said Winslow was bent.'

'Him too? I had no idea it was so prevalent in the force.'

'Winslow's not gay. Kelsey was feeding us a half-truth. Remember the call Clarke got from someone at Rimmington – possibly the duty sergeant – about the body in the reservoir? That a non-existent wife had reported her husband missing? Well, it's the same there: misinformation. Somebody was in the frame – only this time himself. His very words were: "It's difficult to be gay in the police force." He meant it. You got off lightly, just being black.'

Waters rolled his eyes. 'Why, thank you, Inspector.'

'The other thing I wonder now is if it really was Winslow who Miller saw outside the Pink Toothbrush in May.'

'What?'

'You remember there were reports of soliciting from the flats that back on to Baskin's sauna? Hornrim Harry insisted we stake the place out, so we did, and the only thing we saw was the ACC leaving in the small hours. Well, at a distance Kelsey could easily be mistaken for Winslow.' Frost shrugged, clearly enjoying himself. 'Couldn't confuse them on the blower, though, chalk and cheese . . .'

'But, Jack, you're moving off the point – what does it mean? Why would he let you know his sexual inclinations – other than to make a pass at you, and who wouldn't – and what has it to do with Nicholson?'

'I said Nicholson knew that both men were homosexual. He had leverage over Palmer and pushed him to bump off Harry – poor old Pumpy wouldn't have done it otherwise. All he was guilty of was underestimating his sidekick's ambition and taking a bung to fix a snooker match. Take Paul Game the snooker player, for example: Palmer had helped him up the snooker ladder—'

'How?'

'How do you think?' Frost rubbed his thumb and forefinger together. 'Readies. And if not, then some opponents might suddenly find themselves not match fit; yes, by all accounts fingers sometimes got broken.

'Anyway, Palmer gave Game a leg-up, for whatever reason. Shortly afterwards Nicholson squeezed Game into stealing electricals from his day job. You can bet Palmer knew nothing of this – Harry Baskin confirmed as much, when Game came to him for help. Harry tipped me off, and we had the place under surveillance – Nicholson must have clocked this, twigged Game had grassed and killed him.' Frost scratched his beard thoughtfully.

'And Harry himself getting shot – how does that fit in?'

'Don't know for sure, but remember Rachel Rayner works for Harry, she'd have seen Game with Harry. I haven't spoken to Ms Rayner yet, but I figure that although she loathed her old man, she'd slip him the odd nugget like this – that Game had run to Harry – to keep him occupied, thus proving her loyalty, but all the while keeping him off the scent that she would ever plan to do a runner. He did confide in her after all, told her about the payroll job.'

'And Kelsey?'

'Nicholson was becoming too much – taking too many risks; Kelsey had to act before he found himself trapped. He had to bring Nicholson down without implicating himself. If another division, like Denton, was involved, Nicholson couldn't blame Kelsey, and at the same time Kelsey couldn't help Nicholson, should he get arrested. Kelsey would not be compromised.'

'Bugger me.'

'Well, quite. Now then, where are those French chappies?'

'We've put a national alert out for the car, a white Citroën – I got the details from the shop manager. Reckon they'll do a bunk to France.'

'We'll have them if they do.'

The phone's persistence, which had resumed after a pause, had managed to penetrate Frost's disregard for it and he stretched across the desk and picked up the receiver. 'Yep.' Frost's face broadened in surprise. 'What? Downstairs! How bad?' He threw the phone back in the cradle and shook his head. 'Bloody hell.'

'Not another punch-up in the cells?' Waters asked. 'Who – it's not that busy?'

'Sue Clarke has just kicked the crap out of Daley.' Frost raced out along the corridor. Waters on his heel was impressed at the older man's pace as they hammered down the stairs.

They stopped dead in their tracks on reaching the cells; at the far end Clarke was breathing heavily, back against the wall, head bowed. In front of her was the divisional superintendent, bearing down only inches from her face. Waters turned to Frost; the DI looked distraught. Mullett would crucify her if she'd given Daley so much as a whisker of a chance to slip off the hook. This wasn't the same as two football hooligans thumping each other whilst drying out. Waters' heart went out to Frost; they both suddenly realized that the duty officer, who now passed them meekly in the corridor, had tried to circumvent the super getting involved – but they'd not answered the phone.

'You can't breathe for one minute in this job,' Frost muttered grimly, as Clarke and Mullett marched past them both without pause, though the words 'Careful, Inspector' echoed in the stairwell.

Waters followed Frost slowly down to Daley's cell.

They could hear laughter. Frost stopped short, turning away. 'I can't look.'

Waters stepped up to the door and slid back the hatch.

'Boyfriend, was he?' Daley smiled at the door through bloodied teeth, knowing she was being watched.

'It's not that bad. Superficial,' Waters told Frost by way of comfort, though he wasn't so sure – if she didn't clean up all right for the magistrate's hearing tomorrow there'd be hell to pay.

'Sue! Sue!' Frost was wheezing like a man twice his years, and he'd only jogged round the corner to the car park at the rear of Eagle Lane. 'Wait!' he stuttered as his foot slid on an icy puddle. Flaming heck, he thought, you could freeze your knackers off on a night like tonight – wouldn't want to drive far. He caught her getting into the Escort. He bent double, hands on knees trying to catch his breath. 'Wells said . . . Wells said . . .' Frost gasped; the day had finally taken its toll on him, and he broke out into a cough of a dire brutality.

'Bloody hell, Jack,' Clarke said with distaste, her breath tinged with cold. 'What a mess.'

'But I'm getting a new washing machine – I'll be a clean mess.' He stood up. 'With a dryer.'

'Good.' She smiled, hand on the car door. 'I didn't mean that, though; I meant the state of you – hacking away there.'

'Running after you; that's twice in one day I've legged it after you.'

'And too late in both cases,' she said in a tone that reminded him of his wife's mother – or did he mean his wife?

'Bill Wells said you quit.'

'I did,' she said, without emotion.

'Don't worry about Hornrim Harry; Daley will survive – I'm sure—'

'Stuff Mullett and stuff Daley . . . and . . .' She paused. 'Look, Jack, I'd better go.'

'Where are you going?' But she was already inside the car. He rapped on the glass. Once the engine started she wound down the window.

'Essex. To my parents'.' She glanced up at him in the cold autumn night, looking very tired. 'Bye, Jack.' The car started to reverse. Frost stepped back, engulfed in exhaust fumes. The car moved forward, then halted abruptly. Frost ran to the window.

'Yes?' he asked expectantly.

'Look out for David Simms. I know he's in uniform, but all the same. Try, eh?'

Frost followed her tail-lights to the front of the building then watched them disappear into the dark, wet autumn night. A tall silhouette appeared at the police-station entrance.

'Jack,' Waters called out. 'Got something interesting.'

Frost ambled over wearily to the front steps. 'Interesting, you say? Think I've had my fill of interesting for today – tell me something boring instead.'

'Err . . . your mother-in-law has been on the phone

again about her painting – boring enough for you?' Waters clasped him around the shoulder.

'Flaming knickers. Blasted nag is probably in Calais by now.' Frost lit a cigarette. 'Go on, then, I'm all ears.'

'Remember that paperboy found at the bottom of One Tree Hill? A lot of arsing around about whether the kid's death was suspicious or a straightforward hit-and-run?'

'Vaguely – Simms was looking into it.'

'That's the one – well, it transpires the incident was thoroughly investigated and Simms's kid brother has been tying up the pieces as part of some computer synergy bollocks, which I won't trouble your tired brain with. But he's come up with some interesting stuff, and you'll never guess who's in the frame for a hit-and-run . . .'

Acknowledgements

Thanks to Sarah Neal, Elisabeth Merriman, Rachel Rayner, Kate Samano, Bill Scott-Kerr, Sarah Castleton, John Worland, Phil Patterson, Martin Palmer, Krystyna Green, Rob Nichols, Julian Brazier, Steve Moore.

Read the previous book in the series . . .

FIRST FROST
by James Henry

A *Sunday Times* Top 10 Bestseller

*'Frost is back – this is a brilliant read, I can't
recommend it highly enough'*
Martina Cole

Denton, 1981. Britain is in recession, the
IRA is becoming increasingly active and the
country's on alert for an outbreak of rabies.

Detective Jack Frost is working under his mentor and
inspiration DI Bert Williams, and coping badly
with his increasingly strained marriage.

But DI Williams is nowhere to be seen.
So when a 12-year-old girl goes missing from a
department store changing room, DS Frost is
put in charge of the investigation . . .

*'Not only a gripping mystery, but an exclusive look
at Jack Frost's early years'*
David Jason

'The success of First Frost *is incontestable. This is a
palpable hit . . . [a] dark, but glittering pearl'*
Barry Forshaw, *Independent*

R. D. Wingfield's Jack Frost returns in . . .

FATAL FROST

by James Henry

'*A must for all fans of Frost, but also so much more*'
Peter James

May, 1982. Britain celebrates the sinking of the *Belgrano*,
Jimmy Savile has the run of the airwaves and Denton
Police Division welcomes its first black policeman,
DC Waters – recently relocated from Bethnal Green.

While the force is busy dealing with a spate of local
burglaries, the body of fifteen-year-old Samantha Evans
is discovered in woodland next to the nearby railway
track. Then a fifteen-year-old boy is found dead on
Denton's golf course, his organs removed.

Detective Sergeant Jack Frost is sent to investigate – a
welcome distraction from troubles at home. And when
the murdered boy's sister goes missing, Frost and Waters
must work together to find her . . . before it's too late.

'*I can't recommend it highly enough*'
Martina Cole

'*A palpable hit*'
Independent